WITNESS

WITNESS

MANDASUE HELLER

MACMILLAN

First published 2020 by Macmillan
an imprint of Pan Macmillan
The Smithson, 6 Briset Street, London EC1M 5NR
Associated companies throughout the world
www.panmacmillan.com

ISBN   978-1-5290-2426-5

1 3 5 7 9 8 6 4 2

A CIP catalogue record for this book is available from the British Library.

Typeset in Arno Pro by Palimpsest Book Production Ltd, Falkirk, Stirlingshire
Printed and bound by CPI Group (UK) Ltd, Croydon, CR0 4YY

Visit **www.panmacmillan.com** to read more about all our books
and to buy them. You will also find features, author interviews and
news of any author events, and you can sign up for e-newsletters
so that you're always first to hear about our new releases.

For mine and Win's beautiful mums, Jean Heller
and Mavis Ward. Forever in our hearts xxx

Acknowledgements

Eternal love to Win, Michael, Andrew, Azzura, Marissa, Lariah, Antonio, Marlowe, Ava, Amber, Martin, Jade, Reece, Kyro, Diaz, Paul, Silvia, Marvin, Auntie Doreen, Pete, Lorna, Cliff, Chris, Glen, Joseph, Toni, Nats, Dan, Rayne, Amari, Aziah, Val, Jas, Don, Julie, Brian, Amanda – and the rest of our families, past and present. Love also to Liz, Norman, Betty, Ronnie, Laney, Shelly, Kimberley, Katy, John, Rick, Chris, my Hulme buddies, BooksOffice Elaine, Leslie, Brian, Jac, Trixy, Don, Louis, Joe, Gary, Laura, Nicola, Jodie, Neil, Angela, Jason, Alex, Lainey, Amelia, Olivia, Tom, Paul and Iain. Thanks, as always, to Sheila, Wayne, Alex and all at Pan Mac, Emma, Carolyn C, Anne O'B, Cat Ledger (RIP). And, lastly, gratitude to my lovely readers and supportive FB/Twitter/Insta friends – you're the best!

Prologue

The girl's eyes shot open when the back door slammed into the wall below her room, and her heart skittered in her chest when she heard footsteps rushing through the kitchen, the hallway and up the stairs. Unsure if it was the police raiding the house in search of drugs, or one of her stepdad's enemies coming to fight with him again, she did what her mummy had told her to do and wriggled under the bed, burying herself beneath the dusty clothes, shoes and comics that were stashed in the space between the mattress and the floor.

The footsteps reached the landing and she held her breath as she waited for her door to burst open. They went straight past and, seconds later, her mum screamed and her stepdad yelled, 'What the fuck . . . ?'

'Shut it or you're dead,' a deep voice warned. 'You know what we're after.'

Sure now that it wasn't the police, because they always announced themselves and ordered everyone to stay where they were, which usually culminated in the fat lady social worker taking her to stay with strangers for a couple of days, the girl jumped when something heavy hit the wall behind her head.

'Please don't hurt us,' her mum cried. 'I'll tell you where it is.'

'Go get it,' another voice ordered. 'And don't fuck about, or you're dead an' all.'

'Y'ain't gettin' klish!' the girl's stepdad argued, his Jamaican accent thickening with anger. 'Y't'ink me don't know yuh? T'ink yuh can step in me yard wi' yuh face cover an' me won't recognize dem beady lickle ey—'

'Smoke the cunt!' the deep voice barked, and the child shuddered at the sound of a violent struggle breaking out. Glass shattered and wood splintered, then a boom that sounded like a massive firework going off filled the air, and she sucked in a sharp breath when her mum screamed again before abruptly falling silent.

A sinister chuckle broke the silence and the girl bit down on her hand when her mum's bedsprings started squeaking and the head-board banged rhythmically against the wall. She'd been woken by those same noises many times since her stepdad had moved in; and once, when she'd got up to use the toilet in the middle of the night, she had accidentally seen them doing naughties, so she didn't need to guess what was happening.

After what felt like an eternity, the thudding stopped and the girl heard drawers and cupboards being rifled through. Her bedroom door suddenly opened, and in the light spilling in from the landing she saw a pair of feet clad in green trainers. Praying that the man wouldn't hear her breathing as he entered the room and turned in a slow circle before approaching the bed, she shrank further back *when he crouched down and raised the edge of the quilt. Dark eyes peered into the cramped space and, terrified that he would see her, drag her out and kill her, hot piss trickled out from between her legs and soaked her nightgown.*

At the exact moment the man reached out to push the clothes aside, another pair of feet appeared in the doorway behind him, and the deep voice said, 'Got it. Let's go.'

Holding her breath until the man in the green trainers retreated from the room, the child listened as he and the other one jogged down the stairs and left the house the same way they had entered. Scared they might come back, even after hearing the squeal of the rusted hinges on the backyard gate, she stayed where she was for several more minutes before plucking up the courage to crawl out from under the bed.

The house was silent, but she kept a cautious eye on the stairs as she tiptoed out onto the landing and darted to her mum's bedroom at the front of the house. The door was open and the overhead light was on, and her skinny, piss-soaked legs almost gave way when she saw the blood. There was a thick pool of it on the bed, another on the carpet, and a smear on the wall, below which her stepdad was slumped like a broken mannequin, his once-handsome face now unrecognizable.

'Mummy?' she whimpered, tearing her gaze off him and looking round for her mother.

A faint groan drifted up from the other side of the bed and the girl picked a path through the shattered glass and debris. Her mum was lying in the gap between the bedside cabinet and the wardrobe, limbs at odd angles as if she'd fallen off the bed, blood-soaked nightdress pulled up over her stomach. She wasn't wearing knickers and the girl averted her gaze and stared at her face instead, but immediately wished she hadn't when she saw the mess the men had made of it.

Snapped out of her stupor when a bubble of blood popped at the corner of her mum's lips, the girl fled from the room, oblivious to the pain of the glass piercing the soles of her feet as she raced along the landing and down the stairs.

The front door was locked and the top bolt was too high for her to reach it. In a blind panic, she ran to the back door, and a shrill, thin scream started trickling from her throat as she lurched out into the jet-black yard.

'Sshhh!' someone hissed, clamping a rough hand over her mouth. 'Come with me . . .'

PART ONE

1

'Holly, I'm off,' Josie Evans called out as she pulled her coat on and snapped the poppers shut. 'I've got to nip into the office before I start work, and I'm running late so you'll have to make yourself a butty. Go easy on the milk, 'cos there's not much left and I'll want a brew when I get home. Oh, and don't forget I'm doing a double tonight, so I won't be back till morning.'

When no answer came, she popped her head around her daughter's bedroom door. Holly was sitting cross-legged on the bed, her mousy-brown hair hanging down around her face, her gaze fixed on the schoolbooks that were spread out on the grubby duvet.

'Did you hear me?'

'Yeah, you're off.'

'And?'

'I've to make myself a butty and not drink all the milk.'

'And I won't be home till morning.'

'Mmm hmm.'

'Don't open the door. If anyone knocks, ignore it. And if you hear any—'

'*Mum*,' Holly groaned, looking up at last. 'I'm not a kid. I know the rules.'

Josie opened her mouth to point out that, at fifteen, Holly *was* still a child and the rules were there for a reason. But she swallowed the words when she saw the pained expression on Holly's face, and said, 'OK, I'll see you tomorrow. Don't stay up too late.'

Holly looked down at her books without replying and watched from the corner of her eye as her mum shook her head before leaving the room. As soon as the front door clicked shut, she shoved the books aside and flopped back against her pillows. Every night before she left for work her mum trotted out the same list of dos and don'ts, and it did her head in. It was like she thought Holly was going to throw a wild party the minute her back was turned and invite all the local misfits round. Stupid cow!

No longer in the mood for revision, Holly got up when her belly growled and wandered into the kitchen. There were only two slices of bread left and both had green specks of mould on their crusts. Scraping them off with her thumbnail, she took a pack of ham slices out of the fridge. It was three days past its use-by date, but there was nothing else in, and it smelled OK when she sniffed it, so she threw the sandwich together and took a bite out of it as she headed into the living room.

Almost choking on the food at the sound of a loud bang

outside, she switched the light off and rushed over to the window. There had been three shootings on the estate that month, and the victim of the most recent one had collapsed just inside the gates to her block. She had been sleeping at the time, so she hadn't known anything about it until she set off for school the next morning and saw the blood on the path. The victim had survived, but he'd refused to name his attacker, and that, along with the scraps of crime-scene tape that were still attached to the gate and the railings, were a constant reminder that the gunman remained on the loose – maybe living in this very block.

Relieved to see that it was only a group of youths taking turns to pull wheelies on a mud-spattered, backfiring motorbike tonight and not a shooting, Holly took another bite of the sandwich as she watched the bike's tyres churn up the grass at the front of the block. An angry shout suddenly drifted up to her, and she pressed her forehead against the glass when the old man who lived in the flat below came out onto the path brandishing his walking stick.

'Bugger off out of it!' the man bellowed, waving the stick at the lads as he approached them. 'I'm bloody sick of you lot coming round here making a racket. And look what you've done to the grass. You want locking up!'

'Who the fuck d'ya think you're talking to?' one of the lads sneered, shoving him roughly back. 'Piss off inside before I cave yer 'ead in, ya fuckin' nonce!'

The man staggered backwards and then fell, and Holly was

sure that the gang were about to beat him up when they closed in on him.

'Oi, pack that in!' a woman yelled from the floor above. 'And you just wait till I see your mam, Robbie Campbell. If she don't leather you, I bleedin' will!'

The fact that the woman knew one of their names had the desired effect and the lads stopped toying with their prey and took off. About to move away from the window when they'd gone, Holly hesitated when her eye was drawn to the front-room window of one of the old terraced houses directly across the road. The light was on and the blinds were open, and Holly frowned when she saw the woman who had moved in there a few months earlier walking backwards with her arms outstretched in front of her, as if to keep someone at bay.

Shocked when a man she'd seen coming and going from the house lurched into view and slapped the woman across the face, sending her sprawling on the floor, Holly edged behind the curtain and peeped round it in time to see the woman haul herself up to her knees, only for a kick in the ribs to send her flying again. The man leapt on her, and Holly shuddered when he pinned her to the floor and started punching her in the face.

A police car suddenly hurtled round the corner, sirens blaring, lights flashing, and screeched to a halt outside the house. Two male officers jumped out, batons drawn, and rapped loudly on the door. The man opened it seconds later with a bemused expression on his face – as if, Holly thought, he'd been enjoying a quiet night in with his missus and didn't understand why the police were there.

The cops weren't fooled, and one of them yelled at him to come outside with his hands behind his head. No longer smiling, he tried to make a run for it, but a baton-whack to the back of his legs brought him down before he reached the gate, and he let out a roar of pain and anger when one of the cops squirted pepper spray in his eyes.

He rolled around on the path, screaming threats and kicking out at the officers who were now trying to cuff him, and Holly winced when he clamped his teeth around one of their hands and they both started whacking him with their batons. Scared that they might kill him, Holly was relieved when a van pulled up behind the car and another four officers leapt out.

The new arrivals made short work of dragging the man to his feet and tossing him into the back of the van, and the first two dusted themselves down before going inside the house.

Action over, Holly drew the curtains and took another bite of the sandwich as she switched the light back on. Almost immediately, the electric went out, plunging her into darkness again. The emergency credit had already been used, so she lit a candle and carried it into her room. Still thinking about the woman from across the road as she changed into her pyjamas and climbed into bed, she reached for her phone to tell her best mate, Bex, about the fight she'd witnessed. She had no credit, so she sent a text asking Bex to ring her.

When ten minutes had passed with no word from Bex, she

tried their other friend, Kelly. Getting no response from her either, she blew out the candle after a while and settled down for an early night, thinking that she would tell them both when they met up at the park behind Bex's house in the morning.

As soon as Holly's head hit the pillow, a pounding bass beat started up in the flat above, and she groaned when she remembered it was Friday night: party night for the man who'd moved in there a few weeks earlier. The music was already loud enough for the ceiling light over her bed to be swaying and she knew it would only get worse as the night wore on.

Cursing the man under her breath when shouting and raucous laughter signalled the arrival of his rowdy mates, she pulled the pillow over her head to escape the noise. A vision of the woman from across the road immediately flashed into her mind, and she shivered when she recalled the man punching her in the face. Unlike Holly's mum, who rarely made any effort with her appearance, the neighbour was always immaculately made-up and stylishly dressed, and Holly didn't understand why anyone would want to hurt her the way that man had done tonight. But at least now he'd been arrested he wouldn't be able to do it again and the woman would be free to find someone who treated her better.

2

Saturday morning dawned bright, but the sun wasn't throwing off any heat and the icy air bit into Holly's flesh when she climbed out of bed. Still groggy, because the party in the flat above had gone on well into the early hours, she pulled on her dressing gown and stumbled over to the window.

A concrete play area consisting of two broken swings, a rickety slide and a roundabout that no longer turned sat to the left of the glass-littered residents' car park. None of the local parents allowed their kids anywhere near it, because the gangs who hung out there to smoke weed and get pissed had turned it into a no-go zone. Holly didn't even like walking past when the gangs were there, afraid that she would catch their eye and become a target for the abuse they hurled at anyone who dared look their way. Thankfully, the area was deserted now, so she decided to make an early start on her chores.

After washing and dressing, she picked up the cash, electric card and shopping list her mum had left on the hall table. Her mum worked nights – *every* night – and rarely got up before

3 p.m., so the household chores were left to Holly. She kept the flat reasonably tidy throughout the week, but Saturday was the day she did the weekly shopping, the laundry, the polishing and vacuuming. And once those things were out of the way, she was free to go out and meet up with her friends for a few hours. Looking forward to that, because she'd been revising for her GCSEs all week and desperately needed some downtime, Holly tiptoed past her mum's room where she heard loud snores coming from inside and quietly let herself out.

About to cross the road after leaving her block, Holly hesitated when the neighbour she'd seen being beaten up came out of her house carrying two bulging bin-bags. The woman was wearing a black satin dressing gown, and her honey-blond hair was pinned on top of her head, revealing a vivid red mark on her neck and a bruise on her cheek.

Shocked by the blast of a horn, Holly leapt back onto the pavement in time to narrowly avoid being hit by a Transit van. Blushing when it passed and she saw that the woman was looking at her, she dipped her head and scuttled away.

Suzie Clifton dumped the bin-bags on top of the wheelie bin and wiped her hands on her dressing gown as she watched the girl hurry down the road and around the corner. She'd seen her before, at the window of the first-floor flat directly opposite – and, judging by the colour her cheeks had gone when their eyes had met, she guessed the girl must have been looking over last night when Rob went for her.

Suzie didn't blame the girl for staring. She'd have done the same if she had witnessed something like that. And at least the girl hadn't given her a dirty look, as if to say *you must have deserved it*, like that old bitch next door had done when Suzie had gone into the backyard for a fag earlier. That stuck-up cow thought she was a cut above because she owned her house while Suzie was only renting. But fuck her. Suzie didn't give a shit what she or anyone else around here thought about her.

Rushing inside when she heard her phone ringing, Suzie snatched it up. She didn't usually take calls from withheld numbers but she answered this one without hesitation, hoping that it would be the police calling to tell her that they were going to hold Rob over the weekend and then drag his sorry arse in front of the magistrates on Monday morning.

'Suze, it's me, don't hang up,' Rob said. 'They're letting me out, but they brought me to Wythenshawe nick, so I'm gonna need to take a cab home. I'm skint, so make sure you're there with the money when I get back.'

Suzie's hand tightened around the phone. Those coppers last night had told her he would be charged, so why the hell were they releasing him?

Maybe because you let him sweet-talk you into retracting your statement last time, so you've been put on the not-to-be-taken-seriously list . . .

Angrily pushing that thought out of her mind, she said, 'Get lost, Rob. We're finished.'

'Come on, babe, don't give me a hard time,' he groaned. 'I

know you're mad at me, but I've had a really rough night, so sort it out, then we'll talk later, yeah?'

'Are you fucking kidding me?' she spluttered. 'I'm not giving you a damn penny. And we've got nothing to talk about, so don't bother coming here trying to worm your way back in. Your stuff's in bags on top of the bin. Take it and leave me the hell alone.'

'Make sure you've got the cab fare,' Rob said, as if he hadn't heard her. 'And put the kettle on, 'cos the tea's like piss in here and I'm gasping for a proper brew.'

'Do *not* come here,' Suzie repeated. But it was too late; he'd already disconnected.

Tossing the phone onto the bed in disgust, she immediately snatched it up again and did a Google search of local locksmiths. The first two didn't answer, and the third told her he didn't work Saturdays. But he was the closest, and this was urgent, so she pleaded in her best damsel-in-distress voice until he eventually agreed to come out.

In the supermarket, Holly was pushing a trolley along the frozen-food aisle when her mobile rang. Smiling when she saw Bex's name on the screen, she said, 'About time! Why didn't you call me last night?'

'Soz, I was at a party,' Bex said. 'The music was dead loud so I didn't hear your message come through. Then my battery died, and I didn't have my charger, so I've only just seen it. 'S up?'

'Nothing,' Holly said, momentarily forgetting what she'd

meant to tell her as she wondered whose party Bex had been at – and why she hadn't mentioned it at school.

'OK, well, I've got to go,' Bex said. 'See you on Monday.'

'Hang on!' Holly blurted out before Bex could hang up. 'What do you mean, Monday? We're meeting up in a bit, aren't we?'

'Ah, yeah, about that,' Bex said sheepishly. 'Something's come up, so I won't be able to make it.'

'Something like what?' Holly asked, wondering if Bex had copped off with a lad at the party and was blowing her out to spend the day with him instead.

'She's coming to the pictures with me,' a girl piped up in the background.

'Is that Julie Gordon?' Holly demanded, scowling at the sound of the voice.

'Yeah, I'm at hers,' Bex said. 'The party finished really late, so I stayed over.'

'Was it her party? Is that why you didn't tell me about it?'

'No, it was her cousin's. And I didn't tell you 'cos I didn't even know about it till she called round last night and invited me.'

'So why did you have to stay at hers?'

'I didn't *have* to, I *wanted* to. What's your problem, Holl?'

'You're supposed to be my best mate,' Holly said, aware that she sounded like a petulant child but unable to stop herself. 'So why are you sneaking off to parties and going to the pictures with *her*?'

'I just told you, the party was a last-minute thing,' said Bex. 'And her mum gets free tickets for the Multiplex, so what was I supposed to do? Turn it down in case *you* got upset about it?'

'*Yeah! I* wouldn't hang round with someone who hates *you*.'

'Julie doesn't hate you. Why do you always have to be so paranoid?'

'She called me a tramp and said my mum buys my clothes from the charity shop. How's that me being paranoid?'

'God, chill out, you daft cow. She was joking.'

'Well I didn't find it very funny,' Holly muttered.

'*Well I didn't find it very funny*,' Julie mimicked in the background, followed by muffled giggles.

'Have you got me on loudspeaker?' Holly asked, stopping in the middle of the aisle.

'Obvs,' Bex said, as if it was no big deal. 'I can't do my make-up one-handed, can I?'

'I'm not talking to you while *she's* listening,' Holly huffed. 'Ring me when you get home.'

Losing patience, Bex said, 'Grow up, Holly! You're not my only friend, and you can't expect me to stop talking to Julie 'cos *you* don't like her.'

'I didn't talk to Kelly after you and her had that fight the other week,' Holly shot back. 'It's called loyalty.'

'No, it's called being a lesbo stalker,' Julie sneered.

The line went dead before Holly could respond. Furious that she hadn't yet topped up her credit and couldn't call Bex back, she typed a message instead, saying: *If you're gonna pick that stuck-up bitch over me, don't bother speaking to me again! And I hope you both choke on your popcorn!*

Pressing *Send*, she shoved the phone into her pocket and pushed the trolley on up the aisle, angrily tossing items off the list into it. Julie might have fooled Bex into thinking she'd been joking when she'd made those comments about Holly's clothes, but Bex obviously hadn't heard all the other snide things Julie had said, or seen the dirty looks she threw at Holly behind her back. The bitch thought she was special because her parents owned their own house while Holly and her single mum lived in a shitty council flat; and she was always bragging about her expensive clothes and fancy foreign holidays, knowing full well that Holly's mum couldn't afford any of that shit. Bex had claimed that she didn't care that Holly was poor. But she'd also claimed that she didn't really like Julie and only tolerated her because their dads were in the same golf club, yet now she was having sleepovers at the bitch's house *and* sacking Holly off to go to the pictures with her, so that showed what a two-faced cow she was!

Still smarting about the betrayal, but also angry with herself for letting Julie Gordon wind her up and drive a wedge between her and Bex, Holly picked up the last few items and headed for the checkout. She would call Bex later, she decided, when she was sure that Bex was home and able to talk without Julie listening in. The bitch was probably made up that she'd caused them to fall out, but she could piss off if she thought she was stealing Bex away from her for good.

3

Dressed now, the bruises on her face concealed behind a thick layer of foundation, Suzie went out to her front gate and looked both ways along the road. The locksmith was supposed to have been here ten minutes ago, but there was still no sign of him. Agitated when she tried to call him and his phone went to voice-mail, she lit a cigarette and took a deep drag to calm her nerves. Almost immediately, a taxi turned the corner and her heart sank when she saw Rob in the passenger seat. Flicking the cigarette away, she turned to go inside as the car pulled up at the kerb.

'Hang about,' Rob said, leaping out and running to her.

'Don't touch me,' she spat, glaring up at him when he grabbed her arm. 'I thought I told you to stay away?'

'Don't start,' he moaned, rubbing the back of his neck. 'My head's banging.'

'Oh, I'm sorry,' she replied sarcastically. 'Feel as bad as *this*, does it?' She gestured to her bruised cheek.

Rob narrowed his eyes and peered at her, then shrugged. 'I can't see anything.'

'Well, you wouldn't, would you, seeing as I've got about ten layers of foundation on.'

'Nice job,' Rob said approvingly. 'You should switch careers. You'd be a great make-up artist.'

''S'cuse me,' the taxi driver called out through the car's open window. 'I've got to go, and you haven't paid yet.'

Jerking his head at Suzie, Rob said, 'Hurry up and sort him out, babe. I'll go in and put the kettle on.'

'No you won't.' Suzie stepped in front of him when he made to head up the path. 'Go to your mum's. *She* can pay.'

'My mum's still in Spain.'

'I don't care. You're not my problem any more.'

'Someone had better hurry up and pay,' the driver said as the pair stared at each other, horns locked. 'I've got another job to get to, and I can't be sitting here all day watching you two have a lovers' tiff.'

'You what?' Rob snapped his head round and glowered at the man. 'Wanna get out and say that again, mate?'

'You're on camera, *mate*,' the driver replied spikily, staying put.

'Do I look like I give a fuck?'

'That's right, get yourself arrested again and save *me* the trouble of doing it,' Suzie said.

'Shut your mouth,' Rob snapped.

Suzie shook her head in disgust and turned to walk away, but Rob grabbed her shoulder and yanked her roughly back.

'What the *hell*?' she squawked, spinning round to face him. 'You nearly broke my flaming neck!'

'Sorry.' He held up his hands. 'I wasn't gonna hurt you, I swear.'

'That's it, I'm calling the cops,' the cabby said.

'Babe, *please*.' Rob gave Suzie a pained look. 'I know you're mad at me, but if he rings the pigs I'm fucked. And people are watching.'

He jerked his head in the direction of the flats across the road, and Suzie narrowed her eyes when she glanced over and saw a rough-looking bottle blonde with jet-black roots blatantly staring at them from an open window on the second floor. She felt like yelling at the nosy cow to mind her own business, but the woman looked the type to come out fighting, and, thanks to Rob, she wasn't in any fit state to defend herself. So, reluctantly, she marched into the house and took a twenty-pound note out of her purse before walking to the cab and shoving it through the window.

'Thanks, babe.' Rob gave her a grateful smile. 'I'll pay you back as soon as my money comes in.'

'I'm only doing this to get rid of you,' Suzie said sharply. 'You're still not coming in.'

'Can I least have a brew and some painkillers before you kick me out?' he wheedled as the driver handed over her change. 'My head's killing me.'

'No!' Suzie dropped the coins into her pocket as the cab pulled away. 'Your stuff's on top of the bin. Take it and go.'

'Come on, babe, it wasn't all me,' Rob said, following as she walked to the gate. 'You've got to take *some* of the blame.'

'Excuse me?' She drew her head back and gave him an incredulous look. 'How was any of what happened last night my fault?'

'You shouldn't have tried to go out wearing that dress,' Rob said. 'You know I can't stand it when blokes eye you up, and they'd have been all over you in that.'

'You bought me that dress,' Suzie reminded him. 'And what do you expect me to do? Walk around in a bin-bag for the rest of my life because *you* can't handle other men looking at me?'

'No, of course not. But I can't help it if I get jealous sometimes.'

'That's your problem, not mine. And it doesn't give you the right to attack me.'

'I know,' Rob conceded, reaching for her hand. 'But it'll never happen again – I swear.'

'You said that last time,' Suzie said, snatching her hand back. '*And* the time before that.'

'Yeah, but I really mean it this time,' he insisted. 'I love you, and all I want is a chance to make it up to you.'

'How?' She raised an eyebrow. 'Gonna buy me flowers again? Or maybe you'll push the boat out this time and splash out on perfume, or jewellery?'

'Whatever you want, it's yours.' Rob snaked an arm around her waist and pulled her up against him. 'We're made for each, me and you.'

'No, we're not,' Suzie argued, pushing him away. 'Just leave me alone, Rob!'

'Stop shouting,' Rob hissed, no longer smiling as he grasped hold of her wrists. 'You know what these nosy cunts round here are like. You're going to get me arrested again.'

'Good!' Suzie yelled, angrily trying to pull her arms free.

'Suzie, I mean it, pack it in!' Rob said, a warning edge to his voice as he stared down at her. 'I don't want to hurt you, I just want to talk.'

'Well, I don't want to talk to you,' she cried, wincing when his strong hands twisted her skin. 'Get off me!'

On her way home from the shops, Holly hesitated when she saw the couple from across the road on the pavement outside their house. They looked like they were fighting again and, before she could stop herself, she yelled, 'Hey, leave her alone!'

The man snapped his head round at the sound of her voice and glared at her. 'You what?'

Holly's mouth went dry. He was a lot bigger than he'd appeared from across the road, with broad shoulders, muscular thighs and heavily tattooed biceps that were stretching the material of his T-shirt almost to tearing point. But it was the anger in his eyes that really scared her, and she felt the blood drain from her face when he released his grip on the woman and turned to face her.

'Rob, don't!' the woman cried, pulling on the back of his T-shirt when he started walking. 'She's only a kid, and you'll definitely get arrested if you do anything to her. Just go inside and stop being stupid.'

Her words got through to him and he glared at Holly, and spat, 'You're lucky she's here, you nosy little fucker,' before turning and marching into the house.

'Sorry about that,' the woman apologized, walking over to Holly, glad that the woman from the second floor was no longer watching. 'He wouldn't have done anything to you, I promise.'

'What about you?' Holly asked, casting a nervous glance at the front door of the house.

'I'm fine.' The woman smiled. 'He's my boyfriend and we had a row, but he knows he's in the doghouse, so he'll be on his best behaviour from now on.'

Holly very much doubted that after what she'd just seen, but she returned the woman's smile, and said, 'Good luck, then.'

'You live in the flats, don't you?' the woman asked before she walked away.

'Yeah.' Holly hesitated.

'Thought I'd seen you at the window,' the woman said. 'I'm guessing you saw what happened last night?' she added quietly.

'No,' Holly lied, aware that she was blushing. 'Sorry. I, um, need to go.' She readjusted her grip on the bags. 'My mum'll be waiting for the shopping.'

'OK, well, thanks for trying to help . . .'

It took a moment before it sank in that the woman was waiting for her name. 'Holly,' she said. 'Holly Evans.'

'I'm Suzie,' the woman replied. 'And you know where I am if you ever fancy . . .' Tailing off when she spotted a small white van driving up the road, she muttered, 'Oh, shit, I forgot about him. Do me a favour and get rid of him before Rob sees him and thinks I was trying to sneak the guy in for a quickie while he was away. Tell him I'll settle up with him later.'

Frowning when Suzie ran up the path and snatched the bin-bags off the top of the bin before going inside, Holly hitched the shopping bags up and walked round to the driver's side of the van when it had parked.

Still in his seat, typing a message into his mobile phone, the locksmith rolled down the window when he noticed her, and said, 'Sorry I'm late, love. I had to pop over to my workshop for my tools. Give us a sec while I send this and I'll be right with you.'

'No, it's OK,' Holly said quietly, leaning down in case Suzie's boyfriend looked out and saw her talking to the man. 'She asked me to tell you she doesn't need you now.'

'You what?' The man scowled. 'You'd better be joking! I told her I don't work weekends, but she said it was urgent.'

'Please don't cause any trouble,' Holly pleaded when he started unclipping his seat belt. 'Her boyfriend got arrested for beating her up last night, and he'll kick off if he sees you. She said she'll call to settle up when she gets a chance.'

The man peered up at the house as if considering his options. Then, sucking his teeth in disgust, he restarted the engine and slammed his foot down on the accelerator, forcing Holly to leap out of the way.

4

Holly kept an eye on Suzie's house over the weekend, but the blinds had been shut each time she'd looked, so she hadn't seen the couple again. As Sunday drew to a close, her curiosity about the pair was replaced by concern that she still hadn't heard back from Bex despite calling her numerous times and leaving a string of apologetic voicemails and text messages. She'd even tried to call Kelly, hoping that Kelly might speak to Bex on her behalf. But when Kelly also didn't answer, she guessed that Bex must have told her what had happened and the pair had decided to give her the cold shoulder.

Desperate to make it up with them, because they were the only real friends she'd made since moving to the area the previous year, Holly set out for school early on Monday morning in the hope of catching up with them before the bell went. Neither girl was in their usual meeting place when she got there, but Bex was in the same set as her for most lessons, so she headed to their form room and took her seat at the desk they always shared.

When Bex arrived a few minutes later, she walked straight past Holly as if she hadn't seen her and plonked herself down next to Leanne Phillips. A big girl with a reputation for being a bit of a bully, Leanne usually sat alone, and Holly half expected her to tell Bex to sling her hook. But instead, Bex whispered something to Leanne and the girl burst out laughing. Sure that she was the butt of whatever joke Bex had told, Holly struggled to concentrate when the teacher arrived and the lesson got under way.

Bex sat with Leanne again in the next lesson, and the one after that. Upset, but also pissed off by then that Bex was ignoring her because of that stupid little tiff, Holly decided to skip lunch when she walked into the dining hall and saw Bex and Leanne standing together in the queue.

Halfway across the field at the back of the school a few minutes later, she glanced over her shoulder when she heard her name being called, and tutted when she saw Bex running after her.

'What do *you* want?' she asked, turning to face her.

'To talk,' Bex said breathlessly.

'Why? You've been ignoring me all morning, so why stop now?'

'If you're expecting an apology you'll be waiting a long time, 'cos you deserved it after the way you acted on Saturday,' Bex said bluntly. 'But that doesn't mean I want to see you upset.'

'I'm not upset.'

'So how come you're nearly crying?'

'I've got a cold.' Holly sniffed to prove her point and wiped her nose on the back of her hand. Then, dismissively, she said, 'You'd best go back to your new *bestie* before she starts wondering where you've got to.'

'Nah, she'll be too busy stuffing her face.' Bex gave a sly grin. 'You should've seen how many chips she piled on her plate back there. I swear the greedy bitch'd weigh twenty stone by now if she didn't burn it all off shagging Gary Mottram.'

'You what?' Holly frowned.

Still grinning, Bex formed a circle with her hand and poked her finger in and out of it.

'Seriously?' Holly asked, curiosity overriding her determination to play it cool.

'*Seriously*.' Bex nodded. 'She was telling me about it earlier; reckons they've been at it for months. And she doesn't even care that he's still seeing Carla Lewis.'

'Dirty cow.'

'*Dead* cow if Carla ever finds out,' Bex snorted. 'But never mind her, I've got something for you.'

'What is it?' Holly asked, following as Bex forced her way through a clump of bushes at the end of the field, behind which was a tiny clearing where the kids who smoked hung out at break times.

'Ta-da!' Bex said, pulling a pack of cigarettes and a lighter from the bottom of her bag after dusting herself off.

'I don't smoke,' Holly reminded her, perching on a log that

was surrounded by fag ends, chocolate wrappers and crushed soft-drink cans. 'And neither do you.'

'I do now,' Bex said, sitting next to her. 'Julie's mum buys them off someone who smuggles them over from France, and she's got tons of cartons stashed in her wardrobe. Ju nicks them and sells them for a fiver, but she didn't charge me.'

Lip curling at the mention of Julie, Holly said, 'Might've known *she'd* be behind it.'

'She didn't force me,' Bex said, blowing out a thick stream of smoke after lighting up. 'And she's honestly not that bad if you give her a chance.'

'You've changed your tune,' Holly snorted. 'You were slagging her off the other day, saying how much she does your head in, and now you're up each other's arses. What's all that about?'

'I dunno.' Bex shrugged. 'I saw a different side to her at her cousin's party, and we had a right laugh when I stayed over at hers. But that doesn't mean I like her more than I like you, so you don't have to be jealous.'

'I'm not jealous,' Holly lied. 'But Saturday's *our* day, so why did you go to the pictures with her when you could have gone with me?'

'You're always skint, so that was never going to happen,' Bex said. 'But it's done now, so shut up about it and have some of this.'

She held out the cigarette out, but Holly shook her head and stuffed her hands into her pockets. 'You'll get addicted.'

'Nah, I'm not that weak,' Bex said, taking another drag and blowing a smoke-ring. Then, remembering something, she said, 'Hey, did you hear about Kell?'

'No. What about her?' Holly wafted the smoke away.

'Her mum's been sectioned,' said Bex. 'Ju's mum was talking to her friend about it on the phone when she was driving us to the pictures, and she had it on loudspeaker so we heard everything. Apparently, Kell's mum was running round Tesco on Friday night, *stark naked.*'

'No way,' Holly gasped, wondering if that was why Kelly hadn't answered her calls at the weekend – *and* why she wasn't in school today.

'*Way!*' Bex said. 'She was proper going off her head by the sound of it, saying that God told her to assassinate Donald Trump and that he'd sent her to Tesco to find a weapon that wouldn't set off the alarms at the airport. Someone ended up getting a duvet from the bedding section and chucking it over her, then the security guards had to sit on her till the police turned up and called the nut squad in.'

'Wow.' Holly shook her head. 'Poor Kelly. She must be gutted.'

'Nah, she's buzzing. She's always been a daddy's girl, so she's made up that she's being sent to stay with him while her mum's in the loony bin.'

'I thought she'd lost touch with her dad?' Holly frowned. 'She told me she hasn't seen him in years.'

'Yeah, but only 'cos her mum wouldn't let her after he fucked off with another woman,' said Bex. 'Now she's away with the fairies, Kell reckons her dad'll go for full custody. And if he gets it, that'll be the last we ever see of her.'

'Why? She'll still have to come to school, won't she?'

'Yeah, but not this one,' Bex said, taking a last drag on the cigarette before stubbing it out on the log. 'She rang me when I was on my way home from Julie's the other night; told me her dad's moved to Ireland and he's going to try and get her into a school over there.'

'Oh, right,' Holly murmured.

'Never mind,' Bex said, jumping up and pulling Holly to her feet. 'We might have lost her, but we've still got each other.'

Holly nodded, but she was absolutely gutted to think that she might never see Kelly again. She and her mum had moved around so much over the years she'd lost count of how many schools she had attended, and how many friendships she'd made and lost. Her last school had been really rough and she had been badly bullied, but this one was in an affluent area, so her mum had thought she would get on much better; that the other pupils, whose parents all drove posh cars and owned their own houses, would be polite and well behaved. What her mum *hadn't* accounted for was the fact that the posh kids might not want a scruffy estate brat in their midst, and Holly still cringed when she remembered the dirty looks she'd received when she turned up on her first day wearing her ill-fitting, obviously second-hand uniform. If it hadn't been for Bex and Kelly taking her under their wings, she didn't know how she would have coped. But now Kelly was gone and Bex was hanging around with Julie Gordon, Holly felt like her world was shrinking – and she didn't like it one little bit.

5

Suzie prised an eye open and squinted at the clock. Rolling onto her back when she saw that it was almost 3.30 p.m., she yawned and stretched her arms above her head. The combined scents of sex and sweat hung heavy in the air, and she smiled at the memory of Rob waking her that morning with his head between her thighs. When things were good between them, they were *really* good, and it reminded her of why she'd fallen for him in the first place. Not only was he handsome and charming, but no other man had ever come close to pleasuring her the way he did when he made the effort.

And, *boy*, had he made the effort this weekend.

After talking things over, Suzie had agreed to give him another chance, and they had been in bed ever since, only getting up to nip downstairs for food and drink. She truly hoped it was a sign that they had turned a corner in their relationship. But all good things had to come to an end. She had a booking tonight, so it was time to stop indulging herself and start getting ready.

About to sit up, she twisted her head round on the pillow when the door opened, and she smiled at Rob as he walked in.

'Hey, tiger . . . Hope you've made coffee, 'cos I'm gonna need about a gallon to get me—'

'Fuck the coffee!' Rob thrust a mobile phone under her nose. 'What's this?'

'What's what?' She squinted at the screen, her vision too sleep-blurred to see anything in detail.

'Quit stalling and start explaining!' he barked.

'Explain *what*?' She shuffled upright in the bed. 'I can't see anything.'

'Look harder!'

Confused, because he'd been in a great mood after they'd made love a couple of hours earlier and she had no idea why he was so angry now, Suzie blinked and peered at the text message on the screen. Mouth falling open when she realized it was her phone he was holding, not his, she said, 'What the *hell*, Rob! Why are you reading my messages? And how did you get my password?'

'Are you seriously that dumb?' he spat. 'You think I don't know your fucking passwords? Or should I say pass*word*, seeing as you use the same one for every-fucking-thing, you thick bitch.'

'How dare you!' She tossed the duvet aside, furious that he'd violated her privacy. 'You begged me for a second chance, and now I catch you snooping through my phone? Well, that's it! I'm not taking this shit any mo—'

Rob backhanded her across the face before she could finish, and she fell heavily back. Terrified when he lunged at her, she tried to roll out of the way but he was too fast, and she cried out in pain when he seized her wrists and pinned them to the mattress above her head.

'Who is he?' he demanded, his eyes blazing as he stared down into hers. 'And how long's it been going on? Have you been fucking him then coming home and fucking me?'

'I haven't been with anyone!' Suzie protested, struggling to breathe with his full weight pressing down on her.

'Sure about that, are you?'

'Yes, I'm sure, and you need to get off me before this goes too far. I mean it, Rob. Stop it *now*, before you do something you'll regret.'

'The only thing I regret is putting my trust in a lying whore like *you*,' Rob snarled, tightening his grip on her wrists. 'And how many more of these cunts have you been meeting up with behind my back while I've been grafting my bollocks off to give you a life of fucking luxury?'

'I've already told you – *none!*' Suzie yelled, trying to pull her hands free. 'And you've never given me a damn penny. I pay my own way. Always have, always will!'

'Yeah, and we know how you do that, don't we?' Rob sneered. 'Twenty for a blow job, fifty for a shag . . . that what you're charging these days, *whore*?'

'Get the fuck off me,' Suzie cried, blinking to clear the tears that were stinging her eyes.

'You might as well quit struggling, 'cos you're going nowhere till you tell me who this cunt JC is,' Rob said, yanking her arms together and grasping both of her wrists in one hand before reaching for the phone he'd dropped. '*Hey sexy,*' he said, as he read out the message on the screen, '*so good to see you last night, can't wait to do it again.*'

'That's not from a *man,*' Suzie spluttered. 'It's an old school friend. Her name's Jenny. Jenny Corbett. I bumped into her last year and we swapped numbers.'

'*LIAR!*' Rob roared, his face so close to hers that his sour breath scorched her cheeks. 'How about this one, then?' He scrolled to a different message from the same contact. '*You're so hot . . . I can still taste that sweet pussy . . .*' Pausing, he glared down at her. 'That don't sound like no old school friend to me. Unless you're trying to tell me you're a dyke now?'

'She was messing about,' Suzie said, her cheeks blazing. 'That's what she's like. It was a joke.'

'Tell you what, why don't I ring this number and see who answers?' Rob said. 'But be warned,' he added ominously. 'If you make me do this and it turns out to be a bloke, I'm gonna fuck you up.'

Aware that this was going to end badly, Suzie renewed her struggle to get out from under him, but he was too big and heavy to shift.

'OK, I'll tell you the truth,' she gasped. 'They *were* from a man, but they're old messages – I swear. I finished with him before I met you, and I haven't seen him since.'

'Why didn't you tell me that in the first place?'

'Because I didn't think you'd believe me.'

'You were right, I *don't*,' said Rob. 'Now give me the cunt's name.'

'It's the *truth*,' Suzie cried. 'And I don't even care if you think I'm lying. I've had enough, Rob. I can't take this any more.'

'So you're admitting it then?'

'I'm not admitting *anything*. I'm just sick of you trying to control me! This is my house, not yours, and—'

'I'll give you one last chance,' Rob cut in, his voice deceptively quiet. 'I want . . . his fuckin' . . . *NAME!*'

'*FUCK YOU!*' Suzie yelled, thrashing her head from side to side. '*FUCK—*'

'You don't get to tell me what to do, bitch,' Rob hissed, clapping a hand over her mouth. 'I want his name, and I ain't leaving till I get it.'

Unable to breathe, Suzie widened her eyes and tried to shake off his hand. But he either didn't realize or didn't care that he was suffocating her, because he kept it firmly in place.

Next door, May Foster had heard the commotion through the bedroom wall and had called the police. Pacing her tiny hallway as she waited for them to arrive, she gazed at the framed photographs on the walls: the visual timeline of the work she'd done to the house since buying it at auction some years earlier. She had intended to do it up and sell it on, then invest the profit in another property in a slightly better area and do the same again. But she'd been forced to rethink those plans when, a few weeks after committing to the purchase, the company where she worked had gone into liquidation, leaving her unemployed for the first time in years. In her mid-forties by then, she had struggled to find another job in a youth-dominated market. So, ignoring the warnings from her family and friends who had told her she was crazy to consider moving to such a rough area, she had sold the flat she'd been living in at the time and moved into the house. It had been a wreck inside and out, and the repairs had swallowed every penny she'd made from the sale of the flat. But she had settled in nicely over the years, so she'd never regretted her decision.

Until that bloody couple moved in next door.

It was bad enough that she could hear the obscene noises they made whenever they had sex, but their frequent arguments were even worse. The yelling, the screaming, the foul-mouthed insults they threw at each other . . . It was horrendous, and the walls were thin enough that she might as well have been right there in the room with them when they were going at it.

But it wasn't only the noise that set May on edge; it was the feeling of dread that hovered over her during their quieter times as she waited for the next argument to erupt. When the lout had come back to the house on Saturday morning, she'd wondered how long it would be before it all kicked off again. Now, just two days later, they'd had the mother of all bust-ups, and enough was enough. The pity she'd felt for her neighbour when she'd seen the bruises on her face the morning after their last fight was long gone. And this time, if the police didn't hold the thug and that silly girl let him back into the house, she intended to contact their landlord and demand they be evicted.

6

Josie woke in a cold sweat to the repetitive *beep-beep-beep* of her alarm clock going off. She'd had nightmares in the past, but none as vivid and terrifyingly real as the one she'd just had, in which she'd been chased, naked and clutching baby Holly to her breast, through a labyrinth of pitch-dark corridors in a huge abandoned building by a gang of hooded, faceless men.

Her heart was pounding like a jackhammer, and her hand was shaking so violently when she snaked her arm out from under the duvet to silence the alarm that she almost knocked over the glass that was standing beside it. Grabbing it before it toppled over, she sat up and swallowed the stale remnants of the vodka and coke she'd been drinking before she fell asleep that morning. Then, lighting a cigarette, she lay back against the pillows and waited for the booze and nicotine to kick in and soothe her jangled nerves.

Her mobile phone started ringing on the bedside table, waking her from the doze she'd drifted into, and she muttered,

'*Shit!*' when she realized she was still holding the lit cigarette. After taking a last drag on it, she stubbed it out in the overflowing ashtray and reached for her phone. Straightening up when she saw that it was her co-worker, Fiona, calling, she answered quickly, hoping that the woman was ringing to tell her that she'd received a new batch of knock-off vodka.

'Has it come?' she asked, hoping she didn't sound too eager, because the last thing she needed was for that lot at work to think she had a problem. She didn't; she just found it difficult to get to sleep when everyone else was getting up, and a little drink helped her to drop off. That was all.

'Not yet,' Fiona said. 'My usual guy got busted, so I've had to look for another supplier. But I'm hoping I'll get word tonight.'

Disappointed, because her supplies were running low and she couldn't afford shop prices, Josie flopped back against the pillows and massaged her throbbing temples.

'Anyhow, I'm not ringing about that,' Fiona went on. 'Sharon's sacked Petra and she wants you to come in early to cover her shift.'

'Why me?' Josie moaned. 'Can't she ask one of the others?'

'Hey, I'm only the messenger,' said Fiona. 'I can tell her I couldn't get hold of you, if you want? But you know what she's like, so don't blame me if she cuts your hours to nothing to punish you.'

Josie sighed and squeezed her eyes shut. She knew what Sharon was like, all right. The woman was a bitch, and she'd think nothing of doing exactly what Fiona had said if Josie dared to refuse the extra shift.

'What do you want me to tell her?' Fiona's voice cut into Josie's thoughts.

'Tell her I'll be there in an hour,' Josie said.

After hanging up, Josie groped for the vodka bottle that was standing between the base of the bed and the bedside cabinet and gulped down the last inch of liquid from it. Then, pushing the quilt off her legs, she got up and shoved the empty bottle neck-down into the washing basket before heading to the bathroom.

Dressed and feeling a little more human a short time later, Josie had made a cup of tea and was carrying it into the living room when she spotted blue flashing lights outside. Aware that Holly would be on her way home from school, she rushed over to the window, praying that the girl hadn't got caught up in any of the gang-related violence that had been blighting the estate in recent weeks.

Two police cars and an ambulance were parked on the road below, and a gaggle of neighbours were gathered on the pavement a few feet back. The vehicles were obscuring her view, so she couldn't tell if something had happened on the pavement or inside one of the houses. But if it were the latter, she figured it a fair bet that it involved the couple who lived directly opposite.

Josie had never spoken to either of them, but she'd overheard their next-door neighbour gossiping about their noisy sex sessions – and even noisier fights – in the local shop a couple of weeks earlier. It hadn't surprised her to hear that the man was violent. She'd passed him in the street a few times and the tell-tale glint in his eyes had told her that his amiable smile and cocky swagger concealed a dark temper. Handsome men like him, who obsessed over their appearance and spent half their lives in the gym, often harboured deeper insecurities than ugly men, in her experience, and she'd seen how quickly those insecurities could morph into controlling behaviour and extreme violence. So, no, she wouldn't be surprised if those emergency vehicles were attending an incident at that house today.

As her mother watched the scene through the window, Holly turned the corner with slumped shoulders and downcast eyes. She'd been thinking about Kelly all afternoon, wondering why the girl had contacted Bex before leaving, but not her. Even if she hadn't had time to talk, Kelly could at least have sent a text. But the fact that she hadn't bothered to do so made Holly wonder if they had ever been as good friends as she'd thought.

Raising her eyes to check for traffic before crossing the road, she froze when she saw the emergency vehicles parked outside Suzie's house, the spinning blue light on the top of the police car reflecting off the windows of the neighbouring houses. The front door suddenly opened and three police officers walked out followed by two paramedics, one of whom was pushing a wheelchair. Suzie was huddled in the chair with a red blanket wrapped round her and an oxygen mask strapped to her face. They wheeled her into the back of the ambulance, while two of the coppers climbed into the van that was parked behind it. As both vehicles pulled away, the third copper pulled Suzie's door shut and got into his car.

Snapping out of her trance when the car did a three-point turn and drove past her, Holly spotted her mum waving at her from their living room window and scuttled across the road. Two men were trotting down the stairs side by side when she entered the flats' communal hallway, so she waited at the bottom to let them pass.

'What's going on out there?' one of them asked, stopping in front of her. 'It's not another shooting, is it?'

'Don't think so,' she murmured, blushing when she realized it was the party-throwing tenant from the flat above hers. She'd only ever seen him through the window at night before, but up close, with his soft brown eyes, straight white teeth and the hint of stubble on his strong jawline, he reminded her of a younger, sexier Zayn Malik.

'C'mon, Gee, we're gonna be late,' his friend said, brushing past Holly and heading for the door.

The man, whose name she now knew, winked at her before following his mate, and Holly twisted her head to watch as the pair strolled outside. Biting her lip to contain her excitement when they had gone, she rushed up the stairs. Just wait till Bex heard that their celebrity-crush had a lookalike who was living in her block. She was going to be *so* jealous!

* * *

Josie was brushing her hair in front of the mirror on the living room wall. Glancing at Holly when she walked in, she said, 'Who did they put in the ambulance? The man or the woman?'

'Woman,' Holly said, dropping her bag on the sofa. 'What happened?'

'No idea.' Josie shrugged. 'They were already there when I got up. Probably him knocking her about again.'

'What d'you mean?' Holly asked, feigning innocence because she didn't want her mum to suspect that she'd spoken to Suzie. Not speaking to the neighbours was one of the rules, and she could do without the earache she'd get if her mum found out she had broken it.

'Nothing,' Josie said, putting the brush down and taking an elastic band out of the pot on the shelf under the mirror.

Watching as her mum scraped her hair back and tied it into a tight bun, Holly wondered how she couldn't see what an unflattering style it was. Josie's hair was quite nice when it was loose. Not lush and sexy like Suzie's, but a damn sight better than this butch-prison-guard look she seemed to favour.

'What you staring at me like that for?' Josie frowned at her in the mirror.

'I wasn't,' Holly lied.

'Could've fooled me,' Josie muttered, flashing a disbelieving look at her before leaning forward to examine a spot.

Hungry after missing lunch, Holly wandered into the kitchen to see if her mum had made a start on dinner. Disappointed, but not overly surprised to find nothing on the stove, she opened the fridge and took out a pot of yoghurt.

'Put that back,' Josie said, appearing in the doorway as she was about to tear the lid off. 'I was going to microwave one of those little pizzas for you, but you can do it yourself now you're home. I've got to go in early.'

'Again?' Holly asked, replacing the yoghurt in the fridge.

'Excuse me?' Josie's eyebrows knitted together. 'Do you think I work for fun, or something? You don't think I'd rather sit on my arse all night watching telly, like you?'

'Why you having a go at *me*?' Holly asked. 'I didn't even say anything.'

'Yes, you did, you said "again", like I've got a flaming choice,' Josie snapped, snatching her handbag off the ledge.

'Pardon me for breathing,' Holly muttered under her breath.

'Don't get lippy, lady.' Josie gave her a warning look. Then, looping the strap of her handbag over her shoulder and picking her keys up, she said, 'Right, I'm off. Don't stay up too late, and if anyone calls round—'

'Don't answer the door,' Holly cut in wearily.

Irritation flashing in her eyes, Josie said, 'Hurry up and have your pizza, then get on with your revision. Wouldn't want you failing your exams and being forced to clean shitty toilets for a living like me, now, would we?'

Holly waited until the front door slammed shut behind her before blowing out an exasperated breath. Her mother was such a moody bitch, getting on her high horse over a stupid word.

Holly wouldn't have minded so much if it wasn't true, but she *had* been going out earlier since she'd decided to take on extra shifts – *and* coming back later. She claimed she had no choice, but Holly didn't believe that. If she hated her job as much as she claimed to, she could quit and go on benefits. But she obviously didn't want to, because that would mean being forced to spend more time at home. Well, sod her if that was how she felt, because Holly didn't need her.

7

Suzie was restless. The paramedics who'd brought her to A & E had picked up her dressing gown and slippers before leaving the house, but not her handbag or phone. Without the latter to tell her the time, she had no idea how long it was since she'd been plonked in this godforsaken cubicle. She knew the staff were busy, because she could hear them rushing about on the other side of the curtain. The patients who were moaning and groaning in the cubicles on either side of hers sounded like they were dying, and they clearly weren't getting seen any faster than she was. But, even so, they couldn't expect her to wait all night.

Beginning to suspect that she'd been forgotten, Suzie was looking for the buzzer to summon someone when the curtain swished open and a nurse walked in carrying a glass of water and a little plastic cup containing tablets.

'Sorry it's taken so long; we're rushed off our feet tonight,' the woman apologized. 'Here you go.' She held out the glass and the cup.

Suzie was tempted to tell her where to shove the stupid tablets, but she was aching all over and her head was banging, so she took them and stuffed them into her mouth, quickly washing them down with the water.

'Any idea when the doctor's coming to see me?' she asked, wiping her mouth on the back of her hand. 'I've been here for ages.'

'Your guess is as good as mine,' the nurse replied unhelpfully. 'We've had several emergencies come in since you got here, and they take priority, so you'll have to be patient.'

'Is that supposed to be a joke?'

Tutting loudly when the nurse walked out without answering, Suzie flopped back against the pillow. They were taking the piss. She'd been brought in by ambulance with a police escort, yet she wasn't considered an emergency? And they wondered why people complained about the NHS.

An alarm suddenly went off on the other side of the curtain, and Suzie guessed that someone's heart must have stopped when a call went up for the crash team. Wishing it had been whoever was in the cubicle to her left, because their moans were getting louder and more irritating by the second, her patience snapped and she climbed off the trolley and stuffed her feet into her slippers.

Heading outside after stopping off at the desk to tell them she was leaving, she cadged a cigarette off a man who was pacing up and down with his phone glued to his ear. She quickly smoked it before making her way over the road to where two private-hire taxis were parked up, their drivers standing between them having a fag and a chat while they waited for customers.

'Are you supposed to be out here, love?' one of the men asked, looking her up and down when she reached them.

'Don't worry, I'm not a psych case,' Suzie said, aware that she must look a sight in her dressing gown and slippers. 'Which one's front of the queue?'

The man who'd spoken nodded to one of the cars and Suzie clambered into the back of it. Remembering that she wasn't wearing knickers when he got behind the wheel and peered at her in the rear-view mirror, she tugged the hem of her dressing gown down over her thighs, and said, 'Lansdowne Road, please. But you'll have to wait outside for a minute when we get there. I came in by ambulance and they forgot to bring my bag.'

The driver had started to move off, but he slammed his foot on the brake at that and, twisting round in his seat, jerked his thumb at the door. 'Out.'

'Oh, come on,' Suzie moaned. 'I've got the money at home. I just need to go round the back to get my spare key.'

'And leave me sitting out front like a lemon waiting for you to come back?' The driver pulled a dubious face. 'Oldest trick in the book, that, love.'

'I'm not going to do a runner dressed like this, am I?' Suzie reasoned. 'And I'll give you a good tip.'

'No money, no ride,' the driver replied flatly. 'Company policy.'

Suzie tried to appeal to his better nature, but he wouldn't budge, so she gave up and opened the door, muttering, 'Thanks for nothing, you miserable arsehole!'

The walk home was a nightmare, and Suzie couldn't wait to get inside, take a hot bath and fall into bed. It was bad enough that everyone she'd passed along the way had gawped at her, but then a rowdy group of lads on the top deck of a passing bus had chucked a milkshake over her, so she was wet, cold, and thoroughly pissed off by the time she reached the alleyway that led to the estate.

Low-hanging branches from the trees behind the fences on either side of the path formed a creepy canopy over her head, and she shivered when the light from the streetlamps on the main road faded a few steps in. Shivering in the darkness, she was hurrying towards the faint sliver of light at the other end when something shifted in the shadows, and the hairs on the back of her neck bristled when she heard the sound of feet shuffling on the concrete.

Afraid that Rob might have followed her to hospital and then rushed back here to lie in wait when he saw her getting kicked out of the cab, she stopped walking and peered into the gloom. A cigarette lighter suddenly flared, and her fear turned to relief when she saw three pairs of eyes glinting back at her from behind the flame. Guessing that it was a group of kids making their way home from the youth club on the other side of the estate, she released the breath she'd been holding and started walking again.

Expecting the group to move aside when she reached them, she frowned when they spread out in front of her, making it impossible for her to move forward.

'Yo!' one of them said, stepping up to her. 'What you got?'

She could hear that it was a boy, but he had his hood pulled low over his forehead and a scarf wrapped around his lower face, so all she could see were his eyes. Quickly sizing him and his friends up, and guessing from their heights and slight builds that they couldn't be much older than fourteen or fifteen, she drew herself up to her own full height.

'*Move!*' she barked, hoping they were still young enough to have some sort of respect for, or fear of, adults.

A flicker of uncertainty flashed through the boy's eyes, but he immediately blinked it away, and hissed, 'Who the fuck d'ya think you're talkin' to? I axed what you got, and you best hand that shit over.'

'*Axed?*' Suzie snorted, amused by his tough-guy act.

Missing the sarcasm, he said, 'Yeah, that's right. And I ain't gonna axe again, so what you waitin' for?'

Unable to stop the laugh that was bubbling up in her throat from breaking out, Suzie said, 'Fuck off, you little prick! I can see that you're white, so why are you trying to act black? You t'ink you is in da 'hoods, blud?' She adopted a terrible Jamaican accent and threw some hand-signs she'd seen in a gangster movie at them.

'Yo, man, she's off 'er 'ead,' one of the other lads muttered, eyeing her warily. 'Probs on crack, or escaped from the nut-house, or summat. Let's jet.'

'Yeah, that's right, *jet*, before the loony lady really loses her shit,' Suzie sneered. 'Go on . . .' She flapped her hands at them. 'Toddle off before your mummies send out a search party. It must be well past your bedtimes by now, *yo*.'

The boy who was fronting up to her narrowed his eyes and Suzie could tell that his pride was killing him and he wanted to kick the shit out of her. But his mates were clearly spooked by her crazy act, so when they edged past her and scuttled away, he reluctantly followed.

Heart pounding, Suzie watched until the boys had disappeared from view and then ran the rest of the way along the alley. Out on the road, she slowed to a stop when she neared her house and noticed a faint glow of light behind the partially closed blinds at the bedroom window. Biting her lip when the light flickered, realizing it was the flame of one of her scented candles – none of which had been lit when Rob had attacked her – she gazed over at the block of flats on the other side of the road. That girl – what was her name again? Heather? Hannah? *Holly!* That was it. Suzie had spotted her at the window a few times and knew that she lived on the first floor. That window was dark now, but Suzie had asked someone the time on her way home and it had only been 11 p.m., so even if the girl had gone to bed, she might still be awake.

Head down in case Rob was looking out for her, she ran across the road and darted in through the gate at the far end of Holly's block. Then, bending over, she crept alongside the bushes that lined the footpath below the flats until she reached the communal wheelie bin that was standing outside the bin cupboard to the left of the main door.

She slipped behind the bin and squatted down to wait for someone to go in or come out. Luck was on her side and the door started opening. Seizing the opportunity, she lurched out of her hiding place and, pushing past the man who was coming out, darted into the foyer of the flats.

'Hey, what's your game?' the man said, turning on his heel and glaring at her. 'You don't live here.'

'Sorry, I need to see someone,' she said, tightening the belt on her dressing gown when he looked her up and down.

His expression changed from anger to concern when he noticed the bruises on her face, and he took a step towards her.

'Are you all right, love? Is someone after you? Do you want me to call the police?'

'No, I'm OK,' she said, backing away. 'I'm looking for a girl who lives here. I think her name's Holly and she lives on the first floor with her mum. She's about my height, skinny, with longish light-brown hair.'

The man thought about it for a few seconds, then nodded. 'Yeah, I think I know who you mean. Try number sixteen.'

Suzie thanked him and set off up the stairs, tugging the back of her dressing gown down as she went when she felt his eyes following her.

8

Holly had been on the verge of falling asleep when the doorbell rang, and she was alarmed to see that it was just gone 11.30 p.m. when she sat up and checked the time on her phone. Her mum always warned her not to answer the door if anyone called round at night, but this was the first time it had ever actually happened, and she wasn't sure what to do.

Maybe it's Gee, the Zayn lookalike from upstairs?

Her stomach fluttered at the memory of her handsome neighbour winking at her that afternoon, and she bit her lip as she wondered if he'd been thinking about her like she'd been thinking about him. Maybe he had and he'd come down to invite her to his party, which was already well under way judging by the music pounding through the ceiling.

Don't be so stupid, she chided herself. He always had loads of girls his own age at his parties, so why would he be interested in a kid like her who wasn't even allowed to answer the door, never mind go out?

The bell rang again, and then the letterbox cover flapped

open, and a woman's voice called: 'Hello . . . is anyone home? Holly, if you're there, can you open the door, hon? It's Suzie from across the road. I need your help.'

Intrigued, Holly got up and tiptoed out into the icy hallway. She peeped through the spyhole and quickly unlocked the door when she saw Suzie standing on the other side wearing a short dressing gown and slippers.

'What's up?' she asked, rubbing her eyes as she peered out at her.

'Thank God you're still up,' Suzie said, glancing nervously round at the sound of footsteps on the stairs. 'Can I come in for a minute?'

'I'm not really supposed to answer the door,' Holly said. 'My mum—'

'Is she here?'

'No, she's at work.'

'Well, I won't tell if you don't,' Suzie said. Sighing when Holly still didn't open up, she said 'Please, hon. I can't go home till I'm sure Rob's not there. I don't know if you saw what happened earlier, but he put me in hospital and I've just had to walk back like this.' She held out her arms and looked down at herself in disgust. 'Some knob-heads chucked milkshake at me, and then I nearly got mugged in the alley. I wouldn't have bothered you, but you're the only friend I've got round here.'

Flattered to hear that the woman considered her a friend, given that they had only spoken once, Holly said, 'What can I do?'

'I need to use your phone,' Suzie said. 'I left mine at home when they took me to hospital, and I need to check if Rob's there. It'll only take a minute, I promise.'

Holly knew her mum would go mad if she found out that a stranger had been in the flat. But Suzie wasn't a stranger to her, and she couldn't see any harm in letting her come inside for a minute or two.

'You're an angel,' Suzie said, stepping into the hallway when Holly opened the door wider. 'Bloody hell, that's loud.' She glanced up at the ceiling.

'The guy upstairs is always having parties,' Holly told her. 'It'll be like this till three or four.'

'Rather you than me,' Suzie said. Then, shivering, she asked, 'I don't suppose you've got something warm I can put on, have you? I'm getting goosebumps on my goosebumps here.'

'I'll have a look,' Holly said, showing her into the living room before rushing back to her bedroom.

Suzie was at the window, peering over at her house, when Holly came back with the phone, a jumper and a pair of jogging bottoms.

'I didn't realize you had such a good view of my place from up here,' she said. 'I bet you can see straight into my lounge and bedroom when the blinds are open.'

Sure now that she *had* been spotted at the window on the night of the fight, and – worse – that Suzie probably thought she'd been watching them in bed as well, Holly blushed as she handed the items over.

'You OK?' Suzie gave her a questioning look. 'You look a bit flushed.'

'Just hot,' Holly lied, perching on the sofa and slotting her hands between her knees.

'Lucky you, I'm bloody freezing,' Suzie said, quickly pulling the jogging bottoms and jumper on before flopping down beside her. 'Right, let's see where he's at – *if* I can remember my number.'

'I thought you wanted to text Rob?' Holly said.

'It needs to go to my phone,' Suzie said, already typing out the message. 'That's what kicked him off earlier,' she explained when she glanced at Holly and saw the confusion in her eyes. 'He went through my phone and found some old messages from a guy I was seeing before him. I told him it was a girlfriend messing about, but he didn't believe me, and he was threatening to ring the number to see who it was when the police turned up. If he sees this message and tries to ring back on this number, I'll know he's definitely there, and I'll call the police and let them deal with him.'

'Oh, right,' Holly murmured, wishing that she hadn't agreed to let Suzie use her phone now that she knew the plan. The look Rob had given her outside Suzie's the other day had terrified her, and she already knew he was violent. What if he decided to punish her for helping Suzie to trap him?

'What d'you think of this?' Suzie said when she'd finished. '*Hey sexy, are we still on for tonight? Let me know when it's safe to come round. Kiss kiss.* Doesn't sound too girly, does it?'

Holly shook her head and twisted her fingers together nervously when Suzie pressed *Send*.

Rob was standing at Suzie's bedroom window, gazing out along the road through the partially open blinds and wondering where the hell she'd got to.

He'd hidden out at his mum's house after doing a runner earlier, and had spent the day flicking through the news channels, waiting for his mugshot to pop up and to hear that he was wanted for murder. As the day dragged into night with no mention of him or Suzie he'd begun to relax, thinking that maybe he hadn't killed her, after all. A call to the local hospital pretending to be her brother had confirmed his theory, and he'd been massively relieved to hear that she was waiting to be seen and didn't appear to be in a serious condition.

That was when he'd decided to come back to the house: to wait for her and see if they could put this latest tiff behind them. He'd always talked her round in the past, so he was sure he could do it again. Although, by rights, it was *her* who ought to be doing the grovelling, since she was the one who'd cheated.

Those messages had made him see red, and he'd wanted to fuck Suzie up so badly she wouldn't dare *look* at another man again. He hadn't meant to kill her, though, and the realization that he'd almost done exactly that had rapidly brought him to his senses. After thinking it over, he had decided to forgive her – as long as she came clean and told him who JC was. All he needed was a name and address, so he could pay the cunt a visit, then he and Suzie could put this behind them and get on with their lives.

Confident that everything would be fine – and impatient to see her, because make-up sex with Suzie was the best sex ever – Rob had placed another call to the hospital after arriving at the house. Happy to hear that she'd discharged herself by then, he had carried the bottle of whisky and box of chocolates he'd nicked from his mum's up to the bedroom. Scotch didn't really agree with him, but it was all his mum ever drank, and he didn't have enough money to buy anything else, so it would have to do.

Setting the scene for their romantic reunion, he had lit some of Suzie's scented candles and placed them around the bedroom, and then he'd lined up a playlist of her favourite R & B tracks to get her in the mood. But an hour had passed since he'd heard she was on her way home, and she wasn't back yet.

On his third glass of whisky now, and getting a headache from the cloying scent of patchouli, he snatched Suzie's phone off the bedside table when it pinged. An ice-cold rage surged through his veins when he read the message on the screen. So those other messages had been old ones, had they? The lying fucking *bitch*! She was obviously still screwing the cunt and had promised to give him the all-clear when Rob had been arrested and it was safe to come round. Well, he'd get the all-clear, all right. But the sneaky prick was in for a shock if he thought his bit on the side was the one who'd be waiting for him when he got here.

* * *

'What did I tell you?' Suzie said when a reply to her message appeared on Holly's phone screen. '*Hey, baby,*' she read it out with a sneer. '*All clear, come now. Can't wait to see you. Kiss kiss.*'

'I don't get it.' Holly's brow puckered in confusion. 'How does he know it's you?'

'He doesn't. He thinks it's my secret lover. So he's playing smart, pretending to be me to lure the man round to the house.'

'Why?'

'So he can kick the shit out of him and teach us both a lesson,' Suzie muttered, tapping 999 into the phone. 'Police, please . . . Hi, yeah, my ex is on the run for attacking me earlier and I've just come home from hospital and found him in my house . . . No, I'm at a friend's across the road, but he's definitely there . . . Because I left my phone at home, and when I sent a message to it he replied pretending to be me . . . Look, I know it sounds weird, but I haven't got time to explain. I saw him at my bedroom window a minute ago, and he's got a gun . . .'

Eyes wide with fear when Suzie had given her details to the operator and ended the call, Holly said, 'Has he really got a gun?'

'No, course not,' Suzie said, getting up to peek out of the window again. 'But if they *think* he has, they won't mess about. Now shush with the questions and let me watch.'

Terrified that Rob was going to come after her when he found out that she'd helped Suzie to set him up, Holly wished that she'd followed her mum's instructions and ignored the door.

* * *

WITNESS

As Suzie had predicted, the police didn't waste any time responding to her call. Two dark vans arrived a short time later, minus the usual lights and sirens, and parked around the corner, out of sight of the house but in view of the flats. Several officers in riot gear piled out, and some went round the back while the others crept past the fences of the other houses to approach Suzie's from the front.

'*Armed police!*' one of them yelled when they were in position. '*Come out with your hands where we can see them!*'

Suzie and Holly both jumped when a battering ram was slammed into the door. Two booms and it flew open, then the officers rushed inside. Lights went on all over the house and dark figures moved stealthily through the rooms.

'*Got him!*' someone called out. '*Front bedroom! Unarmed . . . Unarmed!*'

More shouts followed, all indecipherable, and Holly chewed on her knuckles as she waited in dread for the sound of a gunshot. Several anxious minutes passed before two police officers appeared, manhandling a handcuffed Rob through the hallway and out onto the path.

'*I haven't done anything!*' he was protesting. '*She's lying about the gun – just like she lied about me attacking her earlier. She likes it rough; that's how she gets her kicks. But I never meant to hurt her, I swear! It was just a stupid sex game that went too far!*'

'Lying bastard,' Suzie spluttered. 'We weren't having sex; he'd gone off his head 'cos of those messages!'

Holly's phone started ringing on the coffee table and they

both dropped to their haunches when the glow of the screen lit up the room behind them. Crawling over to shut it off, Holly accidentally accepted the call instead, and she glanced at Suzie when a woman's voice drifted out, saying: 'Ms Clifton, it's Janet Moore – the police operator you spoke to earlier. If you're there, can you pick up, please?'

Suzie nodded and Holly slid the phone over to her.

'Hello?' Suzie whispered, as if scared that Rob might hear her, despite the fact he was still loudly protesting his innocence outside. 'I know, I'm watching them now . . . Oh, really? Sorry, I honestly thought I saw one . . . Yep . . . No, that's fine. Thank you.'

'What did she say?' Holly asked when Suzie ended the call.

'They didn't find the gun, so they're going to search the house,' Suzie said. 'And they want to talk to me.'

'They won't come here, will they?' Holly asked, worried that one of the neighbours might see them and mention it to her mum.

'I didn't tell them where I was, so they couldn't even if they wanted to,' Suzie said, looking out of the window in time to see Rob being bundled into the back of a police van. Tutting when loud bangs came from inside, she said, 'I bet the idiot's been on the whisky. He always goes crazy when he drinks that shit.'

The bangs faded as the van pulled away, and Suzie released a tense breath before turning to Holly.

'Right, I'd best go and face the music. Thanks for helping me out, hon; I really appreciate it. And thanks for the loan of the clothes. I'll leave them in a bag on top of my bin so you can pick them up on your way to school. *If* I don't get arrested for wasting police time,' she added with a grimace.

Hoping that Suzie wouldn't get into trouble, but relieved that it was over, Holly showed her out – praying, as she closed the door behind her, that the woman would keep her out of whatever came next.

9

As promised, Suzie had left Holly's jumper and jogging bottoms in a plastic bag on top of her bin the following morning. Hoping that no one spotted her taking them and marked her down as a bin-rat, like the junkies from the next block who rooted through everyone's rubbish before the communal bins were emptied on Wednesdays, Holly rushed up the path and grabbed the bag. A sweet floral scent drifted up to her when she opened it and she was embarrassed when she realized that Suzie must have washed the clothes. She'd worn them a couple of times since she'd last done the laundry and hadn't thought to check if they were dirty before handing them over.

Sure that Suzie must think she was a tramp, she was stuffing the clothes into her schoolbag when someone said, 'Morning,' and she blushed when she looked up and saw her neighbour, Gee, crossing the road. He'd spoken in passing, but the mere fact that he'd acknowledged her made her feel giddy, and she couldn't stop grinning as she made her way to school.

* * *

Holly didn't see Suzie again that week, but she was too busy revising and making plans with Bex to worry about her. As she'd suspected might happen, as soon as Bex heard that their celebrity crush's double lived in Holly's block she had offered to meet her on the estate that weekend, instead of making Holly walk the two miles to the park behind her house where they usually met.

It would only be the second time Bex had deigned to visit the estate in the entire time she and Holly had been friends, and her refusal to meet halfway pissed Holly off. But she pushed her irritation aside, happy that Bex was coming – even if it *had* taken a boy to make it happen – and they'd be able to hang out and have a laugh without Julie Gordon sticking her beak in.

Up bright and early on Saturday morning, Holly raced through the shopping, the laundry, the dusting and vacuuming before heading outside to wait for Bex. She took a seat on one of the benches that were scattered around the estate – all facing the road, as if the residents had nothing better to do than sit and watch traffic. A few minutes later, three lads walked round the corner, and her stomach sank when one of them clocked her and started heading in her direction.

'Yo . . .' He stopped in front of her. 'What you got?'

'Piss off,' Holly said, determined not to show fear, but silently praying that an adult somewhere was watching and would chase them off.

'Y'what?' He scowled. 'You lookin' for a slap?'

'Leave her, man,' one of the others said, nodding down at her feet. 'She ain't got nowt. Check the state of them.'

Embarrassed when they all looked down at her grubby, unbranded trainers, Holly self-consciously pulled her feet under the bench.

'Fuck me, d'ya nick them off a tramp, or what?' the first lad jeered. 'Here, go buy yourself a new pair.' He flicked a coin at her. 'But don't go spending your change all at once, eh?'

Laughing, he and his mates walked away, and Holly waited until they'd gone before scooping the coin up off the floor. Pleased to see that it was a pound and not the penny she'd expected, she stuffed it into her pocket and took out her phone to find out where Bex was. Before she had the chance to call her, she heard her name being called, and muttered, '*Great!*' when she looked round and saw Bex strolling towards her arm in arm with Julie. Even from a distance she could see they were both plastered in make-up, and they were dressed almost identically in white skinny jeans, silver puffa jackets, and short pink tops that showed off their fake-tanned bellies.

'Sorry we're late,' Bex said, flopping down on the bench when they reached her. 'This one took forever getting ready.'

'Hey, even perfection needs maintenance,' Julie quipped, flicking her white-blond hair extensions back over her shoulder. Then, frowning, she peered down at Holly, and said, 'Wow, babes, you look really pale. You haven't caught that stomach bug that's been going round, have you?'

'Why are *you* here?' Holly asked, seeing right through her show of concern.

'I asked her to come,' Bex said. 'I wasn't gonna come on my own and get raped or mugged, was I?'

'I could have met you somewhere,' Holly said, grudgingly shifting over when Julie plonked herself on the other side of Bex.

'Told you she'd moan.' Julie rolled her eyes.

'I'm not moaning,' Holly protested. 'I'm just saying I could have met her so she wouldn't have had to walk here on her own.'

'So where is he, then?' Bex changed the subject. 'I haven't dragged myself all the way over here for nothing.'

'He's probably still sleeping,' Holly said. 'His party went on till late last night.'

'Well, he'd better get up soon,' Julie grumbled, taking a pack of cigarettes and a lighter out of her pocket. 'I'm not sitting out here all day freezing my tits off.'

'No one asked you to come,' Holly muttered.

'*I* did,' Bex said, taking a cigarette from Julie and leaning forward to get a light.

'You can't do that here,' Holly said. 'My mum'll stop me hanging round with you if she sees you smoking.'

'God, how old are you?' Julie sneered. 'You sound about three.'

'I'm fifteen, same as you,' Holly replied tartly. 'And I don't see why I should get into trouble 'cos *you* can't wait till you get home.'

'I'm allowed to smoke, actually, 'cos *my* 'rents are cool,' Julie said, defiantly lighting up and blowing the smoke in Holly's direction.

'You're such a liar,' Holly sniped, wafting it away.

'All right, pack it in you two,' Bex said, sliding the unlit cigarette into her pocket. 'I'll save mine for later if it's gonna cause trouble.'

'It's not me, it's *her*,' Holly and Julie said in unison.

'It's *both* of you,' said Bex. 'And I don't wanna hear it, so shut up.'

Holly and Julie exchanged dirty looks and sat back.

Across the road, Suzie's front door opened and Holly glanced over when the woman stepped outside. Her face looked flawless, with no sign of the bruises she'd had the previous week, and she was wearing a figure-hugging red dress that accentuated her tiny waist and showed off her cleavage. Watching as she dropped two empty wine bottles into the recycling bin, Holly smiled when Suzie spotted her and waved before going back inside.

'Who's the slapper?' Julie curled her lip.

'Don't call her that,' Holly said defensively. 'She's really nice.'

'Oh my days, don't tell me she's one of your lesbo crushes?' Julie snorted. 'And there was me thinking you only had eyes for Bex.'

'Get lost!' Holly jumped up.

'Chill out,' Bex said, grabbing her hand and pulling her back down. 'She's only messing – aren't you, Ju?'

'Yeah, course.' Julie gave Holly a smile that didn't quite reach her eyes. 'It's just my sense of humour, babes. I don't mean anything by it – honest.'

Holly didn't believe her, but she didn't want to fall out with Bex again, so she bit her tongue.

At the sound of shouting, all three girls looked round, and Holly smirked when she saw the boys who had tried to mug her earlier being chased off the estate by some older lads.

'Oh my God,' Julie said, clutching at Bex's arm and giving an exaggerated shudder. 'I see what you meant about this place being a war zone, babes. Can you imagine that type of thing going on round our way?'

Holly opened her mouth to tell the snotty bitch to piss off home if that was how she felt, but Bex let out an audible gasp before she had the chance, and she winced when the girl grabbed her hand and squeezed it hard.

'It's him!' Bex squealed. '*Look!*'

She pointed in the direction of the flats, and Holly saw that Gee had come outside and was standing in the porch looking down at his phone.

'Holy shit,' Julie spluttered, her eyes widening when she, too, saw him. 'She was right – he *is* the spit of Zayn.'

'Told you,' Holly said smugly.

'Hey, you two keep your eyes off him, he's mine,' Bex warned them both as she jumped up. 'Come on, you.' She tugged on Holly's hand.

'Where you going?' Holly asked, reluctantly standing up.

71

'You've got to introduce us,' Bex said.

'What? *No!*' Holly pulled her hand free. 'I can't.'

'Why not?'

'I don't know him well enough to go over and start talking to him like that.'

'OK, well, we'll make out like we're going to yours,' Bex said, linking arms with her. 'You say hi, and I'll take it from there.'

'*No,*' Holly protested. 'He'll think we're stupid.'

'Don't be so selfish,' Bex said, dragging her along. 'I'd do it for you.'

'Hey, wait for me,' Julie said, dropping her cigarette and tottering after them.

10

Gee Allen was pissed off. He'd had a massive bust-up with his girlfriend, Kadisha, at the party, and she'd been bombarding him with text messages ever since. They had been abusive to start with, calling him all the dirty, cheating bastards under the sun and threatening to send her brother and his mates round to do him in. Then, at around 4 a.m. – when, Gee presumed, she'd sobered up and realized what she'd done – the tearful apologies had started to flood in: *I'm so sorry, baby, I didn't mean it . . . I just love you so much I can't help getting jealous when you speak to other girls . . . I know I've got a problem, but I'll change, I swear . . .*

Blah, blah, blah.

Gee had heard it all before, and he'd given her one too many second chances already. So, as fine as Kadisha was, he'd had enough.

Determined to get that through to her now, because she didn't seem able to take no for an answer, he sent a curt reply to her latest message, then stuffed the phone into his pocket and set off – not noticing the girl who had just that second appeared in front of him. Their shoulders clashed and she went flying, landing on her backside at his feet.

'God, I'm sorry,' he said, offering his hand to help her. 'Are you OK?'

'Does she look OK?' her friend snapped.

'I'm fine,' the one on the floor said, batting her fake eyelashes at him as she grasped his hand.

'Are you sure?' Gee asked, feeling guilty when he spotted the dirt on the side of her white jeans. 'You're not hurt, are you?'

'I'll live,' the girl cooed. 'And I'm sure you didn't mean it – did you?' She gazed at him from under her lashes and bit her lip.

'Course not,' he said, beginning to feel uncomfortable. 'Right, well, as long as you're not hurt, I need to get going,' he said, sliding his hand free.

'Oi, Zayn,' the girl's friend called after him when he started walking away. 'At least give us your number – in case she gets concussion or something!'

'*Concussion?*' a woman bellowed. 'I'll give you fucking concussion, you slag!'

Gee heard the voice at the same time the girls did, and he groaned when he glanced back and saw Kadisha running across the grass, shoes in hand, face contorted with rage.

'K, don't!' he yelled, rushing back to cut her off. 'They haven't done anything.'

'I've got eyes,' she spat, dodging round him when he tried to grab her arm. 'The little skank was flirting with you!'

'Don't be stupid,' he hissed, jumping between her and the girls. 'They're just kids.'

'Hey, I'm no kid,' one of the girls protested, flicking her blond locks over her shoulder and placing her hands on her skinny hips.

'He wasn't fuckin' talking to you,' Kadisha roared, lunging at her and jabbing a fingernail into her chest. 'Think you're a big woman, do you? Sniffing round my man, trying to get his number. I'll rip your fucking head off, you sketchy tramp!'

'Oh, my God, she's crazy,' one of the other girls spluttered.

'What was that?' Kadisha glared at her. 'If you've got something to say, spit it out, bitch.'

'Pack it in,' Gee hissed, seizing her by the arm and pulling her away. 'You're scaring them.'

'I'll do more than fuckin' scare them,' she screeched, struggling to break free. 'I knew you'd been screwing around, and you'd better tell me which one it is or I'm gonna fuck them all up!'

'See, this is exactly why I can't deal with you,' Gee said, pushing her through the gate. 'You're out of control and I'm done with it.'

'I hate you!' she screamed, beating her fists against his chest.

Gee grabbed her wrists to stop her, but she yanked her arms free at the exact same time he released her, and he winced when she fell backwards and her shoes flew into the road.

Behind them, one of the girls started laughing, and Kadisha let out a roar of anger.

'Ignore her,' Gee said. 'They're only kids, and someone will end up calling the police if you keep threatening them.'

'I don't *care!*' she screeched, tears running down her cheeks.

A car came round the corner and pulled up at the kerb, and two girls leapt out and ran over to Kadisha.

'If you've laid a finger on her, you're dead,' one of them spat, glaring at Gee as they helped her to her feet.

'Don't be stupid,' he snapped. 'I've never hit a woman in my life.'

'Why's she on the floor, then?'

'Because she attacked me and fell over when I pushed her away. Now get her out of here before she does something stupid.'

'I'm not leaving you,' Kadisha sobbed, shrugging her friends off and running to him. 'I'm sorry, baby.' She clutched at his jacket. 'I didn't mean it. I love you.'

'Well, I don't love you,' he replied bluntly, holding her at arm's length. 'Go with your mates and stop making a fool of yourself.'

Wailing, Kadisha sank to her knees and wrapped her arms around his legs.

'Get up!' one of her friends ordered. 'He ain't worth it.'

'Yeah, come on, let's get out of here,' the other girl said, prising Kadisha's hands off him. 'He's a dirty little player, and you can do way better.'

Gee opened his mouth to defend himself, but decided there was no point and snapped it shut again.

'Looks like you had a lucky escape there, Zayn,' one of the girls called out when Kadisha's friends had bundled her into the car and driven away. 'She's off her head!'

Too angry to answer without snapping at her, Gee gave her a withering look before walking away.

'Thanks a lot!' Holly glared at Julie when Gee had gone. 'He'll probably never talk to me again after that.'

'Like he ever talked to you anyway,' Julie sneered. 'He didn't even look at you the whole time he was here. And it was *her* fault, not mine. She's a maniac. Look what she did to me with her fucking claws.' She pulled the neck of her top down to show the red mark the girl's nails had left on her chest.

'You deserved that for mouthing off,' Holly said. 'And you don't live round here, so you're not the one she's going to come after if they get back together.'

'Aw, diddums,' Julie drawled.

'I don't want to be here if she comes back,' Bex said, gazing nervously out along the road.

'Yeah, come on, let's get out of this dump,' Julie said, linking arms with her and setting off up the path. When Holly fell into step beside them, she stopped walking and snapped, 'Where d'you think *you're* going?'

'With Bex,' Holly said.

'No, you're not,' Julie argued. 'We've got plans, and you're not invited.'

'Bex?' Holly looked at her friend.

'Sorry, I meant to tell you when we got here,' Bex said sheepishly. 'Thing is, Ju's mum got us tickets for an art exhibition this afternoon.'

'An art exhibition?' Holly screwed up her face. 'Since when have you been interested in art? It's your least favourite subject.'

'Only 'cos I'm crap at it,' said Bex. 'But this is all Banksy type stuff, so it'll be well cool.'

'So that's it?' Holly stared at her. 'You hardly ever come to see me, and now you're sacking me off for *her* again?'

'Get a grip,' Julie snorted. 'She wouldn't even be here now if you hadn't made out like you and Zayn were mates.'

'His name's not Zayn, you idiot,' Holly snapped. 'And I never said we were mates.'

'As good as,' said Julie. 'And you're the idiot, not me. Look at the state of you, with your trampy clothes and your chip-pan hair. You're an embarrassment, and you wonder why Bex is ashamed to be seen with you?'

'Julie, stop it,' Bex said quietly when Holly's mouth fell open.

'Why should I?' Julie shot back. 'You told me yourself, you only hang out with her 'cos you feel sorry for her.'

'Is that true?' Holly looked at Bex with tears in her eyes.

'Oh, for God's sake, isn't it obvious?' Julie jeered. 'I mean, come on . . . look at *us* then look at *you*.'

'I wasn't asking you, I was asking Bex!' Holly spat.

'Truth hurts, don't it?' Julie replied nastily.

'Get lost!' Holly yelled.

'Make me!' Julie challenged. 'I'll kick your fuckin' head in, you stupid bitch!'

'Holly . . . ? Is everything all right, hon?'

Julie glanced round at the sound of the voice and saw that the woman in the red dress was watching them.

'Oh, look, *hon . . .*' she drawled, turning back to Holly with a sly smile on her lips. 'Your lesbo friend's come out to save you.'

'Fuck off!' Holly cried, slamming her hands into Julie's chest and sending her tottering back on her heels.

'Stop it!' Bex shouted, jumping between them and glaring at Holly. 'This is your fault, not hers. You've been an absolute bitch since we got here, and now she's biting back you're trying to play the victim. It's pathetic and I'm sick of it. We *both* are!'

Unable to hold in the tears any longer, Holly turned and ran to the flats.

Across the road, Suzie watched as Holly ran inside and the other girls walked down the path arm in arm. As they passed on the opposite side, she narrowed her eyes when she heard one of them mimicking Holly in a baby voice. She had no clue what they had been arguing about because she'd only caught the tail end of it, but she'd come up against enough girls like those two to know they were grade-A bitches.

Heading inside when they'd gone, she pulled up the message

she'd sent to her phone from Holly's the previous week, and typed: *Hi, hon, it's Suzie. Just checking you're all right? Xx*

When Holly didn't reply after a few minutes, she sent another, saying: *If you want to talk about it, come over to mine when your mum's gone to work tonight xx*

11

Josie woke with a start when the front door slammed shut, and she sat up when she heard Holly run into her bedroom. Annoyed to see that it was only 11 a.m. when she squinted at the clock, she pulled on her dressing gown and went out to ask Holly what the hell she was playing at.

'What's all the noise about?' she demanded, marching into her room. 'And why are you lying in the dark?' she asked, frowning when she saw Holly curled up in bed with the curtains closed.

'I'm tired,' Holly muttered.

'Are you crying?' Josie walked over to the bed.

'No.'

'You sound like you are.'

'Well, I'm not,' Holly said into her pillow.

Concerned now, because weekends were the only free time Holly had and she didn't usually come home so early, Josie touched her shoulder. 'What's up, love?'

'Nothing.' Holly dragged the quilt up to hide her face. 'Leave me alone.'

'Something's obviously upset you,' Josie persisted, perching on the edge of the bed. 'Have you fallen out with your friends?'

'No.'

'It's not a man, is it?' Josie asked. 'Has a man touched you? You know you can tell me, don't you? Whatever it is, I wouldn't blame you.'

'Nothing's happened,' Holly sniffed. 'I don't feel well.'

'In what way?'

'My stomach hurts.'

'Do you want me to get you some painkillers?'

'No.'

Tutting, Josie stood up, saying, 'Suit yourself, but you're not staying in here all day, so get up.'

'I don't want to,' Holly moaned.

'Don't argue. It's not healthy.'

'*You* do it.'

'Excuse me, lady,' Josie snapped. 'I work nights, so I'm entitled to sleep when I come home. What's your excuse?'

'I haven't got one,' Holly said contritely, wishing she'd kept that last thought to herself. 'Sorry.'

'So you should be,' Josie grumbled. 'Now I'm awake, I might as well get dressed,' she added as she headed for the door. 'And you'd better be up by the time I've finished.'

Cursing herself for making a racket and waking her mum, Holly kicked the duvet off and flopped over onto her back. She lay there until she heard her mum going to the bathroom a few minutes later, then reluctantly got up and shuffled into the living room.

An old black-and-white film was playing when she turned the TV on, and she was flicking through the channel guide in search of something better when her mum walked in.

'Leave this on,' Josie said. 'I love that film.'

'It looks rubbish,' Holly complained. 'Can't we watch *Catfish*, or *Friends* or something?'

'No, they're all repeats,' Josie said, going into the kitchen and coming back with a glass of water. 'Give it a chance, you'll love it.'

'Bet I don't,' Holly muttered under her breath as she curled up at the end of the sofa.

'That bloke went missing after his plane crashed,' Josie said, pointing her glass at a miserable-looking man on the screen. 'She was his wife' – another point – 'and she was going off her head trying to find out what had happened to him. Women didn't earn much in those days and she was struggling, so she married someone else. But then some explorers found her old hubby living with the natives on an island and brought him home, so now she doesn't know if her new marriage is legal or . . .'

Already bored, Holly tuned her mum out and stared unseeing at the screen as her thoughts turned back to the argument she'd had with Julie. She mentally re-ran the whole thing from start to finish, adding the cutting comebacks she wished she'd been quick enough to deliver at the time and visualizing herself beating the bitch to a pulp. She hated Julie and couldn't understand why Bex had started dressing like her and having sleepovers at her place. And as for them calling everyone *babes*, it was pathetic. *They* were pathetic, and she hated them both.

Only she didn't. Not Bex, anyway. They were best mates – or so she'd thought.

'You haven't been listening to a word I've said, have you?'

'What?' Holly snapped out of her thoughts and blinked at her mum, who was walking in from the kitchen, the glass, now refilled, still in her hand.

'I asked if you fancied going into town for a mooch around the charity shops when the film's finished?' Josie said, flopping down beside her. 'See if we can get you some new trainers.'

Holly shook her head. She knew her mum was trying to cheer her up, but it wasn't going to work. Bex's betrayal had cut her to the core and she was never going to get over it.

'OK, we'll stay in then,' Josie said. 'It's been ages since we've spent a whole day together, hasn't it?'

'Mmmm.'

'I've been meaning to take some time off, but we're understaffed so I can't just yet.'

'It's OK. I'm fine on my own.'

'Is that a dig?' Josie's smile morphed into a frown.

'Eh?' Holly pulled a face. 'What you on about?'

'You saying you're fine on your own. Like I'm never here.'

You're not! Holly thought.

'I didn't mean it like that,' she said, scenting alcohol on her mum's breath and realizing that it wasn't water in the glass. 'I meant I'm OK with things as they are, so you don't need to worry about me.'

Josie's expression softened as quickly as it had hardened and she leaned over and squeezed Holly's hand, purring, 'You're a good girl, Holly Wolly. And you know I'd spend more time with you if I could, don't you?'

'Yeah, I know,' Holly said, wishing she'd shut up and concentrate on the film. She always got like this when she'd been drinking, and it was exhausting having to walk on eggshells to avoid saying the wrong thing. She just hoped it wasn't becoming a problem again, because this was the third time in a week that she'd seen her mum drinking during the day. The last time it had got out of hand her mum had gone on a three-day bender with a bloke who lived in the next-door flat at one of their previous addresses, and the pair had got into a massive fight over whose turn it was to pay for the next bottle, culminating in windows getting smashed, the police turning up, and the landlord turfing them out. Her mum had promised never to get in that state again – and, so far, she'd kept to her word. But if she was sliding back into her old ways, Holly didn't know what she would do.

'Oh, here we go,' Josie said, sloshing liquid out of the glass as she pointed at another woman who had appeared on the TV screen. 'She's the new hubby's ex, and she—'

'Mum, just let me watch it,' Holly groaned.

'Well, pardon me for trying to bring you up to speed,' Josie huffed, a look of indignation on her face as she raised the glass to her lips.

The silence only lasted as long as the film did, and Holly felt like she was being tortured when another oldie came on and her mum immediately started a new running commentary.

Hours that felt like an absolute eternity later, Josie headed off to work, at last. The vodka bottle was empty by then and she'd been a little unsteady on her feet as she leaned over the back of the sofa to kiss Holly goodbye – something she only ever did when she was pissed. But she'd walked a reasonably straight line to the door, so Holly figured she'd be OK.

As soon as she was alone, Holly switched the TV off and went to her room with her mum's voice echoing in her head. Still fully clothed, she climbed into bed and checked her phone to see if Bex had messaged or tried to call. There was nothing from Bex, but Suzie had sent two messages: the first asking if she was OK, the second inviting her to go over if she fancied a chat. The only person Holly wanted to chat to was Bex, so she swiped the messages off the screen without replying and logged into her Facebook account.

Bex had been online posting photos of herself and Julie at the art exhibition, and Holly's lip curled as she scrolled through them. They looked like a pair of TOWIE wannabes with their ridiculous fake-tans and duck-lips, and it was obvious they were filtered, contrary to Bex's claim that she never filtered her selfies.

She'd posted loads of photos of the so-called artwork, but

Holly thought it looked more like the graffiti that was spray-painted all over the estate than Banksy's stuff. Bex had gushed that it was all '*Shamaaaazing*', and Julie had commented on every post, even though she was right there and could easily have shared her thoughts with Bex in person. But that was them all over: anything to get a few stupid Facebook likes. It was pathetic, and Holly closed the page down in disgust and pulled her duvet over her head.

12

Suzie had been thinking about Holly all afternoon. The girl still hadn't answered her texts and she was worried about her, so when she saw her mum heading out to work, she rang her.

Holly picked up on the fourth ring, and murmured a wan, 'Hello?'

'Hi, hon, it's Suzie,' she said. 'Didn't you get my messages?'

'Oh, yeah. Sorry. I'm not well, so I'm in bed.'

'Why, what's wrong?'

'I feel sick.'

'Oh, you poor thing. When did that come on?'

'Earlier.'

'Are you sure you're not just fretting about what happened with those girls?' Suzie asked, cutting to the chase. 'Because you know they're probably slagging you off right now while you're lying there feeling sorry for yourself, don't you?'

'Bex is my best mate, she'd never slag me off,' Holly said miserably.

'You don't believe that any more than I do,' said Suzie. Then, more gently, because Holly sounded so unhappy, she said, 'Why don't you forget about them and come over here and chill with me for a bit? I've been cooking, and there's way too much for me on my own.'

'I can't,' Holly said, her voice muffled by the quilt she was hiding beneath. 'I'm not allowed out when my mum's at work.'

'What time does she come home?'

'Depends how many shifts she's got.' Holly sniffed. 'Sometimes two-ish, sometimes five or six.'

'Ah, you've got hours yet,' Suzie said. 'And you'd be doing me a massive favour, 'cos I could really use the company,' she added. 'You're my only friend round here, and I didn't realize it'd be so lonely without Rob. Please, hon. I hate being on my own.'

Holly stayed quiet for a moment. Then, sighing, she said, 'OK.'

'Thank you so much,' Suzie said gratefully. 'I'll leave the door on the latch; come straight in.'

Nervous, because it was the first time she had ever defied her mum and gone out at night, Holly pulled the hood of her jacket up over her head when she crept out of the flats a few minutes later. Scuttling across the road, she gave a tiny knock on Suzie's door before going inside. The warmth hit her as soon as she entered the hallway, and she picked up on the delicious scent of food coming from the kitchen.

'That was fast,' Suzie said, appearing in the kitchen doorway. 'Take your shoes off and go make yourself comfortable while I plate up. And I hope you're hungry, 'cos there's loads.'

Embarrassed when her stomach rumbled loudly in reply, Holly looped her jacket over a peg and then slipped her trainers off before heading into the living room. A black leather settee was positioned against the wall facing the window, and a matching armchair sat in the corner. The floor was laminated, and a flat-screen TV was attached to the wall above the fireplace. Holly and her mum had moved around a lot over the years, carting their possessions from one filthy dump to the next – usually in the middle of the night, when their rent arrears had caught up with them and the bailiffs were breathing down their necks. But they'd never lived in a house as nice or as clean as this one.

'Here we go.' Suzie came in carrying two plates, and handed one to Holly before taking a seat on the sofa. 'It's chicken korma. Hope you like it.'

'Thanks,' Holly said, sitting down and carefully balancing the plate on her lap. Used to the bland microwave meals and frozen foods her mum bought, she was surprised by how good the curry tasted: spicy, but not too hot, with tender chunks of chicken and a heap of fluffy rice.

'Is it OK?' Suzie asked, watching as Holly tucked in.

'Mmmm.' Holly covered her full mouth with her hand and quickly swallowed. 'It's great. Did you make it yourself?'

'Sure did.' Suzie smiled. 'I'll give you the recipe, if you like?'

Holly nodded, but she knew she would never attempt to cook it. She could just about cope with frozen pizzas and oven chips, let alone mess about with real meat and rice.

They ate on in silence, and when they'd finished Suzie took their plates into the kitchen. She came back carrying two glasses and a bottle of white wine.

'How old are you?' she asked as she sat down.

'Fifteen,' said Holly. 'But I'll be sixteen in two months.'

'That's old enough for one little glass,' Suzie said. 'If you want one?'

'Yes, please,' said Holly.

'I'm surprised you're only fifteen,' Suzie said, pouring two glasses and passing one over before settling back in her seat. 'You seem very mature for your age.'

Tickled by the compliment, Holly smiled as she took a sip of wine. She'd had alcohol before, when Kelly had nicked a bottle of brandy off her mum and brought it into school. She, Kelly and Bex had polished it off in the toilets at lunchtime, and she'd been sent home after puking her guts up in maths that afternoon. The teacher had thought it was a stomach bug, so she hadn't got into trouble, but the hangover had been punishment enough and she'd vowed never to drink again. She was sure one glass of wine wouldn't hurt her, though.

'So what was all that about earlier?' Suzie asked, kicking off her slippers and pulling her feet up under her. 'Did you say one of those girls is supposed to be your best mate?'

'Yeah, Bex.' Holly's smile slipped.

'Hey, don't go down on me again,' Suzie said, lighting a cigarette. 'I'm only asking 'cos I saw them walking off after you went inside, and they didn't look that bothered about upsetting you.'

'It was all Julie's fault,' Holly muttered. 'She follows Bex round like a dog, then accuses *me* of being a lesbo. And she proper thinks she's gorgeous,' she added bitterly.

'I take it that's the one with the extensions?' Suzie asked. 'I clocked that about her as soon as I saw her. She's like all the fake bitches I've worked with on the modelling circuit.'

'Oh, are you a model?' Holly asked. 'I did wonder when I saw that.' She nodded at a large framed photograph on the wall, in which Suzie was reclining on a chaise longue wearing a red satin bra and panties. 'It's really nice.'

'It's all right,' Suzie said modestly. 'It's from a shoot I did for a lingerie company. They didn't end up using me, but Rob liked that picture, so I had it blown up and framed for him.'

'How come it's got no glass?' Holly asked.

'Because Rob threw his phone at me, but I ducked and it hit that instead.'

'Why's he so horrible to you?'

'Because he's a knob,' Suzie sneered. Then, sighing, she said, 'He wasn't always like that. I'd been in a few crap relationships before I met him, but he was so sweet and I honestly thought we were good together. I should have finished it the first time he put his hands on me, but we live and learn.'

'Do you still love him?' Holly asked, taking another sip of wine.

'I know I shouldn't after everything he's done, but *yes*, I have still got feelings for him,' Suzie admitted. 'You've only seen the bad side of him, but he can be lovely when he wants to be.'

'Is he in prison?' Holly relaxed back against the cushions as the wine began to soften her edges.

'As far as I know he's still on remand,' Suzie said, twisting round in her seat and resting her elbow on the back of the sofa. 'But enough about him. Finish telling me about the argument with your friends.'

'Julie started it,' Holly said. 'Bex was supposed to be coming over to spend the day with me, 'cos she's been dying to meet my neighbour. But *she* tagged along, even though she knows I can't stand her.'

'Why did Bex want to meet your neighbour?' Suzie asked.

''Cos he's the spit of Zayn,' Holly said. 'Zayn Malik,' she elaborated when Suzie gave her a blank look. 'He used to be in One Direction, and me and Bex fancied him like mad. Well, Bex more than me, but he *is* gorgeous. And my neighbour looks like him, only younger and fitter.'

'Ah, yeah, I think I know who you mean,' Suzie said. 'So did Bex get to meet him?'

'Yeah, but it didn't go how she expected,' Holly snorted. 'She was convinced he would fall for her as soon as he met her, but she made a right tit of herself.' Blushing, she murmured, 'Sorry, I mean she made a fool of herself.'

'Don't censor yourself on my account, hon,' Suzie laughed.

'I swear like a trooper when I get going. So what did she do?'

'She dragged me over to him, but he didn't see us coming and they banged into each other. She fell over, then got all flirty when he helped her up. Julie started gobbing off and asked him for his phone number – in case Bex got concussion, or something stupid like that. But then his girlfriend turned up and went for her.'

'Oh, wow, how did I miss that?'

'It was before you came out. Zayn – I mean *Gee* – stopped the girl from attacking Julie, so she punched him instead. He pushed her away and she fell over, and then her friends turned up and she started crying and begging him to take her back. But he wasn't having any of it.'

'Good for him,' Suzie said approvingly. 'So what happened then?'

'Her friends took her away and he walked off. Then Bex said she wanted to go, so I started walking with them. But Julie said they had plans and I wasn't invited. She said they wouldn't have come if I hadn't lied about being mates with Gee. And then she said Bex is ashamed of me and only hangs round with me 'cos she feels sorry for me.'

'Nasty little cow.' Suzie tutted. 'No wonder you got so upset. I'd have given her what for if I'd heard any of that.'

'She'd only have slagged you off as well,' Holly said. 'She called you a slapper when you came out and waved to me earlier.'

'Did she now?' Suzie raised an eyebrow. 'Well, she'd best not come round here again, or your neighbour's crazy girlfriend will be the least of her worries. It really pissed me off when I heard them taking the mick out of you after you ran inside, and I'll be giving that little madam a piece of my mind if I ever see her again.'

'Why, what were they saying?'

'That Julie one was imitating you in a baby voice, and Bex was laughing like it was a big joke. I could have slapped the pair of them. Wish I had now.'

Upset to hear that Bex had laughed at her after reducing her to tears, Holly took a slug of wine to wash the bitter taste out of her mouth.

'Girls like them are why I've always preferred hanging out with boys,' Suzie went on as she reached for the bottle to refill her glass. 'Subject of, have you got a boyfriend?'

'No.'

'I'm surprised. Pretty girl like you.'

'I'm not pretty.' Holly blushed.

'Yes, you are,' Suzie insisted. 'You've got beautiful eyes and a lovely smile.'

Flattered, but sure that Suzie was only saying it to make her feel better, Holly gazed at the photo on the wall again, and asked, 'Have you been modelling for long?'

'Years,' Suzie said. 'Would you like to see some of my other photos?' Smiling when Holly nodded, she said, 'I keep them in my wardrobe; just give me a minute while I dig them out.'

'Would you mind if I use the loo?' Holly asked as Suzie got up.

''Course not,' Suzie said, already heading for the stairs. 'Come on, I'll show you where it is.'

13

Still in her bedroom when Holly came out of the bathroom, her arms full of photograph albums, Suzie called, 'Give me a hand with these, hon. I'd forgotten how heavy they are.'

Seizing the opportunity to see the bedroom, because she would never have dreamed of asking to be shown around, Holly walked into the room and gazed around. A fitted wardrobe with mirrored doors ranged across one entire wall, and the bed that was facing it had a fancy satin duvet cover and matching pillow-cases. A vanity unit with a large oval mirror sat below the window, and numerous bottles of expensive-looking perfumes were standing on it.

'Wow, this is lovely,' she said.

'It's the landlord's furniture, not mine,' Suzie said, dropping the albums onto the bed. 'We might as well look through these now you're here,' she said, perching on the bed and patting for Holly to sit beside her. 'Save me having to lug them all back up later.'

When Holly was seated, Suzie opened one of the albums

and showed Holly a set of shots in which she was dressed in sportswear.

'This was a campaign I did for the Littlewoods catalogue last year,' she said.

'Really?' Holly was impressed. 'They're amazing.'

'It wasn't that big a deal, to be honest. But it paid well, so I can't complain,' Suzie said. '*This* is the type of work I prefer.' She flipped to another page. 'It was a Fendi campaign, and they flew me to Paris for the weekend.'

'Wow,' Holly murmured, gazing at the photos in awe. In these, Suzie was wearing a variety of glamorous dresses, and she looked absolutely stunning with her glossy hair coiled up and her make-up immaculate. 'Are you a supermodel?' she asked.

'I wish,' Suzie laughed, reaching for her glass.

'You should be,' Holly said, looking through the rest of the photos. 'You're way prettier than any of the models I've seen in magazines.'

'That's very sweet,' Suzie said. 'But if you think *I* look good, you should see some of the other girls I've worked with. And by girls I mean *kids*, 'cos you've got to be fourteen and skinny as a rake to get anywhere these days.'

'You're not giving up, are you?' Holly asked, thinking she would be crazy to do that.

'I don't have a lot of choice at my age,' Suzie said resignedly. 'But even if *I* can't get work, I've got a good eye for talent, so I've decided to set up my own agency. It's a vicious world for young girls to be getting into, but with my experience I'll be able to keep them away from the sharks. Obviously I won't be able to compete with the established agencies, because they use professional photographers and stylists, and I can't afford to do that. But I'm pretty good with hair and make-up, and I've got a decent camera, so now I just need to find a model who's willing to let me practise on her to get me started. Hey, maybe *you* could help me with that?'

'Me?' Holly was confused.

'Yeah, you could be my practice model.'

'No, I couldn't.'

'Yes, you could,' Suzie insisted. 'You'd be perfect. Come over here . . .' She jumped up off the bed and waved for Holly to take a seat at the vanity unit.

'Why?' Holly reluctantly rose to her feet.

'I'm going to give you a little makeover,' Suzie said, lifting a make-up box out from under the unit.

'Oh . . .' Holly hesitated. 'My mum doesn't really like me wearing make-up.'

'I've got wet wipes, so you can take it all off before you go home,' Suzie said, pushing her down onto the stool. 'I just want you to see what *I* see when I look at you.'

When Holly was seated, Suzie swivelled the stool round so her back was to the mirror and studied her face for a few moments before opening the box.

'Right, I'm going to use smoky colours to bring out the green of your eyes,' she said. 'And I'll do a bit of contouring to define your cheekbones, then finish you off with a natural glossy lip.'

'Are you sure it'll come off?' Holly asked nervously when Suzie squirted a huge blob of foundation into the palm of her hand.

'Course it will,' Suzie assured her.

Clasping her hands together in her lap after putting her glass down, Holly closed her eyes and tried not to move when Suzie began to apply the foundation with a soft brush.

'It won't take long, will it?' she asked. 'Only I can't be too late getting home.'

'You said she never gets home before two, so you'll be back way before she is,' Suzie said. 'Subject of your mum,' she went on as she worked. 'Is it just you and her over there? Doesn't your dad live with you?'

'No,' Holly said, trying not to move her mouth too much as the brush tickled her cheeks. 'He took off before I was born, so I've never met him.'

'Oh, I'm sorry.'

'It's OK.'

'No, it's not. Everyone needs a dad. Haven't you ever tried to find him?'

Holly shook her head.

'What's his name?' Suzie asked. 'I'll google him when we've finished, see if he's on Facebook or Twitter.'

'I don't know his name,' Holly admitted. 'My mum wouldn't tell me.'

'Why not?'

'Dunno.' Holly gave a tiny shrug. 'She doesn't really like

talking about private stuff. And she gets mad if I ask too many questions, so I don't bother any more.'

'That's sad,' Suzie said. 'But then, you can't miss what you've never had, can you? And at least you've got your mum. Are you and her close?'

'I suppose so,' Holly murmured.

'How come she's so strict?' Suzie asked. 'I used to be out till all hours when I was fifteen, but you're not allowed out after she goes to work. What's that about?'

'She's just a bit protective,' Holly said guardedly. 'I got bullied at my last school, and the kids are a lot rougher round here, so she thinks it's safer for me to stay in when she's out.'

'Ah, right. I went through something similar when I was your age, so I get where she's coming from.'

'You were bullied?' Holly was surprised. Suzie was so beautiful and self-assured she couldn't imagine anyone having a problem with her – apart from Rob, but he was a thug, so his actions said more about him than Suzie.

'Yep,' Suzie said, her wine-laced breath warming Holly's cheeks as she leaned closer. 'Two horrible bitches like those so-called friends of yours made my life a living hell in fifth year. It started when one of their boyfriends took a fancy to me. I turned him down, so he told her I'd tried it on with him. The silly cow believed him, and her and her mate started following me round school, calling me names and threatening to beat me up.'

'What did you do?'

'They pushed me too far one day, and I went full psycho

bitch on their arses.' Suzie chuckled. 'They'd ambushed me in the girls' toilets and were trying to force my head down the loo. Someone had left a big shit in it, so I grabbed it and slammed it into one of their faces.'

'You didn't?' Holly's eyes popped open.

'Oh, I did.' Suzie laughed. 'It was disgusting, but they didn't come near me again, so it worked.'

'I wish Julie went to my school so I could do that to her,' Holly said.

'Stick with me, kid.' Suzie winked. 'I'll show you how to deal with bitches like her. Now shut your eyes.'

Holly struggled to keep the grin off her lips as Suzie started applying eye make-up. Unlike the brandy Kelly had brought into school that time, which had hit her like a speeding train, the wine was making her feel warm and fuzzy, and she no longer cared so much about all that nonsense with Bex and Julie. They thought they were so cool, but they were just childish and spiteful, and now she had Suzie she didn't need them.

After a while, Suzie swivelled the stool round to face the mirror and asked Holly what she thought. Holly stared at her reflection, unable to believe that it was her. Bex had done her make-up in the past, but the results had been nothing like this. The blend of grey, purple and silver eyeshadows Suzie had used, along with the jet-black fake lashes she'd applied, made her usually dull green eyes pop. And her skin looked smooth and radiant, with all the blemishes she obsessed over whenever she looked in the mirror concealed beneath the creamy foundation.

'It's amazing,' she said. 'I look like a completely different person.'

'No, you look like *you*, but the best version of you,' Suzie said. 'And that's the difference between you and the Julies and Bexes of this world. If you paint a pig, it's still a pig, but paint a pretty girl and you highlight how beautiful she really is. Can you see it?'

Embarrassed to admit that she could, Holly gave a little shrug.

'You're too modest,' Suzie laughed. 'You look drop-dead gorgeous. Or, at least, you *will* when we've done something with this . . .' She lifted Holly's hair off her shoulders and examined the ends. 'When was the last time you had it cut?'

'A couple of months ago,' Holly said, still staring at her reflection.

'By who? A butcher?'

'No, I did it. I watched a video on YouTube and it was dead easy. You tie your hair in a pony on top of your head, then twist it and cut the end off.'

'It's terrible,' Suzie said. 'But don't worry, I can fix it.'

'You can't cut it,' Holly said, panicking when Suzie took a pair of scissors out of the drawer. 'My mum'll want to know who did it, and she'll go mad if she finds out I've been here.'

'I'm only going to take the ends off and shape it a bit,' Suzie promised. 'I doubt your mum'll even notice. But if she does, tell her you copied another vid and did it yourself. It'll look and feel so much better without the dead bits.'

Remembering how Julie had gone on about her hair being

horrible earlier, Holly stared at herself for a few more seconds and then nodded.

'OK. But only a tiny bit.'

Unable to see what was happening when Suzie brushed her hair forward over her eyes and started snipping, Holly crossed her fingers and prayed that she wouldn't get too carried away when clumps began to fall to the floor. After what felt like an age, Suzie sprayed dry shampoo onto the roots and brushed it through before spritzing it with lacquer.

'All done,' she said, standing back.

Relieved to see that her hair still looked pretty much the same length, considering the long bits she'd seen falling to the floor, Holly twisted her head to look at it from all angles. It looked thicker and healthier, and Suzie had moved her usual middle parting slightly to one side and had swept her long fringe over in a replica of the way her own hair was styled.

'I love it,' she said, reaching up to touch it. 'Thank you.'

'You're welcome,' Suzie said, smiling as she put away the brush and scissors before repacking the make-up box.

As Holly continued to admire herself in the mirror, Suzie opened the wardrobe and leafed through the clothes hanging inside. Taking out a deep-purple velvet dress, she said, 'Here . . . try this on.'

The thrill Holly had been experiencing evaporated, and her cheeks reddened at the thought of undressing in front of Suzie and revealing her grubby, stretched bra and the hole in her knickers where the elastic had come away from the material.

'It's, um, getting a bit late,' she said, casting a glance at the clock on the bedside table. 'My mum'll flip out if she gets home and I'm not there.'

'It's only ten o'clock, you've got hours yet,' Suzie said, handing the dress to her. 'Go on, humour me. You can take it straight back off again. I just want to see if it looks as good on you as I think it will. Oh, and what size shoes do you wear?'

'Five,' Holly murmured.

'Ooh, same as me.' Suzie took out a pair of strappy silver shoes with high thin heels. 'Try these.' She handed them over and then walked to the door, saying, 'I need the loo. Give me a shout when you're ready.'

Relieved to be alone, Holly quickly slipped out of her clothes and wriggled into the dress. Taking off her socks, she pushed her feet into the shoes and stood in the space between the bed and the wardrobe.

'Ready,' she called.

Suzie came in and drew back her head. 'Wow, look at you!'

'Does it look OK?' Holly asked, stroking the velvet that was clinging to her hips.

'Are you kidding me?' Suzie said, turning her by the shoulders to face a free-standing mirror in the corner. 'See how gorgeous and sophisticated you look? No one'd ever guess you were only fifteen. And check that figure you've been hiding.'

Blushing again, Holly stared at herself. Suzie was right about her looking older, and the dress caressed curves she hadn't realized were there, giving definition to her waist and hips, and the illusion of larger breasts. Her legs looked good, too, the heels lending tone to her calf muscles.

'I'm going to take some pictures,' Suzie said, slipping her phone out of her pocket and looking around thoughtfully before perching on the dressing table stool. 'Right, sit like this,' she said, placing her elbows on the dresser top and resting her chin on her hands. She gazed up at the ceiling and held the pose for couple of seconds, then looked at Holly. 'Got that?'

'Er, yeah, I think so,' Holly said, feeling awkward again. She'd never liked having her photo taken, and she especially didn't like being made to pose.

After manipulating Holly into the correct position and tilting her head up, Suzie took a series of shots from behind before moving to the side and zooming in on her face. Then she snapped some shots of Holly's reflection in the mirror.

'I knew you'd be photogenic, but these are gorgeous,' she said, scrolling through the images when she'd finished.

She turned the phone round and showed Holly one of the side-profile close-ups in which Holly had been gazing up at the ceiling with an ethereal expression on her face. Smiling when Holly studied the image, she said, 'Told you you'd be perfect, so what d'you say? Will you be my test model while I learn how to use my camera properly? We could make it a regular Saturday-night thing, if you're up for it? Dinner and a photo shoot.'

Tempted by the thought of spending regular time with her new friend, but nervous at the thought of anyone else ever seeing the photos, Holly said, 'I'm not sure.'

'No pressure, it's totally up to you,' Suzie said, slipping the phone into her pocket and handing a pack of wet wipes to her. 'But will you at least think about it?'

Holly nodded, and Suzie said, 'Thanks, hon. Now clean yourself up and get changed while I go and load these onto my laptop.' She patted her pocket. Then, smiling, she said, 'I'm so glad you came over tonight. It's been lovely getting to know you, and even if you decide you don't want to get involved, you've given me the motivation to start putting my website together.'

Returning the smile, Holly waited until Suzie had left the room before changing back into her own clothes.

When Holly left Suzie's house a few minutes later her stomach began to churn, and she prayed, as she rushed across the road, that her mum hadn't come home early. It was unlikely, because she'd never done it before, but it would be just Holly's luck for it to happen tonight.

Hurrying up the stairs after letting herself into the flats, Holly had almost reached the first floor when a shadow fell over her, and she stopped in her tracks and looked up guiltily, fully expecting it to be her mum.

'Steady,' Gee said, reaching out to grab her arm when she swayed backwards.

'Thanks,' she murmured, blushing as she stepped up onto the landing beside him.

'Red or white?' he asked.

'Eh?' Her eyebrows crept together.

'The wine.' He gave a knowing smile. 'Smells like you've had a good night.'

'I, um, had a sip of my friend's,' she lied.

'Hey, it's none of my business.' He held up his hands. 'But you might wanna use some mouthwash if you don't want your mum smelling it.'

'She's at work,' Holly said.

'Ah, you're all right, then.' Gee grinned. Then, more seriously, he said, 'I'm glad I've seen you, actually. I wanted to apologize for all that stuff with my ex earlier. She's a bit of a hothead.'

A bit? Holly thought, remembering the rage in the woman's eyes.

'It's OK,' she said, shrugging it off. 'As long as she doesn't come after me if you get back with her,' she added, trying to make it sound like a joke.

'That's not gonna happen,' Gee said. 'But I doubt she even noticed you, to be honest. She was too busy gunning for the Barbies.'

'The Barbies?' Holly repeated.

'Oh, shit, probably shouldn't have said that out loud.' Gee grimaced. 'It's the way they were dressed, in all that matching gear and make-up. Kinda reminded me of the dolls my sister used to play with when she was little.'

A grin twitched Holly's lips and she sucked it in to keep it from breaking out. So much for Bex thinking she stood a chance with him; he obviously thought she'd looked like a right prat.

'Anyway, I hope they were OK?' Gee went on. 'They didn't deserve her going for them like that.'

Holly disagreed. Julie *had* deserved it for trying to use Gee bumping into Bex as an excuse to get his phone number, and Holly was embarrassed all over again just thinking about the way she'd called him Zayn.

A car horn sounded outside, and Gee said, 'That'll be my taxi, so I'd best make a move. Catch you later. And don't forget the mouthwash.'

Holly watched him jog down the stairs and out through the door before heading home. *The Barbies!* she thought, smirking to herself as she slotted her key into the lock. Just wait till Bex and Julie heard he'd called them that.

In the hallway of the flat, she listened out for the sound of movement in the other rooms, but it was silent apart from the continuous drip of water hitting the bathroom sink. Relieved, she went to her room and quickly undressed before climbing into bed. It had been a crap day, but she was feeling a whole lot better now.

14

'So what happened with Bex?' Suzie asked, curling up at her end of the sofa and lighting a cigarette.

A week had passed, and Holly, despite worrying that she would get caught if she risked sneaking out again, had decided to keep the date with her new friend. And she was glad that she had, because Suzie had served up lasagne with garlic bread tonight. Now they were drinking wine – red, this time, which Holly was finding to be a lot smoother and more palatable than the white they'd had on her previous visit.

Relaxed, her stomach pleasantly full and all thought of her mum catching her out forgotten, Holly relayed the events of the week, starting when she'd gone back to school and had seen Bex for the first time since their argument.

'She was waiting for me by the gate when I got there,' she said. 'Reckoned she felt bad about all that stuff Julie came out with, and totally denied she'd ever said she was ashamed to be seen with me.'

'And yet she laughed when Julie was taking the piss out of you after you ran inside,' said Suzie.

'She said you were lying when I asked her about that, but I told her she's the liar, not you,' Holly said. 'And I said if she's so ashamed of me she needs to look in the mirror, 'cos the way she's started dressing and acting like Julie is pathetic. Then I told her about Gee calling them the Barbies, and how he'd said they looked like kids who'd raided their mummies' make-up bags.'

'Oh, wow! Is that what he said?'

'Nah, he only called them the Barbies, the rest was me.' Holly grinned. 'But Bex doesn't know that, and she was well embarrassed when I told her.'

'See, I knew there was a reason why you and me clicked,' Suzie chuckled. 'You're like me: nice till you're pushed too far, then *bam*! Take that, bitch!'

'I did feel a bit guilty after I said it,' Holly admitted. 'But then I remembered how she stood there and let Julie say all that stuff to me and then blamed *me* for everything, and I decided she deserved it.'

'Too right she did,' Suzie agreed. 'She treated you like crap, and it was about time she got a taste of her own medicine.'

Holly nodded and took a swig of wine. Gazing at her, Suzie said, 'Changing the subject for a minute, I've been meaning to ask about your mum.'

'What about her?'

'When I saw her leaving for work earlier, it occurred to me

that I've never seen her with a man. I know your dad's not around, but hasn't she got a boyfriend?'

'*No.*' Holly pulled a face. 'She had one a few years ago, but they were always arguing so it didn't last long. She's too moody, always snapping people's heads off for no reason.'

'Is that what she's like with you?'

'A bit,' Holly said quietly, sinking lower in her seat before taking another swig of wine.

'It's hard, isn't it?' Suzie said sympathetically. 'Living with someone who's moody, I mean. My mum's bipolar, so I know exactly how it feels.'

'What's that?' Holly asked.

'It's like a chemical imbalance in the brain,' Suzie explained. 'My mum used to have massive highs and do all sorts of crazy stuff, but then she'd crash and wouldn't get out of bed for days on end. It was exhausting even when she was in a good mood, 'cos I was constantly on edge waiting for her to go on another downer.'

'I don't think my mum's got that,' Holly mused. 'She doesn't go up and down, she's narky *all* the time.'

'Does she flip out and kick the crap out of you?'

'No.'

'You're lucky, then,' said Suzie. 'The last time my mum flipped, she battered me and I had to do a runner. And I was only fifteen, like you.'

'Wow, I'd be well scared if I couldn't go home,' Holly said. 'What did you do?'

'My mate let me stay at hers for a few days,' said Suzie. 'But her mum found me hiding in her wardrobe when she was at school and kicked me out, so I had to go to my boyfriend's. He was nineteen and I hadn't been seeing him very long, so I didn't really want to move in with him. But he promised he'd behave, and I believed him – more fool me.'

'Why, what did he do?'

'He got me drunk and tried to have sex with me, but I wasn't as far gone as he thought and I slapped him. That's when I got my first beating.'

'First?' Holly frowned.

'Of many,' Suzie said, sighing at the memory. 'He always said he was sorry straight after and swore he'd never do it again. But that's what they all say, isn't it?'

'Why didn't you leave him?'

'I had nowhere else to go.' Suzie shrugged. 'My mum didn't want me, and I was terrified that the police would put me in care if I went to them, so I stayed with Hank till I was old enough to put my name down for a council flat.'

'*Hank?*' Holly snorted.

'I know! Awful, isn't it?' Suzie grinned. 'I used to call him *Wank* to wind him up when he was getting angry. I figured if he was going to beat me anyway, I might as well push him into it and get it over with. He was always nice to me straight after, but it never lasted long. All I'd have to do was put too much milk in his tea, or not enough salt on his chips, and he'd fly off the handle again.'

'He sounds horrible,' Holly said. 'But if you'd already gone through that with him, why did you stay with Rob after *he* hit you?'

'I've asked myself that same question a thousand times, and I honestly don't know,' Suzie replied. 'There's something about him that really gets to me. I can be mad as hell, but all he has to do is give me those puppy-dog eyes and that soppy smile of his and I fall to pieces.'

'Would you take him back if he turned up?' Holly asked.

Suzie pursed her lips and thought about it. Then, shrugging, she said, 'Possibly. But he'd have to swear never to do anything like that again.'

'Do you think you could ever trust him again?'

'In time, maybe.' Suzie sighed. 'But enough about him.' She glanced at her watch. 'We need to crack on before it gets too late.'

She picked up her cigarettes, her glass and the bottle of wine, and walked out into the hall. But instead of heading up to the bedroom, as she had done the previous week, she opened a door beneath the stairs and switched a light on before descending a narrow flight of steps.

Holly followed her down into a small, low-ceilinged cellar. A clothes rail with a green sheet draped over it stood against the wall opposite the stairs, and a camera on a tripod was facing it. A free-standing light with a square hood attached to it stood in the centre of the room, and a laptop was sitting on a small table in the corner.

'Ta-da!' Suzie spread her hands. 'Welcome to my studio.'

'Did you do it all yourself?' Holly asked, gazing around.

'It's pretty basic, so it wasn't hard,' Suzie said, switching the lamp on. 'I'll pimp it up when I've got more cash, but it'll do for now. Anyway, go and sit on the sheet.'

'Aren't you going to do my make-up?' Holly asked, still standing at the foot of the stairs, wine glass in hand.

'No, I want to do some natural shots tonight,' Suzie said. 'Give myself a clean slate to play around with on Photoshop.'

'OK,' Holly murmured, dreading to think what her pasty, un-made-up face would look like on film. 'You promise no one else is going to see them?'

'Cross my heart,' Suzie assured her. 'Oh, and here . . . these are for you.' She picked up a carrier bag and tossed it to Holly.

'What is it?' Holly asked, catching it.

'Just some bras and knickers,' Suzie said. 'They're a bit small for me, but they're decent, so I didn't want to throw them out. Don't worry, they're all clean, and some have still got tags on.'

'Thanks.' Holly smiled, excited by the thought of owning new underwear. It was over a year since her mum had last bought her a bra, and that had come from a charity shop, so it had already been well worn. She didn't think she'd ever owned a brand-new one.

'I was going to ask if you'd take some pictures of me when we're finished with yours?' Suzie said. 'Nothing fancy, just a few test shots to put on the website.'

'Yeah, sure,' Holly agreed.

'Great,' Suzie said, heading for the stairs. 'Make yourself comfortable while I get changed. I'll be back in a minute.'

Alone, Holly put her glass down on the laptop table and quickly rummaged through the bag. There were several sets of matching bras and panties in it and they were all gorgeous, but she especially liked the red satin ones that looked like the ones Suzie had been wearing in the photo on the living room wall. She hoped they would fit, because she was looking forward to wearing them to school. She had double PE on Monday afternoons, and she usually got changed in the toilets rather than risk the other girls seeing the state of her underwear. But now she had these she wouldn't need to hide away, and she was looking forward to showing Bex that she wasn't such a scruffy embarrassment after all.

Suzie was wearing her dressing gown when she came back down to the cellar, and she'd applied fresh make-up and brushed her hair so it hung in a glossy curtain around her shoulders. After fiddling with the light for a while and running backwards and forwards to the camera to get the focus right, she told Holly to sit on the floor in front of the screen and snapped a series of shots of her from various angles.

Unlike the previous week, when she'd felt awkward and self-conscious, Holly floated through the session. She didn't know if it was the wine, or the sensation of being cut off from the rest of the world down there in the cellar, but she enjoyed following Suzie's directions and striking poses she would have been way too embarrassed to attempt in front of anyone else.

The nerves didn't kick in until her session was over and she swapped places with Suzie behind the camera. Suzie had made it look easy, but there were loads of buttons and levers, and Holly prayed that she wouldn't accidentally press the wrong thing and delete everything.

When, at last, Suzie said, 'OK, let's wrap it up at that,' Holly was only too happy to call it a night. The temperature in the room had plummeted by then, and goosebumps had sprung up all over her body.

'Hey, you've done a great job with these,' Suzie said, scrolling through the last few images after unhooking the camera from the tripod. 'I think I'll put myself on the beach at sunset in this one.'

She showed Holly a shot of herself lying on her back with one knee raised and her arms stretched out above her head. Her glossy lips were partially open and she had a sultry look in her eyes. It was gorgeous, but Holly was confused.

'How will you do that?' she asked. 'It's just green.'

'Wait and see,' Suzie said, smiling as pulled her dressing gown on and switched off the light. 'By the time I've finished, you'll think we were actually there.'

Doubting that, Holly followed Suzie up the stairs and said goodnight before heading home with the bag of underwear stashed inside her jacket.

Relieved to find that her mum hadn't come home early, Holly stuffed the bag under her mattress and then changed into her pyjamas before climbing into bed.

15

Things didn't go quite as planned on Monday, and Holly sensed that something was wrong as soon as she walked into her form room and saw Bex, Leanne and several of their classmates huddled around a desk. They had all been laughing, but they abruptly stopped when they noticed her in the doorway, and she wondered what was going on when she saw Bex and Leanne exchange a hooded look.

Making her way to her own desk on the other side of the room, Holly had just sat down when a shadow crossed her face, and she looked up to find Leanne looming over her.

'You make me sick,' the girl hissed. 'That shit might be acceptable in the slum you come from, but we don't tolerate that kind of thing round here.'

'What are you talking about?' Holly asked, nervous because the girl was taller and a whole lot heavier than she was.

'I'm talking about your prozzy mum,' Leanne spat. 'No wonder you always stink of fish. I bet she's got you at it an' all, hasn't she?'

'*What?*' Holly drew her head back and screwed up her face. 'You're talking rubbish!'

'Hey, Bex, come here a minute . . .' Leanne called out. 'She's trying to make out like she doesn't know what I'm talking about.'

Bex walked over and peered down at Holly with a pitying look in her eyes. 'Sorry, Holls. I know you asked me not to tell anyone, but I don't see why I should keep your dirty little secrets.'

'Why are you lying?' Holly spluttered, staring up at her in disbelief. 'You're supposed to be my best mate.'

'*Ex* mate,' Bex replied coolly. 'And you can deny it all you like, but we both know it's true.'

'Dirty bitch,' one of the other girls muttered. 'You should be ashamed of yourself.'

'Fuck off!' Holly spat, turning on the girl. 'None of you have ever bothered with me anyway, so I don't give a fuck what you lot think.'

'Yeah, 'cos you're a scruffy little weirdo and we can't stand you,' sneered Leanne.

'I'd rather be a weirdo than a fat slag,' Holly shot back, too angry by then to hold her tongue. 'What was it you said about her, Bex? She's a greedy bitch who'd probably weigh twenty stone by now if she didn't burn it all off shagging Gary Mottram?'

A collective gasp went up among the other girls, and Bex's face drained of colour when Leanne glared at her.

'I never said that,' she spluttered.

'So how comes she knows about Gary when you're the only one I've ever told?' Leanne hissed, whacking her in the shoulder and almost knocking her over.

'I don't know!' Bex flapped her hands helplessly and edged behind the desk. 'She must have been listening when we were talking that day. You know how sneaky she is.'

'You're the sneaky one, you two-faced bitch,' Leanne spat. 'I should've known I couldn't trust you.'

'Told you she's a liar,' Holly said triumphantly.

'You shut your mouth,' Bex cried.

'Why should I?' Holly retorted. 'It's true!'

'You're just jealous 'cos you know I like Julie more than I ever liked you,' Bex yelled.

'I don't give a shit about you and Julie,' Holly yelled back. 'But don't you ever talk about my mum like that again, or I'll kill you!'

'Holly Evans, go to the Head's office immediately!' the teacher barked, walking into the room at that exact moment.

'But, miss . . .' Holly protested.

'*Now!*' the teacher said sharply. 'And the rest of you sit down. I'll be back in a minute.'

As she gathered her things together, Holly flashed a glance at Bex and felt a twinge of remorse when she saw how scared she looked as she sat down beside a still-scowling Leanne. They had been best friends for a long time and she had trusted her more than she had ever trusted anyone, so it hurt that Bex had said that about her mum. But if this was how she wanted to play it, she could get lost, because Holly was never going to talk to her again.

Holly didn't bother trying to defend herself when the teacher told the Head what she'd done. She was an outsider, and she knew the teachers looked down their noses at her as much as the other pupils did, so she stayed silent while the Head lectured her about bullying and zero tolerance, and she didn't argue when he ordered her to go to the exclusion zone and think about her actions.

Secretly relieved that she wouldn't have to face Leanne and Bex again, Holly kept her head down for the rest of that morning. But she knew she wasn't off the hook when, at lunch-time, she heard a group of girls excitedly discussing a fight Leanne was planning to have after school. In no doubt that she was the intended victim, she made sure she was ready to run as soon as the home-time bell rang that afternoon.

16

Josie was coming out of the bathroom when the front door flew open, and she jumped back in fright, spluttering, 'What the *hell*?' when Holly ran in.

'Sorry!' Holly gasped, bending over and placing her hands on her knees.

Concerned when she saw that Holly was struggling to catch her breath, Josie said, 'What's happened? Is someone chasing you?'

'Ran home,' Holly gulped. 'Trying to . . . keep fit.'

'By half killing yourself?' Josie frowned.

'Didn't realize it was so far.'

'Idiot.' Josie tutted. 'Hurry up and get changed. You're dripping sweat on the lino.'

Muttering, 'Sorry,' again, Holly dropped her bag and took off her damp blazer.

Josie narrowed her eyes and peered at Holly's chest. 'Where'd you get that?' she demanded.

Holly looked down and blushed when she saw that her

sweaty shirt had become transparent and the red bra was visible. There was no way she could tell her mum that Suzie had given it to her, so she said, 'Oh, erm, Bex gave it to me.'

'Why?'

'It didn't fit her, so she asked if I wanted it. I can give it back if you want?'

'You might as well keep it now you've worn it,' Josie grumbled. 'But don't take anything else off her. We're not charity cases.'

She turned and walked into the living room at that, and Holly shook her head as she went to her room, wondering why she'd made such a big deal out of it if she wasn't going to make her give it back.

After changing into jeans and a jumper and hanging the damp shirt on the back of the door to dry out, Holly sank down on her bed and chewed her thumbnail. She'd made it home safely today, but what about tomorrow and the day after that? With Leanne and Bex both gunning for her, her life was going to be hell, and the thought of facing them at school tomorrow was making her nauseous.

Pretend you're ill!

The thought came to her in a flash, and she seized it with both hands. If she could bag a few days off school by convincing her mum that she was sick, Leanne might have found someone else to pick on by the time she went back.

Thinking that it had to be worth a shot, she wrapped her arms around herself and hobbled into the kitchen where her mum was rinsing a glass out at the sink.

'Mum, I don't feel well,' she said.

'Why, what's up with you?' Josie asked.

'I've got stomach ache.'

'It'll be a stitch from running home,' Josie said, wiping her hands on a tea towel.

'It's been aching all day, but it's getting worse,' Holly groaned. 'I think it might be appendicitis.'

'Don't talk rubbish.'

'But it's really sore, and I feel sick.'

'Drink some water and sit down till it passes,' Josie said distractedly as she rooted through her handbag. 'Where's my purse? You haven't seen it, have you?'

Holly shook her head, and Josie brushed past her and went into the living room. Still clutching her stomach, Holly leaned on the door frame and said, 'I think I'd best stay off school tomorrow.'

'What?' Josie said, tossing the sofa cushions aside.

'I said I should stay off school tomorrow,' Holly repeated. 'I'm sure there's something wrong.'

'You've over-exerted yourself, that's all,' Josie replied gruffly. 'Stop being such a drama queen.'

Figuring that honesty might be the best policy since the lies were getting her nowhere, Holly said, 'Mum, *please* let me stay off. Bex isn't talking to me, and she's turned everyone else against me. And now this other girl's after me, 'cos Bex told me a secret about her and I got mad and let it out.'

'Serves you right for gossiping,' Josie said unsympathetically.

'I'm always telling you to keep your mouth shut, but you never listen, so you'll have to deal with it.'

'I *can't*,' Holly moaned. 'She's the hardest girl in our class. Please, Mum—'

'For God's *sake*!' Josie snapped, plunging her arm down the back of the sofa. 'Don't you think I've got more important things to worry about than you and some stupid girl having a fucking falling-out? If I don't find my purse I'll have to walk to work, and I'll probably end up losing my job for being late!'

Holly shot a resentful look at the back of her mum's head and half-heartedly helped her to look for the purse. Any other mother would have consoled their child and tried to help them find a solution to their problems, but *her* mum cared more about her stupid job than her own daughter. And she wondered why Holly didn't feel able to confide in her. *Bitch!*

Desperate to talk to the only person who would understand or care about her predicament, Holly sulked in her room until her mum had left for work. Snatching up her phone as soon as the door closed behind her, she rang Suzie.

'My mum's a total cow!' she complained when Suzie answered.

'Oh dear. What's she done?'

'I told her I don't feel well and asked if I can stay off school tomorrow, but she won't let me.'

'What's wrong with you?'

'I've had a horrible day, and it's made me feel really sick. And now I've got a headache as well.'

'Another run-in with Bex?' Suzie asked perceptively.

'Her and everyone else,' Holly moaned. 'She told them my mum's a prostitute.'

'Oh, that's awful. Why would she do that?'

''Cos she's a bitch,' Holly spat. 'But that's not the worst of it. I got mad and told the hardest girl in our class something Bex had told me about her, and now she's got it in for me too. I heard some other girls going on about a fight after school, and I know Leanne was going to jump me. I managed to get out before her today, but she'll get me tomorrow, and I don't know what to do.'

'Hey . . .' Suzie said when Holly started crying. 'Calm down before you make yourself ill for real. It'll be OK.'

'No it won't,' Holly sobbed. 'Leanne's massive, and she'll batter me if she gets hold of me. All I wanted was a couple of days off to let it die down, but my mum doesn't give a toss.'

'Did you tell her why you wanted to stay off?'

'Yeah, but she said it was my own fault for gossiping. I wish I was dead!'

'Hey, that's enough of that,' Suzie said firmly. 'Nothing's ever that bad, and don't let me hear you say that again.'

'But Leanne's gonna *kill* me,' Holly wailed, as if her friend hadn't grasped the seriousness of the situation.

Suzie was quiet for moment. Then, sighing, she said, 'OK, here's what we're going to do. Get ready for school as usual tomorrow morning, then come round to mine. I'll leave the back door open for you.'

'Why?' Holly sniffed.

'If you need a couple of days to let things blow over, I'll ring your school and pretend to be your mum,' said Suzie. 'I'll tell them you've come down with a stomach bug or something.'

Holly's heart momentarily leapt before immediately sinking again. It sounded like the perfect solution, but she'd never wagged school in her life, and the thought of getting caught and dragged in front of the Head again terrified her almost as much as the thought of being gripped by Leanne.

'I can't,' she said. 'I'll get into trouble.'

'Trust me, you won't,' Suzie insisted. 'Me and my mates used to do it all the time and we *never* got caught. Now quit worrying and get some sleep. I'll see you in the morning.'

17

After a restless night, Holly felt like death warmed up when she got up the next morning, and she groaned when she saw her pasty complexion and the dark circles under her eyes. Wondering if it might be worth waking her mum to ask again if she could stay off, she shuffled out into the hall, but changed her mind when she heard deep rumbling snores coming through her mum's door.

Back in her own room, she picked her phone up off the bedside table when it beeped as she was pulling her uniform on, and her stomach turned to water when she read the message on the screen.

I'm waiting, bitch. See you soon!

It had come from a withheld number, so she didn't know who had sent it, but she figured it had to be Leanne, which meant that the girl was probably intending to ambush her on her way to school.

Jumping when another message pinged onto her phone, Holly gazed down at it and was relieved to see that it was from Suzie this time.

Morning, hon, are you coming over? X

Holly bit her lip and stared at it for a few seconds, trying to decide what to do. Then, her heart racing, she typed *Be there in a minute X* and quickly pressed *Send* before she could change her mind.

Suzie's back gate was unlocked and Holly found herself in a small, neat garden when she stepped through it. Ahead of her, the kitchen door was standing ajar, and she could see Suzie moving around in the kitchen wearing the same black satin dressing gown she'd seen her in on the morning after Rob had attacked her. Still nervous about skipping school, she contemplated leaving before Suzie spotted her. But it was too late. Suzie walked over to the sink at that exact moment and waved to her through the window.

'I was starting to think you'd lost your nerve,' Suzie said, kissing Holly on the cheek when she came inside.

'I nearly did,' Holly admitted.

'Glad you didn't,' Suzie said, moving over to the counter when four pieces of golden brown bread popped out of the toaster. Dropping them onto a plate, she said, 'Be a pet and butter those. Unless you prefer yours dry?'

'Oh. Is some of that for me?' Holly asked.

'I had a feeling you might skip breakfast if your stomach was still iffy, so I'm making enough for both of us,' Suzie said, switching the kettle on before cracking three eggs into a frying pan. 'You don't have to eat it if you don't want to, but it'll go in the bin if you don't.'

'It's OK, I'll have it,' Holly said, smiling to herself as she took a tub of margarine out of the fridge. It had been a long time since anyone had made breakfast for her. She presumed her mum must have done it for her when she was younger, but she genuinely couldn't remember.

When the food was plated and the tea was brewed, they sat at the table facing each other.

'This is nice,' Suzie said, sprinkling salt onto her eggs. 'You probably won't understand, 'cos you've got your mum, but I miss having someone to eat with now Rob's gone.'

'My mum's always asleep when I go to school, so we never have breakfast together,' Holly said, covering her mouth with her hand to avoid spitting crumbs onto the table.

'What about dinner?' Suzie asked, taking a tiny bite of toast.

Swallowing loudly, Holly said, 'She eats at work, so I usually make a butty or stick a pizza in the microwave.'

'That's a shame,' Suzie said. 'But at least you know how to take of yourself. I was a mess when I left home; took me ages to figure out how to use a cooker.'

'I've been doing it ever since I can remember,' said Holly. 'I do all the cleaning and washing as well.'

Suzie heard the pride in her voice and smiled. 'Independent little thing, aren't you?'

Holly shrugged and shoved another forkful of egg into her mouth.

'Any word from Bex?' Suzie asked.

Holly shook her head. 'No, but I got a message off Leanne. There was no number, but I know it was her.'

'What did it say?' Suzie reached for her cup and took a sip of tea.

Mouth full again, Holly lifted her phone out of her blazer pocket and, bringing up the message, showed it to Suzie.

Leaning forward, Suzie squinted at it and said, 'Bloody hell, your screen's a mess, hon. What have you been doing with it?'

'It was like that when I got it.' Holly blushed. 'My mum found it at work and they let her keep it.'

'Ah, well, as long as it works, who cares?' Suzie said. Then, tutting softly when she'd read the message, she sat back and said, 'Ignore it. She's only trying to scare you.'

'It's worked,' Holly muttered, wiping her mouth on the back of her hand. 'I was going to go in before that came.'

'Try to forget about it for now,' Suzie counselled, pushing her plate away and lighting a cigarette. 'I'll get dressed when I've had this, then we'll go down to the studio and work on those photos we took the other night. I've already edited a few, and they're looking really good.'

'Can we ring school first?' Holly asked, glancing at the clock. 'The bell goes in fifteen minutes, and they'll text my mum to ask why I'm not there if I miss registration.'

'Oh, yeah, I forgot about that,' Suzie said, picking her phone up off the table. 'Do you know the number or should I google it?'

'Google,' Holly said, feeling nervous again.

'Relax, it'll be fine.' Suzie smiled. 'What's the name?'

'Holly Evans.'

'I meant the name of the school.'

'Oh, sorry. Parkside High.'

'Ooh, get you.' Suzie arched an eyebrow. 'One of my old friends went there. *Very* posh.'

'I hate it.' Holly pulled a face. 'They all think they're better than me 'cos they're rich.'

'Hey, you're as good as them all day long, and don't you forget it,' Suzie said. 'Money isn't everything. You're clever and kind, and I'd rather have you for a friend than some snobby little cow.'

Holly smiled and shoved the last piece of toast into her mouth.

'I know what you mean about hating school, though,' Suzie went on as she typed the name of Holly's school into her phone. 'I wagged most of my last year and missed most of my exams. I was lucky I got taken on by the first agent I approached, or I'd probably be stacking shelves or cleaning bogs right now.'

'That's what my mum reckons I'll end up doing if I fail mine,' Holly said, gathering their plates and forks together. 'She's always nagging at me to revise so I don't end up like her.'

'Oh, is she a cleaner?' Suzie asked. 'I was wondering what she did. And does she always work lates?'

'Yep.'

'Don't you get scared being on your own every night?'

'I'm used to it.' Holly shrugged. 'And I still wouldn't see much of her even if she worked days, 'cos she always goes straight to bed as soon as she comes home.'

She carried the plates to the sink, and Suzie watched her thoughtfully as she washed them and the frying pan before wiping the cooker and the counter. She was guarded when it came to talking about her mum, but some of the things she'd let slip during their conversations gave Suzie the impression that she'd pretty much been left to bring herself up – which probably explained why she was forbidden from going out or answering the door when her mum was out: in case someone realized she was being left alone overnight and reported her mum for neglect. She might be almost sixteen now, but who knew how young she'd been when it had first started happening?

Still, it was their business, not hers, so she tore her gaze off the girl and phoned the school.

'Oh, hello, is this Parkside High? I'm calling to let you know that my daughter won't be coming in today. Her name's Holly Evans and she's in year ten.'

'*Eleven!*' Holly hissed, snapping her head round.

'Sorry, I mean year eleven,' Suzie corrected herself. 'I've been up half the night and I'm not thinking straight. Anyway, she's been sick and her temperature's still high, so I'm waiting for a call back from the doctor. I'll let you know how we get on.'

'What did they say?' Holly asked, wiping her hands on a tea towel when Suzie had finished the call.

'That they hope you'll be feeling better soon, and to let them know if you're going to be off for more than a few days so they can arrange to have some work sent home for you,' Suzie said, smiling as she stubbed the cigarette out and got up. 'Now relax and make us another brew while I get dressed, then we'll go downstairs.'

Nodding, Holly refilled the kettle and switched it on, then rinsed out their cups and put a new teabag in each. As she waited for the water to boil, a new message pinged onto her phone. It was just one word this time: *Shithouse!* Staring at it, she chewed on her lip. It was definitely Leanne, because she'd never heard Bex use that word, and she dreaded the thought of what would happen when she went back to school. But the girl couldn't get to her while she was here, so she determinedly pushed it out of her mind and made the teas.

18

Down in the cellar, cut off from the rest of the world, Holly forgot her troubles for a few hours as she and Suzie went through the photos. As Suzie had promised, the edited ones really did look as if they had been shot at various exotic locations around the world, and Holly wished she could post some of them onto her Facebook page so Bex and Julie could see how gorgeous Suzie had made her look. But her mum checked her page and would want to know where and when they had been taken, so she couldn't risk it.

The photos of Holly weren't going on the website, so they concentrated on separating Holly's shots of Suzie into sets of *definites, maybes* and *hell nos!* Uploading the 'definites' turned out to be a little trickier than they had anticipated, and they wasted a fair bit of time messing about with the dimensions before they got the hang of it.

All too soon, it was time for Holly to go home, and the dread she'd pushed to the back of her mind resurfaced as she left the artificial light of the cellar and emerged into the bright daylight of the kitchen.

'Don't worry, it'll be fine,' Suzie said, giving her a hug before she left.

'Hope so,' Holly replied, her stomach already churning at the thought of facing her mum.

Holly took a deep breath before inserting the key into the lock when she reached the flat, and she did a quick mental run-through of what Suzie had told her to say if her mum had found out that she'd wagged school. She was to say that she *had* gone, but that, because of the messages she'd received, she'd been too scared to go inside when she saw Leanne and a gang of girls waiting for her at the gate. Then, to keep Suzie out of it, she was to say that *she* had phoned the school and pretended to be her mum, and had spent the rest of the day hiding in the park. And if her mum got mad, she was to start crying and ask if her mum would have preferred for her to come home in an ambulance – because that was what would have happened if Leanne and the others had got their hands on her.

Praying that she wouldn't slip up, she entered the hallway and hung her blazer on a peg. She could smell food, and she was surprised to find a pan of stew bubbling on the stove when she went into the kitchen. Her mum rarely cooked, and never from scratch, and she wondered what the occasion was.

'I thought I heard the door,' Josie said, walking into the room behind her. 'How was school?'

'OK,' Holly said warily, wondering if it was a trick question; that her mum knew she'd wagged it and was giving her the chance to confess before the axe fell.

'That's good.' Josie smiled and patted her arm. Then, apologetically, she said, 'Sorry about yesterday, love. I wasn't in the best of moods, but I shouldn't have taken it out on you. How did you get on with that girl you were talking about? Did she give you any trouble?'

Holly shook her head.

'Well, let me know if she does and I'll go in and make sure the Head puts a stop to it,' Josie said, picking up a spoon and stirring the stew.

Scared of her mum going to the school and finding out that she had supposedly rung them that morning, Holly said, 'No! It's fine now. I, um, sorted everything out with Bex and she told Leanne to back off.'

Josie put the spoon down and peered at her. 'You've never told Bex anything you shouldn't, have you? About *us*, I mean.'

'No, of course not,' said Holly. 'We don't really talk about our parents. It's more about homework and what we've watched on telly, and that.'

'I hope that's the truth, 'cos all it'll take is for someone to say the wrong thing and we could lose everything. You know that, don't you?'

'I know,' Holly murmured, averting her gaze when she felt her cheeks heating up. 'I, um, need to get changed,' she said, edging towards the door.

Josie glanced up at the clock, and said, 'Hurry up, then. I haven't got long.'

In her bedroom, Holly leaned back against the door and breathed a sigh of relief. Her mum definitely didn't know she'd skipped school, so she'd got away with it. But the tension of not knowing had made her feel sick, and she didn't think she could go through it all again tomorrow. So, as scared as she was of Leanne, she was going to have to go to school and try to avoid the girl. There were numerous ways to get onto the school grounds, and Leanne and her mates couldn't guard them all, so all she had to do was slip in and out without them catching her, and then make sure she was always in view of a teacher during break times, and she would be OK. It would only be for a couple of months, until the exams were out of the way; after that she would never have to see any of the stupid bitches again.

Josie was sitting on the sofa with a bowl of stew on her lap when Holly went back to the living room after changing out of her uniform. Holly's bowl was on the coffee table, alongside a plate of buttered bread.

'Like it?' Josie asked when Holly dipped a piece of bread into the stew and stuffed it into her mouth.

'Mmmm.' Holly nodded and swallowed. 'It's lovely.'

'It was your favourite when you were little.' Josie smiled. 'I should try to do it more often.'

'That'd be good,' Holly said. 'Suzie says . . .' Pulling herself up short when she realized what she'd said, she flashed a glance at her mum out of the corner of her eye to see if she'd picked up on it.

She had, and she gave Holly a quizzical look. 'Suzie?'

'Um, Bex's mum,' Holly lied, hoping she'd never mentioned that Bex's mum was actually called Tina. 'She reckons home-cooked food is healthier than shop-bought.'

'Does she now?' Josie rolled her eyes. 'Easy to say when you can afford to buy fresh every day. Stuck-up cow.'

Holly didn't answer and they ate on in silence. Josie finished first and took her bowl into the kitchen, leaving it on the ledge beside the sink before pouring a glass of vodka and lemonade. Bringing it back to the sofa, she caught Holly flicking a disapproving glance at the glass and said, 'What?'

'Nothing,' Holly murmured, picking up on the edge to her mum's voice and wanting to avoid an argument.

Josie took a defiant swig of the drink and then lit a cigarette and settled back in her seat, asking, 'So what did you do today?'

'At school?' Holly asked, wary again.

'Where else would I be talking about?' Josie gave her a bemused look.

'Er, maths, history, geography and RE,' Holly said, mentally visualizing her timetable in case her mum had already checked it.

'Got any homework?'

'No, they want us to concentrate on revising.'

'The amount you've been doing lately, you should fly through your exams,' Josie said, smiling again as the vodka and nicotine kicked in. 'Who knows, you might even get into uni after sixth form. Imagine that, eh? If you get a degree and land a good job, you'll be able to take care of me in my old age.'

Holly nodded, but she had no intention of staying on at school *or* going to uni. She was going to work for Suzie. She wouldn't be doing much to start with, just making tea and pouring wine for the models who came in for photo shoots. But Suzie had said that she would promote her to office manager when the agency was established, so she would be taking phone calls and arranging meetings and auditions. It sounded really exciting and glamorous and she couldn't wait. But she wasn't going to mention it until it actually happened, because she knew her mum would only try to pull the plug on it.

As Holly carried on eating, Josie turned her attention to the quiz show that was playing on TV. 'Leonard Nimmo,' she said in answer to the question the host was asking one of the contestants. 'Leonard Nimmo,' she repeated irritably when the contestant said 'Pass.'

'Leonard Nimoy,' the host said.

'Close enough.' Josie shrugged and took another swig from her glass. Then, her gaze still on the screen, she said, 'There's been rumours of cut-backs at our place.'

Holly swallowed the food in her mouth too quickly and winced when a chunk of potato caught in her throat. Coughing to shift it, she said, 'You're not going to lose your job, are you?'

'No, of course not.' Josie took another swig. 'They'd fall apart without me.'

'So why'd you say it like that? Like your neck's on the line?'

'I was only saying there's been rumours.'

Holly frowned as she ate the last spoonful of stew. Was that why her mum had talked about her going to uni and getting a good job: because she knew she was about to lose hers? It didn't seem likely, because she'd have to know that it would take years for Holly to graduate. But *something* had to be worrying her to make her mention cut-backs out of the blue like that. And that, in turn, worried Holly, because they always ended up moving when her mum lost a job, and she didn't want to. Not now she'd met Suzie and made plans for the future.

Josie downed what was left of her drink and took one last drag on her cigarette before stubbing it out. Then, sighing, she stood up and said, 'I'd best get ready for work. Put the rest of the stew in the fridge when you've finished washing up; we'll have it again tomorrow. Oh, and don't be worrying about my job. It's safe, I promise.'

Holly nodded, but she wasn't sure she believed her.

Across the road a short time later, Suzie watched through her living room blinds as Josie exited the flats and headed off down the road. Reaching for her phone when the woman had disappeared from view, she rang Holly.

'Hey, hon, I just saw your mum setting off. How did it go? Did she say anything?'

'No, nothing,' said Holly. 'She was being really nice and I thought it might be a trick – like she was waiting for me to admit it or something. But she definitely would have said something before she left, so I think I got away with it.'

'See, I told you it'd be OK.'

'Yeah, but I can't do it again, so I've decided to go to school tomorrow.'

'That's up to you, hon. As long as you think you can handle Bex and that other girl.'

'Leanne,' Holly said, shivering at the thought of her. 'I've got no choice, so I'm just going to try and avoid them until I've got through my exams.'

'Good for you,' Suzie said. 'But, anyway, forget about them for tonight. What you up to?'

'I'm in my room revising,' Holly told her. 'Why?'

'I need you to come over,' Suzie said. 'And try not to be long.'

'OK, but I'll need to get dressed 'cos I've got my pyjamas on.'

'Hurry up, then,' Suzie said before hanging up.

Thinking that she probably wanted to do more work on the website, Holly closed the history book she'd half-heartedly been studying and pushed the quilt off her legs.

19

Glancing at her watch as she hurried through the estate, Josie picked up speed when she saw that her bus was due in five minutes. When she reached the alleyway that led to the main road, she hesitated and pulled the zip of her coat all the way up to her throat. Spring had been an absolute washout so far, and the sky was darker than usual for the time of year. That, and the branches of the trees hanging over the fences on either side of the narrow path, made the alley look like a long black tunnel, and she contemplated walking round the block instead. But the buses to her workplace only came once an hour, and her boss would go on the warpath if she was late. So, biting the bullet, she clutched her handbag tightly to her side and set off down the alley.

Halfway along she hit what felt like a brick wall and fell sideways into the fence, clipping her ankle on a brick as she went down. Tears sprang into her eyes and she cursed under her breath as she rubbed her ankle before trying to stand up. Freezing when she heard a shuffling noise, the hairs on the back of her neck stood on end when she looked up and saw a man dressed all in black and wearing a balaclava looming over her.

'Keep it shut or I'll kill you!' the man hissed, clamping a leather-gloved hand over her mouth as he hauled her roughly to her feet.

Josie's eyes bulged when he wrapped a muscular arm around her, and she felt the toes of her boots scrape along the path as he half carried, half dragged her towards a broken section of fence a few feet ahead. Guessing that this wasn't a mugging, because he'd have grabbed her bag and legged it if that was his intention, she tried to dig her heels into the soft earth between the concrete of the alleyway and the overgrown grass and weeds on the other side of the fence. A brain-rattling punch to the side of her head knocked the fight out of her, and she was powerless to resist when her attacker hauled her through the gap and tossed her roughly down into the undergrowth.

Still reeling, Josie blinked to clear her vision, hoping to get a look at the man's face, but all she could see was the glint of his eyes through the cut-out in the balaclava. And then he brought his fist down again, and she knew she was about to die when stars exploded in her head.

20

Suzie was dressed up to the nines when she opened the door. Surprised, Holly said, 'Oh . . . are you going out?'

'I'm not, *we* are,' Suzie said, pulling her inside.

'What d'you mean?' Holly gave her a questioning look.

'We're going to a club,' Suzie explained, taking the jacket off Holly's shoulders and hanging it up. 'And I've already booked the cab, so we need to get a move on.'

'I'm not old enough to go to a club,' Holly said as Suzie propelled her up the stairs and into the front bedroom.

'You'll look old enough by the time I've finished with you,' Suzie replied breezily, pushing her down on the dressing-table stool. 'Now shush and let me get on with it.'

Squirming when Suzie slapped foundation onto her cheeks, Holly said, 'But what if my mum comes—'

'She won't,' Suzie cut her off. 'And it's time we had a bit of fun, so stop worrying and get your party head on. I've arranged to meet someone.'

'Oh?' Holly gazed up at her.

'His name's Sam, and I used to work at his club between modelling gigs,' Suzie told her. 'His wife got cancer, so he sold up and took her home to Ireland where she could be near her family. She's dead now and he's back in town, and he rang me this afternoon to ask if I fancied meeting up.'

'Why do you want me to come if you're going on a date?' Holly asked.

'It's not a date,' Suzie said, brushing blusher onto her cheeks before reaching for a tube of lip gloss. 'But he might *think* it is, so that's why I need you there: to make sure he knows it's just business.'

'Business?'

'Yeah, he's loaded, and I'm going to ask if he'll invest in the agency,' Suzie said, slicking the gloss onto Holly's lips before taking a brush to her hair. 'Truth is, I'm running a bit low on funds, so I was thinking about trying to get a bank loan. But it'll be a lot easier if I can get Sam to come on board.'

'Do you think he will?'

'No idea. But he's generous, so we'll get a good night out of it if nothing else.'

The wail of sirens suddenly drifted in through the partially open window. As they grew louder, someone yelled, 'Over here!' and, seconds later, blue flashing lights strobed through the blinds.

'I hope that's not another shooting,' Suzie said, moving over to the window and pushing it open. 'Looks like something's happened in the alley,' she said when she saw a crowd gathering at the far end of the road. 'Bet it's got something to do with those little shits who tried to mug me on my way home from hospital.'

'My mum goes that way to catch her bus,' Holly said, getting up and joining her at the window as another police car whizzed past, followed by an ambulance.

'It won't be her,' Suzie said. 'She went out ages ago.'

Holly glanced at the clock and relaxed when she saw that it had just gone seven. It was over half an hour since her mum had left the flat, so she'd be long gone by now.

Downstairs, after Holly had changed into the dress and shoes Suzie had picked out for her, Suzie poured two glasses of wine and handed one to Holly. Still nervous at the thought of going to a nightclub, sure that she would be asked for ID and turned away when she couldn't produce any, which would be *mega* embarrassing, Holly perched on the sofa and sipped her drink.

Jumping when the doorbell chimed a couple of minutes later, she said, 'Oh, God, what if it's my mum?'

'Relax,' Suzie said, walking to the door. 'It's probably the cab. Hurry up and finish your drink. I'll tell him to give us a minute.'

Holly nodded and took another swig as Suzie went to answer the door. A woman's voice drifted through the hall, and Holly's heart leapt in her chest when she heard her say: 'I need to speak to the girl.'

Holding her breath when Suzie said, 'What girl?' Holly got up and tiptoed to the door.

'Don't act dumb, love,' the woman replied tartly. 'I saw her coming over here earlier, and I need a word. It's about her mam, and it's urgent.'

Stomach flipping, Holly slammed her glass down on the table and rushed out into the hall. She recognized the woman immediately as the neighbour from the second floor who had warned the gang off on the night she'd seen Rob attacking Suzie.

'What about my mum?' she asked.

'Ah, you haven't heard then?' the woman said, her excitement at being the one to deliver the news battling against the concern in her eyes. 'Some lads disturbed a bloke attacking her on the wasteland behind the alley a bit ago.'

'No . . .' Holly clutched the doorframe when her legs turned to jelly.

'Sorry, love,' the woman said, touching her arm. 'I saw them putting her in the ambulance and thought someone needed to tell you. Why don't you come over to mine for a bit? I'll call the police and see if we can find out which hospital they've took her to.'

'It's OK, I'll do it,' Suzie said.

'I'm only trying to help,' the woman said, narrowing her eyes and looking Suzie up and down. 'She's me neighbour, and that's what we do round here. Not that you'd know, mind, seeing as how you never bother with no one apart from that man of yours.'

Flashing a cold smile at her, Suzie closed the door in her face. The letterbox immediately flapped up, and the woman shouted, 'You know where I am if you need owt, love. I'm at number twenty-eight. The name's Carol.'

'Nosy cow,' Suzie muttered, ushering Holly back into the living room.

'What should I do?' Holly asked, panic in her eyes.

'It might not have been your mum, so let's not jump to conclusions,' Suzie said calmly.

'But what if it was?' Holly paced the floor. 'Oh, God, I knew I shouldn't have come out tonight. It was asking for trouble.'

'Hey, you couldn't have known this was going to happen,' Suzie said, taking hold of her shoulders to stop her. 'And we still don't know for sure that it was your mum. It's dark out there; your neighbour might have got it wrong. Just let me cancel the cab and let Sam know I'm not coming, then I'll ring the police and find out what's going on.'

'I need to go,' Holly said, wriggling free and heading for the door.

'Wait, I'll come with you,' Suzie said as she rushed out into the hall. 'This will only take a minute.'

Holly continued on her way without answering.

Gee was coming out of the flats when Holly reached the door, and he smiled and stepped back to let her enter.

'Thanks,' she murmured, fumbling her front-door key out of the tiny clutch bag Suzie had lent her to go with the outfit.

Catching a glimpse of her pale face when she brushed past him, Gee called, 'Is everything all right?' as she rushed up the stairs. Frowning when she didn't answer, he held the door for a few more seconds, then let it go and went after her.

'Hey, what's up?' he asked, concerned when he saw how badly her hand was shaking as she tried to slot her key into the lock. 'Has something happened?'

'Someone's been attacked in the alley and the woman upstairs reckons it was my mum,' Holly gabbled. 'Suzie says it can't be her, 'cos she'll be at work, but I've got a horrible feeling.'

'Have you tried ringing her?' Gee asked, scooping her key up off the floor when she dropped it.

Wondering why she hadn't thought of that, Holly yanked her phone out of the bag and dialled her mum's number. It rang out before going to voicemail.

'She's not answering,' she said, gazing fearfully up at Gee.

'She's probably not allowed to take calls while she's working,' Gee said. 'Leave a message asking her to ring you back when she's on a break.'

Hands still shaking, Holly pressed redial. Blushing when Gee unlocked the front door, exposing the shabby lino in the hallway, the dustballs in the corners, the dirty skirting boards and the ever-present stench of damp, she said, 'I, um, can't let you in. My mum—'

'It's cool.' Gee passed the key to her and held up his hands. 'I only wanted to make sure you got in OK.'

Thanking him, Holly rushed inside with the phone clamped to her ear and flashed an embarrassed smile at him as she closed the door.

'Mum, it's me,' she said when the phone clicked into voice-mail. 'Something's happened in the alley and I need to know you're all right. Ring me back when you get a break. *Please.*'

Jumping when the doorbell rang, she hurriedly opened the door after she'd looked through the spyhole and saw that it was Suzie.

'I rang my mum and asked her to call me back,' she said.

'Good. Now stop worrying,' Suzie said. 'I brought your clothes back, so go and get changed while I make a coffee.' She handed over a plastic bag. 'When you're ready, I'll ring the police.'

Feeling a little calmer now that she was home, Holly said, 'You don't have to stay. Go and meet Sam, see if he can help you out.'

'I've already arranged to see him next week,' Suzie said, slipping her jacket off. 'And I don't want to leave you on your own while you're upset, so I'll stay until you hear from your mum. OK?'

Nodding, Holly went to her room and took off the dress. As she was pulling her jeans on the doorbell rang, and she pressed her ear against her door when she heard Suzie answer it.

'Is this Josie Evans's flat?' a man asked.

Unable to hear Suzie's reply, Holly pulled her jumper on and went out into the hall just as two uniformed police officers stepped inside.

'Oh, God,' she croaked. 'It was my mum, wasn't it?'

'Let's go and sit down,' Suzie said softly, taking her arm and leading her into the living room.

'Just tell me,' Holly pleaded, tears stinging her eyes as she sank onto the sofa. 'Was it her?'

'It looks like it,' Suzie said, sitting beside her and taking hold of her hand. 'But don't panic. They've taken her to the MRI and she's being well looked after.'

The officers were in the room by then, and one of them took a seat facing Holly while the other looked around before walking over to the window and gazing out at the police cars that were still parked at the far end of the road.

'I'm PC Dan Spencer, and this is my colleague, PC Jack Bennett,' the seated man introduced them. 'We've spoken to your aunt, so we know you're aware of the incident earlier tonight.'

'Aunt?' Holly repeated.

'I told them we'd seen the ambulance and wondered what was going on,' Suzie said, squeezing Holly's hand and giving her a pointed look.

Holly nodded mutely. She recognized the look, because it was the same one her mum always gave her whenever she wanted Holly to go along with something she'd said without questioning her.

'You aunt tells us it's just you and your mum living here,' Spencer went on. 'Can I ask how old you are?'

'Fifteen,' Holly murmured.

'Does your dad live locally?'

Holly shook her head, and Suzie said, 'He took off before she was born. Josie hasn't seen him since, and Holly's never met him.'

'I see,' Spencer said, narrowing his eyes thoughtfully as he peered at Suzie. 'You look familiar,' he said after a moment.

'Do I?' She gazed innocently back at him.

'Ah, that's it.' He clicked his fingers. 'You live across the road, don't you? We attended an incident a couple of weeks back.' He flicked a hooded glance at Holly, before adding, 'Altercation with your partner?'

'*Ex* partner,' Suzie corrected him. 'And I'm still waiting to hear back from you on that.'

'He was up in court last week,' PC Bennett said from his position at the window. 'Two years suspended.'

'You're kidding me?' Suzie spluttered. 'Why wasn't I told about this?'

'The charges weren't related to you, so you wouldn't have been marked down for notification,' said Bennett.

'Of *course* they were related to me,' Suzie argued. 'I'm the one he attacked, and it was me who called you to tell you he was in my house while you were out there looking for him.'

'There wasn't enough evidence to proceed with your case,' Spencer interjected, sounding as uncomfortable as he was beginning to look. 'But he kicked off after we removed him from the house, so he was charged with assaulting an officer and damaging police property.'

Suzie was outraged. 'So he half kills me and then breaks into my house to finish the job, but that's all right as long as he doesn't damage anything belonging to *you* lot?'

'I want to see my mum,' Holly blurted out.

Visibly relieved by the interruption, Spencer said, 'I'm afraid that won't be possible right now.'

'She – she's not going to die, is she?' Holly swiped at a tear that was slithering down her cheek.

'No, of course not.' Spencer gave her a reassuring smile. 'But they need to do a thorough assessment of her condition before anyone can see her.'

At the window, Bennett was talking quietly into his radio. Turning to Spencer when he'd finished, he said, 'We need to get going, mate.'

Spencer rose to his feet and, looking down at Suzie, jerked his head towards the door, saying, 'Could I have a quick word?'

Suzie squeezed Holly's hand, and said, 'Won't be a sec,' before following him out into the hall.

'I need to know your real relationship to Holly,' Spencer said quietly when she'd closed the door.

'I've already told you, I'm her aunt.' Suzie folded her arms.

'I'm not calling you a liar, but I know how these things work,' Spencer said. 'Everyone called their mum's mates auntie or uncle when I was a kid, and if that's what's going on here I need to know so we can contact an actual relative.'

Sensing that he would ask for proof if she persisted with the lie, Suzie said, 'All right, I'm only a friend. But she hasn't got any family apart from her mum, so what happens now?'

'Because she's a minor and we don't know how long her mum's going to be in hospital, we'll need to place a protection order on her,' Spencer said. 'Social services will take over from there.'

'Is that really necessary?' Suzie asked. 'She's nearly sixteen. Can't she stay with me?'

'That's the procedure in these cases, I'm afraid,' Spencer said. 'And, to be honest, I'm not sure you'd be given clearance to take her even if you *were* her aunt, given the history of violence with your ex.'

'That was him, not me,' Suzie replied sharply, annoyed that she was being judged because of Rob's actions. Then, swallowing the irritation, she said, 'Look, you just said you don't know how long her mum's going to be away, so can't you wait for one night before escalating it? Unless there's something you're not telling me?' she added, when it occurred to her that this might be worse than he was letting on. 'She's not *dead*, is she?'

'No.' Spencer shook his head. Then, lowering his voice, he said, 'Holly doesn't need to hear this, but we recovered a knife from the scene.'

'She was stabbed?' Suzie's eyes widened. 'Christ, that's awful. Did you catch him?'

'Not yet. He legged it when he was disturbed, and the lads couldn't give us much of a description because he was wearing a balaclava. But we will.'

'I hope so.' Suzie shuddered. 'There's enough weirdos round here without adding a knife-wielding maniac to the list.'

'Well, now you know what we're dealing with, I'm sure you'll understand why we need to put safeguarding measures in place for Holly,' Spencer said.

'Yeah, but does it have to be tonight?' Suzie asked. 'She's already traumatized, and sending her to spend the night with strangers will feel like a punishment. Josie wouldn't want that, and neither do I, so please let me look after her. If you're worried about my ex turning up, I'll stay here.'

Spencer breathed in deeply and ran a hand through his dark hair. Then, sighing, he said, 'All right, here's what I'll do. You told me you're her aunt and Holly didn't dispute it, so that's what I'll put in my report. But if her mum ends up being kept in for more than a couple of nights, it'll be out of my hands.'

'Thank you.' Suzie touched his arm. 'She'll be safe with me. And if any awkward questions get asked, I'll take the blame so you don't get into trouble.'

'Let's hope it doesn't come to that,' he muttered, sounding like he was already regretting his decision.

'It won't,' Suzie said, mentally crossing her fingers. 'But you'd best take my number, just in case.'

After saving her number into his phone, Spencer went back into the living room.

'OK, Holly, we're going to leave you with your aunt for tonight,' he said. 'I've got her number, so I'll ring as soon as we've got any news about your mum. Try not to worry.'

'She'll be fine,' Suzie said, putting her arm around Holly. 'I'll look after her.'

Spencer nodded and said goodbye, then he and his colleague saw themselves out.

'What am I going to do?' Holly whimpered. 'What if she dies?'

'That is *not* going to happen,' Suzie said firmly, peering into her eyes. 'She'll be home soon, and you need to pull yourself together or you'll be no use to her. I persuaded PC Spencer to let me stay with you tonight, but if social services get wind of it and come sniffing round, you need to show them that you're mature enough to cope with this. Do you understand?'

'Yeah,' Holly whispered, wiping her nose on her hand.

'Good girl,' Suzie said, giving her a quick hug. 'Now I need to nip home and get a few bits. Will you be all right here till I get back, or do you want to come with me?'

'I'll stay here.'

'OK, I won't be long.'

Holly forced a tiny smile, but it slid off her lips as soon as Suzie had gone, and she stared at the cushion where her mum had been sitting when they ate dinner earlier. The coppers hadn't told her much, but she knew it had to be bad for them to tape the road off, and she felt guilty that she hadn't followed her instincts and gone down there. It would have been too late to stop her mum from getting attacked, but at least she could have comforted her and gone in the ambulance with her. Now her mum was alone, and she couldn't even go to see her. And if she died . . .

Fresh tears burned her eyes at the thought of never seeing

her mum again, but she swiped them away at the sound of the doorbell ringing. Assuming it must be Suzie, she went out into the hall to let her in – and cursed herself for not checking first when she saw that it was actually Carol from the second floor. Too polite to close the door in the woman's face, she pushed it to until there was an inch-wide crack and peered out at her.

'Are you all right, love?' Carol asked. 'I saw the coppers and her from across the road leaving and wanted to check on you.'

'I'm OK,' Holly said.

'Not being funny,' Carol said conspiratorially, casting a quick glance back along the corridor, 'but does your mam know you're knocking about with that tart? Only I'm not sure I'd be happy if one of *my* kids got mixed up with her sort.'

'She's not a tart,' Holly bristled.

'What's going on?' Suzie asked.

'Fuck's sake!' Carol yelped, spinning round to face her. 'What you sneaking up on me for? You're lucky I didn't lamp you one.'

'Is that right?' Suzie gazed coolly back at her.

Carol narrowed her eyes and looked her up and down, clocking the pyjama pants beneath her coat, and the wine bottle sticking out of the carrier bag she was holding. Then, turning back to Holly, she said, 'You seem like a nice girl and I'd hate to see you get led astray, so watch yourself, yeah?'

'Suzie's my friend,' Holly shot back indignantly. 'And you don't even know me, so why're you—'

'It's all right, I'll deal with this,' Suzie said, pushing Holly inside and pulling the door shut.

'Oh, you think you can deal with me, do ya?' Carol sneered, rolling her sleeves up as if preparing for a fight.

'Why are you here?' Suzie asked, maintaining her cool. 'You can see she's upset, so leave her alone.'

Carol's lip curled into a sneer, and she said, 'You proper think you're special, but you don't fool me, and I doubt them coppers'd be too happy if they knew what kind of woman was looking after her in there.' She nodded at the door.

'And what kind of woman would that be?' Suzie raised an eyebrow.

'A *whore*,' Carol hissed, pushing her face into Suzie's. 'I knew it the minute I clapped eyes on you, and I ain't having no tart look down their nose at me, so I'd quit before yours gets re-arranged, if I was you.'

'And I'd quit making threats, if I was *you*,' Suzie replied icily. 'Unless you wouldn't want the drug squad to hear about that little business you're running in your flat.'

'You what?' Carol drew her head back. 'You're talking shit.'

'Am I?' Suzie challenged. 'Well I guess you won't have anything to worry about when they pay you a surprise visit, will you?'

Carol's fat jowls quivered and her mouth flapped open as if she wanted to continue the argument. Then, seeming to think better of it, she clamped her mouth shut and gave Suzie a murderous look before stomping away.

Pacing the hallway, chewing her thumbnail, Holly said, 'What was all that about?' when Suzie came inside. 'She looked like she wanted to kill you.'

'Oh, she did,' Suzie chuckled, closing the door. 'But I doubt she'll bother us again now she knows that *I* know about her little sideline.'

'Sideline?' Holly repeated, following when Suzie headed into the kitchen after hanging up her coat.

'She's a dealer,' Suzie said, twisting the lid off the wine bottle and looking around for glasses.

'How do you know?' Holly took two out of the cupboard and passed them to her.

'I haven't been sleeping too well since Rob left, and I see a lot of people coming in and out of here at odd hours,' Suzie explained as she poured the drinks. 'They never stay for long, so I figured someone in here must be supplying them. I didn't know it was her for sure, but her reaction when I threatened to report her to the drug squad confirmed it.'

'Wow.' Holly shook her head. 'And she had the cheek to warn me about hanging round with you.'

'I don't give a toss what she thinks of me,' Suzie said dismissively. 'Anyway, forget her and go and wash that mascara off your face, then put your jimmies on while I find us a film to watch.'

21

Josie opened her eyes, but immediately wished she hadn't when a harsh overhead light blinded her. Raising her arm to block it out, she felt something tug at her skin and squinted in confusion at the bulky plastic thing taped to the back of her hand. She followed the clear plastic tube coming out of it to a drip standing beside the bed, and her heart lurched when she realized she was in hospital. But why?

Swallowing dryly when a vague memory nudged into her consciousness, she closed her eyes and tried to grab onto it. She'd made lamb stew, she remembered. It was Holly's favourite meal when she was little, and she'd made it because she felt guilty for not listening when Holly had told her she was being bullied and had asked for time off school. She'd got up early and gone to the shop, then she'd made the stew and eaten with Holly before heading out to work. And then . . .

Nothing. Just empty black space.

Struggling to sit up, she cried out when a sharp pain tore through the back of her head.

'Take it easy,' a voice cautioned.

A nurse appeared at the side of the bed, and Josie gazed up at her. 'Why . . . why am I here?' she asked, her voice raspy to her own ears.

'The police will explain,' the nurse replied evasively. 'I'll give them a ring and let them know you're awake. Now, how are you feeling?'

'Like I've been hit by a train,' Josie said truthfully.

'The meds you were given when you came in are probably wearing off, so I'll get you some more,' the nurse said. 'And would you like a drink?'

'Yes, please.'

'Won't be a sec.'

The nurse left the room and Josie looked around. There were three more beds in the room, all occupied by frail-looking old ladies who, with the exception of the one in the far corner whose gaze seemed transfixed by something on the ceiling, were fast asleep and snoring softly. Quietly, to avoid disturbing them, Josie lifted the sheet off her legs and gingerly sat up again. A dark bruise had spread out across the back of her hand, and she winced when she accidentally jabbed the tender flesh with her thumbnail while trying to peel off the tape that was holding the cannula in place. Distracted by the sight of yet more bruises running up her arms, she sucked in a sharp breath when she noticed dark blood on the front of the gown she was wearing.

The nurse came back into the room carrying a jug of water and two tablets in a small plastic cup. Rushing over to the bed when she saw Josie teetering on the edge of the mattress, she put the items on the table and eased her back against the pillows, saying, 'Try not to move around too much. If you need the toilet, I'll fetch you a bedpan.'

'I – I need to go home,' Josie said, licking her dry lips. 'My daughter—'

'The police have spoken to her and she's safe with her aunt,' the nurse said, pulling the sheet over her legs before drawing the curtain around the bed. 'Now stop worrying and try to relax.'

Josie's heart thudded painfully in her chest and the blood rushed to her head. 'I've got to go home,' she gasped, struggling to sit up again. 'I need to see her.'

'What you *need* is to keep still,' the nurse said firmly, placing a hand on her arm to hold her in place. 'You're in no fit state to go anywhere, and Doctor Ross will be in to see you shortly, so—'

'You don't understand,' Josie said, her voice rising in panic. 'Holly hasn't got an aunt. I don't know who she's with.'

'Calm down,' the nurse said patiently, holding her arm. 'It's perfectly normal to feel confused when you've suffered a trauma to the head, but things will start settling down if you relax and give your body a chance to heal. OK?'

Josie did feel confused, but one thing she knew for certain was that Holly did *not* have an aunt. Not one that Holly knew of, anyway. No one from the past knew where they lived – Josie had made sure of that. And if she wanted it to stay that way, she needed to be very careful right now, because the last thing she needed was for the nurse to alert the police that something might be wrong and have them start digging. That would open a huge can of worms, and Josie couldn't risk that.

'Sorry,' she murmured. 'It freaked me out, waking up in here, but I'm OK now. It'll be my, um, sister. Holly must have rung her and asked her to go round.'

'That'll be it.' The nurse smiled and patted her shoulder. 'Now let's get you comfortable.'

Resting against the pillows after the nurse had raised the back of the bed up, Josie swallowed the tablets and then gulped the water down to douse the flames in her throat.

'Better?' the nurse asked, taking the tumbler from her hand and placing it on the table.

'Yes, thanks. How long have I been here?'

'A few hours,' the nurse said, gazing at the watch that was pinned to her tunic as she checked Josie's pulse.

'Can't you tell me what happened? Everything hurts. Was I run over?'

'The police will explain when they get here.'

Someone on the other side of the curtain gave a small cough as the words left her mouth, and she smiled when she pulled it back and saw two police officers standing there.

'Speak of the devil,' she said, waving for them to come in. 'PC Spencer?' She looked at each of the men in turn.

'That's me,' Spencer said. 'And you're Lorraine?'

'I am.' She smiled. 'And this is Josie.'

Josie sank lower in the bed and eyed the officers warily.

'Try not to overdo it,' Lorraine said quietly to Spencer. 'She was a bit confused when she woke up.'

'We won't keep her long,' Spencer promised.

Lorraine gave Josie one last look then left them to it, swishing the curtain shut behind her. Spencer pulled a chair up to the side of the bed and sat down. He introduced himself and his colleague to Josie, and asked if she was up to talking to them.

She nodded, her gaze flicking from him to PC Bennett, who had moved to the end of bed and was blatantly reading her notes.

'Do you know what happened?' Spencer began.

'No,' she murmured. 'The nurse said you'd tell me.'

'You were assaulted,' Spencer said, watching her face closely as he spoke.

'*Assaulted?*' Her eyes widened in shock. 'W-what do you mean? I thought I'd been run over. That's what it feels like.'

'A man attacked you in the alleyway leading off the estate,' Spencer told her. 'Some lads disturbed him and he got away. They weren't able to give a description because his face was covered, but we hoped you might remember something.'

A murky vision flashed into Josie's mind and she closed her eyes and gripped the edge of the mattress when the bed lurched beneath her.

It was pitch-dark in the alley and she didn't want to go down there, but the bus was due . . .

'Josie?' Spencer's voice cut into her thoughts. 'Are you OK?'

'I – I feel a bit dizzy,' she mumbled.

'Do you need me to fetch the nurse?'

She shook her head and swallowed loudly, her tongue sticking to the roof of her mouth. 'I just want to go home,' she whispered.

'You've got a nasty bump on the back of your head, so I think you'll be staying here for a couple of nights, at least,' Spencer said. 'You're lucky those lads came along when they did or it could have been a lot worse.'

'The next one might not be so lucky,' Bennett said, slotting her notes back into the cradle. 'And the sooner we catch him, the faster we'll get him off the streets, so we need you to really think about what you might have seen or heard. Was he black, white, Asian? Were there any logos or colours on his jacket? Did he speak . . . ?'

Josie's head throbbed as the man fired the questions at her without giving her a chance to answer, and a shiver rippled down her spine when she closed her eyes and saw another hazy vision.

She'd been walking fast, trying to get to the main road, then she hit a wall and fell over. Only it wasn't a wall, it was a man, and he'd covered her mouth with his hand and dragged her through the fence. And then . . .

'Josie? Are you feeling dizzy again?'

Josie opened her eyes when Spencer's voice filtered through the haze. His colleague was right: they needed to catch her attacker before he did this to somebody else. But if she told them that she remembered it, they'd keep coming back for more. And if they somehow managed to catch him, they'd expect her to go to court. She couldn't risk that, so she shook her head, and said, 'I was trying to remember, but there's nothing. I'm sorry.'

'It's fine,' Spencer said, trying to mask his disappointment. 'We'll leave it at that for now, but if you remember anything, no matter how small or insignificant you might think it is, let one of the nurses know and we'll come back.'

'I will,' Josie lied.

'I'll give your daughter a call and let her know you're awake,' Spencer said as he stood up. 'Her Aunt Suzie's staying with her while you're here,' he added, giving her a meaningful look.

Suzie . . . Josie frowned as she silently repeated the name. She didn't know anyone called Suzie, so why was it ringing a bell?

Holly had said it earlier! When they were eating, she'd said it was Bex's mum's name!

Relief washed over her, only to be instantly replaced by dread. Oh, God! The rich bitch was at her flat. What if she'd taken a look around and decided that Holly was being neglected because it was squalid compared to her posh house?

'How are we getting on?' Lorraine popped her head round the curtain.

'We're leaving,' Spencer said. 'I'm sure her daughter will want to see her when she hears she's awake, so when should I tell her to come?'

'Visiting starts at two,' Lorraine said. 'But if she wants to pop in a little earlier with some of her mum's things, that'd be fine.'

'I'll let her know,' Spencer said. Then, to Josie, he added, 'I'll try to call in again tomorrow, but if you remember anything in the meantime—'

'Tell the nurse,' Josie murmured.

Nodding, Spencer smiled and said goodbye, then he, his colleague and the nurse left her.

Unable to see past the curtain, she listened as their footsteps receded. The pain in her head was becoming duller and she guessed the tablets must have started to kick in. Grateful for that, but aware that she didn't have much time as a sluggish feeling began to creep over her, she was about to sit up when she heard something beeping on the other side of the room. Footsteps entered and she heard muffled voices, then the curtain billowed inward as another bed was wheeled quickly past the end of hers.

When silence fell over the room again, she sat up and eased her heavy, bruised legs over the side of the mattress. She looked around for her clothes but they weren't there, and she guessed the police must have taken them to check for traces of her attacker's DNA. Her shoes were under the chair, however, and her handbag was inside the bedside cabinet when she checked. Pulling it out, she rooted her phone out from the mess of tissues and receipts inside, intending to call Holly and tell her that she was coming home and warn her not to let Bex's mum snoop around.

The battery was flat, and she muttered a curse under her breath when she remembered that she'd forgotten to charge it; she'd been too busy shopping and then cooking the stupid stew to think about it. Dropping the phone back into her bag, she was relieved to find that her purse hadn't been stolen and the small amount of money she'd had in it was still there. A quick count told her that she had just enough for a taxi home, so she put it away and carefully slid off the bed and peeked out into the room.

There were no nurses in sight, either in here or out on the corridor. Bending over as far as her sore stomach and the pain in her side would allow, so that the woman who was still staring up at the ceiling in the corner bed wouldn't see her and raise the alarm, she crept out from behind the curtain and made her way over to the cabinet beside the now missing bed. She eased the door open, keeping an eye on the other beds and the door, and her heart leapt when she saw a neatly folded coat on top of a pile of clothes on the bottom shelf. Sliding it out, she quickly closed the door at the sound of approaching footsteps and hobbled back to her own bed, stashing the coat in her cabinet seconds before the nurse came through the curtain.

'Hey, what are you doing?' Lorraine chided, taking hold of her arm. 'I told you I'd bring you a bedpan if you needed the toilet.'

'I'm not going to the toilet, I'm going home,' Josie snapped, shrugging her hand off.

'I don't think so,' Lorraine said. 'Doctor Ross will be in to see you soon; she'll decide when you're ready to be discharged.'

'Am I under arrest?' Josie asked, irritated by the woman's school-marmish manner.

'No, of course not.'

'Then I'm going,' Josie said, reaching for her handbag. 'And, don't worry, I'm not nicking your gown. I'll fetch it back when I've washed it.'

'I'm not concerned about that, I'm concerned about you,' Lorraine argued. 'You've had a trauma to your head and we need to monitor you for the next twenty-four hours, make sure there are no complications.'

'I'll be fine,' Josie insisted.

A young female doctor appeared. Hesitating when she saw Josie on her feet, she glanced down at the folder in her hand, before asking, 'Is this Ms Evans?'

'Yes, and she's trying to leave,' said Lorraine. 'I've told her it's not advisable.'

'And I told you I'll be fine,' Josie interjected.

'We can't force you to stay,' the doctor said, 'but I'd be a lot happier if you did.'

'I can't,' Josie said, hitching the strap of her bag over her shoulder. A pain seared through her side as she did it, and she put her hand down on the bed and breathed in deeply.

'I need to take a look at that,' the doctor said, gesturing for her to get onto the bed. 'Your coat stopped the knife from going in too far, but it did pierce your skin, so we don't want to be taking any chances with it.'

'Knife?' Josie repeated, gaping at her. 'He stabbed me?'

'As I said, your coat took the brunt of it, but we don't want you opening the wound and getting infected, so if we could just take a look?'

Too shocked to argue, Josie lay down. The nurse lifted the gown over her stomach and the doctor gently peeled back the dressing Josie hadn't noticed until then. Arching her neck to look, Josie sucked in a breath when she saw the angry wound in the flesh above her left hip. It was tiny, but the dried blood around it and on the dressing told her that it must have bled out for some time.

'It looks OK, but I think we'll redress it,' the doctor said. 'And I'd still prefer to keep you in overnight, Ms Evans – just to be on the safe side.'

Sensing that they were going to keep hassling her until she agreed, Josie sighed, and said, 'Fine. Whatever.'

'Good girl,' Lorraine smiled.

Flashing a furious look at the bitch from beneath her lashes, Josie turned slowly onto her side until she could no longer see her.

Another nurse popped her head around the curtain, and said, 'Sorry for interrupting, Doctor Ross, but you're needed in Resus.'

The doctor immediately scooped up the folder she'd laid on the bed and rushed out, leaving Lorraine to get Josie back into bed.

'Leave me,' Josie said. 'I'm tired and I just want to lie like this for a while.'

'OK, I'll check on you in a bit then,' Lorraine said, backing out. 'Ring the buzzer if you need anything.'

Josie nodded, and closed her eyes. In the gap beneath the curtain, she saw Lorraine's feet walking towards the bed next to hers, then heard her walk over to the bed on the other side of the room, and ask, in a loud, slow voice, as if speaking to a deaf person or an idiot, 'Are you feeling any better, Agnes?'

No reply came, so she said, 'Why don't you close your eyes for a bit, my love? They'll get sore if you keep staring like that, and we'll have to use those drops you don't like. Shall I turn the light off and see if that helps?'

Still no reply. Lorraine walked past Josie's bed again, the overhead light went out, and then all fell silent in the room. Waiting a few seconds to make sure she wasn't coming back, Josie got up and took the coat she'd stolen out of the cabinet. It was a little tight around the arms, but it buttoned up all right; and it fell to just below Josie's knees, so the bloodstained gown was completely covered. Shoes back on, her handbag over her shoulder, she peeped out into the corridor to make sure Lorraine wasn't standing guard, and then headed quietly towards the door marked *Exit*.

The Resus room was situated at that end of the corridor, and Josie glanced in through the open door as she passed. The old lady whose coat she was wearing was lying flat on the bed, her head angled back, her mouth wide open. Doctor Ross and three nurses were standing around the bed and Josie instinctively knew from their downbeat expressions that the woman hadn't made it. At least she wouldn't get done for stealing the coat, she thought, doubting that the grieving relatives would notice it was gone when they came to collect the woman's belongings. Thankful for that, she quickly crossed herself before pushing out through the exit door.

22

Suzie and Holly were huddled on the sofa in their pyjamas, watching a horror film. Jumping when her phone started ringing, Suzie reached for it, her gaze still fixed on the TV screen.

'Hello?'

'Is this Suzie?'

'Depends who's asking,' she replied cagily, not recognizing the voice.

'It's Dan,' the man said. 'PC Spencer.'

'Oh, hi . . .' Suzie sat up straighter and flapped her hand at Holly to lower the TV volume. 'Is everything OK? We weren't expecting to hear back from you so soon.'

'I just wanted to let you know that Josie's awake and I've spoken to her,' Spencer said.

'Oh, that's good,' Suzie said, smiling at Holly who was watching her anxiously. 'And how was she?'

'A bit groggy, but the nurse said she'd just had pain meds before we got there, so that's to be expected, said Spencer. 'She doesn't remember anything, but it'll probably start coming back to her when she's slept and her head's a little clearer.'

'Let's hope so,' Suzie said. 'He needs catching before he does this to someone else.'

'We'll get him,' Spencer assured her. 'Anyway, they said Holly can visit her tomorrow, and they've asked if she can take some stuff in – nightie and toiletries, and what have you.'

'No problem,' Suzie said. 'And thanks for letting us know.'

'You're welcome.'

Spencer paused, as if, Suzie thought, he wanted to say something else, and she wondered if he was going to ask her out. Given the way he'd looked at her earlier, and his blush when she'd touched his arm, it wouldn't surprise her; and he was a good-looking bloke, so she couldn't deny it would be flattering. But she wasn't sure she was ready to start seeing anyone so soon after Rob, so she was relieved when Spencer said, 'Right, well, I'll leave you to it, then. Night.'

'Night,' she said. 'And thanks again.'

'What did he say?' Holly asked. 'Is my mum OK?'

'He's spoken to her and she's fine.'

'Really?' Holly's eyes lit up for the first time that night. 'Can I go and see her?'

'Tomorrow,' said Suzie. 'And we need to take a nightie and some toiletries in for her, so I'll help you to pack a bag when the film's finished.'

'I'll do it,' Holly said, jumping up off the sofa and rushing into the kitchen to grab a plastic bag.

Suzie smiled, happy that the cloud of gloom had lifted off Holly's shoulders – and even happier to hear that Josie was on the mend, because the thought of spending the night in this grubby, soul-destroying little flat was already bringing her out in hives. She felt itchy just sitting on this stinking sofa, but she'd promised PC Spencer she would stay here, so that's what she would do. But she was going to count off the seconds until she could escape and take a long hot shower.

Out in the hall, Holly hesitated before entering her mum's bedroom. She wasn't allowed in there, because her mum said it was the only private space she had, and she'd always respected that. But this was an emergency, so she opened the door and switched on the light.

Unprepared for the sight that greeted her, her mouth fell open. Her mum nagged her to keep her own room clean and moaned if the rest of the flat wasn't spotless after she'd cleaned up at the weekend, yet *her* room was an absolute tip. Dirty clothes were strewn across the floor, and the air reeked of stale smoke and sweat. The duvet cover and pillowcases looked grubby, and an overflowing ashtray was sitting on the bedside cabinet surrounded by dirty cups, glasses and scrunched-up tissues. A laundry basket without its lid stood in the corner, and Holly shook her head when she spotted the empty vodka bottles sticking out of it. She'd suspected her mum was drinking too much again, but she hadn't realized it was *this* bad.

'Holy *shit!*'

Jumping at the sound of Suzie's voice, Holly's cheeks blazed when she saw the disgust in her friend's eyes.

'I'm sorry, hon,' Suzie said, pulling a face as she looked around. 'I know I said I'd stay over, but there's no way I'm sleeping in here. It needs fumigating.'

'We can't touch anything,' Holly said, feeling nervous when Suzie started rolling up the sleeves of her pyjama top, as if she intended to start cleaning. 'My mum'll go mad if she finds out you've been in here. She doesn't even let *me* come in.'

'And how will she feel if social services come round and you get taken into care because she couldn't be arsed cleaning up?' Suzie asked bluntly. ''Cos that's what'll happen if they see this, I guarantee it.'

Holly shuddered at the thought of being sent to a children's home. A girl at her last school had been sent to live in a home after her mum died, and she'd told Holly it was worse than prison.

'Right, forget it, we're going to mine,' Suzie said decisively. 'I know I told PC Spencer I'd stay here, but I doubt we'll hear from him again tonight, so grab some underwear and toiletries while I look for a nightie, then we'll get going.'

Squirming with shame when Suzie walked over to the bed and gingerly lifted a pillow with her fingernails, as if afraid that she might catch something from it, Holly rifled through the dressing table drawer and tossed a bra and a couple of pairs of knickers into the plastic bag before going to the bathroom to get her mum's toothbrush.

There was no nightdress beneath the pillows, so Suzie went over to the wardrobe. A heap of clothes tumbled out as she opened the door, and an old, square biscuit tin fell out from the middle when she tried to catch them. The lid came off when it hit the floor and a pile of photographs and papers spilled out at her feet.

Scooping them together as Holly came back into the room, she peered at the photograph on the top of the pile as she straightened up. It was of a pretty young woman with long blond hair and sparkling blue eyes, and she was smiling widely at whoever was holding the camera.

'Is this your mum?' she asked, showing it to Holly.

'Yeah, I think so,' Holly murmured, studying the face. 'She looks so young though, and I've never seen her with blond hair before. It really suits her.'

'It does,' Suzie agreed, leafing through the other photos. 'Ooh, she doesn't look so happy in this one.' She turned it round for Holly to see.

Looking at it, Holly frowned. Her mum looked a lot older in this shot: her cheeks gaunt, her eyes dull, and the blond grown out to the extent that she looked like she was wearing a black skullcap on top of a straw wig. Wondering if it had been taken when she was pregnant and Holly's dad had dumped her, Holly felt a twinge of guilt when she realized that she might have been the cause of their break-up and her mum's subsequent misery.

'Aw, this is sweet.' Suzie showed Holly another image, this

time of Josie smiling down at the newborn baby in her arms. 'Is that your sister?'

'I haven't got a sister,' Holly said, her frown deepening as she took the photo from her. 'I'm an only child.'

'Well, it doesn't look anything like you,' Suzie commented.

Holly agreed: it didn't. Her hair was mousy brown but the baby's was a lot darker, and its nose was a completely different shape than hers. But her name and date of birth were written on the back when she turned it over, so it had to be her.

'God, I was an ugly baby,' she muttered.

'At least you're pretty now,' Suzie said, plucking a folded age-yellowed newspaper cutting out of the bundle and opening it out on the bed. 'Hey, look at this.'

'What is it?' Holly asked, putting the photos down and looking over Suzie's shoulder.

CHILD MISSING FROM SCENE OF DOUBLE MURDER, the headline read. *An investigation has been launched after an anonymous tip-off led police to the scene of a double murder in the Shaw district of Oldham in the early hours of Wednesday morning. The bodies of Anna Hughes and her partner Devon Prince were found in a blood-spattered bedroom at Ms Hughes's home. Both victims had been shot at close range in what police are describing as a targeted attack. Concerns were raised when it was discovered that Ms Hughes's four-year-old daughter from a previous relationship, Charlotte, was missing from the house, and an intensive search is taking place in Shaw and surrounding areas. Detective Chief Inspector Andrew Forster has asked anyone who knows of Charlotte's whereabouts to contact—*

The paper had been torn at that point and the rest of the article was missing.

'Did your mum know these people?' Suzie asked.

'No idea.' Holly shrugged. 'She's never mentioned them to me if she did.'

'It's probably someone she knew before she had you. Or maybe she was related to one of them.'

'Yeah, maybe.'

'I wonder if they ever found the girl,' Suzie said, pulling her phone out of her pocket to google the names in the article.

Before she had the chance, Holly heard a key being inserted into the lock of the front door. Panicking, because it could only be her mum, she shoved Suzie out into the hall, then switched off the light and pulled the door shut a millisecond before the front door opened and Josie limped in looking like death warmed up.

23

'*Mum!*' Holly snapped out of her trance. 'What are you doing home? The police told us they were keeping you in hospital tonight.'

'I discharged myself,' Josie muttered, holding onto the hall table for support as she waited for the room to stop swaying and her heart to stop pounding. Unable to find a taxi, she had walked home, stopping off at the late shop on the way to pick up a pack of cigarettes and a cheap bottle of vodka with the money she would have spent on her fare. A couple of slugs from the bottle outside the shop had made her legs feel a little less sluggish, and the hit of nicotine had shifted the fog inside her head. But she was exhausted now.

'You look terrible,' Holly said, her young face creased with concern as she took in Josie's swollen eyes, the bruises on her cheeks, the split lip and the blood on the neck of the gown she was wearing beneath the unfamiliar coat. 'What did he do to you?'

'Stop fussing, I'm fine,' Josie said irritably, slapping her hands aside. Then, staring at the woman who was standing behind Holly, she frowned, and said, 'Where's Bex's mum?'

'Bex's mum?' Holly repeated. 'Why would *she* be here?'

'The copper told me someone called Suzie was with you.'

'Yeah, that's right. *This* is Suzie.'

'You said that was Bex's mum's name.' Josie was confused.

Blushing guiltily when she recalled the lie she'd told at dinner earlier, Holly said, 'Er, yeah, it is. They're both called Suzie.'

'Sorry, we haven't been introduced.' Suzie stepped forward. 'I live across the road.'

'I know who you are,' Josie said, eyeing her warily. 'But why are you here?'

'I heard what happened and wanted to make sure Holly was OK,' said Suzie. Then, smiling, she reached out to take Josie's arm, saying, 'You shouldn't be on your feet, love, so let's get you sat down. Holly, go and fetch your mum's quilt while I make her a cup of tea.'

'I don't want tea.' Josie snatched her arm away. 'I want you to leave.'

'*Mum!*' Holly protested. 'She's only trying to help.'

'We don't need help,' Josie snapped.

'*I* did,' Holly argued. 'The police would have called social services and had me taken into care if she hadn't been here, so you should be thanking her.'

'It's all right, hon,' Suzie said softly. 'Your mum's had a rough night and needs to rest, so I'll go home. You've got my number if you need me.'

She went into the living room and gathered her things together, then said goodnight and let herself out. When she'd gone, Holly folded her arms and gave her mum a reproachful look.

'You didn't have to be so rude.'

'How do you know her?' Josie demanded. 'And don't say you don't, 'cos it's obvious this isn't the first time you've met her. And what's all this *hon* business?'

'I've seen her on the street a few times and said hello. And she calls *everyone* hon.'

'You're lying.' Josie narrowed her eyes.

'No, I'm not,' Holly replied sulkily. 'God, why don't you ever belie—'

The slap was swift and sharp, and Holly gaped at her mum in shock as she covered her stinging cheek with her hand.

'What was that for?'

'You brought a stranger into our home!' Josie yelled, grabbing her arm. 'Have you any idea the damage you could have done?'

'I had no choice,' Holly cried, wincing when her mum's nails dug into her flesh. '*OW!* You're hurting me!'

'What have you told her?' Josie shook her roughly. 'Tell me what you said!'

'*Nothing!*' Holly protested, yanking her arm free and rubbing the sore spot. 'And I haven't done anything wrong, so I don't see why you're flipping out like this.'

'You broke the rules!' Josie glared at her.

'The rules are stupid,' Holly shot back, too angry and upset to hold her tongue any longer. 'I'm nearly sixteen, but you won't let me answer the door or talk to anyone. It's not normal.'

'I let you hang around with Bex and that other one – Kelly, or whatever her name is,' Josie argued. 'It's only these nosy bastards round here I don't want you getting friendly with.'

'Why? What's wrong with talking to your neighbours? Everyone else does.'

'You *know* why. It's dangerous.'

'But Suzie's not like the others. She's really nice, and she doesn't even talk to anyone round here.'

'Shut up about fucking *Suzie*!' Josie roared, balling her hands into fists. Then, breathing in deeply through her nose, she lowered her voice and said, 'You're not to talk to her again, and that's the end of it. Now go to bed and give me some bloody peace.' She brushed past Holly and went into her room, closing the door firmly behind her.

Sighing, Holly shook her head in despair and went to her own room. Her mum ought to be glad Suzie had stepped in and stopped her being put into care, but, as usual, all she cared about was herself and her stupid rules.

Josie switched the light on and dropped her bag onto the bed before shrugging the coat off and flinging it aside. In need of another drink, she took the bottle of vodka out of her bag and poured a measure into the dirty glass on her bedside table. Knocking half of it back in one mouthful, she gently rolled her head to ease the tension in her shoulders. When she noticed the wardrobe door standing open, her body instantly stiffened again, and her heart leapt into her throat when she saw the biscuit tin lying open on the floor, the photographs and papers it had contained strewn around it.

'*HOLLLYYYY!*' she bellowed.

'What's up?' Holly rushed in, her eyes wide. 'You haven't hurt yourself, have you?'

'Who's been in here?' Josie demanded.

'No one,' Holly lied. Then, frowning when she noticed the glass in her mum's shaking hand and the bottle on the table, she said, 'You shouldn't be drinking. You've only just come out of hospital.'

'Stop trying to change the subject,' Josie hissed, her eyes blazing. 'You've had that bitch in here, haven't you?'

'No.' Holly shook her head.

'Explain *that*, then!' Josie pointed at the photos and papers.

Holly winced when she realized she'd forgotten to put them back in her haste to get Suzie out of there.

'OK, it was me,' she admitted. 'The copper told me to bring some stuff to hospital for you tomorrow, and everything fell out of the wardrobe when I was looking for a nightie. But I didn't look at it, I swear.'

'Yes, you did,' Josie said quietly, her chest heaving beneath the bloodstained gown. 'It's written all over your face. So, come on, then . . . what did you see?'

'Nothing,' Holly insisted.

'And what about Lady Muck?' Josie jerked her chin up. 'Did she have a good nosy an' all?'

'No, it was only me, I swear.'

'You *swear*,' Josie sneered, taking a swig of her drink and wiping her mouth on the back of her hand. 'I don't know why I thought I could trust you; you've always been a sly little cow. That's why you looked so guilty when I walked in: 'cos you knew you'd been caught.'

Upset that her mum had called her sly when she genuinely hadn't meant to snoop, Holly felt the prick of tears behind her eyes as she watched Josie swallow her drink and toss the glass onto the bed before stumbling over to the wardrobe.

'God damn it,' Josie cried, clutching at her side when a pain tore through it as she bent to scoop up the photos. She squeezed her eyes shut and leaned against the wardrobe until it had passed, then crammed the photos back into the tin and pushed the lid firmly into place, muttering, 'I can't do this any more. All I've ever done is try to protect her, and she's ruined everything.'

'Protect me from what?' Holly asked, confused.

'*Them!*' Josie said, tossing the biscuit tin into the wardrobe and slamming the door shut. 'You've got no idea how fucking hard it's been for me, have you? Having to hawk you around and work my arse off for shit wages to keep you safe. Well, that's it. We can't stay here after this.'

Concerned that the combination of alcohol and medication was affecting her badly, Holly said, 'Why don't you go to bed, Mum? You'll feel better if you get some sleep.'

'It's too late for that,' Josie said, a wild gleam in her eyes as she looked around the room. 'We need to get out of here. Go and pack a bag.'

'What?' Holly screwed up her face. 'It's nearly midnight. Where are we supposed to go?'

'Stop arguing and get your things,' Josie ordered, sifting through the clothes on the floor and flinging some aside and others onto the bed.

'No.' Holly stood her ground. 'I like it here. I'm not leaving.'

'Do as you're fucking *told*!' Josie roared, lunging at her and pushing her out into the hall.

'*No!*' Holly pushed her back. 'This is stupid, Mum! I've got my exams in a couple of months. I can't change schools again.'

'If you hadn't let that bitch in here we wouldn't have to,' Josie screeched, her hands bouncing off Holly's raised arms as she tried to slap her. 'They're probably on their way here already, you stupid girl! And they won't just kill me, they'll kill you as well! It's you they're after, not—'

She abruptly stopped speaking and her face twisted with pain as she clutched at her side again. Alarmed when sweat started trickling down her deathly white face and she sank to the floor, Holly rushed to her.

'Mum, what's wrong? Are you OK?'

'Need to . . . go . . .' Josie mumbled, her eyes flickering before rolling back.

Scared now, Holly raced to her bedroom to call an ambulance. Her phone wasn't there, so she ran into the living room and looked around. Unable to find it, she tore back out into the hall where her mum was still slumped against the wall. Edging past her, she went to the bed and rifled through her mum's handbag for *her* phone. It was dead, and a whimper of fear slipped from Holly's lips as she dropped it and rushed out into the hall. She didn't know what to do, but Suzie would, so she grabbed her key off the hall table and charged out of the flat.

Suzie had jumped into the shower as soon as she got home and had scrubbed her skin and double-washed her hair to erase the stench of mildew that was clinging to her. In a fresh pair of pyjamas now, her clean hair lying damp on her shoulders, she was heading to the kitchen to get a drink when the doorbell rang, followed by a volley of raps on the knocker. Concerned when she peeped through the spyhole and saw Holly in tears on the step, she quickly opened the door.

'Hey, what's wrong?' she asked when Holly fell into her arms. 'Is it your mum? She didn't take a bad turn after I left, did she?'

'She – she went mad after you left,' Holly cried, the words tumbling out of her mouth. 'She knew we'd been in her room and seen those photos and she flipped. She said we had to leave 'cos someone was coming to kill us, and we were arguing. Then she went funny and collapsed and her eyes rolled back. I thought she was dead and I didn't know what to do. I couldn't find my phone, and hers was dead, and—'

'OK, calm down,' Suzie said, taking control. 'I'm sure it's not as bad as you think. She probably came out of hospital too early, that's all. Just give me a sec and I'll come over with you.'

Praying that she was right, Holly swiped at her tears and hopped from foot to foot as Suzie grabbed her coat off the hook and ran upstairs.

When they got back to the flat, Holly unlocked the door with shaking hands and rushed inside. She stopped dead when she saw that her mum wasn't where she'd left her, and Suzie ran into the back of her, almost knocking her over. Her first thought was that her mum had done a runner to escape the imaginary killers she was expecting to arrive at any minute, and her heart was pounding so hard she didn't immediately hear Suzie calling her name.

'*Holly* . . .' Suzie hissed, a little louder this time. 'She's in here.'

She pointed through Josie's open bedroom door and Holly took a faltering step towards it, scared that she was going to see her mum lying dead on the floor.

'See, I told you it wouldn't be as bad as you thought,' Suzie whispered, stroking Holly's arm as the shivering girl stared at her mum, who was lying in the bed now, the grubby quilt pulled over her.

'I – I thought she was . . .' Holly tailed off and swallowed loudly as the fear began to subside, leaving a nauseous feeling in its wake. 'She looked so bad, Suzie. Really sweaty and pale, like a ghost.'

Tiptoeing into the room, Suzie went over to the bed and peered at Josie's face before lightly touching her cheek.

'She is a bit clammy,' she whispered when Holly crept up beside her. 'But she's been through a lot today, and it'll have taken a massive toll on her.'

'You don't think we should call for an ambulance – just in case?' Holly asked.

Suzie pursed her lips and peered at Josie again. Then, shaking her head, she said, 'If the doctors at the hospital had thought there was anything seriously wrong they wouldn't have let her discharge herself, so let's wait and see how she is when she wakes up, eh? Chances are, she's exhausted and needs to sleep. And *that* won't have helped, if she's had any since she got home,' she added, indicating the bottle of vodka on the bedside table.

'Yeah, she has,' Holly said, hugging herself as she recalled the way her mum had been knocking it back before flying off the handle.

'No wonder she's out cold, then,' Suzie said. 'She took quite a beating by the look of it, and they would have given her strong painkillers at hospital. Them and alcohol don't mix, so you're not supposed to drink while you're on them.'

'Do you think she'll be OK?' Holly asked.

'I'd say so,' Suzie said, backing away from the bed. 'But she'll probably have a massive hangover, so make sure she drinks plenty of water when she wakes up.'

Nodding, Holly followed when Suzie went back out into the hall.

'Thanks for coming over,' she said, feeling daft for panicking now she knew it was the booze that had sent her mum funny.

'You don't need to thank me, hon,' Suzie said, heading for the door. 'We're friends, and I'm happy to help. Now try to get some sleep, 'cos your mum's not the only one who's had a rough night. If anything happens or you get worried, ring me. OK?'

'If I can find my phone,' Holly said.

'Last time I saw it was when we were watching the film,' Suzie told her. 'I think you shoved it down the side of the cushion.'

'Oh, yeah,' Holly murmured. 'Thanks.'

When Suzie had gone, Holly retrieved her phone and turned it on. She hadn't told Suzie, but she had turned it off earlier, sick of seeing the messages that had been coming in throughout the day and evening – all along the same threatening lines as those that had been sent to her that morning. There were several new ones when the screen lit up, and she was deleting them when she saw that the last two were from Bex, along with four missed call notifications.

Hey Holls, are you OK? the first message began. *Ju's mum told her someone's been attacked round your way. I tried to ring but you're not answering. Please let me know you're all right xx*

Holls ring me!!!! the second, more urgent message read. *Ju's mum's friend is married to a copper and she said it was a woman called Josie who got attacked. It wasn't your mum was it???? Please ring me babes xx*

Blinking when unexpected tears welled in her eyes, Holly went to ring Bex but stopped herself when she realized her friend would be fast asleep. About to reply to her messages instead, she snapped her head up at the sound of a groan coming from her mum's room.

Josie had rolled onto her back and the quilt was on the floor beside her. Holly picked it up and was gently laying it over her when she rolled over again. The hospital gown had ridden up, and Holly's gaze was drawn to a large bruise on her thigh between a cluster of smaller ones. It was purple and black, and had fainter lines zig-zagging through it, like the sole of a trainer. Upset to think that the beast who had attacked her mum must have stamped on her, she wondered if the police had noticed it. In *CSI: Miami*, one of her favourite TV shows, the detectives were always finding footprints in soil outside windows and in pools of blood at crime scenes, and they always took photos to determine the shoe size and type of footwear. It invariably led them to the killer, and she wondered if she ought to take a photo of this imprint on her phone and ask Suzie to pass it on to that nice copper who'd come round earlier.

Josie flopped over again before Holly had a chance to open her phone camera. She was agitated, thrashing her head from side to side, and Holly remembered what Suzie had said about making sure she had something to drink after she woke up when she saw how dry and cracked her lips were.

Josie started mumbling. Unable to make out the words, Holly touched her arm, and said, 'Mum . . . ? Are you awake?'

'No . . .' Josie croaked, her eyes still closed.

Thinking it was a reply to her question, Holly said, 'I'm going to get you a drink; won't be a sec.'

'*No!*' Josie said again, more forcefully. 'You can't have her, she's mine! Leave us alone . . . !'

Holly gazed down at her and wondered if she was dreaming or delirious. She was shivering, even though she was still sweating, and a small patch of what looked like fresh blood had appeared on the side of the gown – the side she'd kept clutching at earlier. Curious to see where it was coming from in case it needed attention, Holly tentatively lifted the gown to take a look. A square dressing had been applied to the skin above her mum's hip, but one of the pieces of tape holding it in place had come loose, and she could see a small wound beneath it. Blood and pus had oozed out, but it didn't appear to be bleeding now, so she carefully pushed the tape back down before laying the quilt over her mum.

She placed a glass of water on the bedside cabinet. Then, drained and in need of sleep herself, she took the bottle of vodka into her room and stashed it in her underwear drawer before climbing into bed – leaving the door open so she would hear if her mum started moving around in the night.

24

Suzie had gone straight to bed after leaving Holly's flat for the second time, but as tired as she was her brain refused to switch off. Instead she found herself staring at the silhouettes of the bottles of perfume, hairbrushes and assorted tubes of make-up on the dressing table as she thought about everything that had happened tonight.

She wasn't sure why Josie had taken such an instant dislike to her, but it was clear from the things Holly had said after her mum collapsed that Josie wasn't in her right mind. All that stuff about them having to leave because someone was coming to kill them both was bizarre. And that – added to her controlling behaviour in not allowing Holly to talk to their neighbours, go out, or even answer the door – made Suzie wonder if Josie was bipolar, like her own mum. That level of paranoia wasn't normal, so *something* was definitely wrong with her, and Suzie pitied Holly for having to deal with it. The poor girl had enough problems at school, where even her so-called friends looked down their noses at her. Home was supposed to be a safe haven away from all those outside pressures, but that flat was no haven for Holly. It was a prison.

The doorbell rang, and Suzie frowned when she glanced at the clock and saw that it was almost 2 a.m. She had told Holly to ring if anything happened, but there were no missed calls on her phone. Hoping it wasn't something serious, because she wasn't sure how much more she could cope with tonight, she got up and pulled her dressing gown on before making her way down the stairs.

She'd been sure that it would be Holly, so it was a shock to see Rob on the step when she peeped through the spyhole. It had been almost three weeks since she'd seen or heard from him, and she wondered if he had been laying low on purpose, lulling her into a false sense of security before turning up to finish what he'd started the last time he was here. But why would he knock if that was his intention? Wouldn't he be worried that she would call the police as soon as she saw him?

Still mulling this over, she jumped when Rob turned his head and stared straight at the spyhole. He gave a tentative smile which told her that he knew she was there, and said, 'You not going to open it?'

'What do you want?' she called through the wood.

'To talk,' he said.

'About what?'

'If you open up, I'll tell you. I won't keep you long, I promise.'

He smiled again, and Suzie tutted softly before unlocking the door and peering out at him.

'What are you doing here, Rob? It's late.'

'Sorry.' Rob's smile morphed into the puppy-dog look that had always melted her heart. 'I just wanted to see you.'

Irritated when her stomach gave an involuntary flutter, Suzie folded her arms defensively. She'd forgotten how handsome he was, and her head was still swimming at the unexpected sight of him.

'I've missed you,' he went on wistfully.

'Well, I haven't missed you,' she lied, determined not to let him sweet-talk her. 'And you got me out of bed, so . . .'

'Don't be like that,' Rob sighed.

'Like what?' she shot back. 'You didn't seriously think you could turn up in the middle of the night and I'd welcome you back with open arms, did you?'

'A man can hope, can't he?'

'You nearly killed me, Rob.'

'I know, and I'll never forgive myself for that,' Rob said, contrite now. 'It probably won't make any difference, but I've been working on my temper while I've been staying at my mum's. I've done an anger-management course and it's made me see things differently.'

'Really?' Suzie rolled her eyes.

'On my life,' he insisted. 'That's why it's taken so long for me to come round. My mentor said I needed to sort my head out before I spoke to you.'

'And what makes you think *I* want to speak to *you*?'

'Well, you opened the door, and you haven't slammed it in my face yet, so that's a good start.'

'That can easily be rectified.' Suzie placed her hand on the wood.

'OK, I get it, you're not interested,' Rob said. 'I only came round to apologize, but you don't have to worry about me bothering you again, 'cos I'm moving to Scotland.'

'At this time of night?' Suzie asked, noticing the heavy-looking rucksack over his shoulder for the first time. 'I didn't think trains ran this late.'

'I'm going tomorrow,' Rob said. 'But I needed to get out of my mum's place, 'cos it's getting a bit . . .' He paused and narrowed his eyes, as if searching for the right word. Then, shrugging, he said, 'Let's just say I'm not her favourite person right now.'

'Why, what've you done?'

'Nothing. I've been good as gold.'

Suzie snorted her disbelief. 'If that was true, you'd be home in bed now, not standing on my doorstep at two in the morning in the freezing cold.'

'Scout's honour.' Rob held up two fingers. 'It's not me, it's her new bloke. The guy's a total bell-end; sits around all day in his vest and boxers, drinking cider and ordering her about like some kind of skivvy. I pulled him up about it earlier and he squared up to me, so I had to have a word.'

'You mean you went for him?'

'No, I didn't touch him – I *warned* him. The daft cow thinks she's in love, so she took his side and now I'm the bad guy. But I swear I didn't hit him. I'd have been out of there in a few hours anyway, so I thought I might as well save myself the aggro and leave early.'

He sounded sincere, but Suzie wasn't sure if she believed him. She knew from bitter experience how fast he could snap, and she couldn't see him backing down if someone fronted up to him – especially someone who was supposedly treating his mum like crap.

Watching her face as the thoughts went through her mind, Rob said, 'It wasn't easy to walk away, but I did it, and I'm proud of myself for that. I don't expect you to believe me, but I wanted you to know that I've changed – even if it's too late to make a difference for us. Anyway . . .' He hefted the strap of his rucksack higher on his shoulder. 'I'll get out of your hair and let you get back to bed. Take care, yeah?'

He tugged his collar up around his throat and walked up the path. It had started to rain while they were talking, and the wind was whipping rubbish around the road behind him as he stepped out onto the pavement and pulled the gate shut.

Shivering in the doorway, Suzie said, 'Where are you going to sleep if you can't go back to your mum's?'

'I'll find a bench to kip on,' Rob said, squinting at her through the raindrops clinging to his eyelashes.

'In this?' Suzie pulled a face. 'Haven't you got any friends who'll put you up?'

'Nah, I don't want to be bothering anyone at this time of night.'

'You weren't worried about bothering me,' she snorted.

'Yeah, sorry about that,' he apologized. 'I wanted to see you, but it was selfish. I shouldn't have come.'

Sighing, Suzie said, 'You're here now, and I'm awake, so you might as well come in and have a brew while you wait for this to die down.'

'It's all right, I'll get something at the station,' Rob said. 'Thanks for caring, though.'

'I didn't say I cared,' she replied, irritated to realize that she did. Then, before she knew she had even thought it, she heard herself saying, 'And I suppose you could sleep on the sofa tonight if you've really got nowhere else to go.'

'Cheers, but I don't think that's a very good idea,' said Rob. 'I don't want you thinking I'm taking advantage of you.'

'I offered,' Suzie reminded him, unsure why she was trying to persuade him to stay when she ought to be glad to see the back of him.

'I know, and I appreciate it, but I think I'd rather sleep on a bench.'

'Charming!' Suzie was offended and it showed.

'I didn't mean that the way it sounded.' Rob chuckled. 'Truth is, it'd be hard sleeping under the same roof, knowing I've blown it with you. Best I save you the aggro and *me* the regret, and walk away while it's good, eh?'

'Stop playing the bloody martyr and come in,' Suzie said brusquely. '*Now*, before I change my mind.'

Rob tilted his head to one side. 'Are you sure?'

'*Yes*,' she said, already wishing she'd kept her mouth shut.

She hadn't had sex since they'd broken up, and he had a way of getting under her skin like no man before him ever had, so she probably wouldn't sleep a wink knowing he was in the house.

Rob put his hand on the gate latch, and a panicked voice in Suzie's head hissed, *What are you doing, you idiot? Tell him you've changed your mind! Quick, before—*

'OK, if you really don't mind.' He pushed the gate open. 'But I'll be gone first thing.'

'Mmmm hmmm,' she murmured, closing her eyes when he brushed past her and the combined scents of his aftershave and personal musk enveloped her.

About to follow him inside, she hesitated when someone called, 'Excuse me . . .' and she looked out across the road and saw Holly's neighbour, Gee, climbing out of the back of a taxi.

'How's the girl?' he asked, pulling his hood up and jogging over to her. 'Sorry, I don't know her name.'

'It's Holly, and she's OK,' Suzie told him, conscious of Rob standing in the hallway behind her, his eyes burning into her neck. Her talking to another man – especially one as good-looking as Gee was close up, with his warm eyes, his beautifully shaped mouth and chiselled cheekbones – was exactly the kind of thing that made him see red in the past. But if he dared try any of that shit on her tonight, she would kick his arse out so fast his head would spin.

'That's good,' Gee said, stuffing his hands into his pockets and hunching his shoulders against the wind. 'She was in a bit of a state when I saw her earlier. Something about her mum getting attacked?'

'Yeah, but it wasn't as bad as we thought. And her mum's home now, so it's all good.'

'Cool. I'm glad it worked out for her.'

'Me, too,' Suzie said, thinking what a genuinely nice guy he was to take the time to check on Holly like this when he barely knew her.

'Night, then,' Gee said, smiling as he backed away. 'Tell Holly I said hi.'

'Will do. Night.'

Turning when he'd gone, Suzie looked at Rob and raised an eyebrow when she saw an all-too-familiar glint in his eyes. 'What?' she asked, staying put in the doorway in case she had to make a run for it.

The glint disappeared as fast as it had appeared, and Rob smiled, all innocence and light again. 'You mentioned a drink?'

Eyeing him warily for a second and deciding that she had probably imagined the glimpse of the old him, Suzie said, 'I'll put the kettle on.'

'I'd rather have beer, if you've got any?' Rob said, following her into the kitchen and looking around when she went over to the fridge. 'It's funny how much you can miss a place when you haven't been there for a while, isn't it?' he said, running his hand over the back of a chair. 'I used to love eating in here with you.'

Giving him a look as if to say, *You're the one who got yourself thrown out,* Suzie passed a can of lager to him – quickly snatching her hand back when his fingertips brushed her flesh and her stomach tingled.

'So what was that about just now?' Rob asked, peeling the tab off the can. 'Who's Holly?'

'The girl you nearly went for when you got back from the police station the other week,' Suzie said, flapping her hand at him to move so she could take a clean glass out of the cupboard.

'The one from the flats?' Rob took a seat at the table and eyed her over the rim of the can as he sucked the froth off the beer. 'Why's he asking *you* about her?'

'Her mum got attacked in the alley and rushed to hospital,' Suzie explained, pouring a glass of wine for herself. 'She was in a state, so I offered to stay with her. I would have brought her here, but the police wouldn't let me,' she added, frowning when she remembered that *he* was the reason for that.

'You don't even know her, so why would you put yourself out like that?' Rob asked.

'Actually, I've spent a lot of time with her since you left,' Suzie informed him. 'She's nice, and I was glad of the company,' she added, deciding not to mention what she and Holly had been doing. He'd belittled her when she had told him her plans to start the agency a few months back, asking why any girl with half an ounce of what it took to be a model would want *her* for an agent when she'd never even managed to land a major campaign for herself. Anyway, if she told him about the photo sessions, he'd ask to see the pictures, and she wasn't sure she wanted him to see the ones Holly had taken of her in her lingerie.

It might be ridiculous, since he had already seen every inch of her body in intimate detail. But that was when they'd been a couple. And now they weren't, it didn't feel right.

'Hey, it's your business who you hang out with,' Rob said, smiling slyly as he added: 'As long as it's a girl and not some hunky dude.'

Aware that he was talking about Gee, Suzie gave him a stern look. 'He was asking about Holly, not me. They're neighbours and he was concerned about her.'

'Sorry,' Rob apologized. 'It was meant to be a joke. Like I said, none of my business.'

Unused to him apologizing before a fight, because he usually reserved that for after, Suzie said, 'It's freezing in here. Why don't you go and turn the fire on while I get the spare quilt? And, here, take this.' She handed her wine glass to him.

Standing up when she headed upstairs, Rob went to the living room and turned on the lamp and the fire. Then, kicking off his trainers, he sprawled on the sofa and put his feet up on the coffee table.

'Make yourself comfortable, why don't you?' Suzie muttered when she came in, flashing a look at his feet as she placed the bedding she'd brought down for him onto the armchair.

'Sorry.' He quickly sat up and dropped his feet to the floor. 'Keep forgetting I don't live here any more.'

'No, I'm sorry,' Suzie sighed, flopping down at the other end of the sofa and reaching for her wine. 'It's been a long day; didn't mean to be narky.'

'You look wiped,' Rob said, lighting two cigarettes and passing one to her.

Thanking him, Suzie took a drag and then a swig of wine before resting her head back against the cushion. 'I haven't been sleeping very well,' she admitted. 'That's why I answered the door so fast when you rang.'

'Haven't you got any of those tablets the doctor gave you last time?'

'No, I ran out. But it's OK. It usually only lasts a few nights.'

'You work too hard.' Rob placed an ashtray on the cushion between them. 'How many bookings have you had this week?'

'A couple,' Suzie lied, embarrassed to admit that she hadn't had a single one since he'd left – and her agent hadn't replied to any of her calls, so she doubted she'd be getting any in the foreseeable future. She had to face facts: she'd hit the top of the mythical hill and was well and truly on the slide down the other side. That was why she desperately needed to get her agency up and running: before her savings ran out and she ended up homeless as well as jobless.

Rob settled back in his seat and looked around as the heat from the fire lifted the chill off the room.

'It's so peaceful in here,' he sighed, resting the beer can on his stomach. 'I'm grateful my mum let me stay at hers, but she's so stuck in the past it was like being trapped in a coffin at times.'

'Don't talk about her like that,' Suzie chided. 'She's nice.'

'She says the same about you,' Rob said – lying through his

teeth, because his mum had done nothing but slag Suzie off since finding out she'd had him arrested.

'Really?' Suzie was surprised. 'I always got the impression she didn't like me.'

'Are you kidding me?' Rob laughed. 'If she had her way, we'd be married with a house full of kids by now. But you'd have to be the barefoot-and-chained-to-the-cooker type wife, or she'd be round here every day training you how to show proper respect to your man.'

He grinned and Suzie gave an exaggerated shudder. 'God forbid,' she muttered, gulping her wine.

'Have you ever thought about it?' Rob asked, propping his elbow on the back of the sofa and resting his cheek on his hand. 'What our kids might look like if we'd stuck it out, I mean?'

'*No.*' Suzie pulled a face. 'It's never even crossed my mind.'

'I have,' Rob said. 'I reckon the first would be a girl who looked like you, and then we'd have a lad who looked like me.'

'And would they tear each other to shreds like us?' Suzie sniped. Immediately feeling guilty when Rob withdrew his arm and took a swig of lager without answering, she said, 'Sorry. That was uncalled for.'

'No, it wasn't,' he replied quietly. 'I was a cunt, and you've got every reason to be glad we never got that far.'

'We both had our faults. It wasn't all you.'

'Yeah, it was. You were the best thing that ever happened to me, and I blew it big time. Worst thing is, I don't even know why I treated you like that. You hear people talking about a red mist coming down when they get mad, but with me it was like a raging inferno, and I couldn't see or hear anything till I snapped out of it. I know it's too late for us, but I *am* sorry. I hope you can believe that.'

His gaze was intense, and Suzie nodded and looked down into her glass. He sounded sincere and her instincts were telling her that he genuinely meant it. But she was starting to feel a little tipsy and wasn't sure she could trust her own judgement.

'I think I'd best go.' Rob sat forward. 'I came to apologize, not rake up all that old shit and make you feel uncomfortable.'

'You're not making me uncomfortable,' Suzie insisted. 'It's all water under the bridge now. Forget about it.'

'Wish I could,' he said wistfully. 'Truth is, you're all I've thought about for weeks. That's why I'm moving to Scotland: 'cos my mentor told me I need to get away from you.'

'Cheeky sod!'

Amused by her indignation, Rob said, 'He meant for your sake, not mine. He reckons you deserve the chance to move on without worrying about seeing my ugly mug every time you turn round. Anyway, I bumped into an old mate who works on the rigs and he told me they were hiring, so I applied online. They rang yesterday and asked me to go over for an interview. If I get it, I'll be starting straightaway.'

'On the rigs? As in *oil* rigs? In the middle of the sea?'

'Well, that's where the oil is, so, yeah. My mate reckons the weather gets a bit hairy at times, so I'm not looking forward to that. But the money's top whack, and I won't have any expenses while I'm offshore, so I'm sure I'll get used to it.'

'Sounds good,' Suzie lied, unable to think of anything worse.

'Not so good for the old love life, though, eh?' Rob quipped. 'Subject of, how's yours these days?' Laughing when Suzie almost choked on her wine, he sat back and crossed his legs. 'I'm asking as a friend – honest. You deserve a bloke who treats you good, and I'll be made up for you if you've found someone.'

'I'm not looking for anyone,' Suzie said, plucking a tissue out of the box on the table and wiping wine off her chin.

'Same here. No one'll ever match up to you, so what's the point?'

'Don't say that. You've got a lot to offer the right woman.'

'Already had her and lost her,' said Rob. Then, grinning again, he said, 'But I thought we were supposed to be giving that subject a swerve, so what did you think of the match the other night? Cracking goal, wasn't it?'

'*Seriously?*' Suzie screwed up her face.

'Neutral ground, baby.' Rob winked at her. 'Unless you've turned into a secret City fan behind my back? 'Cos that'd be a step too far, that.'

'Idiot,' Suzie snorted.

Laughing, Rob drained the last of the lager out of his can and nodded at her glass. 'Don't suppose you've got any more of that knocking about?'

'The bottle's in the kitchen,' Suzie told him. 'Help yourself.'

'Not gonna join me?'

'No, I've had enough. And it's getting late, so I think I might try to get some sleep.'

'Awww, don't go yet,' Rob moaned. 'I'm wide awake here. Have one last drink with me. *Please?*'

He jutted out his bottom lip and gave her the puppy-dog eyes, and Suzie felt the butterflies stir in her stomach again.

'OK,' she heard herself agreeing as she rose unsteadily to her feet. 'One more, then I'm definitely going to bed.'

That one last drink had inevitably turned into two, and then three, until, before Suzie knew it, they had finished two bottles between them and it was almost 4 a.m.

The alcohol, added to the cosiness of the room – and Rob's presence in it – had slowly dismantled the wall Suzie had built around herself in his absence. She'd found herself relaxing as they reminisced about the past – focusing on the good bits while studiously avoiding the not-so-good. The sexual tension in the air had been so thick by the time the wine was finished, she fully expected Rob to make a move on her. But he was now stretching, and she guessed she'd read it wrong when his gaze drifted to the clock on the wall.

Think yourself lucky, the sensible part of her brain whispered. *You're pissed, and you'd regret it big time if you slept with him.*

Unsure if that was true, because her body was crying out to be touched, Suzie drained the dregs of her wine and placed her glass on the coffee table.

'You look as tired as I am, so I think it's time we called it a night,' she said, half hoping Rob would disagree.

'Yeah, you're probably right,' he said, covering a yawn with his hand. 'I need to make an early start.'

'Do you want me to set my alarm to wake you?' she offered, trying not to let her disappointment show as she pushed herself up to her feet.

'No, it's OK, I'll set my phone alarm,' he said, also standing.

Suzie froze, her nerve endings sparking with anticipation. Was this it? Was he going to take her in his arms and . . .

'Just need to use the loo before I hit the hay.' Rob nodded towards the door, the path to which she was blocking.

'Oh, sorry . . .' She moved aside, feeling foolish. 'I'll, um, leave you to it, then. Night.'

'Night,' Rob said. Then, touching her arm lightly before she moved, he said, 'Thanks for tonight, Suze. I really appreciate you letting me kip on the sofa, and it's been great catching up with you.'

Catching up . . . Suzie mentally repeated the words as she made her way up the stairs ahead of Rob. Was that all tonight had meant to him: a chance to apologize before he left the country, and – bonus – salvage a bit of friendship from the ruins of their relationship?

They said goodnight again when they reached the landing, then Suzie went to her room while Rob headed into the bathroom. Climbing into bed, she heard the flush of the toilet a couple of minutes later, followed by the pad of his feet on the carpet as he went down the stairs, and the click of the living room lamp being switched off.

Sighing when silence fell over the house, Suzie rolled onto her side and pulled the quilt up over her shoulders, trying to ignore the yearning in the pit of her stomach.

It's the wine, she told herself firmly. *If you were sober you wouldn't even be thinking these things. You split up with Rob for a reason, and you've been doing fine without him, so stop this pathetic pining and go to bloody sleep!*

Downstairs, lying on the sofa in his boxers, his arms behind his head, the spare quilt draped over his legs, Rob stared up at the ceiling and listened to the creak of the bedsprings as Suzie settled down for the night in the room they had once shared.

Given the way things had ended between them, he hadn't really expected Suzie to open the door, so he'd been pleasantly surprised when she not only invited him in but had also offered him a bed for the night. Her guard had been high to start with, but the booze had gradually lowered it, and by the time they'd finished the second bottle – most of which *she* had necked – Suzie had been giving him the full-on *fuck me* eyes.

He could have taken her up on it. He could have had her right here on this sofa and then carried her upstairs and fucked her all night. And he'd wanted to – *God*, he had wanted to! But he had resisted – for her sake as much as his.

He hadn't realized how much he'd missed her until he saw her tonight, and he wished he could turn back the clock and start over with her. But if he was to stand any chance of getting back with her, it had to be her decision – and a sober one, at that, so she couldn't accuse him of taking advantage of her further down the line.

A buzzing sound coming from under the coffee table interrupted Rob's thoughts, and he leaned over and dragged his rucksack out from under it. There were several messages and missed call notifications on his phone screen, none of which he'd heard because his attention had been focused on Suzie. It was too late to reply to them now, so he slipped the phone into the bag and lay back down, casting one last glance up at the ceiling before closing his eyes.

25

The door slammed into the wall below the girl's room, and her heart skittered in her chest when she heard footsteps rushing through the kitchen, the hallway and up the stairs. Remembering what her mummy had told her to do if anyone ever came into the house while they were sleeping, she quickly rolled off the bed and wriggled under it, unsure if it was the police looking for drugs, or the bad men coming to fight with her stepdad again.

She didn't understand why those horrible men always wanted to hurt him, because he was really nice to her and her mummy. Most of the time. When he had money and smokes and they weren't arguing and throwing things at each other. But, as scary as it was when the bad men came, at least she didn't get sent away to stay with strangers afterwards, like she did whenever the police turned up looking for drugs and made her go with the fat lady social worker.

Under the bed now, trying not to sneeze as dust went up her nose, she bit down hard on her hand to stop herself from crying out when the footsteps ran past her room and her mummy screamed . . .

PART TWO

26

Holly woke in a cold sweat. The room was pitch-dark and all she could hear was the jackhammer of her heartbeat pounding in her ears. As it began to settle she heard a dull thud coming through the wall behind her headboard, and she jumped up when the memories of the previous night rushed back to her. Stumbling out into the hallway, groping for the light switch as she went, she tiptoed into her mum's room and quietly approached the bed.

Josie's mum was still out of it, her closed eyes rolling inside their lids as if she was dreaming deeply – but not peacefully, judging by the way her legs were jerking. She was mumbling and Holly leaned closer to listen. Most of the words were inde-cipherable, but one leapt out loud and clear, and Holly pulled her head back and stared at her mum open-mouthed.

She'd said Charlie. Short for Charles – or *Charlotte*, the name of the missing girl.

It was too much of a coincidence for it not to mean anything, and Holly crept over to the wardrobe to take another look at the newspaper cutting. She eased the door open, scared that the hinges might squeak and wake her mum, then carefully lifted the tin box out and carried it back to her room.

She spread the cutting out on her bed and re-read it before typing the names of the murdered couple into a Google search. A stream of articles appeared on her phone screen and she quickly scrolled through them. Most pretty much mirrored the story in the cutting, with occasional updates on the progress – or lack of – in the search for Charlotte. The last article was dated three months after the original, and Holly's heart sank when she read that the search had been called off. A piece of clothing, believed to belong to the missing child, had been recovered from the bottom of the Rochdale canal a mile away from the murder scene, and Charlotte was now presumed to be dead. In light of that, a police spokesperson had said, they were now focusing their efforts on finding her remains, which were believed to have been swept away during the recent floods in the area.

There was no further mention of the case and Holly assumed they had never found Charlotte's body. It saddened her to think the police had given up on her so fast, and she hoped Charlotte hadn't suffered too much – especially if there was a possibility that they had been related, as Suzie had suggested.

She scrolled back to one of the earlier articles which had contained an image of the murdered woman and her child, and enlarged the picture. It was grainy, and the facial features weren't very clear, but she scrutinized it closely, looking for similarities between the woman and her mum. There didn't seem to be any. Her mum's hair was brown, but the woman's was fair; and her mum's eyes were dark blue, whereas the woman's looked a lot lighter – although it was impossible to tell their actual colour since the photo was black and white. The shape of their faces was also quite different: her mum's longer, her jaw more square than the woman's.

It seemed pretty clear to Holly that her mum and the woman weren't related, so she switched her gaze to the child instead, wondering if the link might be between her mum and the girl's father. Charlotte's hair looked almost white-blond and was tied up in pigtails secured by ribbons. She was really cute, with a heart-shaped face, a button nose and a wide, happy smile. The individual features revealed nothing significant, but there was something familiar in the image as a whole, something that stirred a hazy, distant memory and made Holly's stomach feel funny.

She told herself to stop being ridiculous. This was wishful thinking, that was all. She was so desperate to know there was more to her life than her mother and this boring, claustrophobic flat, she was trying to force Charlotte and her mother into the blank family photo of her imagination, and it was pathetic.

Deflated, she closed her phone and refolded the article before putting it back into the box and sliding it under her bed. She was too tired to replace it in the wardrobe tonight, so she would do it tomorrow, she decided as she reached out to switch off the light.

27

Suzie felt bright and energized when she woke the next morning, so much so that she was shocked to see she had only slept a couple of hours when she glanced at the clock. She had been going through the motions for the last few weeks, each boring day an exact replica of the one before: waking up, pottering about, eating, drinking – *so* much drinking – then sleeping again . . . But, today, she felt like she'd broken out of the rut, and she smiled when she heard Rob whistling along to the music that was drifting up from the kitchen.

Last night, she had seen the man she fell in love with for the first time in a long time: the lovely, caring, easy-going Rob who could charm the birds out of the trees and turn her legs to water with one sexy smile. She wasn't so stupid that she had forgotten the other side to him: the possessiveness, the irrational jealousy, the rages . . . But the anger-management course he'd taken during their separation certainly seemed to have had an impact, and she was glad they could be friends again.

And, who knew . . . ? she mused. If he stayed like this, there might even be a possibility of them reuniting further down the line.

She'd been disappointed by the way things ended last night, but, in hindsight, she was glad that Rob hadn't tried it on with her. She was also glad that he was heading off to Scotland today. Not because she wanted him gone, but because it would give them both time and space to think about what they wanted. If they decided they still loved each other, then they could make a go of it when he came home from the rigs. But if not, they would have been apart for so long by then that it wouldn't really hurt either of them.

The smell of bacon drifted up to her now, and she climbed out of bed and pulled her dressing gown on over her pyjamas when her stomach rumbled. After nipping into the bathroom to use the loo, brush her teeth and wash off last night's make-up, she headed downstairs.

'Morning, gorgeous.' Rob smiled when she entered the kitchen. 'Hope you don't mind me raiding the fridge, but I wanted to make breakfast for you before I left – to thank you for letting me stay.'

'There was no need, but thanks,' Suzie said, returning the smile as she took a seat at the table. 'Did you sleep all right?'

'Like a log,' Rob said, slotting bread into the toaster. 'Oh, and I had a shower when I got up. Hope that's OK?'

'Course it is,' Suzie said, amused that he was being so respectful when it was only a matter of weeks since he'd lived here and wouldn't have thought he needed permission.

'I'll tell you what, I'd forgotten how comfy that sofa is,' Rob went on as he pulled out the grill-tray and turned over the bacon strips that were sizzling on it. 'It wrecked my back, sleeping on my old bed. But it was better than a bench, I suppose, so I'm not complaining.'

The mention of benches reminded Suzie that he'd intended to sleep on one at the station last night, which also reminded her that he hadn't told her what time his train was due.

'Two o'clock,' he said when she asked. 'But I want to get there early, so I'll head off as soon as we've eaten.'

'It's only quarter past eight,' she said, glancing up at the clock. 'You've got hours yet.'

'Yeah, but I told you I'd be gone first thing, and I don't want you to think I'm taking the piss,' Rob said, walking over to the fridge to get butter for the toast.

'You don't need to rush off on my account,' Suzie said, admiring the way his muscles rippled beneath the material of his T-shirt as he moved, the gloss of his newly washed hair, the curve of his sexy backside encased in the tight jeans, his masculine thighs . . .

Blushing when Rob turned and looked at her, she dipped her gaze and pulled her phone out of her pocket when it beeped.

'Something wrong?' Rob asked, carrying their plates and the cups of tea he'd made to the table and taking the seat facing hers.

'Message from Holly,' she said.

'Oh . . . ?' He raised a questioning eyebrow. 'Everything all right?'

'She said her mum seems a bit better, but she doesn't want to leave her, so she's asking if I can ring her school and let them know what's happened.'

'Why can't she do it?'

'She's got enough on her plate. And I don't mind.'

'Hey, I wasn't trying to tell you what to do,' Rob said softly. 'I know what a big heart you've got, and I worry about you getting taken advantage of. But it's your business, not mine, so I'll butt out.'

Suzie nodded and typed out her reply to Holly. She was glad Rob wasn't going to keep on at her, because that was what he'd always done in the past whenever she'd tried to help someone out: either guilt-tripping her into seeing things his way or, if that didn't work, outright accusing her of putting whichever friend it was before him – and God help her if that friend happened to be male. Still, he'd backed off this time – another point in his favour – so, after sending the message, she rang Holly's school.

'Oh, hi,' she said, lowering her tone by an octave when a woman who sounded like the one she'd spoken to the previous day answered. 'This is Holly Evans's, um, aunt.' She felt Rob's curious gaze on her as the lie slipped out, and she avoided looking at him as she went on: 'She's still sick, and her mum got attacked last night, so I've had to come over to look after them both. I'll let you know when she's ready to come back . . . Thanks, I will do. Bye.'

'Aunt?' Rob raised an eyebrow when she'd finished the call.

'It's a long story.' Suzie sighed. 'Holly's technically a minor, so when her mum was taken into hospital last night the police were going to hand her over to social services. I told them I was her aunt so she could stay with me instead.'

'You lied to the police?' Rob frowned.

'What was I supposed to do?' Suzie asked. 'She didn't know if her mum was dead or alive, and she was terrified.'

'I hope you know what you're doing,' Rob said. 'The cops aren't stupid, and they don't mess about when it comes to kids.'

'Well, her mum's home now, and – hopefully – she's going to be OK, so it shouldn't be an issue,' Suzie murmured, reaching for her fork.

Rob didn't reply to that, but Suzie could tell from his expression that he thought she was crazy for getting involved. It was understandable, because he didn't know how close she and Holly had grown. As far as he knew, Holly and Josie were virtual strangers to her, so he was bound to be concerned that she had lied to the police on their behalf. And she couldn't deny that she was a bit worried about that herself. But it was done now, so there was no point dwelling on it.

A phone started ringing and Suzie automatically reached for hers, which was face-down on the table.

'I, er, think it's mine,' Rob said, smiling sheepishly as he pulled his phone out of his pocket. 'I changed it to your ringtone, 'cos it reminded me of you.'

Flattered, Suzie lifted a slice of toast to hide her smile as Rob got up and went out into the hall to take the call.

'Morning, mate,' his voice carried back to her. 'I'll be setting off in a bit. Train's at two, so I should be with you around . . .'

He tailed off, and Suzie tipped her head to one side when, after a pause, he said, 'You're kidding me? Nah, man, that's bang out of order; you've fucked me right up. Forget the ticket, I've given up my room, so what the fuck am I supposed to do now?'

Unable to hear any more when he went into the living room and closed the door, Suzie noticed her hands were trembling when she reached for her cup and took a sip of tea. Whatever the caller had said, Rob was clearly furious, and his harsh tone made her wonder if he'd really changed after all.

Rob came back to the kitchen minutes later and Suzie eyed him warily as he flopped down onto his chair. Relieved that the anger she'd heard in his voice wasn't reflected in his eyes when he looked at her, she said, 'Bad news?'

'You could say that,' he replied, a resigned edge to his voice. 'That was the bloke who was supposed to be interviewing me for the job today. Seems he's offered it to someone else, so that's me fucked.'

'Oh, no,' Suzie murmured.

'Ah, who cares?' Rob shrugged. 'To tell you the truth I didn't fancy being stuck at sea with a load of smelly bastards anyway, so it's probably for the best.'

'But you've left your mum's, so where are you going to stay?'

Rob exhaled loudly and ran his hands through his hair. Then, sighing, he said, 'Don't worry about it. I'll figure something out.'

'But—'

'It's fine,' he insisted, smiling again. 'I'm a big boy; I can deal with it. Now eat your breakfast before it gets cold. I didn't slave over a hot stove all morning to have you chuck it in the bin.'

Returning his smile, Suzie picked up her fork and pushed the scrambled egg around on her plate, but her appetite was as dead as his hopes of making a fresh start seemed to be. He might now be claiming that he hadn't fancied it, but he'd given up his home to make a go of it, and she hoped the disappointment wouldn't send him on a downer after he'd worked so hard to get back on his feet.

28

'Holly . . . ? *HOLLLYYYY . . . !*'

Holly heard her name being called and jumped up off the sofa, sending her revision notes flying as she ran to her mum's bedroom. Relieved to see that her mum was awake and looked more alert – even if she was still deathly pale beneath the livid bruises – she said, 'Are you OK? Do you want me to get you anything? Water? Tea? Toast?'

'Where's my tin?' Josie demanded, her voice as dry as her cracked lips looked.

'Tin?' Holly repeated innocently, mentally cursing herself for forgetting to replace it that morning.

'Don't play games with me,' Josie barked. 'I can see it's not there, so where is it?'

Swallowing nervously when she glanced at the wardrobe and saw that the door had swung open, Holly murmured, 'Oh, yeah, sorry. I, um . . .'

'You, *um*, what?' Josie glared at her. 'Thought you'd sneak it out behind my back after I told you to keep your big nose out of my private things?'

'I only wanted to see if those people who got murdered were related to us,' Holly admitted, her voice so quiet she could barely hear herself.

'You had no right!' Josie spat, her bloodshot eyes blazing. 'Did *she* put you up to it? Lady Muck?'

'Suzie? *No!*'

'I bet she did, nosy bitch,' Josie muttered as she struggled to sit up. 'Well, that's it, we're out of here!'

'You're not well,' Holly said. 'You need to rest.'

'How am I supposed to rest, knowing I could get shot at any fucking minute?' Josie bellowed. ''Cos that's what'll happen now you've opened your big mouth, you idiot! How many times have I told you we can't trust *anyone*?' she went on, as she shoved the dirty quilt off and dropped her bruised legs over the side of the bed.

She started muttering under her breath after that, asking what she'd ever done to deserve the shit Holly was putting her through, but Holly was still fixated on what she'd said at the start of it. If she thought she was going to get shot in her bed, then she *must* have known the murdered couple. But why was she scared the same was going to happen to them when so many years had passed since it had happened?

'Who were they?' she asked, the question slipping out before she had a chance to stop it.

Josie snapped her eyes up and Holly shivered when she saw

the anger in them. But she'd started now, and she needed to know, so she pressed on: 'Were they related to us? Was . . . was Charlotte my cousin?'

Josie's already white face turned another shade paler at the mention of Charlotte, and she dropped her chin onto her chest and inhaled deeply through her nose, before saying, 'Stop asking questions and bring me the tin. You're a child; you don't need to know the ins and outs of everything.'

Irritated that her mum was trying to shut her down, like she always did when she didn't want to answer questions, Holly said, 'I'm not a child. I'm nearly sixteen.'

'I don't care how old you are, it's still none of your business.'

'It is if it involves me.'

'Well, it doesn't, and I don't want to talk about it any more, so stop interrogating me and fetch my fucking *tin*!'

'No.' Holly defiantly raised her chin. 'Not until you tell me the truth.'

'You'd better stop this right now,' Josie warned. 'I'm your mother, and you'll do as I say or—'

'Or *what*?' Holly cut in, tears of frustration and defiance welling in her eyes. 'What you gonna do, Mum? Keep me locked up for the rest of my life, not letting me talk to anyone in case they find out what an absolute fucking nutjob *you* are?'

Furious that Holly had cursed at her, Josie forgot her pain and, rearing up off the bed, slapped her across the face before grabbing the front of her jumper.

'Don't you ever dare speak to me like that again, you ungrateful little bitch!' she yelled, her sour spittle dotting Holly's face. 'Everything I've done, I did for *you*, and I won't have you talking down to me like that *whore*—'

She abruptly stopped speaking and clamped a hand over her mouth, her eyes wide and fearful.

'What d'you mean?' Holly asked, instincts prickling. 'Who are you talking about?'

'I wasn't talking about anyone,' Josie said quietly, swivelling her eyes away. 'Forget it.'

'You're lying.'

'No, I'm not. It's the tablets; they've confused me. I need to think.'

Something clicked in Holly's mind, and she gasped, 'Oh, my God, you were talking about that woman in the paper, weren't you? You *did* know her.'

'No, I didn't,' Josie said sharply, straightening up and taking hold of Holly's shoulders. 'Now stop this nonsense and do as you're told, because we haven't got much time.'

Holly jerked free of her and stepped back, suspicion gleaming in her eyes.

'For God's *sake!*' Josie threw her hands up in exasperation. 'Stop reading things into everything I say!'

'Stop lying to me, then,' Holly cried. 'I'm not stupid, and if you don't tell me what's going on, I swear to God I'll leave and you'll never see me again.'

'No, you won't, because I won't let you,' Josie argued,

lumbering after her when she backed out into the hall. 'You might think you know everything, but you're just a – *Aggh!*'

Her foot caught in some of the clothes on the floor and she went flying, knocking the laundry basket over on her way down. The empty vodka bottles rolled out across the floor, and Holly's eyes widened in shock when she saw how many there were.

'Don't look at me like that, you self-righteous little cow,' Josie hissed, scrabbling to get back on her feet. 'This is *your* fault!'

Holly stared down at the woman who suddenly felt like a stranger, and her life flashed before her eyes. All the times she'd been woken in the middle of the night to be told they had to leave whichever dump they were living in . . . Being forced to change schools mid-term so she always felt like an outsider . . . Her mum getting drunk and talking about things in the past that Holly had no recollection of – then insisting, when she was sober, that she'd never said it, that Holly had imagined it . . .

Her entire life had been built on secrets and lies, and if she didn't get out she would end up as crazy as her mum.

'Get back here!' Josie yelled when Holly darted into her bedroom and grabbed her key and her phone before yanking the front door open. 'I'm warning you, Holly. *HOLLLYYYY . . . !*'

29

Suzie was sitting at the kitchen table scrolling through Facebook when the doorbell rang, and she frowned when whoever it was immediately started hammering on the small glass pane in the centre of the door. Rob had nipped out to the shops to get cigarettes, but she'd given him a key to get back in so it couldn't be him. It had to be Holly. And, judging by the panicked knocking, something bad must have happened.

Hoping it wasn't too serious, Suzie rushed out into the hall and opened the door. Holly stumbled inside, her face wet with tears.

'She's been lying to me!' she cried.

'Who? Your mum?' Suzie closed the door. 'About what?'

'I don't know,' Holly wailed, already beginning to doubt what she'd thought she had figured out. '*Everything!* That – that stuff we saw in the paper . . .'

'About the couple and the child?'

Holly nodded and wiped her nose on her sleeve.

'What about them?' Suzie asked, trying not to grimace as she led her into the kitchen.

WITNESS

Holly slumped down on a chair and dropped her head into her hands. She had been so sure she was onto something back there at the flat, but it now seemed ludicrous.

'Talk to me, hon.' Suzie squatted down beside the chair and handed her a piece of kitchen roll.

'I think Charlotte might have been my cousin, like you said,' Holly gulped, swiping her eyes before loudly blowing her nose.

'Did your mum tell you that?'

'No. I asked her, but she went off her head.'

'OK, let me make a brew,' Suzie said softly. 'Then when you've calmed down, you can go home and try to talk to her again. OK?'

Holly nodded her agreement, although she didn't see what good it would do to try and talk to her mum again, because all she would get was more lies.

Teas made, Suzie sat down and asked Holly to tell her exactly what had happened after she left her the previous night.

Starting from when she'd sneaked the biscuit tin out of her mum's room after she'd heard her say the name Charlie in her sleep, Holly explained how she'd googled the names of the murdered couple, curious to know if the missing child had ever been found, and how she'd scrutinized the image of the mother and daughter, hoping to see something that would tell her they were related to her and her mum.

'The mum didn't look anything like mine, but I thought there was something familiar about the girl, so I thought it might have been the dad who was related to us.'

231

'That's possible, I suppose,' Suzie said.

'I don't think so,' Holly said glumly. 'The way my mum reacted when I asked her about Charlotte made me think she probably *had* known the mum, but I don't think they were friends, 'cos she called her a whore. But why's she got to be so secretive about it? Why won't she just tell me?'

'The way they were killed was pretty horrendous, so it would have affected your mum if she had known them – even if they hadn't been particularly close,' Suzie reasoned. 'Death has a way of making us forget the bad things people have done, and she might have felt guilty if they'd had a falling out before it happened. That's probably why she doesn't want to talk about it. It might be too traumatic for her.'

Holly shook her head slowly. 'I don't think she's traumatized, I think she's scared the same thing's going to happen to her – to *us*. But it happened years ago, so why would she think that?'

'Did those articles tell you if they ever caught the person who shot them?' Suzie asked.

'I don't think so. Why?'

'If she did know them, and she knew the killer was still on the loose, I think it would be natural to be scared that they might come after her, as well,' Suzie said. 'Hell, if someone *I* knew got shot and they didn't catch the guy, I'd probably want to emigrate.'

Holly pursed her lips thoughtfully. If Suzie was right, it would certainly explain why her mum was so jumpy all the time. But surely she'd have got over it by now?

'It sounds to me like your mum's totally stressed out, which is understandable,' Suzie went on. 'And drinking while she's on painkillers will have confused her, so maybe you should lay off with the questions for a bit. Give her a chance to get better before you talk to her about this again.'

'What's the point?' Holly replied flatly. 'She won't tell me anything. She'll just say what she always says. "*You're a child*,"' she mimicked. '"*And you'll do as I say, or else!*"'

Before Suzie could reply to that, they heard the scrape of a key in the front door.

'That'll be Rob,' she said, standing up.

'*Rob?*' Holly's eyes widened in fear.

'He came round last night to tell me he's moving to Scotland,' Suzie explained. 'He'd had a row with his mum and had nowhere else to go, and it was raining, so I let him sleep on the sofa.'

'You're not getting back with him, are you?'

Suzie realized that it must seem odd to Holly that she had let him in after everything he'd done. And she couldn't blame her, because she'd feel the same if a friend told her they were entertaining a violent ex. But this was different – *Rob* was different – so she said, 'No, I'm not, but he's been working on his temper and I think he deserves a break.'

'I should go home.' Holly scraped her chair back.

'You don't have to do that,' Suzie said.

'You won't tell him about my mum, will you?' Holly asked. 'Please, Suzie. I don't want anyone to know. They'll say she's crazy, and I'll get taken away.'

'I won't say anything,' Suzie assured her. 'But you'd better put your face straight, or he'll know something's wrong and start asking questions.'

The front door opened and Holly jumped when a blast of cold air circled her ankles. Suzie seemed to think Rob had changed, but Holly hadn't forgotten the scary way he'd looked at her the first time they'd met, and she was terrified that he might have found out she had helped Suzie to set him up that night.

'Only me,' Rob called out as he came inside.

'I think I'd best go,' Holly whispered, rising to her feet.

'Don't be daft,' Suzie said, waving for her to sit back down. 'It'll be fine, I promise.'

'Sorry I've been so long,' Rob went on. 'I walked down to the offy to replace that wine we drank last night, and – *Hey!*' His voice suddenly changed, and Suzie frowned when he said, 'Who the fuck are you?'

'I need to see my daughter!' a woman answered, and Holly's stomach flipped when she realized it was her mum.

'Wait there, I'll talk to her,' Suzie said, going out into the hall and pulling the door to behind her.

'Where is she?' Holly heard her mum yell. 'I know she's here, and you've got no right to stop me from seeing her. She's *my* daughter, not yours.'

'No one's disputing that,' Suzie replied. 'But she's upset, so why don't we—'

'So she *is* here?' Josie cut her off angrily. '*HOLLY?* Get out here right now! You're coming home!'

The kitchen door opened and Holly, who had been leaning towards it, jerked away when Rob walked in. He hesitated when he saw her. Then, smiling, he closed the door, saying, 'I take it that's your mum?'

Holly nodded and eyed him warily as he put the bag he was carrying onto the counter.

'Don't worry, Suzie'll calm her down,' he went on as he took two bottles of wine and two packs of cigarettes out of the bag before crunching it into a ball and stuffing it in a drawer. 'She looks a bit rough, mind. Has she been in a car crash or something?'

'She got attacked,' Holly said. 'Last night in the alley.'

'Oh, yeah, I think Suze mentioned that,' Rob said, taking a cigarette out of the open pack on the table and lighting up. 'Must have been quite a shock for you.' He squinted at Holly through the smoke. 'How are you feeling?'

'OK,' she murmured, twisting her hands together nervously.

In the hall, Josie was shouting again, and Holly heard Suzie tell her to quieten down – that some of the neighbours were watching and one of them might call the police.

'I don't give a *fuck*!' Josie roared. 'I'll scream the whole fucking street down if you don't fetch my daughter out!'

Holly winced. Her mum swore at *her* when she got mad, but she'd never heard her swear at anyone else, and it was embarrassing.

'Right, here's what I'm going to do,' Suzie was saying. 'I'm going to ask Holly if she wants to talk to you, and if she does,

I'll let you in. But if you so much as raise a finger to her, you're out. Do you understand?'

Groaning when her mum screeched that this was none of Suzie's business and she had no right to kidnap her daughter, Holly pulled the door open and went out into the hall.

'Stop it,' she cried, feeling guilty for bringing trouble to Suzie's door when she saw her mum trying to force her way inside. 'It's not her fault.'

'Do you want me to let her in?' Suzie asked, glancing at Holly over her shoulder as she held Josie back. 'I'll send her away if you don't. Your choice.'

Holly nodded and then folded her arms defensively when Suzie let go of her mum.

'Baby, I'm sorry,' Josie cried, stumbling into the hallway and rushing to her. 'I didn't mean to scare you. Come home.'

'I don't want to,' Holly said, disentangling herself when her mum pulled her into an awkward embrace. 'You'll try to make me leave again.'

'We've got to,' Josie hissed, flicking a hooded glance at Suzie. 'It's not safe here any more.'

'Why?'

'You know why.'

'No, I don't, 'cos you won't tell me.'

'Right, I've had enough of this,' Josie said through gritted teeth. 'You're coming home, and that's the end of it!'

'Get off me,' Holly protested, wincing when her mum seized her wrist and started dragging her towards the door.

'OK, that's enough,' Suzie said, jumping between them.

Josie cried out in pain when Suzie grabbed her bruised arm, and tears flooded her eyes as she cradled it.

'I'm sorry if I hurt you,' Suzie apologized. 'But I won't let you force her to do something she doesn't want to do.'

'Need a hand?' Rob appeared in the kitchen doorway, a halo of smoke around his head, his broad shoulders blocking out most of the light coming through the window behind him.

'I've got this,' Suzie said curtly, waving him away.

Holly shivered when she saw anger flash into Rob's eyes. But he blinked it away as fast as it had appeared, and held up his hands before retreating into the kitchen.

'Let's go in here,' Suzie said, ushering Josie and Holly into the living room. 'I'll make coffee, and then we can—'

'I don't want your coffee.' Josie scowled. 'And this has got nothing to do with you, so stay out of it.'

'Don't talk to her like that.' Holly jumped to Suzie's defence. 'She's done nothing wrong.'

'She's interfering,' Josie argued. 'And she already knows too much.'

'She doesn't know anything – and neither do I,' said Holly.

'I don't know why you think you can talk to me like this all of a sudden,' Josie said under her breath, her stare fierce. 'But I'm your mother, and I won't—'

'I wish you *weren't* my mother!' Holly cried, cutting her off mid-sentence. 'You're embarrassing!'

Josie's head jerked as if she'd been physically slapped. Then, whispering so Suzie couldn't hear, she said, 'I didn't want to come over here, but you left me no choice when you ran out. These people are strangers, and this is none of their business, so do as you're told and come home. We'll talk about this in private.'

'You won't talk, though, will you? You'll just tell me it's none of my business, like you always do,' Holly replied bluntly. 'You treat me like a baby, and I'm sick of it.'

'If I treat you like a baby it's because you *act* like one,' Josie hissed.

'This is getting us nowhere,' Suzie said, stepping between them again and peering at Josie. 'You look terrible, so why don't you go home and get some rest before you end up back in hospital? Holly can stay here for a bit, give you both a chance to calm down.'

'I'm not leaving her with *you*,' Josie spat. 'You're trying to turn her against me.'

'I promise you I'm not,' Suzie insisted. 'But she's told you she doesn't want to go home with you, and I think she's old enough to make that decision for herself.'

'You only met her two fucking minutes ago, and now you think you know her better than *I* do?' Josie sneered. 'You've got no idea, you stupid cow!'

'She knows me way better than you, 'cos *she* listens,' Holly said, swiping tears off her cheeks. 'All *you* care about is your stupid job and trying to stop me from having a normal life! I *hate* you!'

'Get back here!' Josie yelled when Holly fled from the room and ran up the stairs.

'Leave her,' Suzie said. 'She's upset, and shouting clearly isn't helping.'

Josie gritted her teeth and balled her hands into fists, and Suzie braced herself for the punch she felt sure was coming. Instead, Josie's body suddenly deflated, as if all the fight had been sucked out of her, and she sank down on the sofa with an expression of resignation on her blood-drained face.

'Go on, then, get it over with. Call the police. I know you want to.'

'What?' Suzie frowned. 'Why would I do that? I'm trying to help.'

'If you wanted to help you wouldn't have told Holly she could stay. She'd have come home if you hadn't said that.'

'I doubt that,' said Suzie. 'And you must see this isn't going to get resolved by shouting over each other. Why don't you let Holly stay here tonight? She'll be safe with me, and you can talk to her again tomorrow when you've both had some rest.'

'What's the point?' Josie muttered dejectedly. 'She hates me.'

'No, she doesn't,' Suzie insisted, beginning to feel sorry for the woman. 'Look, I know you don't know me – and probably don't want to – but how about I make that coffee? I'm a good listener, and I promise I won't judge you.'

Josie bit her lip, as if considering it. Then, shaking her head, she stood up, saying, 'You wouldn't understand.'

'Try me,' Suzie urged. 'Holly knows you're keeping something from her, and she's not a child any more so you can't blame her for wanting answers. Whatever happened in the past, I'm sure she won't hold it against you. She's a smart girl.'

'Yeah, she is,' Josie agreed, her chin quivering as a tear slithered down her cheek. Brushing it away, she looked Suzie in the eye, as if seeing her for the first time, and said, 'I can see why she likes you, and I'm sorry for going off on you like that.'

'It's fine,' Suzie said. 'I understand.'

'No, you don't,' Josie countered. 'But . . . tell her I love her.'

'She loves you, too,' Suzie said, concerned by the way this was going.

'No, she loves who she *thought* I was,' Josie said sadly. 'Look after her for me.'

'Wait!' Suzie cried, following Josie out into the hall. 'You're her mum; you can't just leave her. It'll break her heart.'

Josie left without answering and pulled the door firmly shut behind her. Determined to make her see sense before this went any further, Suzie reached for her coat to go after her.

'Is it safe to come out now?' Rob asked.

'*What?*' Suzie snapped, twisting her head round. Immediately feeling guilty when she saw his hurt expression, she said, 'Sorry. I didn't mean to jump down your throat. I'm just worried about Holly and her mum.'

'Look, I know you probably don't want or need my advice,

but I'd leave them to it if I was you,' Rob said. 'You were fine when I went to the shop, but look how stressed you are now, and they were only here five minutes.'

'I can't leave them to it,' Suzie said. 'It's a mess, and Holly's—'

'Her mum's problem, not yours,' Rob said firmly. 'You did your best, but this isn't your fight, and you need to walk away before you get dragged down by it.'

Suzie closed her eyes and breathed in slowly to calm her jangling nerves. Rob was right: Holly wasn't her problem, and she didn't need the stress this was causing her. But she was the only friend Holly had right now, and she couldn't just abandon her in her hour of need.

'It's time you stopped worrying about other people and started thinking about yourself,' Rob said, walking to her and pulling her into his arms. 'This is their problem, not yours, so let them deal with it.'

Biting her lip when a shiver ran through her, Suzie rested her head against his chest and closed her eyes. Josie was upset, but she wouldn't really leave Holly. She just needed to rest and recover from her ordeal, then she would come back and sort everything out.

After a few blissful seconds, a floorboard creaked overhead and Suzie reluctantly broke free of the embrace, murmuring, 'Oh, God, I forgot Holly was still here.'

'Didn't she go with her mum?' Rob frowned.

'No. They needed time to sort their heads out, so I said Holly could stay the night,' Suzie told him. 'I know you probably don't agree,' she went on when she saw the disapproving look in his eye. 'But it's complicated.'

'It's quite simple from where I'm standing,' Rob argued. 'Her mum needs looking after, and you should have made her go with her.'

Suzie glanced up the stairs to make sure Holly wasn't listening before gesturing for him to come into the kitchen with her. She took a seat at the table after closing the door, and said, 'Look, I promised Holly I wouldn't tell you, so you've got to promise you won't say anything to her.'

'Course I won't,' Rob said, lighting a cigarette.

'Holly's been coming over a lot since you left,' Suzie started.

'I didn't leave,' Rob interrupted. 'You kicked me out.'

Suzie gave him a look that clearly said, *And you know exactly why I did that, so don't even go there.*

'Sorry,' he said, holding up his hand. 'Go on.'

Brushing her irritation aside, Suzie said, 'As you probably gathered from that row just now, they've got a weird relationship. Holly's cagey when it comes to talking about her mum, so I don't know the full extent of it, but Josie's really secretive, and she doesn't let Holly talk to the neighbours or answer the door when she's out.'

'Can't blame her for that,' Rob said, blowing smoke into the air. 'There's a lot of freaks round here.'

'I think it goes deeper than that,' Suzie said quietly, unsure if she fully understood it herself. 'I think her mum's paranoid. And I don't mean a *bit*, I mean the full-on conspiracy theory kind of paranoid that people end up getting sectioned for. She's a drinker, as well.'

'Nothing wrong with that,' Rob grinned, waving a hand at the bottles of wine he'd bought, which were standing on the counter behind her. 'I was going to make you a brew, but you look like you could use something stronger.'

'It's too early for that,' Suzie said, waving for him to stay put. 'Thing is, something happened last night, and—'

A tap came at the door before she could finish and Suzie whispered, '*Don't say anything*,' to Rob, before calling: 'Come in, hon.'

The door opened and Holly shuffled in. Her eyes were swollen and red, and she was wringing a sodden strip of toilet tissue between her hands.

'Feeling any better?' Suzie asked. Smiling when Holly nodded, she patted the chair next to hers, and said, 'Come and sit down.'

'Has my mum gone?' Holly asked, casting a wary glance at Rob, who was peering at her through narrowed eyes.

Suzie flashed a hooded look at Rob. Holly caught it and frowned.

'What's wrong?'

'Nothing,' Suzie said innocently. 'I think the attack must have hit her harder than she realized, that's all. I'm sure she'll be fine when she's had a rest.'

'You should probably go home,' Rob said, his gaze still fixed on Holly. 'Aren't you supposed to be looking after her?'

Holly's chin wobbled and she gazed up at Suzie. 'You said I could stay.'

'And you can,' Suzie assured her. 'But she's your mum, and Rob's right: you should be with her.'

'I don't want to go back' Holly gulped, as the tears began to fall. 'You don't know what she's like when she gets mad. She scares me.'

'Oh, hon, don't get upset again.' Suzie hugged her. 'I told her you could stay here tonight, so why don't you go and have a lie-down? I'll go over with you later and we'll talk to her together. OK.'

Frowning when Holly nodded her agreement, Rob said, 'I'm not being funny, love, but this isn't Suzie's problem, and you shouldn't be putting it on her like this.'

'*Rob!*' Suzie hissed. 'I told you I could handle this.'

'And I'm sure you think you can,' he replied smoothly. 'But I know you better than anyone, and I can see what it's doing to you. It's not right.'

'Holly's my friend and I offered to help,' said Suzie. 'You don't know what she's been through, so please don't interfere.'

Rob's eyes stayed locked on hers for several long moments. Then, shrugging, he said, 'My mistake,' and pushed himself up to his feet. 'I'll leave you to it.'

Suzie gave a curt nod and watched as he left the room. She had assumed he would go into the living room to give them privacy but, seconds later, she heard him come back out into the hall and pull his jacket on before leaving the house, slamming the door behind him.

'I'm sorry,' Holly sniffed.

'Don't apologize, it's not your fault.' Suzie sighed. 'He shouldn't have waded in like that. Anyway, come on . . .' She stood up and held out her hand. 'You look wiped. Why don't you go and have a lie-down, then we'll talk later.'

30

Rob was fuming as he strode away from Suzie's house with his rucksack over his shoulder. He'd come so close to getting his feet back under the table before that little cow turned up and ruined everything. Now he was out on his arse and *she* was still in there, lapping up the attention Suzie should have been lavishing on him. He felt like marching back in, picking the cuckoo up by the scruff of her scrawny neck and physically booting her out of his nest. And it *was* his nest. His and Suzie's. He'd paid his way, and he had more right to be there than Holly did.

All right, so maybe he hadn't contributed all that much *financially*. But he'd sure as hell supported Suzie in other ways, and he didn't appreciate the way she'd turned on him in favour of that whingeing little bitch. Well, fuck her if that was how she wanted to play this. Fuck the *pair* of them!

As he turned the corner at the end of the road, his heart leapt when he heard his phone ringing in his rucksack. It had to be Suzie. Him walking out must have given her a wake-up call and made her realize that he was more important to her than her so-called friend.

It wasn't Suzie, and he almost chucked his phone at the wall in frustration when he saw the name on the screen. Resisting the urge, because he couldn't afford to replace it, he decided to answer it instead.

'About time!' Angie Scott cried before he had the chance to speak. 'Where are you? Why haven't you answered any of my calls or messages? I was trying to get hold of you all night.'

'I was busy,' he replied coolly. ''S up?'

'Are you coming home?' she asked, the whine in her voice instantly setting his teeth on edge. 'We need to talk.'

'About what?' He slung the rucksack back over his shoulder and walked on.

'*Us*,' Angie said. 'You really hurt me yesterday, but I know you didn't mean to be so rough.'

She paused, obviously waiting for him to apologize. When he stayed silent, she sighed, and said, 'Look, I know you were pissed off with me for going through your phone, but those messages upset me, Rob. We live together, so how did you expect me to react?'

'We don't live together,' he sneered, stopping at the mouth of the alleyway behind Suzie's block. 'I was a guest.'

'*Was?*' Angie picked up on his use of the past tense. 'Does that mean you're not coming back?'

'Haven't decided yet,' Rob said, feigning boredom. 'Anyway, is that it? Only I've got stuff to do.'

'Are you with *her*?' she demanded. 'That *tart* who's been messaging you?'

Amused that she was directing her anger at the girl he'd met at the pub a few nights earlier, even though she'd read all the messages and must have known that it was him who'd done all the chasing, Rob said, 'It's none of your business who I'm with. And I'm going now, so—'

'Please don't leave me!' Angie blurted out. 'Please, Rob. I love you, and I'm sorry. Just give me a chance to—'

Smirking, Rob cut the call and chucked the phone back into his rucksack. Then, lighting a cigarette, he took a deep drag and slid his gaze along the row of windows until he located Suzie's.

Suzie's spare room was smaller than Holly's room at the flat, with barely enough space for the single bed, bedside cabinet, tiny vanity table and slim wardrobe it contained. But where Holly's room reeked of mildew, this one smelled fresh; the bedding looked clean, and the curtains fitted properly so there were no gaps at the top or bottom.

'Try to put everything out of your mind and get some sleep,' Suzie counselled. 'I'll fetch you some pyjamas so you can get comfortable.'

Holly smiled, but it slipped as soon as Suzie left the room, and she tested the mattress with her hand before wandering over to the window. Rob's words were still going round in her head, and she felt guilty for dragging Suzie into her mess. Suzie had insisted she didn't mind her being here – and she must have meant it, because she'd been angry when Rob tried to make her go home. But it was nothing compared to the anger she'd seen in Rob's eyes before he walked out, and she dreaded to think what he'd do if their paths ever crossed again.

Still, he was gone now, so she did her best to put him out of her mind and, opening the blinds, she leaned on the windowsill and gazed down at the garden. A square of grass with a narrow flagstone path leading from the back door to the gate, it was the same size as every other garden on the block. But, unlike the others, which all had flowers and plants lining their borders and were decorated with birdhouses and pretty garden furniture, Suzie's was plain, as if she couldn't care less about it.

A red and yellow plastic swing set and matching slide occupied the garden to the left, alongside a Disney Princess-style Wendy house, and Holly felt a twinge of envy in her stomach as she looked down at them. She and her mum had never lived in a house with a garden. The closest they'd come was a junk-cluttered backyard at one of the terraced houses her mum had rented a couple of years back, but it had been overrun with rats so she'd never dared open the back door, let alone attempt to play outside.

Mind drifting, she wondered how different her life might have been if her dad had stuck around. He must have been nice for her mum to have been so heartbroken over losing him, and she imagined he would have had a really good job – like Bex's dad, who spoiled her rotten because he could afford to. They'd have lived in a big posh house, like Bex's; with a monkey-puzzle tree and a two-car driveway at the front, and a massive garden at the back where her dad would play with her when he came home from work; building a tree house for her, while her mum – who would still smile like she had in the old photo – cooked dinner for them and washed and ironed his and Holly's clothes for work and school the next day. And . . .

The fantasy evaporated when she caught a movement in her peripheral vision, and she jerked back from the window when she saw Rob standing at the mouth of the alleyway. He was staring straight at her, sucking on a cigarette, and she shuddered when he gave her a sly smile before walking away.

Unnerved, she quickly closed the blinds – at the exact same time the door opened behind her.

'Here you go.' Suzie handed her a pair of black satin pyjamas. 'And you left these in the bathroom.' She passed over Holly's phone and key. 'Your screen lit up when I picked it up. I think someone's been trying to call you.'

Thanking her, Holly clutched the items to her stomach.

'Don't look so worried, hon,' Suzie said softly, stroking her cheek. 'We'll get this sorted, I promise.'

Holly nodded, but she couldn't see how this was ever going to get resolved. She'd felt justified for arguing with her mum earlier, but now all she wanted to do was go home, crawl into bed, and forget any of this had ever happened.

The doorbell rang and Holly jumped.

'Don't panic,' Suzie said. 'If it's your mum, chances are she'll have calmed down. But stay up here, just in case. I'll call you down if I think she's ready to be reasonable.'

Suzie backed out onto the landing and closed the door, then jogged down the stairs, fluffing her hair with her hands as she went. She thought it probably would be Josie, but she was hoping it might be Rob. She didn't blame him for walking out after she'd as good as told him to keep his nose out, but this was Holly's business, and the girl had asked her not to tell him anything, so her hands had been tied.

It was neither Josie nor Rob, it was PC Spencer, and Suzie's stomach clenched at the sight of him. Had Josie reported her for keeping Holly here against her wishes? Oh God, why hadn't she listened to Rob and sent the girl home? Kidnapping was a serious offence, and she didn't want to end up in prison because she'd been too stubborn to admit Rob was right.

'Hi.' Spencer gave her a nervous smile. 'Hope I'm not disturbing you, but we called in at the hospital to see Ms Evans and they told us she discharged herself last night. No one's answering at the flat, so I wondered if she might be here?'

Relief washed over Suzie, and she shook her head. 'No, they're not here,' she said, hoping that Holly didn't decide to come downstairs and prove her a liar. Spencer had allowed her to get away with pretending to be Holly's aunt last night, but if he got wind of what had happened since and decided to hand the case over to social services, she was screwed.

'OK, we'll try again later,' he said. 'If you see her in the meantime, can you ask her to give us a call?'

'Yeah, sure,' Suzie agreed. 'Any news on her attacker?'

'One of our units picked up a guy who was acting suspiciously in the park at the back of the estate in the early hours,' Spencer told her. 'The lads who disturbed Ms Evans's attacker didn't get a look at his face, and she can't remember anything about it, but his height and build matches the lads' general description, so we want her to take a look at some mugshots – see if it sparks any memories.'

'Oh, she'll be pleased about that.' Suzie smiled. 'And I'm sure she'll be happy to help if it means he gets what's coming to him. If I see her before you, I'll let her know.'

Spencer nodded his thanks and backed up a step, as if about to leave. Then, hesitating, he lowered his voice and said, 'Can I ask how well you know Ms Evans?'

Suzie remembered Rob's warning about the cops not messing about when it came to kids, and decided that it might be wiser to put a bit of distance between herself and Josie.

'We're not overly close,' she admitted. 'I've only lived here a few months so, obviously, I don't know her all that well. Why?'

'I hope I'm not speaking out of turn,' Spencer said. 'But does anything about her strike you as . . . *odd*?'

'In what way?' Suzie tilted her head.

Spencer pursed his lips as if considering whether to tell her what was on his mind. Then, seeming to decide against it, he shook his head and said, 'Nothing, forget it. Just ask her to give us a call.'

'Will do,' Suzie said.

As she watched Spencer walk over to his car, which was parked across the road, she frowned when she noticed his colleague, PC Bennett, staring at her from the passenger seat. Something about the man unnerved her. It was like he could see right through her lies, and she had no doubt that he'd have called social services in last night, if it had been up to him.

Quickly closing the door, she chewed her lip as she mulled over the implications of Spencer's question. The man had only spoken to Josie once, as far as she knew, and, given that Josie had just regained consciousness at the time, he surely couldn't have expected her behaviour to be 'normal'. But he'd obviously seen something *ab*normal about her for him to ask if Suzie thought there was something odd. She could easily have told him that she didn't think Josie was odd so much as barking mad, but he was likely to slap that protection order on Holly if he thought she was in danger, and Suzie could end up in a heap of trouble if they found out that the woman had left her here and Suzie had covered for her.

'*Damn it!*' she muttered, wishing again that she had listened to Rob.

'Was it her?' Holly whispered from the top of the stairs.

Looking up, Suzie sighed and shook her head. 'No, it was PC Spencer. They think they might have caught the bloke who attacked your mum and they want her to look at some photos, but she's not answering the door.'

Holly came down a few steps, and Suzie could see the fear in her eyes when she asked, 'You don't think she's done something stupid, do you?'

'No, of course not,' Suzie reassured her. 'She's probably sleeping and didn't hear them. But maybe I should take your key and go over, just in case. Not because I'm worried,' she added quickly when Holly's face fell. 'I just want to make sure she hasn't collapsed again. OK?'

Nodding, Holly went back to the spare room and fetched the key.

Carol was jogging down the communal stairs with a dog on a leash when Suzie entered the foyer of the flats, and Suzie leapt back in fright when it lunged at her.

'Tyson, *heel*!' Carol ordered, using both hands to hold it in check. Then, scowling at Suzie, she said, 'If it's the girl's mam you're after, she ain't in. I saw her go out five minutes before the coppers showed up.'

'Thanks,' Suzie murmured, eyeing the dog as she slid her back along the wall. 'Don't suppose you know where she was going?'

Snorting softly, Carol said, 'No, 'cos I ain't nosy like *some* I could mention, and I don't spend all my time spying on me neighbours and threatening to dob them in for stuff they haven't done.'

She stalked away at that, and Suzie blew out a breath of relief and straightened herself up before heading up the stairs.

Gee turned the corner just as she reached the last step.

'Oh, hi,' he said, smiling down at her, his straight white teeth gleaming. 'We'll have to stop meeting like this or people are gonna start talking.'

Struck again by how handsome he was – even more so than Zayn Malik, who she'd googled after Holly had remarked on their likeness – Suzie returned his smile and self-consciously touched her hair.

'I was, um, coming to see Holly's mum,' she said. 'Your neighbour – the big woman with the dog from the second floor – said she saw her going out. But I've got Holly's key, so I thought I'd check everything's OK while I'm here.'

'Were those coppers looking for her?' Gee asked. 'I wasn't being nosy, but I noticed them calling at yours after they left here.'

'Yeah, they think they might have caught the bloke who attacked her, and they want her to look at some mugshots.'

'That was fast.'

'Yeah, it was,' Suzie agreed. 'Josie doesn't really remember anything, but they're hoping something might click if she sees his face.'

'Finger crossed it's him, then, eh?' Gee said. 'Beasts like that need castrating. Sorry if that sounds extreme,' he added when Suzie's eyebrows rose. 'But I can't stomach blokes who think it's all right to abuse women.'

'Same here,' Suzie murmured, wondering what he would think of her if he knew she'd let Rob back into the house after he nearly killed her.

'Right, well, I'd best let you get on,' Gee said, stepping aside to let her ascend the last step. 'Have a good day.'

'You too,' Suzie said, watching as he trotted down the stairs and out through the door.

Remembering why she was there, she walked along the corridor to Holly and Josie's flat and rang the bell. No one answered, so she knocked a couple of times and then called through the letterbox to let Josie know it was her. Still nothing, so, after looking around to make sure none of the neighbours were watching, she slotted the key into the lock.

'Josie . . . ?' she called out as she entered the dingy hallway and closed the door.

She waited for an answer and listened out for the sound of movement, but all she could hear was a tap dripping. Wrinkling her nose at the stench of damp, which seemed to get stronger every time she came in here, she tapped on Josie's partially open bedroom door. Again, no answer came, but she could see the bed through the crack and Josie wasn't in it, so she pushed the door a little wider.

'Bloody hell . . .' she muttered under her breath as she gazed around at the mess, which, impossibly, seemed even worse in the cold light of day. 'You are one lazy bitch, Josie.'

Her foot clipped an empty vodka bottle when she stepped further into the room, and she shook her head in disgust when it clinked against the others and she saw how many there were – all one litre, with an unreadable Russian-looking name on their labels. It was no wonder Spencer had thought Josie odd; the silly cow's brain had probably been addled drinking that toxic shite.

After checking the floor on the other side of the bed to make sure Josie wasn't lying there, dead or dying, Suzie was about to head out and check the other rooms when something caught her eye and made her stomach clench. The dressing table drawer, which had been crammed full of underwear when she'd seen Holly bag a few things from it for her mum, was now empty. And the wardrobe, when she switched her gaze to that, seemed to contain fewer clothes than it had last night.

'Oh, Josie, what have you done?' she whispered. 'You stupid, *stupid* woman!'

31

Still angry about Holly fucking his plans up, Rob called in at a pub after leaving the estate. Further irritated when he reached the bar and remembered he'd spent the last of his money on the fags and wine he'd left at the house, he looked around for someone to tap and smiled when he spotted Kev Burton sitting alone at a table in the corner. The man was a friend of a friend and Rob had only met him a couple of times. But they had got on OK, so he made his way over.

'All right, Kev?' he greeted the man breezily. 'Long time no see. How's it going, mate?'

Kev glanced up from the phone in his hand and narrowed his eyes when he saw who it was. 'Fuck're you talking to me for, dickhead?' he grunted. 'Thought I was a cunt and you wouldn't piss on us if I was on fire?'

'You what?' Rob screwed up his face as if he didn't know what Kev was talking about. 'Who told you that?'

'Don't bother denyin' it,' Kev snarled. 'Decca told us, and I'd believe him over you any day of the week, so do one before I put me foot up your arse.'

As big as Rob was, Kev was bigger – and hard as fuck – so Rob held up his hands and quickly backed off. Just wait till he saw Decca, he fumed as he made his way back to the bar where he'd left his rucksack. *He* was the one who'd slagged Kev off after he'd found out the cunt had shagged his ex, and Rob had only agreed with him to make him feel better. So much for loyalty, the two-faced bastard!

Pissed off that no one else he knew was around to ease his thirst, Rob gave up and set off for his mum's place, hoping that she might have got bored of Reg and chucked him out by now. He didn't really want to stay there, because his old bed had fucked his back up the last time he'd slept on it, and his mum's nagging had almost driven him insane. But he was starting to feel hungry again, and she was a great cook, so he figured he could put up with her for a bit. Plus, it was her benefit day, so she'd be ripe for tapping up for a few quid.

Reg was still there, and Rob's blood instantly started bubbling when the man answered the door and tried to send him away with a flea in his ear, telling him he wasn't welcome and that his mum didn't want to see him.

'Where is she?' Rob demanded. 'If she don't wanna see me, she can tell me herself.'

'She's not in,' Reg said, blocking the doorway with his obese frame. 'And I won't have you *or* your lady friends coming round here trying to bully her. She's your mother and you ought to have more respect.'

'Bully her?' Rob repeated, pulling a face. 'Behave, you fat twat.'

'You don't scare me, boy,' Reg spluttered, his jowls wobbling.

'Listen here, *Churchill*,' Rob sneered, thinking the man looked like the nodding dog from the advert. 'She's *my* mam, and I ain't having a cunt like you, who thinks shagging her gives him some sort of rights, keep me out of the house I grew up in. So, if I was you, I'd back the fuck up or—'

A vehicle pulled up at the kerb behind Rob before he could finish, and he groaned when he glanced round and saw that it was a police car.

'What's going on?' one of the two officers who got out asked as they walked up the short path.

'Sorry for calling you out when I'm sure you have far more important things to be dealing with,' Reg said, his ingratiating tone bringing a snort of derision from Rob. 'This young man is my partner's son, and there was an unfortunate incident last time he was here and she was forced to eject him. She's out shopping at the moment and I'm under strict instructions not to let him in if he turns up – which, as you can see, he *has*. I anticipated trouble, so I rang you as soon as I saw him coming through the gate.'

'And has he given you any trouble?' one of the coppers asked, hooking his thumbs into the sides of his stab-vest and staring at Rob.

'He threatened me,' said Reg. 'He seems to think I don't have the authority to keep him out, even though I live here and his mother *told* me not to let him in.'

'You're a fucking liar,' Rob spat, glaring at him. 'I haven't threatened you, and my mum would *never* bar me from the house. What you even doing here, anyhow, you ponce?'

'OK, sir, let's calm down and get some details,' the second officer said.

Rob narrowed his eyes. He recognized the man as having been part of the crew who had arrested him for beating Suzie up, and he knew exactly how this would pan out if he didn't simmer down. These jokers would slap the cuffs on him and chuck him in a cell – revenge for him only getting a suspended sentence after landing a tasty punch on their mate's nose and booting the fuck out of the van when Suzie had falsely reported him for having a gun in the house.

'It's all cool, lads,' he said, holding up his hands and backing out onto the pavement. 'I only wanted to see my mum, but I'll ring her instead. Sorry for inconveniencing you,' he added, flashing an insincere smile as he pulled the gate shut.

Turning without waiting to hear what the coppers might have to say, he hitched his rucksack over his shoulder and walked briskly down the road, cursing Reg under his breath as he went.

Before he knew it, he was standing outside the block of flats where Angie lived, and he sighed as he gazed up at her living room window on the fourth floor. He hadn't wanted to come here, and the thought of Angie slobbering over him in a desperate attempt to win back his heart – which had never been, and never *would* be, hers – sickened him. Suzie was the only woman he wanted, but she hadn't tried to call him so she clearly hadn't come to her senses yet. She would in time, he was sure. But, until that happened, he needed somewhere to kip. And as annoying as Angie was, she kept a good stock of decent booze in, so he figured there were worse places to wait it out. Plus, he could do with some dosh, and the careless bitch always left money lying around.

32

The screaming had stopped and the girl squeezed her eyes shut when she heard the rhythmic thud of the headboard banging against the wall in the next room. She knew exactly what that sound signified, because she had been woken by it many times since her stepdad had moved in. And, once, when she had crept out to use the toilet in the middle of the night, she had seen him and her mum doing naughties.

After what felt like an eternity the noise stopped, and the girl shuddered when she heard a low, deep chuckle. Her bedroom door suddenly creaked open and she bit down on her hand to keep from crying out when light spilled in from the landing and she saw a huge pair of feet clad in green trainers with black writing on the side enter the room. They turned in a circle before approaching the bed, and she felt hot piss trickle out from between her thighs and soak into her nightie when the duvet that was hanging over the side was lifted and a pair of dark eyes peered straight at her . . .

* * *

'Holly . . . ? Holly, wake up, hon.'

Holly's eyes snapped open and she sucked in a sharp breath when she saw a hazy figure hovering over her.

'It's only me.' Suzie placed a gentle hand on her shoulder when she lurched up in the bed. 'You were crying out in your sleep. Bad dream?'

'Mmm hmm.' Holly shivered when she gazed around the dark room and saw the silhouettes of unfamiliar furniture. 'Wh-where am I?'

'My spare room,' Suzie reminded her.

'What time is it?' Holly sank a little lower beneath the quilt to try and get warm.

'Nearly twelve.'

'At night?' Holly was shocked. 'Have I been sleeping all day?'

'No, you had a couple of hours when I went over to see your mum, but then you came down and watched telly with me. I sent you back up at eight when you started falling asleep again. Don't you remember?'

Holly frowned and then nodded when it started to come back to her. 'Yeah, I think so. Have you seen my mum yet?'

'Not yet.' Suzie stroked her hair. 'But she knew you were staying the night, so I reckon she's probably gone to visit a friend and clear her head.'

That was what Suzie had told herself after going over to the flat that morning, but she didn't believe it – and Holly clearly didn't either, because she said, 'She hasn't got any friends; only people she works with.'

'Well, maybe she decided to go back to work to take her mind off things,' Suzie suggested, even though she already knew that hadn't happened, because she'd rung the agency while Holly was sleeping and they hadn't seen Josie. 'Wherever she is, I'm sure she'll be home tomorrow, so try not to worry about her.'

'I can't help it,' Holly whimpered. 'I feel like something awful's going to happen.'

'You're bound to feel like that after a nightmare,' Suzie reasoned. 'I've had them in the past, and it takes ages to shake the feeling off. Might help if you talk about it?'

'It – it was really scary,' Holly said, licking her dry lips. 'I was sleeping and some men broke in and woke me up. I hid under the bed and heard them going past my room, then I heard a load of shouting and my mum screamed. Only it wasn't my mum.' She paused and looked up at Suzie with wide eyes. 'Not *this* mum, anyway.'

'It'll be all that stuff about the woman in the paper playing on your mind,' Suzie said. 'I wouldn't read too much into it.'

'But I've had it before, when I was little,' Holly said, her chin quivering as tears pricked her eyes. 'My mum started giving me tablets to help me sleep, and I didn't have any bad dreams for ages. But I had it again the other night, and this was the same one. I remember it.'

'Dreams are made up of all the stuff we see, do and think about during the day,' Suzie said. 'It's the mind's way of putting things into perspective, that's all.'

Holly desperately wanted to believe that, but she knew she'd had the same dream before, and the realness of it terrified her. It was like she had actually been under that bed, and she could almost taste the dust in the back of her throat and feel the piss-wet material of her nightie between her legs.

'How about I make some hot chocolate to help you get back to sleep?' Suzie offered.

Suzie was wearing nightclothes and, guessing that she must be tired and eager to get back to her own bed, Holly murmured, 'Yes, please.'

When Suzie had left the room, Holly sat up and switched the bedside lamp on before reaching for her phone. Bex had sent a couple of messages, but she must have been asleep when they came in because she hadn't heard them. The first one was a long one, and Holly smiled when she read it.

Babes, I'm worried about you, please call me. I missed you at school today, and I wanted to let you know it's all cool with Leanne now. Gary Mottram's girlfriend got suspended for attacking her, then Gary finished it and asked Leanne to go steady with him, so she's not mad at us any more. She actually thanked me for telling you – can you believe that??!! She reckons he wouldn't have done it if you hadn't let the secret out, so now we're like her new besties. Cool, eh? Anyway, call me when you get this and let me know you're all right xxx

WITNESS

The second message was shorter, the tone more clipped.

OK, so I'm guessing you don't want to talk to me. That's fine, but I think it's a bit rude to ignore me when I was only trying to make sure you were all right. I know it was your mum who got attacked 'cos Ju's mum's friend who's married to the copper told her it was. I hope she gets better soon. Take care x

Feeling bad that she'd forgotten to ring Bex as she'd intended to after receiving her previous messages, Holly typed out a quick reply, even though she knew Bex would be sleeping and wouldn't see it until morning.

Sorry couldn't get back to you earlier, it's been a weird couple of days, she wrote. *That's great about Leanne, bet you're buzzing! My mum's home from hozzy, but we had a massive bust-up this morn and now she's*

She paused and bit her lip, then deleted the last part, and wrote:

My mum's OK, thanks for asking. See you when I come back to school xxx

PS miss you.

Pressing *Send* before she could change her mind, she checked to see if she'd had any missed calls from her mum. She hadn't, and that upset her. She probably wouldn't have answered if her mum *had* called, but the fact that she hadn't bothered spoke volumes, and Holly swallowed the lump that was forming in her throat. All that stuff her mum had said about loving her and wanting to protect her – from God only knew what or *who* – was crap. She didn't give a shit about anybody but herself, and Holly had never felt more alone in her entire life.

Downstairs, waiting for the kettle to boil, Suzie sat at the table and scrolled through the article she'd been reading on her laptop when she had heard Holly crying out in her sleep.

After coming home from Josie's flat that morning to find Holly asleep, she had intended to spend some time in the basement, working on the website. But she'd been too pre-occupied by everything that had happened with Josie and Rob to concentrate, and had found herself staring blankly at the screen, seeing not the photos that were actually on it, but a montage of images from earlier. The fury on Josie's bruised face when she'd tried to force her way in . . . The anguish in Holly's eyes as she had struggled to stand up for herself against the woman who had, until then, controlled every aspect of her life . . . The disappointment in Rob's eyes when she had taken Holly's side over his . . . Rob walking out . . . Josie's empty underwear drawer . . .

With all that going round in her head, along with the fear

that she wouldn't be able to hear the doorbell down there and might miss Josie or Rob, she had brought the laptop up to the kitchen, thinking that she might be able to work better there. Holly had come down shortly after, so she'd been forced to abandon her plans, and the day had been pretty much wasted watching films.

Holly had started to fall asleep after dinner, so Suzie had told her to go back to bed. She had then come into the kitchen and turned her laptop back on, and she'd been sitting here ever since, chain-smoking and working her way through the wine Rob had left behind as she searched for Josie on Facebook, Twitter and Instagram.

Frustratingly, none of the Josie Evanses that came up were the right one, and Suzie guessed that Holly's mum must be one of those rare people who didn't like social media. Suzie embraced it as a way of keeping up with the lives of friends from the past who she no longer saw in person, but she knew there were people out there who steered well clear of it, because Rob was one of them.

'*Why would anyone be stupid enough to put all their personal shit out there for the whole world to see?*' he'd asked her once when discussing what he classed as her 'obsession' with Facebook. '*Don't you think the government spies on us enough already without handing it to them on a fucking plate?*'

Suzie was a little more cautious than Rob gave her credit for and rarely posted anything, and she truly doubted the government would be interested in the photos of peoples' dinners, babies and funny pet videos that clogged up her timeline. But, just as in real life, it seemed that men were far less interested in that stuff than women, and only a handful of her male friends and colleagues had online accounts, whereas *all* of her female friends did. That was why she had expected to find Josie on at least one of those sites, but the woman was a virtual ghost.

Holly had said that her mum was secretive, but this level of secrecy seemed unusual to Suzie, and she wondered what the woman was hiding. Or was it, she mused, that *Josie* was trying to hide?

The more Suzie thought about it, the more likely that latter theory seemed. Holly had told her that she and her mum were always moving around and never settled anywhere long enough for her to make any lasting friendships. To Suzie's mind, that was the classic behaviour of someone who had escaped from a violent relationship and desperately didn't want the ex to find them. And that made her wonder if Holly's father had abandoned her mum before she was born, as she'd been told. Maybe he'd been violent and Josie had fled *after* Holly was born, and the nightmares Holly claimed to have suffered from a young age were actually memories of traumatic things that she'd seen or heard.

That seemed like a pretty logical explanation to Suzie, but she wasn't sure how it linked in with the murdered couple. And there clearly *was* a link, judging by Josie's over-the-top reaction to Holly reading the article and questioning her about it. But what was it?

A chill ran down Suzie's spine when something occurred to her. Holly claimed she had never met her father and knew nothing about him, but what if he was the one who had shot that couple, and Josie had known about it and run away with Holly because she was terrified he would try to silence her?

Most of the articles concentrated on the search for the missing child, but Suzie had delved a little deeper into the couple tonight and she had learned that the dead man, Devon Prince, had a criminal past involving drugs and gang-related activities. So maybe Holly's father had been a rival dealer, and he had killed the pair because Devon Prince had ripped him off or threatened to bring him down. In which case he'd probably had an accomplice, which would explain why Josie had told Holly that '*they*' were going to kill them.

If Suzie was right, she understood why Josie had been so desperate to get Holly away from her. The woman had kept herself and Holly under the radar for years, moving from place to place and never allowing anyone to get close enough to discover their secret. And now Holly had brought Suzie into their lives, exposing them – in Josie's mind – to danger.

Holly's instincts had told her there was a connection between herself and those people in the article, and she'd been right – but not in the way she'd thought. *They* weren't related to her, the killer was!

Sure that she had solved the mystery, Suzie wondered if she ought to tell Holly. She got why Josie wouldn't have wanted her to know her father was a murderer, because no child needed to grow up with that knowledge. But now Holly was growing up and starting to rebel against Josie's rules, it would surely be safer for them both if Holly knew *why* her mum had set those rules in place. Not only would it bring them closer, it might also put a stop to Holly's nightmares if she understood what was causing them.

But Josie was the only one who knew the absolute truth, and she was Holly's mother, so if anyone was going to tell Holly, it had to be her. And Suzie decided that she would tell her that when – *if* – she came back.

'You better had, Josie,' she muttered under her breath as she stirred milk into the hot chocolate she'd promised Holly. 'You better bloody had . . .'

33

The sound of glass clinking against glass jerked Josie out of the light doze she had fallen into, and she groaned when she lifted her stiff neck off the bag of clothes she'd been using as a pillow. Her head was pounding, and every muscle in her bruised, battered body was screaming for pain relief. The packet of paracetamol she'd picked up on her way out of the flat had barely touched the sides, and they had run out hours ago – although the bitter taste of the last three she'd dry-swallowed was still coating her tongue.

At the sound of a low male voice and a woman's soft laugh, she dragged herself up onto her knees and crawled out of the stinking bin cupboard she'd been hiding in all day. The dull light coming from the shabby porch of the semi-detached house attached to the cupboard seared her eyes, and she shielded them with her hand and saw two shadowy figures wrapped around each other in the hallway beyond. The door was open, so she hauled herself up to her feet and staggered towards it.

'Holy fucking *shit*!' Fiona Morgan squawked, almost jumping out of her skin when she turned to shut the door at the exact moment Josie stepped inside the porch.

'What's up?' the man she'd been kissing moments earlier asked, his hard-on bulging in his jeans as he pushed past Fiona and raised one of the two wine bottles he was holding into the air.

Cowering, scared that he was about to smash it over her head, Josie looked at Fiona, and croaked, 'I need help, Fi.'

'Josie?' Fiona frowned, only then recognizing her. 'Oh, my God, what's happened to you?'

'I – I got attacked,' Josie said. 'A man . . . a man jumped me in the alley.'

'Bloody hell, was that *you*?' Fiona asked, grabbing Josie's arm and pulling her inside the house before switching the hall light on and examining her face. 'Christ, he's made a right mess of you. Me and the girls were talking about it at work earlier, but we had no idea it was you. Should have clicked when you didn't come to work, but we thought you were skiving 'cos you were pissed off about the extra shifts Sharon dropped on you.'

Behind them, still holding the bottles, the man cleared his throat.

'Oh, sorry, Bri,' Fiona said. 'This is one of my workmates, Josie. She got attacked.'

'I heard,' he replied, giving her a pointed look before jerking his head towards the stairs to remind her they were supposed to be on their way up to the bedroom.

'Sorry, love, you go on up,' Fiona said. 'I'll be with you when I've finished here.'

'Don't be long.' He gave her a lusty smile. Then, nodding at Josie, he said, 'Hope you get better soon,' before heading upstairs.

'Who's that?' Josie asked, hugging herself to stop the violent shivering. 'I didn't know you had a fella. You've never mentioned him.'

'I don't tell my business to people I work with,' Fiona said coolly as she slipped her jacket off and looped it over the newel post. 'Anyway, what you doing here?' she asked, folding her arms. 'Shouldn't you be in hospital, or home in bed, or something?'

'I – I needed to see you,' Josie said.

'Why?' Fiona frowned again. Then, drawing her head back, she gave Josie a knowing look, and said, 'Please don't tell me you've come all this way to get booze? Fucking hell, girl. That should be the last thing on your mind at a time like this.'

'It's for the pain,' Josie replied, her eyes brimming with tears. 'And – and I could do with some of those tramadol I got off you when I twisted my ankle that time, if you've got any?'

Fiona pursed her lips and stared down at her. Squirming under the scrutiny, sure that Fiona thought she was an alcoholic and was about to tell her to sling her hook, Josie put her hands out in a prayer-like gesture, and said, 'Please, Fi, I'm begging you. I only need enough to get me through the night till I can get to the doctor. *Please?*'

At the sound of banging on the floorboards above, Fiona tutted, and said, 'OK, I'll give you one bottle and enough caps for *two* nights – in case you can't get an appointment that fast. But my name had better not leave your mouth if you get sick, else you're dead.'

'I'd never grass you up,' Josie insisted. 'We're mates.'

'Being workmates don't make us buddies,' Fiona countered. 'And I'm telling you this for your own good, 'cos it won't be *me* who comes after you if I get raided, it'll be my supplier – and he doesn't fuck about. Do you understand what I'm saying?'

Desperate to get her hands on the painkillers and vodka, Josie nodded her agreement and licked her lips when Fiona walked into the kitchen, pushing the door shut behind her. She'd waited all day for this, and Fiona's threats weren't about to put her off. Where she would go once she got what she needed, she didn't yet know. Her knee-jerk reaction after the argument with Holly had been to run away and never look back, but her conscience had stopped her and she had found herself here instead. She was exhausted and wanted to go home, but she couldn't risk it until she knew what Holly had told Suzie. But she had no way of finding out while Holly was refusing to leave the woman's house and Suzie had taken it upon herself to act as some sort of mediator. She'd already tried to force her to leave, and that hadn't worked. And she couldn't ask the police to intervene and risk raising *their* suspicions, so it looked like she was going to have to leave Holly where she was for now.

'Here you go . . .' Fiona came back from the kitchen with a bottle of vodka and a half-strip of tramadol capsules. Giving Josie a stern look as she handed them over, she said, 'Don't forget what I said. If anything happens—'

'It won't,' Josie assured her, clutching the bottle tightly after sliding the silver strip into her pocket.

'Er, I think you're forgetting something,' Fiona said sharply when she turned and made for the door. 'That'll be twenty-five quid.'

'Twenty-five?' Josie gulped, turning back to her.

'That's what I said.' Fiona held out her hand.

'Can – can I give it to you tomorrow?' Josie asked. 'I left my purse at home, and it'll take an hour to walk there and back.'

At the sound of yet more banging from upstairs, Fiona yelled, 'I'll be up in a sec, Bri.' Then, muttering, 'Fuck's sake,' she turned back to Josie, and said, 'OK, you can pay me tomorrow, but I want it first thing. If I'm not up when you get here, post it through the letterbox. And don't let me down, or it'll be the last thing you ever do.'

'I won't,' Josie said, scrabbling to open the door. 'First thing, I promise.'

Outside, Josie stood in the shadows at the side of the house and listened as Fiona locked and bolted the door. When the porch light went out, followed a few seconds later by the hall light, she peered at the houses on the opposite side of the road to check that none of Fiona's neighbours were watching, then crawled back into the bin cupboard, pulling the door shut behind her.

As infuriating as it was that she couldn't get to Holly tonight, there was nothing she could do about it, so she would see to her own needs and then go back round there tomorrow, when she felt stronger. And this time, Holly would leave with her – whether she liked it or not!

34

Suzie had taken the hot chocolate up to Holly and was on her way back down to the kitchen when someone tapped lightly on the front door. Guessing, from the timidity of it, that it was Josie, that the woman, embarrassed about her behaviour that morning, had come back with her tail between her legs to apologize, she was surprised to find Rob on the step.

'Hope it's not too late to call round?' He gave her a sheepish smile. 'I thought you might be in bed when I didn't see any lights on, but then I saw your shadow through the glass and thought I'd take a chance.'

'I've been sitting in the kitchen, that's why the other lights are off,' Suzie told him, shivering in the cold night air.

'I thought we should talk,' he said. 'But I'll come back tomorrow, if it's not convenient?'

Noticing that he, too, was shivering, and that his teeth were tightly clenched, Suzie said, 'No, don't be daft. You're here now, so you might as well come in.'

'Cheers.' Rob stepped inside. 'I know you've got a lot on your hands right now, but . . .' He paused and gave a tiny shrug. 'Truth is, I felt bad about walking out in a strop earlier. I was jealous, and I acted like an idiot.'

'Jealous?' Suzie was bemused. 'Of Holly?'

'Yeah, I know, I'm a dick.' He grimaced. 'But we'd been getting on so well, and . . . I dunno. I just thought we were getting somewhere – you know?'

Suzie wasn't listening. She had spotted three angry red marks on his neck and, concerned that he'd been fighting, she said, 'What's happened?'

'What?' Rob looked confused.

'Your neck,' she said, turning him to face the mirror on the wall. 'They look like scratches.'

'Oh, right . . .' he murmured when he saw them. 'That was me. Don't laugh, but I was sitting in a cafe earlier, thinking about you, and the bloke at the next table kept itching like he had fleas or something. It set *me* off, and I guess I must have got carried away.'

'You're not kidding you got carried away,' Suzie said, shaking her head. 'They're pretty nasty. I'm surprised you didn't notice.'

'Ah, well, it'll teach me not to let my nails grow so long in future.' Rob grinned. 'Anyhow, I only came to say sorry, so I'll let you get back to whatev—'

'Rob, shut up.' Suzie sighed.

'Sorry,' he apologized. 'I wasn't trying to—'

'I said shut *up*,' Suzie repeated, stepping closer to him. 'And bloody kiss me.'

'What?' He tipped his head to one side and gave her a questioning look.

'You heard me,' she purred, sliding her arms around him and gazing up at him. 'Unless you don't want to? Because I—'

Rob pressed his lips down on hers before she could finish and, holding her against him with one strong arm, shrugged the rucksack off his shoulder and wriggled out of his jacket. Dropping both to the floor, he lifted Suzie off her feet, his mouth still covering hers, and walked her backwards towards the stairs.

'Not up there,' Suzie whispered, pulling her head back. 'Holly will hear us.'

Rob glanced up the stairs, as if expecting to see the girl standing there. Then, kissing Suzie again, he turned and walked her into the living room, kicking the door shut behind him.

Falling onto the sofa, Rob tugged Suzie's pyjama bottoms down while she unzipped his fly.

'God, I've missed you,' he groaned, climbing on top of her.

'I've missed you, too,' she gasped, arching her back when he bit her neck and slid his hand under her top to caress her breasts.

'ROB!' a woman bellowed, followed by a flurry of raps on the window pane. 'GET OUT HERE, YOU CHEATING BASTARD!'

Suzie's eyes popped open, and a cry escaped her lips when she saw that the blinds weren't fully closed and a woman was staring at them while hammering on the glass with her fist.

'What the *fuck* . . . ?' she spluttered, grabbing a cushion to cover herself when Rob leapt up and grabbed his jeans off the floor. 'Who is she?'

'Stay there,' he growled, shoving his legs into the jeans and heading for the door. 'I'll deal with this.'

Suzie wanted to know who the woman was and why she was here, so she pulled her pyjama bottoms on and followed him out into the hall.

'I *knew* it!' Angie Scott roared, glaring at Rob when he opened the door. 'I fuckin' *knew* you were still screwing her, you lying piece of shit!'

'I don't know what you're talking about, you crazy bitch,' Rob hissed, physically pushing her away from the door.

'*Fuck you!*' Angie yelled, her alcohol-laced spittle covering his face when she slammed her hands against his chest and pushed him back. 'This is why you started that fight with me earlier, isn't it? So you could nick my money and sneak round here to shag your bit on the side!'

'What's going on?' Suzie asked, looking from the woman to Rob.

'Nothing,' Rob said through gritted teeth.

'He's my *boyfriend*,' Angie cried at the same time.

'Rob?' Suzie gaped at him.

'Tell her,' Angie ordered. 'Tell her you're with me!'

'You're pissed,' Rob said, gazing down at her in disgust. 'I suggest you go home and sleep it off.'

'Is that a bruise?' Suzie frowned and pushed past Rob when

she spotted a flash of purple beneath the mascara streaking the woman's cheeks.

'Yeah, it is,' Angie spat, glaring at Suzie now. 'He punched me – because of *you* and those filthy messages you've been sending him! Why can't you leave him alone, you home-wrecking whore? You must have known he had a girlfriend?'

'What messages?' Suzie was genuinely confused.

'Don't pretend you don't know,' Angie yelled. 'I've *read* them, you stupid bitch!'

Embarrassed when she noticed Carol from across the road watching with a smug grin on her face, Suzie said, 'I haven't sent him any bloody messages, and I don't appreciate you coming round here making a scene.'

'And *I* don't appreciate you fucking my *BOYFRIEND!*' Angie screeched in her face.

'When are you going to get it into your thick head, I am *not* your boyfriend?' Rob yelled, shoving her away from Suzie when she swung her arm back to hit her. 'Now quit stalking me and get a life, you fucking nutjob!'

'You weren't calling me that when you were screwing me earlier, were you?' Angie cried, whacking his arm. 'I should've known you were only using me to get at my money, you lying bastard!'

'Rob, what's going on?' Suzie asked, suspicion in her eyes. 'I want the truth.'

Turning to her, his own eyes angry, Rob took a deep breath and held up his hands. 'OK, I'm not gonna lie,' he said quietly.

'I did have a one-night stand with her. But it only happened once, and it was after we split up. I was pissed out of my head, or I would never have touched her, I swear. I felt sick straight after and told her it was a mistake, but she won't let it go. She's been following me, and harassing my mum.'

'You *liar*!' Angie squawked.

'Oh, really?' Rob pounced. 'I'm lying, am I? How come she messaged me about it last night, then?'

He scrolled through his messages until he found the one he'd received from his mum the previous night – the one he had initially missed, because it had come in the middle of the flurry of messages from Angie.

'"*Robert*,"' he read out loud, '"*whoever that woman is who turned up here shouting the odds and demanding to see you, I'd appreciate it if you could tell her not to bother us again. Reg has a bad heart, and he doesn't need the stress. Mum.*"'

He turned the phone round when he'd finished, so Suzie could see that he hadn't made it up.

'OK, so maybe I did go round there,' Angie spluttered, her face scarlet. 'But only because I thought you'd gone there after we had that fight about your phone last night. I admit I shouldn't have done it, but I'd had a drink and I wanted to see you.'

'Save it for your therapist,' Rob said coldly. 'I've tried to be polite, but you've gone too far this time, and if you don't leave me the fuck alone I'm going to apply for a restraining order.'

'Rob, please don't leave me, I'm begging you,' Angie cried, grabbing his arm and trying to drag him back out when he made to go inside the house. 'I'm sorry for following you here, but I had to see you. Please . . . I'll do anything—'

'Go *home*,' Rob hissed, shaking her off. 'You're making a show of yourself.'

'Do you think we should call someone to come and get her?' Suzie asked when Angie threw herself onto the floor at his feet.

'No, leave her,' Rob said, pulling Suzie inside and slamming the door in Angie's wailing face. 'Seriously, babe, she's been driving me mental. I just hope she'll see sense now she knows I'm with you and quit stalking me.'

Suzie followed when he walked into the living room and watched as he drew the blinds before closing the curtains.

'Were you telling the truth out there?' she asked. 'Was it really only once? You haven't been living with her?'

'Babe, I swear on my life,' Rob said, making the sign of the cross on his chest. 'You saw her face when I caught her out about going to my mum's. She's a fantasist.'

'I know she lied about that, but—'

'Listen,' Rob said, peering down into her eyes. 'I didn't have to tell you I'd been with her, 'cos we weren't even together when it happened, but I wanted to be honest with you. If I'd known she was going to go this far, I'd have had her arrested at the start of it, but I honestly thought she'd quit if I ignored her for long enough.'

'Why, what's she done?' Suzie asked, sitting down.

'Texts, phone calls, following me,' Rob said, sighing as he sat beside her. 'I tried to let her down gently, but she must have taken that as a sign that I liked her and was playing hard to get, or something. I've been avoiding her, but today . . .'

'What happened today?' Suzie prompted when he paused.

'OK, I said I'd be honest, so I will,' Rob said, reaching for her hand and stroking her fingers with his thumb. 'I've been keeping my phone on silent since she started harassing me, 'cos she goes on one when she's drinking – as you just saw. Anyhow, I checked it after I left here this morning and she'd sent another load of messages. As I was deleting them, I saw the one from my mum, and I thought I'd best go round to check she was OK and apologize for getting her caught up in it. She wasn't in, so I walked into town and mooched about for a bit before going to the pub. I was in there a while, but Angie must have followed me, 'cos she was waiting when I came out. She was pissed and she started yelling at me, and people were watching. I felt like a right cunt, so I tried to walk away, but she went mental and attacked me.'

'Is that where those scratches on your neck came from?'

'Yeah.' Rob nodded and dipped his gaze. 'I didn't want to tell you 'cos I was ashamed, and I didn't think you'd believe me.'

'Answer one thing – *honestly*,' Suzie said, peering into his eyes. 'Did you punch her?'

'No, I didn't,' Rob insisted. 'I don't blame you for thinking it after what happened with *us*, but I meant it when I said I've changed. Losing you broke me and I hated myself for what I'd done. That's why I took that anger management course. I didn't think it was going to work, but it did, and now, if someone pisses me off, I walk away instead of flying off the handle – like I did earlier when I went into that strop over Holly. Knowing Angie – and I wish to God I *didn't* – I wouldn't put it past her to have done it herself after she saw me coming in here. She probably thought it'd put you off me. But I hope it hasn't worked, 'cos I couldn't bear to lose you again so soon after getting you back.'

Suzie stared down at their hands entwined on her lap and thought everything over. The woman had sounded really convincing and she would probably have believed her if Rob hadn't proved her to be lying about going round to his mum's place. Her instincts were telling her that Rob *had* slept with the woman more than the one time he'd admitted to, but if it had happened while they were apart it was none of her business.

'No, it didn't work,' she said after a while, aware that Rob was holding his breath beside her. 'But if anything like this ever happens again, you need to tell me so I'm prepared, because that was horrible.'

'Believe me, if I'd known she was going to turn up like that I *would* have told you,' Rob said. 'And I swear I'll tell you if anything else happens. But hopefully she'll give up now she's had her card marked.'

'She better had, or it'll be *me* who punches her next time,' Suzie said, only half joking.

'My little warrior queen,' Rob chuckled, leaning towards her and planting a soft kiss on her lips. 'I don't know about you, but I could really do with a drink. Don't suppose there's any of that wine left?'

'One and a bit bottles,' Suzie said, getting up when he did.

'You mean you necked the rest by yourself?' Rob gave her a mock-disapproving look.

'It's your fault for walking out and leaving it with me,' Suzie said, walking over to the window and peeking out through the blinds. 'She's gone.'

'Good,' Rob grunted, following as she made her way to the kitchen. 'And let's hope she *stays* gone.'

The laptop was still open on the table, and Suzie hurriedly closed the lid on it before taking another glass out of the cupboard and filling it for Rob before topping up her own.

'Hiding something?' Rob teased, nodding at the laptop as he took a seat. 'Don't tell me . . . you've been ogling naked men on the Net again, haven't you?'

'Behave!' Suzie tutted.

'Well, you closed that pretty fast, so there must be *something* on it that you didn't want me to see,' Rob persisted. 'I thought we were going to be honest with each other from now on – or does that only apply to me?'

He was smiling when Suzie looked at him, and there was no anger in his eyes, only curiosity. She knew Holly didn't want her to tell him anything, but it would be good to get his opinion on her theory about Josie's connection to the murdered couple.

'OK, I'll tell you,' she said. 'But you've got to promise you won't mention it to Holly.'

'My lips are sealed,' Rob said, pulling his chair up beside hers when she sat down and opened the laptop.

Suzie showed him the article she'd been looking at before he arrived. After quickly reading it, he said, 'I thought you said it was about Holly, but there's no mention of her.'

'It's not about her, but we think it involves her,' Suzie said, taking a swig of wine before lighting a cigarette.

Rob did the same, and then settled back in his seat as Suzie outlined the events of the previous night, starting when she and Holly had been in Josie's room packing a bag to take to the hospital and had come across the biscuit tin.

'Holly didn't recognize their names and was curious to know why her mum had kept the newspaper clipping,' she went on. 'Like I told you earlier, Josie's really secretive and won't tell her anything about her family, so I think she was hoping they might turn out to be relatives. Anyway, I was about to google their names when Josie turned up. She'd discharged herself from hospital and looked terrible, and I was trying to get her to sit down before she fell down, but she as good as kicked me out. I came home, but I hadn't been here long when Holly ran over in tears, saying her mum had collapsed. She said Josie had gone mad at her for letting me into the flat, and that she'd ordered Holly to start packing 'cos they had to leave before someone came and killed them.'

'Eh?' Rob's eyebrows crept together. 'Who?'

'I'm not sure, but I think it relates to this.' Suzie pointed at the article on the screen. 'But I'll get to that in a minute . . .'

She picked up the story where she and Holly had gone back to the flat and found Josie in bed, and how she had told Holly to call her if anything else happened.

'You came round not long after I got home,' she went on. 'And I didn't hear from Holly again until she turned up in tears again this morning after you went out to get the cigs and wine. She was telling me what had happened when you came back and Josie tried to force her way in. Anyway, after Josie left and you walked out, Holly went for a lie-down and I went over to the flat to try and talk to Josie. But she wasn't there, and . . .' She paused and glanced at the door before whispering, 'I haven't told Holly this, but some of her clothes were missing.'

'She might have gone to the launderette,' Rob suggested.

'No, she'd *gone*,' Suzie said with certainty. 'You don't empty your underwear drawer for a trip to the launderette, do you? And the biscuit tin wasn't where Holly told me she'd left it.'

'So what did you do?'

'I left a note asking Josie to ring me when she got home. But I haven't heard from her, and she hasn't turned any lights on all day, so I'm guessing she hasn't come back yet.'

She paused and took a drag on her cigarette, then shook her head, saying, 'How can any woman do that to their own child? Holly's upset now, but can you imagine how she's going to feel when she finds out her mum's abandoned her?'

'Do you think that's what she's done?'

'I honestly don't know.' Suzie shrugged. 'I hope not, because I can't keep Holly here forever. She'll have to go back to school soon or they're likely to send the welfare officer round. And if they find out Josie's gone and left Holly with me . . .' She tailed off and shook her head again. 'It could get really messy, Rob.'

'I don't want to say I told you so, but I did try to warn you not to get involved,' Rob said softly. 'If it was me, I'd call the police and let them handle it.'

'I know I'll probably have to do that eventually, but I want to give Josie a chance. You saw the state she was in earlier. She's traumatized, and she can't be thinking straight. But she'll have to snap out of it at some point.'

'And what if she doesn't?'

'She will,' Suzie said, as much to convince herself as Rob. 'She's already gone to extreme lengths to protect Holly, so there's no way she'd leave her if she genuinely thinks she's in danger. That's where the dead couple come in . . .'

She told Rob her theory about Holly's nightmares stemming from repressed memories of her childhood; how the father she believed she had never met might actually have been abusive towards her mum, and Josie had fled with her in fear of their lives after finding out that he'd murdered the couple.

'That's some twisted shit you've dreamed up there,' Rob said bemusedly when she'd finished. 'Ever thought about writing a book?'

'Don't take the mick,' Suzie chided. 'I've been thinking about it all night and it's the only thing that makes sense. It explains why Josie's moved Holly around so much, making it impossible for her to get close to anyone in case she let something slip and her father was able to track them down. And when she said they had to leave because it wasn't safe here any more, I reckon she thought Holly must have confided in me and put them in danger.'

'And had she?' Rob asked.

'No.' Suzie shook her head. 'She doesn't know anything *to* tell me, bless her. She's always believed her dad abandoned her mum before she was born, and Josie's never even told her his name.'

'Have you told Holly any of this?'

'No, it's not my place. Josie obviously thinks she's protecting her by keeping her in the dark, but I think they'd both be safer if Holly knew what they were dealing with, so I'm going to try to persuade her to tell her when she comes back.'

'*If* she comes back,' Rob said ominously.

Suzie wanted to reiterate that Josie *would* come back, but she honestly wasn't sure any more. It was obvious the woman had issues, and the attack had probably unbalanced her already unstable mind. Added to which, Josie clearly had a drink problem, and maybe even a drug habit. But if Josie had gone to such great lengths to protect Holly so far, would she really give up on her now?

Clinging to the hope that she wouldn't, Suzie said, 'If she's not back by morning, I'll talk to Holly – see if she can think of anyone her mum might be staying with. She must have at least *one* friend she trusts.'

'Doesn't sound like she trusts anyone, from what you've told me,' Rob said, scrolling through the article again. 'But if you're right, and this murder is connected to whatever's going on, you seriously need to think about handing Holly over to the police before these phantom killers come after you, as well.'

The image on the screen suddenly changed to one of the sultry shots Holly had taken of Suzie, and Suzie blushed when she realized that Rob must have accidentally clicked back to the website, which she'd minimized instead of closing down before going online.

'Whoa, what's this?' Rob's eyes lit up.

'Nothing,' she said, trying to click back to the article.

'Hang about,' Rob said, batting her hand away. 'Who took it?'

'Holly,' Suzie said. 'It's for the website I told you about.'

'The modelling agency?' Rob said, his gaze fixed on the image of Suzie lying on a beach with one knee raised, the other leg outstretched; lips parted, eyes half closed, her glossy hair cascading down her back. 'I reckon you'd be better sacking that off and setting up as a webcam babe instead, 'cos blokes would pay through the nose to have a one-on-one with you looking like this.'

Suzie frowned. Given the violent way Rob had reacted in the past to men simply looking at her in bars, she was surprised he would even suggest such a thing.

'Babe, I was joking,' Rob said when he saw her expression. 'But seriously, these are gorgeous.'

'Thanks,' Suzie murmured, quickly closing the laptop down. 'They're only test shots for me to experiment with. I'll replace them with photos of the models who sign up to the agency before I launch the website.'

'I know you think you're past it, but you're still the most beautiful woman I've ever met,' Rob said.

Certain that he *had* been joking about the webcam thing, Suzie smiled and reached for her drink.

'So what now?' Rob asked, taking a swig of his drink and stubbing his cigarette out in the ashtray. 'Reckon she'll be asleep yet?' He flicked his eyes up at the ceiling.

'Probably,' Suzie said, realizing that she hadn't heard any movement from up there in a while. 'She was pretty wiped when I left her.'

'Want to chance it?' He gave her a wolfish grin. Then, seeming to think better of it, he said, 'That's if you still want to? If you need time to think about it, I can leave and come back tomorrow. Or I'll sleep on the sofa. Whatever's best for you.'

Suzie bit her lip and stared into her almost empty glass. She was the one who had initiated things tonight, and she had no doubt they would already have made love by now if Rob's crazy ex hadn't turned up.

'You can stay,' she said, looking up after a moment. 'But if we're going to give this another go, you need to be sure it's what you really want.'

'I'm sure,' Rob said, stroking her cheek with the back of his fingers. 'But are *you*? I don't want you to feel like I'm rushing you into it.'

'Shut up and kiss me,' Suzie said, repeating what she'd said earlier. 'And this time, don't stop,' she added huskily.

35

Josie still hadn't been in touch by the following morning, and there was no sign that she'd been home when Suzie and Holly went over to check the flat. The air smelled as bad as always, and dust motes rose up into the air in each of the rooms they entered.

'What if she's been attacked again?' Holly fretted, as they went back through the rooms they had already checked, looking in cupboards and checking under the beds. 'Or been run over, or fallen into a ditch and been too weak to climb out of it?'

'I'm sure nothing's happened, or we'd have heard by now,' Suzie reassured her, trying to ignore her own nagging doubts about Josie's wellbeing. 'She's most likely gone to a friend's place, so is there no one you can think of? She must have mentioned *somebody*?'

'No.' Holly shook her head. 'I've already told you, she hasn't got any friends; just people she works with.'

'I find that really hard to believe,' Suzie said. 'What about boyfriends?'

'There's only ever been one that I know about,' said Holly. 'I thought I'd told you about him? She met him in the cafe she was working in and we moved in with him, but she was too moody so he kicked us out after a few months.'

'Yeah, I think you did mention it,' Suzie said.

'There hasn't been anyone since that,' Holly said adamantly. 'Even if she was trying to hide it from me, she wouldn't have time between working and sleeping.'

'OK, so maybe it's not a boyfriend,' Suzie conceded. 'But *someone* must know where she is.'

'Can we phone the hospital again?' Holly asked.

Suzie took out her phone and reluctantly perched on the sofa, which looked grubbier than ever in daylight. She had called all the hospitals in Manchester a couple of times already, and Josie hadn't been admitted to any of them. But if it put Holly's mind at rest, she supposed it wouldn't hurt to try again.

Ten minutes later, the phone hot in her hand, she said, 'Nothing. So stop worrying, because she would have been found by now if anything had happened, I promise you.'

Holly nodded and chewed on her thumbnail.

'I'll try the agency again,' Suzie said. 'I doubt she'll be working in her condition, but they might know if she's friendly with any of the women she works with. While I do that, why don't you go and make a brew,' she suggested, struggling to contain her disgust when Holly's thumbnail-chewing drew blood and she started sucking it.

Holly got up without argument and sloped into the kitchen. When she'd gone, Suzie rang the agency.

'Barker's cleaning contractors,' a woman answered.

'Oh, hi,' Suzie said. 'I rang yesterday . . . about Josie Evans?'

'Oh, yeah?' the woman said guardedly.

'I'm a friend of hers,' Suzie went on. 'Well, more a friend of her daughter's, actually. But, anyway . . . I know you're aware that Josie was attacked the other night.'

'Yeah, I know,' the woman said. 'Made a right mess of her.'

'Oh, have you seen her?' Suzie asked.

The woman went quiet, and Suzie's instincts told her that she knew something.

'Look, I promise I won't tell Josie you told me,' she said carefully, so as not to alarm the woman if she had a reason for not wanting to talk about Josie. 'Thing is, she's gone missing, and we're really worried about her. Like you said, the attacker made a mess of her, and she collapsed when she came home from hospital, so if you *have* seen her and know where she is, please tell me. Holly – her daughter – is out of her mind with worry.'

After another few seconds of silence, the woman spoke again. But her voice was muffled now, as if she'd moved away from whoever might be around her because she didn't want them to hear. 'I want my name kept out of this,' she said.

'Absolutely,' Suzie agreed, even though she didn't actually know the woman's name, because it hadn't been offered. 'So you have seen her?'

'Yeah. Last night. She came round to mine.'

'Really?' Suzie's heart leapt. 'Did she stay? Is she still there?'

'No, she ain't,' the woman replied coolly. 'We're not mates, or anything. But she seemed fine, so . . .'

'Why did she come to you?' Suzie asked. 'I'm not being nosy,' she added quickly. 'I'm just trying to figure out where her head's at, and where she might have gone after she left yours. Do you know if she's got any other friends at work she could be staying with?'

'She's not the sort to make friends,' the woman replied gruffly, echoing what Holly had already said. 'But me and her have got a little . . .' She paused, as if reconsidering her decision to discuss this with a stranger. Then, sighing, she said, 'Right, I'm only telling you this for the kid's sake, and I'll deny it if you try and drag me into it, 'cos I've got kids of me own to think about.'

'I won't repeat anything you tell me,' Suzie assured her. 'You have my word.'

The woman muttered an audible *Hmph!* as if Suzie's word meant jack-shit to her, before saying, 'She was after booze. Booze and painkillers.'

'Ah . . . I see,' Suzie murmured. 'And did you give her any?'

'A bottle of voddy and a strip of trammies,' said the woman. 'And if you see her before I do, you'd best tell her to get her arse round here and pay for it, 'cos she was supposed to drop the money off this morning.'

She hung up at that, and Suzie stared at the phone thoughtfully. So Josie had gone off in search of booze – no surprises there, given how many empty bottles she'd had stashed in the laundry basket. Holly and the woman both claimed that Josie didn't have any friends, but Suzie suspected she probably had at least one drinking buddy. Most alcoholics did, in her experience, and she figured that Josie's buddy would have been only too happy to let her stay if she turned up on their doorstep with a bottle of booze in her hand.

'Anything?' Holly asked, coming through from the kitchen carrying two steaming cups.

Making a snap decision not to tell Holly about the booze, or her suspicion that Josie might be holed up somewhere with a fellow alcoholic, Suzie said, 'One of her workmates saw her last night and said she seemed fine.'

'Did she say where she was?' Holly's eyes lit up. 'Is she coming home soon?'

'She didn't say, but at least we know she's OK,' Suzie said, grimacing when she saw bits of stale milk floating in the tea Holly handed to her. Placing the cup on the table, she said, 'Tell you what, let's forget this and go back to mine for breakfast.'

'But what about my mum?' Holly asked. 'Shouldn't we wait here for her?'

Already on her feet, desperate to get out of there, Suzie said, 'I need to get back, hon.'

'To see Rob?' Holly asked.

'How did you know he was there?' Suzie asked, sure that she couldn't have heard them last night, because they'd been careful to keep the noise down. And she couldn't have seen him this morning, because he'd still been sleeping when they came over here.

'I heard you and him talking last night, and some woman shouting,' Holly admitted, hoping that Suzie wouldn't think she'd been eavesdropping. 'And his jacket and rucksack were in the hall when I came downstairs, so I figured he must have stayed,' she added.

'Proper little detective, aren't we?' Suzie said, rolling her eyes. 'Oh, well, seeing as you've figured it out for yourself, you might as well know we've decided to give it another go. Don't look so worried,' she added when she saw Holly's frown. 'He *has* changed. In fact, he's like he used to be when I first got with him, and I think you'd like him if you gave him a chance.'

Holly nodded, but Suzie could tell she wasn't convinced. Sighing, she said, 'So what do you want to do? You're welcome to come with me, but I'll understand if you'd rather stay here.'

Holly looked around. This was her home and she'd spent more time alone there than she had ever spent with her mum. But her mum's weird warnings about people coming to kill them were fresh in her mind, and she didn't think she'd feel safe on her own.

'I'll come back to yours,' she said, placing her cup next to Suzie's.

Rob was up, dressed, and making a brew when Suzie and Holly arrived back at the house, and he raised an eyebrow at Suzie when the girl scuttled up the stairs at the sight of him.

'I take it there's no sign of her mum yet?'

'Nope,' Suzie said, resting her head on his chest when he

pulled her into his arms. 'Hey, pack it in,' she giggled, squirming out of his grasp when he nuzzled her neck. 'Holly might see us.'

'So?' Rob placed his hands around her waist and pulled her towards him.

'Stop it,' Suzie chided playfully, grinning as she pushed him away.

'What's the plan?' Rob asked, folding his arms and leaning back against the counter when she sat down and lit a cigarette.

'Same as before – waiting for Josie to come back,' Suzie said, opening her laptop. 'Oh, have you been using this?' she asked when she saw that it was already switched on.

'Yeah, I was checking the job centre website to see if there was anything worth applying for,' Rob said. 'Don't mind, do you?'

'No, of course not,' Suzie said, clicking into the local news sites.

'Looking for something?' Rob glanced at the screen.

'I rang the hospitals again and Josie hasn't been admitted,' Suzie told him quietly, looking out into the hallway to make sure Holly hadn't come down the stairs. 'Then I rang the agency she works for and spoke to one of her colleagues. She told me Josie turned up at hers last night asking for booze and pain-killers. It seems she sold her some, but she doesn't know where Josie went from there, so I'm checking to see if there are any reports of women getting arrested for drunken behaviour.'

'Wouldn't it be quicker to call the police?' Rob suggested, turning to finish making the brews.

'I don't really want to talk to them until it's absolutely necessary,' Suzie said, speed-reading the news articles. 'If I tell them Josie's missing and we're worried about her, they'll start sniffing round Holly again.'

Before Rob could respond to that, the doorbell rang. 'Want me to get it?' he offered, putting the spoon down.

'No, I'll get it.' Suzie leapt up. 'If it's Josie, she might get spooked if she sees you, and I don't want her running away again.'

She went out into the hall, pulling the door shut behind her, and then quickly opened the front door.

'Morning.' PC Spencer smiled at her from the step. 'I don't suppose you've seen Ms Evans yet, have you? Only she hasn't called, and she's not answering the door.'

'Ah . . . yeah, I saw her last night,' Suzie lied, thinking on her feet. 'She popped over to tell me she was taking Holly to stay with a friend for a couple of days.'

'I see.' Spencer looked disappointed. 'You wouldn't happen to know where this friend lives, would you?'

'Sorry, I don't,' Suzie said, folding her arms when she noticed Bennett watching her from the car again. There was something about the way he looked at her that made her nervous.

'Never mind,' Spencer said. 'Thanks, anyway. I'll try her again in a few days.'

'To be honest, I'm not sure she's going to tell you anything even if you do catch up with her,' Suzie said. 'She told me she doesn't remember anything and pretty much wants to forget about it.'

'Can't say I blame her,' said Spencer. 'But we need *something* or the guy we picked up is going to walk.'

'Oh, I see,' Suzie murmured, feeling guilty for trying to throw him off the scent if it meant the attacker got away with it. But Josie was so secretive, Suzie genuinely doubted she would tell Spencer anything even if she had perfect recall of the attack.

'OK, I'll get off, then,' Spencer said. 'But when you see her, could you tell her I'd still like to speak to her?'

'Of course.' Suzie smiled.

When she'd seen him off, Suzie went back to the kitchen. The door was ajar, and she guessed Rob had been eavesdropping when he asked who she'd been talking to.

'It was one of the cops who came round to tell Holly her mum was in hospital that night,' she told him as she sat down. 'They've been trying to get hold of her because they want her to look at some mugshots, so I told him they'd gone to stay with friends for a couple of days.'

'A couple of days?' Rob frowned. 'I thought you said she'd been seen and she was OK?'

'Yeah, but we don't know where she is, or what her plans are, so I thought I'd best buy some time – just in case,' said Suzie. 'She stayed out last night, and there's no guarantee she won't do the same again tonight.'

'And if she does?'

'I don't know.' Suzie shrugged. 'I suppose Holly will have to stay here again.' Giving him a sheepish look when she saw the disapproval in his eyes, she said, 'Please don't be angry with me. You didn't see her face when I asked if she wanted to stay over there and wait for her mum. She obviously doesn't want to be on her own. And she's only a kid.'

'Someone *else's* kid,' said Rob. 'And what if her mum doesn't come back?'

'I don't know,' Suzie groaned, resting her elbows on the tabletop and dropping her head into her hands.

'Babe, you need to face facts,' Rob said, placing a cup of tea in front of her and taking a seat. 'I know you think you're helping, but she's not your responsibility, and the longer you keep her here, the harder the police are going to come down on you when they find out.'

'They're not going to find out,' Suzie said. 'As soon as Josie comes back—'

'Stop saying that like it's a done deal,' Rob cut her off, his expression serious. 'You said she went looking for booze and painkillers last night, so what if she took an overdose? She could be dying for all you know, and they won't find her in time because *you* told that copper she's staying with a mate.'

'Well, I couldn't tell him the truth, could I?' Suzie argued. 'Holly would definitely get taken off her if they heard that.'

'And so she should be, if her mum's more concerned about getting pissed than looking after her.'

'That's not fair. She's bound to be struggling after everything she's been through. And she knows Holly's safe.'

'Does she, though?' Rob asked bluntly. 'I'm not being funny,

Suze, but you've only met the woman a couple of times. You could be a serial killer, for all she knows.'

'That's a bit extreme.'

'No, it's the truth. And if she cares so little about Holly that she'd leave her with a virtual stranger, what makes you think she's going to come back for her? She's probably halfway to Spain by now, thanking her lucky stars that she found a mug to take the kid off her hands.'

'She wouldn't do that.'

'I'm not trying to make you feel bad,' Rob said. 'But promise me you won't leave it too long before you call the police? I've only just got you back, and I don't want to lose you again because you end up getting arrested for harbouring a fugitive.'

'Fugitive?' Suzie snorted, unable to stop herself from laughing.

'You know what I mean.' Rob grinned. 'Just think about it, yeah?'

Glad that the atmosphere had lifted and Rob wasn't going to pressure her into handing Holly over to the authorities immediately, Suzie said, 'OK, I'll make a deal with you. If she's not back in a week—'

'A *week*?' Rob's eyes widened.

'I know it seems like a long time, but I'm going to speak to that woman she works with again, see if she knows more than she was letting on.'

'And what about Holly? Are you planning on keeping her here while you're waiting?'

Suzie gave a tiny shrug and gripped the cup between both hands. 'I can't make her stay over there on her own, can I?'

'What about school? They're bound to start asking questions if she stays off for too long.'

'If Josie isn't back by Monday, I'll ring them and tell them what I told the copper: that they've gone to stay with a friend.'

Rob breathed in deeply and shook his head. 'I hope you know what you're doing, Suze.'

'One week,' Suzie reiterated. 'And if I haven't found Josie by then, I promise I'll do it your way. OK?'

'I don't know why you're asking what *I* think, 'cos you've obviously made up your mind,' Rob said, standing up.

Scared that she'd asked too much of him and he had decided he wanted out, Suzie said, 'You're not leaving, are you?'

'I'm going to get some more fags,' he said, nodding at the almost empty pack lying between them on the table.

Relieved, Suzie rose from her seat. 'You bought the last lot, so let me get these.'

'It's cool, I've got it.' Rob waved for her to sit back down. 'Need anything else while I'm there?'

'We could do with some more wine.'

Rob nodded, and Suzie smiled when he said he'd be back in a minute. The smile slipped as soon as he'd gone, and she frowned as she thought over the implications of her decision. If Josie really had done a runner, as Rob seemed to think, how the hell was she supposed to tell Holly that she was handing her over to the police when the week was up? The girl trusted her, and it would feel like a double betrayal if Suzie abandoned her as well. But Rob was right when he'd said that she couldn't keep Holly here indefinitely. Not only could it potentially land Suzie in a heap of trouble with the law, it was bound to impact on her relationship with Rob, who had already made his opinions on the subject quite clear.

It was a mess, and all she could do was pray that Josie *did* come back soon. Because if push came to shove and she was forced to choose, Holly's heart was going to break into a thousand pieces.

Outside, Rob zipped up his jacket and stared thoughtfully over at the flats before setting off to the shops. He wasn't happy about Suzie bringing the girl back to the house, and he had no intention of letting her stay a full week. He'd put a lot of effort into winning Suzie back, and he wasn't going to allow anyone to come between them. For whatever reason, Suzie had taken a real shine to the girl, and it pissed him off to know that they formed such a tight bond in his absence. And what was with those sexy photos Holly had taken of her?

Suzie had done lingerie photo shoots in the past and she knew he didn't like it – even if he *had* helped her to spend the money she'd earned from them. But those ones he'd seen today were too intimate by far, and he'd struggled to contain his jealousy when he'd looked through them – hence his jibe about her setting up a webcam business instead of an agency.

She might as bloody well, if that was the kind of thing she'd been getting up to behind his back. If he didn't know better, he'd swear there was something more going on between her and that girl than just friendship. He'd seen how uncomfortable Suzie had looked when he'd stumbled across the photos. It was like she'd wanted to keep them strictly between her and Holly. Their little secret from which he was excluded.

Whether or not there was any truth to his suspicions, Rob didn't like the girl and wanted her out. He'd seen the sly looks the little bitch kept giving him, and it had pissed him off when Suzie had said that Holly had asked her not to tell him what was going on with her and her stupid, neglectful mother. And it didn't matter that Suzie had eventually told him. It was the fact that she had considered *not* telling him which infuriated him.

One way or another, he needed to get rid of Holly. He'd tried to scare Suzie into seeing sense by warning her that the police would come down on her like a ton of bricks if she didn't hand the girl over to them, but she had stubbornly dug her heels in on that one, so he'd had to let it go. He knew she would be furious if he went behind her back and talked to the police himself, and he didn't want to risk getting kicked out again now he'd burned his bridges with Angie. So he would just have to find another way around this.

Brain ticking over as he walked, Rob's thoughts turned to Josie. Suzie seemed convinced that the woman would come back for Holly soon, but there was no guarantee that was going to happen. But if Suzie was right and she had spent all these years trying to protect her child, would she really abandon the girl? Suzie didn't think so, and neither did Rob – despite what he'd told Suzie. No, Josie was lurking somewhere nearby, he was sure of it. He just needed to flush her out.

Still thinking about that when he arrived at the shops, he bought wine and cigarettes using the money he'd stolen out of Angie's drawer, and then headed back to the house. Suzie's research into the background of the dead man had led her to believe that the murder was drug-related. Whether or not that was true, the killer had never been caught, according to the articles Rob had read. In his experience, those types of criminals rarely committed only one offence, so it was likely that the man was still operating. And he had to be pretty high up in the game to have evaded capture for so long.

Rob had reached the corner of Suzie's road, but he abruptly stopped walking when another thought struck him. If Josie had spent all these years on the run fearing that the killer wanted to silence her, then it had to be a genuine threat. In which case, the killer would probably be prepared to pay a nice sum of money to find her.

Narrowing his eyes thoughtfully as the idea took root and began to blossom into a get-rich-quick scheme, Rob pulled his phone out of his pocket and scrolled through his contact list.

'Decca, it's me,' he said when his call was answered. 'Don't sound so nervous, mate, I'm not calling to have a go at you for grassing me up to Kev. It did piss me off, but he *is* a cunt, so I couldn't give a shit. Anyhow, listen . . . remember when we were both in the Strange three years back and I was padded up with Harry Cox? The old dude, yeah, that's the one. I left before you, and I forgot to ask for his number. Don't suppose you got it, did you – or know anyone else who might have it? Cheers, mate, that'd be great. Give us a bell as soon as.'

Grinning when he'd finished the call, Rob glanced over at the flats again before walking on. Decca was lucky he had contacts or Rob would have kicked his arse next time he saw him. But if he managed to get hold of Harry Cox's number, they were even.

It was 4 p.m. before Rob's phone rang. It was a withheld number, and he'd got into the habit of ignoring those in case it was Angie drunk-dialling for another argument. But he'd been waiting all day for Decca's call, and he didn't want to miss it if it was him, so he got up off the sofa, where he and Suzie had spent the afternoon watching DVDs, and went out into the hall to answer it.

'Is this Robert?' a man asked.

'Harry!' Rob grinned, instantly recognizing the fifty-rollies-a-day rasp of his old cellmate's voice. 'Wow, man, it's been a long time,' he said, heading into the kitchen and closing the door. 'How you doing?'

'All good,' Harry said. 'So, a little birdie tells me you've been asking for my number?'

'Yeah, that's right,' Rob said, guessing that Decca must have given his number to his contacts and one of them had passed it on to Harry. 'Hope you don't mind, but I need a favour, and you were the go-to man inside, so . . .'

'How much you after?' Harry asked bluntly.

'It's not money, or anything,' Rob assured him. 'It's, um, personal,' he said, reluctant to say too much over the phone, because he was wary of who might be listening in. 'I thought maybe we could meet up and discuss it over a pint? My treat.'

'Personal, eh?' Harry repeated, sounding intrigued. 'Tell you what, give us your address and I'll pop round when I get some spare time.'

'I'd rather come to you, if that's OK?' Rob said, lowering his voice as he added, 'The missus doesn't know about this, and I'd rather she didn't find out.'

'Like that, is it?' Harry chuckled. 'And when were you thinking of?'

'Sooner the better,' Rob said hopefully.

After arranging to meet up with Harry later that evening, Rob went back to the living room.

'Everything all right?' Suzie asked, looking up at him with concern in her eyes. 'It wasn't that crazy bitch again, was it?'

'No, it was a bloke about a job,' Rob grinned. 'I didn't tell you this morning, 'cos I didn't want to get your hopes up, but I applied for something while you were out – when you asked if I'd been using the laptop – and they want me to go for an interview.'

'That's great.' Suzie smiled. 'When?'

'Six.'

'Tonight?'

'Yep, so I'd best start getting ready,' Rob said, glancing at the clock. 'Fingers crossed, eh?'

'You don't need luck, you're bound to get it,' Suzie said. 'Where's the interview being held?'

'Wythenshawe,' Rob lied. 'It's a bit of a trek, and I'll have to switch buses a few times so I might be back late. You don't mind, do you?'

'Of course I don't,' Suzie said without hesitation. 'I know how important this is for you after losing out on the rig thing.'

'It's important for *us*,' Rob corrected her, planting a kiss on her lips. ''Cos if I get this we'll be quids in, and you can forget about the agency and let *me* look after *you* for a change.'

He winked at her before leaving the room and jogging up the stairs, not noticing the flicker of a frown that crossed her brow as she watched him go. He knew she thought of herself as an independent woman, but now they were back together, he was fucked if he was letting her take her clothes off in front of another man – *or* woman – again.

36

Rob hadn't been to Oldham in years, and he remembered why he'd been in no rush to return when the bus trundled past row after row of boarded-up shops and scruffy houses at six that evening. Although it was within ten miles of Manchester, the atmosphere was so alien to him it might as well have been another planet. And the feeling of uneasiness increased the closer he got to his destination, so that by the time the bus driver told him he'd reached his stop, he was beginning to regret not asking Harry to meet up on his turf instead.

Reminding himself that he'd done it this way so that he could kill two birds with one stone and try to make contact with the killer while he was up here – providing Harry knew who it was – he squinted when he stepped off the bus and the wind hurled a swirling cloud of dust into his eyes. He was standing at the end of a long narrow road of two-up two-down terraced houses, at the far end of which he could just about make out the dully lit sign of the Dog and Partridge pub where Harry had asked to meet. A squat single-storey building, it sat alone in the centre of its deserted car park, and dark wasteland stretched out into the distance behind it.

Looking up when he heard the dull thwack of a football hitting concrete, Rob picked out the shadowy figures of several small boys playing footie at the end of the road. The sky was already dark enough to make them look like they'd stepped straight out of a Lowry painting, and he wondered if he'd made a mistake choosing the designer leather jacket and trainers he was wearing. He had bought them off a junkie shoplifter for fifteen quid apiece, but they were probably worth more than any of the tatty cars that were parked along the road, and it showed. Still, he could hardly go and get changed now, so he lowered his head in an effort to make himself inconspicuous as he set off along the road.

As he neared the boys, he instinctively ducked when he saw the football flying towards his head out of the corner of his eye.

'What d'ya do that for, dickhead?' one of the boys spat when it glanced off his shoulder and smashed into the door of a house. 'Me dad'll kick your fuckin' 'ead in if you've woke 'im.'

Rob felt like belting the lippy fucker, but he was out of his territory, so he decided it would be wiser to keep his mouth shut and walk on. Jaw clenching when the ball whizzed past his head again, followed by raucous laughter from the boys, he strode across the road and pushed through the pub's paint-peeled door.

The strong scent of weed smacked him in the face, and he tried not to breathe too deeply as he looked around the pub's dingy interior. Three burly, hard-faced white men who were propping up the bar turned their heads and eyed him with suspicion, as did the group of black lads who were openly flouting the smoking ban by sucking on fat spliffs at the pool table in the far corner. Two women, who looked to be in their fifties but obviously thought they looked much younger in their sparkly low-cut tops and plastered-on make-up, had been cackling loudly at a table in the centre of the room, but they both went quiet and stared at him.

Again regretting his decision to insist on meeting Harry on his turf, Rob was about to skulk away when he heard the growl of a high-powered motor pulling into the car park behind him. Stepping aside so the door wouldn't smack him in the back when he heard two sets of footsteps approaching, he was relieved when he saw that it was Harry and a young woman.

Harry rasped a greeting to the other customers, and Rob, noting the respectful way they all acknowledged him, guessed that he had as much clout on the outside as he'd seemed to have in the Strange, where no one, not even the younger gang-bangers who had fought like wild dogs to assert dominance, ever so much as crossed their eyes at the man they had all called *Uncle* Harry.

Harry placed a hand on his companion's back and, nodding towards the table where the only other women in the place were sitting, said, 'Go and sit with your pals, darlin'. I'll send a bottle over in a minute.'

When she'd gone, Harry turned and looked at Rob for the first time, a slow grin lifting his thin lips.

'Robert . . .' he rasped, using Rob's full name as he had done throughout the six months they had been padded up together. 'As handsome as ever, ya little fucker.'

Rob grinned as he felt the tension slipping off his shoulders. Harry had always looked ancient, but he appeared to have aged twenty years in the three since they had last met, with his watery, faded blue eyes, and the wrinkles cutting grooves in his deeply tanned face. Age clearly hadn't robbed him of his strength, though, and Rob forced himself not to grimace when Harry pumped his hand with a vice-like grip.

'Good to see you,' Harry said, releasing Rob's hand at last – and nearly breaking his shoulder when he clapped a gnarled hand down on it. 'What took you so long?'

'I've been meaning to get in touch for ages,' Rob lied, surreptitiously cradling his hand when Harry steered him over to the bar. 'But you know how it is . . . life got in the way.'

'More like you've been too busy slinging your cock around to remember your old Uncle Harry, eh?' The man gave a leery grin and clicked his fingers at the barman, who jumped to attention. 'What you having?'

'Er, whatever you're having,' Rob said. 'But I'll get it.'

'Don't insult me,' Harry said, pulling a thick wad of twenties out of his pocket and slapping several down on the bar top. 'Two fat Hens,' he told the barman. 'And a bottle of red for the ladies.'

'Is that your wife?' Rob asked, glancing over at the woman Harry had arrived with and wondering how the man had managed to pull her. Not only was she was much closer to Rob's age than his, she was also surprisingly attractive – way too attractive for an ugly old bugger like Harry.

'Mistress,' Harry said, his eyes glittering as he, too, looked over at her. 'Not bad, eh?' He winked at Rob and jabbed him in the ribs with a rock-hard elbow before scooping up one of the glasses the barman had placed on the bar and throwing the double measure into his mouth. 'Same again,' he said, slamming the empty glass down. 'And keep 'em coming,' he added, before jerking his head at Rob and heading over to a table in a quiet corner.

Following, with his own as-yet untouched drink in his hand, Rob sat down.

'So what brings you all the way out here on a shit night like this?' Harry asked, his faded eyes still as sharp as a tack as he peered into Rob's.

'Like I said, I need a favour,' Rob started.

Harry held up a hand to silence him when the barman came over with a bottle of Hennessy. Gesturing for the man put it down and go, Harry took a pack of tobacco out of his pocket and rolled a cigarette.

'Go on, then,' he said, looking at Rob again after lighting up. 'You said you ain't after money, so what is it? Drugs? Passport? Driving licence . . . ?'

Shocked to hear how easily the items rolled off Harry's

tongue, as if he'd have no problem supplying any or all of them, Rob said, 'I, um, wanted to sound you out about some people who got murdered.'

'Murdered?' Harry raised a bushy grey eyebrow. 'Pals of yours, were they?'

'No, I didn't actually know them,' Rob admitted. 'It was a while back, and they lived not far from here, so I was hoping you might know something about it.'

'Journalist, are you?' Harry asked. 'Or a private dick?'

'No, nothing like that,' Rob said, catching the glint of suspicion in the old man's eyes. 'I'm actually looking into it for a friend.'

'Who got snuffed?' Harry asked, taking a deep drag on his roll-up.

'It was a couple,' Rob told him. 'Woman and her boyfriend. They got shot in her bedroom.'

He took out his phone and brought up the article he'd googled after reading it on Suzie's laptop. Harry quickly read it and passed the phone back.

'Do you know them?' Rob asked.

'Not personally,' Harry said guardedly. 'What are they to this friend of yours?'

Rob gave him the edited version that he'd rehearsed on the way over, leaving Suzie out of it and making himself out to be a friend of Josie's who was trying to help her to get her life back on track. Harry listened in silence, and was frowning by the time he'd finished.

'So let me get this straight,' he said. 'You think this Josie bird's fella offed Devon Prince and *his* bird, and you're trying to find out if he's banged up so you can tell her she's safe to stop running?'

'Exactly,' Rob said.

'And this kid of hers, is she white or black?'

'White,' Rob said, taking a swig of his drink.

'Well, she deffo ain't the killer's daughter, then,' Harry said. ''Cos he's black as night.'

'You know him?' Rob's heart leapt.

'Never said that,' Harry said, the guarded look coming back into his eyes. 'Tell me more about this Josie bird.' He changed the subject. 'What's *she* look like?'

Rob gave him a brief description, and Harry pursed his lips. 'Interesting. And how old's the kid?'

'Fifteen,' Rob said. 'Why? Do you know them?'

Harry shook his head. 'Nope.'

'Are you sure?' Rob asked, convinced he had seen a spark of recognition in Harry's eyes when he'd described Josie.

'I'm sure,' Harry said, downing his second drink and twisting the lid off the bottle to refill both their glasses. 'I thought I recognized the names for a minute, but it can't be the ones I'm thinking of, 'cos that Holly died when she was two.'

'Died?' Rob repeated.

'Yep.' Harry nodded and sucked on his rollie, which was now wet at the end and turning a deep shade of nicotine brown in his matching fingers. 'The mam was a smackhead, and the kid got hold of her methadone when she was gouched out and drank the lot. Little fucker didn't stand a chance.'

'So she definitely died?' Rob asked, thinking it a bit of a coincidence that there could have been a different Josie and Holly living in the same area as the murdered couple if *his* Josie and Holly had a connection to it. And they obviously did, because why else would Josie have kept that newspaper clipping about them?

'Far as I know.' Harry shrugged. 'My missus reckoned the mam disappeared soon after, but I suppose you'd have to be on a death wish to stick around in a place where everyone knew you'd as good as killed your own baby, wouldn't you? Remember what happened to that nonce who got put on our wing that time?' he added, giving a sinister chuckle as he reached for his drink.

Rob remembered the man all right, and he shuddered at the memory of watching him being dragged into a cell and raped with a broom handle before being doused in lighter fluid, set alight and flung over the walkway – in full view of the screws, who had pretended they hadn't seen anything until the last minute, despite the man screaming the place down.

Rob pushed the horrible images out of his mind and took a sip of his drink. Harry reckoned the Holly *he'd* known of had died but he hadn't seemed certain, and Rob wondered if that was because she hadn't, and was currently sleeping in Suzie's spare room.

'Do you know the bloke's name?' he asked, figuring he still

had a chance of turning the situation to his own advantage. 'The one who killed that couple?'

'And why would you want to know that?' Harry asked sharply. 'I thought you only wanted to find out if he was banged up?'

Sensing that he'd been too forward and had made Harry suspicious again, Rob said, 'I just thought it might help Josie if I could tell her the name.'

'I thought you said it was her ex?' Harry replied smoothly. 'In which case she already knows his name, don't she? And if you're such good friends, wouldn't she have told *you*?'

Rob felt his cheeks reddening. 'I, um, wanted to be sure it was the same one.'

'Tell me the name she told you, and I'll tell you if it's the same one,' Harry said, his stare intense. Snorting softly when Rob's mouth flapped open but nothing came out, he said, 'Never try to kid a kidder, son. Now what's the *real* reason you want his name?'

Shifting in his seat, feeling like a dick for getting caught out so easily, Rob said, 'I just . . .' He tailed off, then murmured, 'I thought I might be able to make some money out of it.'

'And you thought, *Oh, I know, I'll ask good old Uncle Harry for the bloke's name, 'cos he's the kind of dickhead who whistles on command.* That it?' Harry asked.

'No, course not.' Rob's cheeks felt like they were on fire.

The lads who had been playing pool suddenly downed cues and headed for the door, and Rob's stomach clenched when they glanced over at him on their way out. He had a horrible feeling they would be waiting for him when he left to catch his bus – which he would soon have to do if he hoped to get home before Suzie became suspicious about how long the interview was taking.

As if reading his mind, Harry said, 'You still living in Manchester?' When Rob nodded, he said, 'I'll give you a lift home.'

'No, it's OK,' Rob said miserably. 'I don't want to put you out.'

'I need to see a man about a dog, anyway,' Harry insisted. 'So drink up while I have a quick word with Cheryl, then we'll get going.'

Harry got up and walked over to his mistress, and Rob watched as the man peeled some notes off the wad and pushed them into her hand. She smiled and leaned her head back for a kiss, which Harry dutifully planted. Grimacing, Rob quickly averted his gaze when the man headed back to their table.

'Let's go,' Harry said, wiping his mouth on the back of his hand after sinking his drink.

Reluctantly, Rob finished his own drink and followed Harry outside.

'Address?' Harry said when he and Rob were sitting in his plush Mercedes.

Wary of giving his real address, because he didn't want Harry to take it upon himself to start visiting, Rob gave the name of a road a hundred metres from Suzie's. *Good old Uncle Harry* wasn't the kindly old man he had recast him as in his hazy memories. They had rubbed along all right at the time, but it was hard not to form some kind of friendship when you were locked in a cell with someone for twenty-three hours a day. Now, after less than an hour in the man's company, he knew they had absolutely nothing in common and he couldn't wait to see the back of him.

After a nightmare journey, during which Harry had kept his foot to the metal on the motorway, swerving from lane to lane and blasting his horn at every driver who didn't get out of his way fast enough, almost causing multiple pile-ups, Rob released his grip on the sides of the leather seats when Harry, at last, pulled over.

'Which one's yours?' the old man asked, gazing out at the semi-detached houses.

'The one at the end,' Rob lied.

'Not going to invite me in for a brew?'

'Sorry, mate, I can't,' Rob said, feigning regret as he unclipped his seat belt with shaking hands. 'The missus thinks I've been for an interview, and I don't want her to know I was lying. We only just got back together, and I'm still on probation. You know how it is.'

'Special, is she?'

'Very. And I've already fucked it up once, so I don't wanna risk losing her again. Maybe next time, eh? I'll give you a ring. Maybe meet up for dinner, or something?'

'Mebbe.' Harry winked at him.

'Anyway, it was good to see you.' Rob held out his hand.

'You too,' Harry said, giving it a quick, hard shake. 'And good luck with the missus.'

Rolling his eyes as if he fully expected to get a rollicking, Rob climbed out of the car and tapped on the roof. Harry raised his hand in a farewell gesture and pulled away from the kerb, and Rob released a long, tense breath as he watched the car go.

He stayed where he was until he could no longer see it, then pulled up his collar and walked quickly down the road. Head down as he turned the corner, he didn't notice the Mercedes idling in the shadows ahead.

Harry had killed the lights and was watching Rob in the rear-view. When he'd turned the corner, Harry reversed smoothly back and then jumped out of the car. Ducking down at the side of the wall encircling a glass-littered car park, he watched as Rob looked furtively around before entering one of the terraced houses on the opposite side of the road. When he'd closed the door, Harry squinted at the number of the house on the corner and then counted backwards in twos until he reached Rob's house.

Back in his car, he made a phone call.

'It's me,' he said when it was answered. 'I need you to get me a number, ASAP . . .'

Suzie was sitting on the sofa when Rob let himself in, and she smiled up at him when he came into the room after hanging his jacket up.

'How did it go?'

'Bit shit, to be honest,' Rob lied, leaning down to kiss her. 'There were about forty of us after the same job, and some of them have been in the building trade for longer than I've been alive, so I don't reckon I'll stand much chance.'

'Surely they'll consider you if the others are that much older?' Suzie said, getting up and heading into the kitchen where she'd been keeping his dinner warm in the oven. 'I thought you needed to be fit to work in construction?'

'I'm not sure I'd want it even if they offered it to me,' Rob said, sitting at the table and smiling when she placed his plate in front of him. 'It sounded like they expect their crews to travel long distances at short notice.'

'Oh, wasn't it a fixed position?' Suzie asked, taking a can of beer out of the fridge and opening it for him.

'Nope.' Rob shook his head and stuck his fork into the food. 'What is this?'

'Chicken chasseur,' Suzie told him, wrinkling her nose as they both looked at the congealed mess on the plate. 'It looked a lot better than that when I served it up.'

'My fault for taking so long,' Rob said, scooping a forkful into his mouth and giving her the thumbs up.

'You don't have to pretend you like it,' she laughed. 'I can make you a bacon butty instead, if you want?'

'It's fine,' Rob insisted, taking a swig of beer to wash the weird taste out of his mouth. 'So what did you get up to while I was out?'

'Apart from mucking dinner up? Not a lot.' Suzie shrugged.

'Me and Holly watched telly for a bit, then she had a bath and went to bed, and I came in here to work on those photos.'

'Get much done?' Rob forced another mouthful of glop down.

'Not really. I wasn't in the mood, so I decided to leave it for now and concentrate on looking for Josie instead.'

'Any luck getting hold of that woman?'

'No. And the one I spoke to tonight wouldn't even tell me her name, so I'll have to keep trying until she answers the phone again. I'm sure I'll recognize her voice when she does.'

'And how's she been?' Rob jerked his chin up at the ceiling.

'Quiet,' Suzie said. 'But that's to be expected, I suppose. She feels safe here with us, but I'm sure she'd rather be at home with her mum.'

Rob nodded and ate one more forkful of food before pushing his plate away. 'Sorry, babe, I can't eat any more.'

'I didn't really expect you to eat as much as you have,' Suzie said, smiling as she scraped the residue into the bin and washed the plate. 'Want me to make that butty?'

'Nah, I think I'm ready for bed.' Rob yawned and stretched his arms above his head.

'Don't be thinking you're going straight to sleep.' Suzie gave him a meaningful smile. 'We've got a lot of catching up to do.'

'If I *have* to,' Rob sighed.

Laughing, Suzie flicked soap suds at him and then quickly dried her hands before sitting on his lap and wrapping her arms around his neck.

'Thanks for letting Holly stay,' she said, as if she'd given him a choice in the matter. 'I know it's cramping your style having her here, but—'

'Sshhh . . .' Rob placed a finger over her lips. 'I don't want to talk about her any more tonight.'

'OK,' Suzie agreed. 'Let's talk about the agency instead. I've been thinking about what you said earlier, and I'm not sure I like the idea of letting you work while I sit at home doing nothing. I've put a lot of thought into this, and I really think I can make a success of it. But I don't want it coming between us, so I was thinking . . . how about you come in on it with me?'

Rob made a face as if that was an interesting prospect. But he had other things on his mind, so he said, 'I'd rather talk about . . .' He pulled her head down and whispered the rest, and Suzie leapt up and reached for his hand.

'Come on, then, lover boy . . . what you waiting for?'

Two long but very pleasurable hours later, when Suzie had, at last, fallen asleep, Rob slid his arm out from under her and, easing himself out of bed, pulled on her dressing gown before creeping downstairs.

After quietly closing the kitchen door, he sat at the table and booted up Suzie's laptop. When Harry had shut him down at the pub, refusing to give him the name he'd wanted, he had realized that his original plan might not have been such a good idea, after all. He'd greedily thought the killer would be happy to pay for Josie's address, but, in hindsight, the man was more likely to have put a bullet in his head after getting the info, to prevent him from warning her or passing his name to the police. But something about Harry's story regarding the other Holly overdosing as a baby was still niggling him, and he needed to figure out what his instincts were trying to tell him.

37

'What the *fuck* . . . ? Josie? *JOSIE!*'

Jolted from her sleep by a sharp kick in the leg, Josie cried out when pain shot through her body.

'Never mind whingeing,' Fiona barked. 'Get the fuck out of my bin cupboard, you little tramp!'

Unsure where she was, Josie gazed confusedly out at her from the cramped, foul-smelling interior of the cupboard.

'Have you been in there since I gave you that?' Fiona asked, staring in disgust at the now-empty vodka bottle lying next to Josie. Then, pulling a face when she saw the front of Josie's coat, she said, 'Ewww . . . is that puke?'

Josie gazed down at herself and, smelling the vomit before she saw it, covered her mouth with a filthy hand when her stomach heaved.

'Don't you dare throw up again,' Fiona warned, taking a step back and holding the cupboard door wide. 'It's gonna take me ages to clean that up as it is.'

Josie's head felt like it was stuffed with cotton wool, and her limbs felt like lead weights as she scrambled onto her knees and crawled out onto the path. It was dark, and Fiona was wearing a dressing gown and slippers, her hair sticking up around her head as if she'd just got out of bed.

'What time is it?' she croaked, rising unsteadily to her feet.

'One a.m.,' said Fiona.

Confused as to why she was so angry, Josie rubbed her eyes, and said, 'I haven't been here long.'

'You came here *yesterday*, so that's more than twenty-four hours,' Fiona corrected her. 'If I hadn't heard you rustling about just now and thought a fox was raiding the bins, you could have *died* in there.'

When Josie gazed blankly back at her, Fiona sighed and folded her arms. 'How many of those caps have you got left, or have you taken them all?'

'I – I haven't taken anything,' Josie said, not remembering that at all.

'Jeezus, Josie, it's no wonder your daughter's worried about you,' Fiona tutted. 'You need serious help.'

'H-Holly?' Josie stuttered, the mention of her daughter breaking through the fog in her mind. 'Has she been here?'

'No, but I've had your mate on the phone asking questions while I was working, which was bad enough.'

'What did you tell her?' Josie asked, guessing that it must have been Suzie.

'That I'd seen you and you were fine.'

'Did – did she mention the police?'

'No, she just wanted to know where you were, 'cos they're worried about you,' Fiona said. Then, her expression softening a little, she said, 'Look, I know you've had a rough time of it, but you really need to sort yourself out. If social services get wind of this, they'll have that girl of yours in a home before you can blink.'

'You're not going to report me, are you?'

'I *should*. But, no . . . I won't.'

'Thank you,' Josie said gratefully.

'Just go home,' said Fiona, her tone pitying now.

Nodding, Josie reached into the cupboard and pulled out her bags, both of which were coated in vomit, before shuffling away.

Fiona shook her head as she watched her go, and then closed the bin cupboard door and went back to her bed.

The walk home seemed to take forever, and Josie's legs felt like they were going to give out on her by the time she got there. The cold night air had cleared more of the fog from her brain, and she was acutely aware of her surroundings as she made her way through the estate.

When she reached her road, she hesitated and looked around. She had half expected to see a load of police and forensic vehicles parked outside the flats and crime-scene tape blocking access at each end of the road, but all was quiet and no one was around. Relieved to think that Holly must still be safe, she slipped quietly into the flats.

Apart from the drip of the bathroom tap, the flat was silent when she let herself in, but she held her breath and listened out for sounds of movement or breathing which would tell her if anybody was hiding. Relaxing when she'd heard nothing after a couple of minutes, she put down the vomit-stinking bags and double-locked and bolted the front door before slipping her coat off. A foil strip fell out of the pocket, and she frowned as she picked it up and read the print on the back: tramadol. Fiona had asked her if she'd taken all the caps. This must be what she'd meant, but Josie didn't recall taking anything last night. Three of the five blisters in the strip were empty, so she assumed she must have taken them. Maybe that was why she'd slept so long and couldn't remember a thing between arriving at Fiona's and leaving?

Glad that she still had some to ease the aches and pains, she checked Holly's room. The bed was empty, and she guessed that Suzie must have invited her to stay another night. It wasn't ideal, but it was better than Holly falling into the clutches of social services, as Fiona had warned her would happen if she didn't sort herself out. But Suzie already knew too much, and the longer Holly was there, telling her God only knew what, the more risk there was of Suzie figuring things out and reporting her to the police. So, tomorrow morning, come hell or high water, Josie was going to get Holly out of there and take her far, far away from here.

As she turned to leave the room, thinking that she should probably take a bath before going to bed, her eye was drawn to Holly's partially open underwear drawer, and her heart leapt when she spotted the red cap and neck of the bottle of vodka she'd bought on the way home from hospital sticking out between the bras and knickers. She realized that Holly must have confiscated it to keep her from drinking any more, and that saddened her, but she knew she didn't have as big a problem as Holly obviously thought she did. Still, she made a silent vow to cut down on her drinking as soon as they were settled in a new place and she had secured a new job.

But that was then and this was now, and she needed a drink to help her sleep. So, forgetting about the bath, Josie headed to her own room and poured a glassful.

38

Gee gazed out through the window of the cab as it carried him home. It was 2.30 a.m. and he had just finished his third shift manning the doors at the newly refurbished nightclub Zenith in the fashionable Northern Quarter. He had been working as a security guard at a shopping centre for the last two years, chasing petty shoplifters and directing shoppers to stores they could easily have found for themselves if they'd bothered to check the information boards. It had paid the rent, just about, but it had also bored the arse off him, and he'd been terrified that he would end up like the old codgers he'd worked alongside, who seemed proud to have devoted forty years to a job that rewarded them with shit pay and no chance of promotion. So when his mate had told him Zenith was advertising for door staff, he'd jumped at the chance to escape the life-sucking drudgery of the Arndale.

His body hadn't fully adjusted to the switch from days to nights yet, but the work was way more exciting, the hours were shorter and the pay was better. But he had earned every penny of that extra pay tonight. The club had been packed, and it had been all hands on deck when a massive fight broke out on the dance floor. With blokes throwing wild punches, screaming girls pulling hair extensions clean out of other screaming girls' heads, and tables and chairs flying all over the show, it was a miracle he and his colleagues hadn't received any significant injuries. But just as they'd got that one under control and were ejecting the instigators, another far more serious fight had erupted on the pavement outside, this time involving two rival gangs.

Outnumbered, and fearing for their own safety as well as that of their customers when they saw the array of weapons being brandished, Gee and the others had herded everyone back inside and locked the doors before calling the police. One of the guys had been caught by a machete before escaping, and Gee shuddered when he recalled the deep gash he'd seen in the man's shoulder when they had cut his jacket and shirt off. The club's designated first-aider had stemmed the blood as best she could until the police arrived and the man had walked to the ambulance – so he was going to be OK – but it had shaken Gee nevertheless.

Still, he'd managed to avoid getting injured himself, so he figured he'd be fit to do it all again tomorrow night.

As the cab neared his estate, Gee twisted his head when they passed the derelict church that had been used as a community centre for the estate's residents until a council pen-pusher decided it was no longer cost-effective and closed it down. It had been boarded-up for a couple of years, and the land around it had become something of a rubbish dump for old mattresses, sofas and shopping trolleys, so Gee was curious to know why the BMW with blacked-out windows they had just passed was parked in the shadows of its driveway. He hadn't seen the car around here before, and it looked like an expensive one, so he doubted it belonged to any of the estate residents.

No longer able to see the Beemer when the cab turned the corner, Gee shrugged it off, figuring that the car probably belonged to some rich developer who was planning to buy the plot and erect more flats. It was a damn shame, because there were precious few old buildings left in the area, but there was no stopping progress, he supposed.

Climbing out of the cab after paying his fare, Gee took out his keys and made his way inside the block. As tired as his body felt, his head was still wide awake, so he was going to take a shower when he got in, then pour himself a glass of Chivas from the bottle one of his mates had left behind after his last party, and roll a nice spliff before hitting the sack.

As he climbed the communal stairs, he saw what looked like chunks of vomit on the steps. Grimacing, he sidestepped them and continued on up to his flat.

'Reckon he clocked us?' Austin Gordon asked, leaning forward in the passenger seat of the BMW to scan the road through the tinted windscreen.

'So what if he did?' Dom Cooper shrugged. 'He's a brother,

so he ain't gonna think nutt'n 'bout bred'rin chillin' in a motor.'

'I s'ppose,' Austin conceded. 'So what now?'

'We wait till the lights go out, then go see what's what,' Dom murmured, his dark eyes glowing red as he sucked on his spliff.

'D'ya reckon this dude knows anything?'

'The old man seems to think so.'

'What if he don't?'

'Then we'll have a lickle chat and leave him be.'

Dom grinned and passed the spliff over. Austin took a tiny toke on it before passing it back. He avoided coming to Manchester as a rule, and he felt jumpy enough already without clouding his mind with Skunk. He also wasn't happy that there were only two of them here, because if something went wrong and they got separated, he'd be fucked for getting home.

'Not long now,' Dom said when he spotted another light going out along the row of houses he'd been watching.

Austin rolled his head on his shoulders, trying to ease the tension that had gripped him when Harry Cox's call had come through. His bird was due any day, and he'd promised to be at the birth, so he hoped this was going to be fast and easy.

39

Rob leaned forward in his seat and stared at the image on the laptop screen. It wasn't the clearest of shots, because it had obviously been taken on a phone from a distance, and the woman in it had her face turned sideways on to the camera. But he was certain it was Josie.

Suzie had told him that she'd searched for Josie on all the social media sites she could think of, but if she'd searched for Josie on Google as well, instead of focusing all her attention on the dead couple, she might have made the same discovery as Rob – and her mind would have been blown, just like his currently was.

It had taken a while, because there were loads of women called Josie Evans on the Net, and Rob had waded through hundreds, if not thousands, of links to beauticians, florists, hairdressers and other businesses using the name. There were also numerous links to various social media profiles, but he ignored those, figuring that Suzie must already have checked them out.

Bored and on the verge of giving up at 3 a.m., he had decided to try one last search, this time entering Holly's name along with Josie's. Annoyed with himself for not thinking to do that at the start when a stream of articles had appeared on the screen, he'd quickly read through them. They all confirmed what Harry had told him in the pub: that a two-year-old child called Holly Evans, daughter of former heroin addict Josie Evans, had died of an overdose after drinking the bottle of methadone her mother had left open on the table while taking a nap.

The coroner had classed it as a tragic accident and Josie hadn't been charged. Luckily for her, that story had been buried by news of the murder of Anna Hughes and Devon Prince five weeks later, and the subsequent search for Anna's missing daughter, Charlotte – whose clothes had been recovered from the Rochdale canal, but whose body had never been found.

The last article about Holly, the one that contained the photograph, was a short piece about her council-funded funeral. The date and venue had been kept strictly under wraps for Josie's protection, but somebody had obviously found out about it and had managed to capture this image of Josie coming out of the crematorium escorted by a police officer and a woman who looked too official to be a family member.

Rob was 99 per cent certain that the Josie *he* knew was the same one Harry had mentioned, and he was also sure that she *had* been connected to the murdered couple, as Suzie had theorized. A cross-reference of the two stories had revealed that Josie and Anna had actually been next-door neighbours, but Josie was believed to have gone into hiding before the murder after receiving death threats, so she wasn't named as a person of interest.

That all made sense to Rob, but one thing still didn't quite fit: if Josie's Holly was dead, how could she be here right now?

The answer came to him in a flash. Of course! Josie must have given birth to *this* Holly after the death of the original one, and she'd given her the same name to keep the other one's memory alive. It wasn't something Rob would do, because he thought it a bit ghoulish. But women were a different species when it came to stuff like that.

Tired by then, Rob decided to call it a night. He couldn't wait to tell Suzie what he'd found out, but he would keep Harry well out of it. If she found out he'd lied about the interview and had actually gone looking for information that could have potentially put her little friend in danger, she would boot his arse out for good this time.

After closing the laptop down, he got up and stretched. Tensing when he heard a scuffling noise outside the back door, he slowly lowered his arms and looked behind him. The blinds were drawn at the window, so if someone *was* out there they wouldn't be able to see him. A block of carving knives stood on the counter to his left, and he slid the largest one out of its slot and gripped it firmly in his hand before creeping towards the back door.

Before he reached it, there was a dull thud and the glass from the panel next to the door handle fell onto the tiled floor. A gloved hand snaked through the gap before he had time to react, and he watched in horror as the key was turned – the key he was forever warning Suzie to take out before she went to bed at night.

The door opened and two hooded figures stepped inside; one white and holding a metal baseball bat, the other black and pointing a handgun at his face.

'You must be Robert?' the black man said, his deep voice sending a shiver down Rob's spine.

'Wh-what do you want?' Rob stuttered, taking a step back, trying to put the table between them. 'There's no drugs or money in the house.'

'Put the knife down,' the man said, walking further into the room as his friend re-locked the back door before pocketing the key.

Sweating, his mind whirring as he tried to think who he'd upset enough to send heavies after him, Rob said, 'Has – has Angie sent you?' as he placed the knife on the table. 'I didn't mean to hurt her,' he went on, holding up his hands. 'And I'll pay back the money I took, I swear.'

'I don't know any Angies,' the man said, looking at his mate. 'How 'bout you?'

'Nah.' The white man shook his head and slapped the bat onto the palm of his other hand.

'Rob . . . ?' Suzie appeared in the doorway wearing only her pyjama top and rubbing sleep from her eyes.

'Well, hello there, darlin' . . .' the gunman drawled, a glint of lust in his eyes as his gaze slid down her body. 'Come to join the party, have you?'

'Suzie, don't come in,' Rob said. 'Go back to bed.'

Suzie blinked in confusion as she looked from Rob to the men, and the blood drained from her face when she saw the gun and the baseball bat. Then, snapping out of the daze, she said, 'Who the hell are you, and why are you in my house?'

'Feisty,' the one holding the gun chuckled, walking over to her and peering down into her eyes. 'I'm going to have fun gettin' to know you, *Suzie*.'

'Don't fucking touch me,' she spat, jerking her head away when he slid the barrel of the gun beneath her hair.

'Don't argue with him,' Rob croaked. 'Angie's sent them.'

'Shut the fuck up and sit down!' the other man barked, whacking the back of his legs with the bat.

'Leave him alone!' Suzie yelled, instinctively trying to go to Rob when his knees buckled.

'Now, now,' the gunman purred, wrapping a muscular arm around her waist and pulling her against him. 'We only want a lickle chat with your man, so be a good girl and mek us a drink, eh?'

'Get out of my house right now,' she hissed, forcing herself to return his gaze.

'Suzie, shut the fuck up and do as he says!' Rob spluttered, his teeth bared with pain as he sank onto a chair.

'Didn't your mam teach you it's rude to speak to women like

that?' the other one snarled, ramming the end of the bat into his stomach.

'Stop it!' Suzie cried when Rob doubled over, clutching his stomach. 'Just tell us what you want and go! *Please*.'

On the landing above, Holly bit down hard on her hand when she heard the fear in Suzie's voice. She'd been sleeping fitfully and had woken several times throughout the night, her heart pounding, a dread feeling in the pit of her stomach.

She had been awake when a floorboard creaked outside her door a couple of hours earlier, and she'd cowered beneath the quilt when it had brought back memories of the nightmare. When whoever it was had passed and she heard them going downstairs, she had forced herself to calm down, reminding herself that she was safe and that it must be Rob or Suzie going down for a drink.

She had gone back to sleep after that, but voices drifting up from the kitchen a few minutes ago had roused her again, and she had slid out of bed and come out onto the landing to listen, worried that Rob and Suzie were arguing and he was going to hurt her again.

But it wasn't only them down there. She could hear two more voices, one of which sounded familiar, although she couldn't remember where she'd heard it before.

A low chuckle from below made every hair on Holly's body stand on end, and the blood in her veins turned to ice.

It was *him* – the man from her nightmare! He was real, and he'd come for her!

More terrified than she had ever been in her life, Holly edged back into the bedroom and snatched her phone off the bedside table. Then, nervously watching the stairs, she crept along the landing to Suzie's room and, carefully sliding the wardrobe door open, she slipped inside and hid at the back behind the long dresses before sliding the door shut again.

Covering her mouth with her hand when she heard an angry shout followed by a cry of pain, she fumbled with her phone, switching it to silent before making the call.

The phone rang once before clicking into voicemail.

'Mum?' she whispered, keeping an ear open for sounds of someone coming up the stairs. 'Mum, if you're there, pick up! The – the man's here . . . he's going to kill me! *Please*, Mum, I'm scared!'

40

Josie's phone hadn't been charged since the battery had died after she discharged herself from hospital, so she had plugged it in before climbing into bed. The slug of vodka she'd taken from the bottle had relaxed her and, aware that she needed to be clear-headed when she faced Holly if she was to stand any chance of persuading her to leave, she decided that she would allow herself one more little drink to wash the tramadol capsule down before going to sleep.

That had been her intention, but temptation had got the better of her and, before she knew it, she'd polished off two full glasses, neat, and had swallowed not one but both of the capsules.

Dead to the world now, she didn't hear the phone vibrating on her bedside table, and nor did she hear when it clicked to voicemail.

Across the road, shivering wildly in the wardrobe, Holly stared at her phone, willing her mum to call her back. When several minutes had passed with no response, a sob escaped her lips and she swiped at the tears that were cascading down her cheeks. Her mum didn't care about her. She'd gone and she wasn't coming back, and she'd blocked Holly's number to stop her from pestering her. How could she *do* that?

Downstairs, Dom was getting fed up, and he walked round behind Rob's chair and yanked his head back by the hair.

'I'll give you one last chance,' he growled. '*Why* were you looking for me?'

'I've al-already told you,' Rob spluttered as blood from his broken nose slid down his throat. 'I th-thought you were looking for J-Josie and Holly.'

'And I've already told *you* I don't know any Josies or Hollys,' Dom yelled, whacking him on the side of his head with the gun. 'So, let's start again . . .'

'I *swear*!' Rob cried. Then, switching his tearful gaze to Suzie, who had been ordered to sit on the other side of the table, he said, 'Tell him, Suze . . . tell him what Holly told you about – about Josie being on the run!'

Unable to believe what she had heard in the last few minutes, Suzie stared back at him with an unreadable expression in her eyes.

'Suzie, *please*,' he implored. 'They're gonna *kill* me!'

'I don't know what you're talking about,' she said quietly.

A loud bang and an agonized scream made Holly cover her ears, and she buried her face in her knees to keep from crying out. When it went quiet again, she tried to phone her mum again, but an automated voice informed her that she had insufficient credit. About to try and message her instead, she whimpered, '*Nooooo* . . .' when the *No Signal* notification appeared in the top left corner of the screen.

Next door, May Foster was having no such troubles with her phone. She'd been rudely woken by noises she was all too familiar with coming through the wall, and she was furious that her neighbour had let that man back into the house to abuse her all over again. The woman was clearly one of those idiots who thought they could change the men who beat them. The police ought to tell her that women who took their offending partners back time after time invariably ended up dead.

With that in mind, May, who had been sorely tempted to stay out of it this time and let the silly girl learn her lesson the hard way, dialled 999 – praying that the police hadn't put her name on a 'Timewaster' list because of her previous complaints.

41

Gee had fallen asleep on the sofa listening to music after taking a shower. Woken by the sound of a vehicle pulling up outside, and the heavy clunk of two doors opening and closing, he saw blue lights strobing the walls of his still-dark living room when he opened his eyes. A glance at his phone told him that it was 3.45 a.m., and he cursed under his breath when he sat up and saw that the spliff he'd been smoking had burned a hole in his dressing gown. Relieved that it hadn't done any more damage, he brushed the ash off himself as he wandered over to the window.

Two coppers were walking up Suzie's path and one of them started banging on the door while the other, shielding his hands with his eyes, peered through the living room window. Curious to know what was going on, because there were no lights on in the house, Gee rested his arms on the window ledge and relit the spliff.

Austin had opened Suzie's kitchen door a crack when the knocking had started. Quickly closing it again when he saw blue flashing lights through the glass panel of the front door, he hissed, 'It's the pigs,' as another volley of raps echoed around the hall.

Rob lifted his bloodied head at this and opened his mouth.

'Don't even think about it,' Dom warned, grabbing a tea towel off the counter and stuffing it into his mouth. Then, gesturing with the gun for Suzie to get up, he said, 'Go get rid of them.'

'Like this?' Suzie said, indicating her bare legs as she stood up.

'It's perfect,' Dom said. 'It'll make them think you just got out of bed. No stunts,' he warned, holding the gun to Rob's head.

Shivering, Suzie nodded and opened the kitchen door – almost falling through it when Austin came up behind her and pressed the tip of the knife he'd picked up off the table into her back.

'I'll be listening,' he whispered into her ear. 'So be very very careful what you say.'

'OK,' she gulped.

Austin followed her up the hallway and slipped into the shadows at the side of the door, and Suzie took a deep breath before opening it and peering out. Spencer and an officer who wasn't his usual colleague were standing on the step. She rubbed her eyes as if they'd woken her and gave them a questioning look.

'Sorry to get you up,' Spencer said. 'We had a report of a disturbance. Is everything OK?'

'Yeah, it's fine,' Suzie said, forcing a sleepy croak into her voice. 'I was sleeping.'

'We were told there was a lot of noise coming from in here,' the other officer said.

'Oh . . . it must have been the TV,' Suzie lied. 'I was watching a DVD when I fell asleep. *Die Hard*,' she elaborated, thinking of the loud action movie she and Rob had watched that afternoon. 'I must have rolled onto the remote and turned the volume up while I was sleeping. I, um, had a couple of drinks and a sleeping tablet,' she added, feigning sheepishness. 'Not been sleeping too well lately.'

Spencer was peering closely into her eyes. 'You sure you're OK?' he asked quietly.

Suzie's throat constricted when she realized he was giving her the opportunity to alert him if something was wrong. All it would have taken was a blink and he'd have understood, she was sure. But she couldn't risk it. Not only because Rob would get shot, but because Spencer and his colleague would probably get hurt as well. She knew they carried batons, but they weren't equipped to tackle criminals armed with guns.

'I'm absolutely fine,' she said, forcing a natural smile onto her lips. 'I'm sorry you were dragged over here at this time of night for nothing. You usually work days, don't you?'

'I alternate,' Spencer told her, seeming to buy her assurances. 'We'll let you get back to bed, then. Night.'

'Night,' Suzie murmured, the smile still on her lips.

The men walked away and Suzie closed the door, leaning her forehead against the wood when her legs almost gave way.

'Proper little actress, ain't we?' Austin grinned, pushing her back into the kitchen.

* * *

Gee watched as the coppers climbed into their car and turned off the blues before pulling away. Yawning, he pushed himself upright and was about to turn away when he caught a movement at Suzie's bedroom window.

'What the *fuck*?' he muttered, staring at the ghostly figure of Holly waving her arms, desperately trying to attract the police officers' attention. The car didn't stop and her head snapped round as if she'd heard something behind her, then she disappeared.

Shaking his head, unsure if he'd imagined it, Gee looked over again and knew he hadn't when he saw some of the vertical blinds swinging. Something was going on over there, and Holly must have called the police. But what could it be, and why had she looked so scared?

Determined to find out, he pulled on his jeans and a jumper and, grabbing his keys, let himself out of the flat.

Carol opened her door as he passed. 'Did you see what I just saw?' she asked, stepping out into the corridor.

'I think so,' he muttered.

'It was the girl from the first floor, wasn't it?' Carol asked, tugging the belt of her grubby dressing gown tighter around her belly as she pulled her door shut.

'Holly, yeah,' Gee said, walking on.

'What d'you think's going on?' Carol asked, falling into step beside him. 'Those coppers must have turned up for a reason, and she didn't look too happy when they drove off.'

'I know, I thought the same,' Gee said. 'I'm going to go over and see if everything's all right.'

Carol gave him a doubtful look. 'Not being funny, love, but that dark-haired copper's been paying blondie a lot of visits recently, and I've seen the way they smile at each other, like they're all pally pally, so I reckon she would have told him if something was up. Unless she *couldn't*.'

'What d'you mean?' Gee asked, frowning as they jogged down the stairs side by side.

'Her bloke moved back in the other day,' Carol said, pausing to catch her breath when they reached the first-floor landing. 'And he's got form for beating the shit out of her, so he's probably at it again. I bet the girl heard it and called the cops, and he forced blondie to tell them she was OK.'

'You reckon?' Gee gazed down at her.

'Happens all the time, love,' Carol said, something in her expression telling Gee that she might have been in the same predicament in the past.

'Shouldn't we call the police and tell them that?' Gee suggested.

'No point.' Carol shrugged. 'They won't come back now they've seen her and she's told them she's OK. We could ring the girl, though. See what *she's* saying.'

'Have you got her number?'

'No, but her mam will,' Carol said. 'I saw her sneaking in earlier, so she's deffo home. Come on . . .'

'You do know it's nearly four o'clock, don't you?' Gee asked as he reluctantly followed her to Holly's flat.

'She won't care,' Carol tossed back over her shoulder as she walked on, her slippers scuffing across the tiles. 'She's proper protective of her, so she'll want to know if summat's up. *I* would.'

She had reached the door by then, and Gee flinched when she jabbed her finger on the bell several times before rapping on the knocker.

'Keep it down,' he whispered, looking round. 'You'll have the whole block up at this rate.'

Ignoring him, Carol rang the bell again, then leaned down and yelled, 'Hellooo...' through the letterbox. 'Anyone home?'

About to ring the bell again, she hesitated at the sound of movement inside. Bolts were drawn back and, seconds later, a pale bruised face peered out at them.

'Sorry for waking you, love,' Carol said, wrinkling her nose at the stench of damp that drifted out. 'We think your girl might be in trouble.'

'She – she's in bed,' Josie said, confusion in her eyes.

'No, she's over the road,' Carol said, wondering if the girl had slipped over to see her friend while her mum was sleeping, as she'd seen her do many times after the woman left for work of an evening. 'Me and...' She paused and looked at Gee.

'Gee,' he said.

'Carol,' she replied. Then, back to Josie: 'Me and Gee both saw her at the window. The police was there and she looked proper scared.'

'What?' Josie's face scrunched up, as if she couldn't make head nor tail of what Carol was saying. 'But she's only a baby.'

Carol exchanged a hooded look with Gee. Then, turning back

to Josie, her tone gentler now, as if talking to somebody who was mentally impaired, she said, 'Let's go and give Holly a quick ring, eh? If she's OK, we can all go back to bed.'

'Who – who are you?' Josie asked, her movements jerky and uncoordinated as Carol guided her inside.

'This your room, is it?' Carol asked, ignoring the question as she ushered Josie inside the first bedroom. She sat her down on the bed and then picked up the phone that was sitting on the cabinet.

'Has *he* sent you?' Josie asked, eyeing her warily. 'She doesn't know anything . . . she was only a baby, she doesn't remember.'

'I'm sure she doesn't, and no one's sent me,' Carol said. 'I'm your neighbour, and I'm here to help. Here we go . . .' The screen had lit up, showing a missed call from Holly and a voice-mail notification. 'She tried to call you twenty minutes ago.'

Josie gazed blankly back at her, caught in the fog between sleep and consciousness. Recognizing the look, because she'd seen plenty of stoned people in her time, Carol lifted Josie's hand and touched her thumb to the screen to open it, then listened to the message Holly had left.

'Who – who are you?' Josie asked, blinking as if struggling to focus her mind.

'A friend,' Carol said, frowning as she replayed the message a second time. The girl had said that a man was going to kill her, and that, added to this woman asking if *he'd* sent her, had set off an alarm bell in her mind. Telling Josie to stay there, she went back out into the corridor and played the message to Gee.

'Christ, she sounds terrified,' he said. 'I really think we should call the police.'

'Even if they come back, they'll take their time about it,' Carol said, then added quietly: 'Besides, her mam's clearly not the full shilling, and it could be hereditary, for all we know.'

'Holly seems pretty normal to me,' Gee said. 'And you saw her face. She was genuinely scared.'

'OK, let's call her back and ask her what's going on,' Carol suggested. 'Then if we still think we need to call the cops, I'll do it.'

Gee nodded and watched as Carol returned the call.

'It's gone straight to voicemail,' she said. 'That usually means the battery's died, or she's got no signal.'

Behind them, Josie had wandered out of her room and was calling for Holly, telling her that she needed to pack. Giving Gee a loaded look, as if to say *Does this look normal to you?*, Carol went inside and guided the woman back into the bedroom.

'It's all right, lovie,' she said in a sing-song voice. 'You're dreaming, so let's get you back into bed. And how's about we have a little drink to send you back to beddybyes?' she went on, twisting the lid off the bottle of vodka and tipping the last couple of inches into the empty glass. 'Here we go . . .' She placed the glass in Josie's hand and guided it towards her lips.

Josie spluttered when the liquid entered her mouth, but she swallowed it all.

'There's a good girl,' Carol crooned, taking the empty glass from her before pushing her gently down on the bed. 'Now close your eyes . . . there we go.'

'Is she all right?' Gee asked worriedly when Carol came back out into the corridor a few minutes later.

'She was rambling on about murderers coming to get them, and how *she* must have told him where they were,' Carol said. 'I gave her a drink to relax her, and she's flat out now.'

'Are you sure that's safe?' Gee frowned. 'She's not long out of hospital and she's probably on painkillers.'

'I reckon she can handle it, judging by the amount of empties on the floor,' Carol replied unconcernedly. 'Anyhow, shush while I call my lads.'

'Why you calling them and not the police?'

''Cos I need to find out what's going on before I waste their time. If you want to make yourself useful, go take a look out of the window and see if anything's happening over there.'

Carol flapped a dismissive hand at him, and Gee sighed as he went into the flat to do as she'd ordered. She had taken over and was clearly determined to do things her way, and he was annoyed with himself for going along with it instead of heading over to Suzie's place, as he'd intended – or calling the police, who would surely be here by now if they'd done it when he first suggested it. He wasn't overly happy about the way she'd dealt with Holly's mum, either. The woman was in a bad way, and he didn't approve of Carol encouraging her to drink. But it was done now, so he supposed there was no use arguing about it.

WITNESS

The living room was dark, but the curtains were open and a hint of moonlight was shining through the window, so he managed to avoid crashing into any of the furniture. There were still no lights on at Suzie's place, and he didn't see any movement at any of the windows, so he headed back out to Carol, at the exact moment her call was answered.

'About time!' she said. 'Get your arses over here. Come the back way and fetch your tools. And hurry up.'

Turning to Gee when she'd hung up, she said, 'They only live a few blocks away, so they'll be here in a minute. Let's go down and wait for them.'

Gee followed her down the stairs into the foyer. A couple of minutes later they heard a tap on the fire exit door, and four strapping lads with sleep-blurred eyes and messy hair squeezed inside when Carol pushed the bar down.

'Told you they'd be quick,' she said proudly to Gee.

'What's going on, Ma?' one of the lads asked, staring at Gee. 'He giving you trouble?'

Alarmed when the lad moved his jacket aside to reveal the grip of a handgun sticking out from the waistband of his jeans, Gee held his hands out in front of him and took a step back.

'Behave!' Carol barked, slapping her son's arm. 'He's me neighbour.'

'So what d'you call us round for?' one of the others asked, wiping sleep-crust from the corner of his eye. 'You made it sound like an emergency.'

'It is,' said Carol. 'A girl who lives on the first floor is in

357

trouble. We're not sure what's going on yet, 'cos her mum's not all there and she wasn't making a lot of sense. But she was going on about someone trying to kill them, and the girl left her a voicemail telling her the man was there.'

'What man? Where?'

'The girl's at a woman's house across the road,' Carol explained. 'Her mam got attacked in the alley the other night and took to hospital.'

'I saw that,' one of her sons said. 'Not the attack, obviously, or I'd have cut the fucker's head off, but the Five-O and the ambulances and that.'

'Can I finish?' Carol gave him an impatient look. Continuing when the lad nodded, she said, 'The girl went over to stay with the woman across the road, and me and Gee both saw her at the bedroom window. The cops were there and she was waving at them, but they didn't notice. She looked proper scared, so me and Gee went to talk to her mam. Only she's a bit loopy loo, so I took her phone to call the girl, and that's when I heard the message saying the man was there and he was going to kill her.'

'Have you called the police?' the son with the gun asked, earning himself a nod of approval from Gee. He was taller than the others and looked a little older, and was clearly the brains of the outfit.

'No, I figured we'd be better off finding out what's going on first,' said Carol. 'That's why I called you.'

'Let's go, then,' another of her sons said, sliding a Samurai sword out from under his coat.

'Whoa,' Gee muttered, unnerved by the sight of it.

'Put it away,' the older one snapped. 'We don't know if anyone's there yet.'

'I think I should go and take a look round the back,' Gee said. 'It's all dark at the front, so if anyone is there they must be in the kitchen or back bedroom.'

'Good idea,' the lad said. 'But it's probably best if you go out the fire door and cut down the side of the car park, just in case.'

At the mention of the car park, Gee remembered the BMW, and said, 'I passed a Beemer with blacked-out windows on my way home from work tonight. It was parked up outside the old church and I thought it was a bit suss, but now I'm wondering if that's got something to do with this.'

'Was anyone in it?'

'Two blokes in the front, but there could have been more in the back.'

'Black or white?'

'I didn't get a good enough look,' Gee said, frowning. 'But what difference does that make?'

'Chill, mate, we ain't racists,' the lad replied. 'But the only white guys who drive Beemers round these ends are under-cover cops, and we don't wanna be getting gripped while we're tooled up.'

'Fair point,' Gee said sheepishly. 'Sorry.'

'Right, Davy and Ben go with Gee,' Carol said, resuming control. 'Steve and Pete can stop here with me and keep an eye on the front of the house. If youse see owt dodgy going on, I don't want no heroics,' she added firmly. 'Come back here and we'll decide what to do.'

Nodding his agreement, Gee followed Carol's sons out through the fire exit door.

42

Dom Cooper was frowning as he circled the chair Rob was tied to, which he and Austin had dragged out into the middle of the kitchen floor to give them more room. Harry Cox's call had taken him by surprise, and it had pissed him off to hear that some random dickhead ex-cellmate of the old man had been asking about him, trying to get his name. Harry had told him that the guy had been talking about Devon Prince and his bird, and how he'd claimed to have information about some woman and her daughter which he'd seemed convinced Dom might be willing to pay for.

The names Josie and Holly had rung no bells for Dom, so when Harry had told him that the only ones *he* knew by those names were a mother and daughter who had lived near to Devon's bird, and that the kid had died of an overdose five weeks before they were shot, he had assumed that the bloke had mentioned their names in order to make it look like he knew something.

Whatever the reason, it was thirteen years since Dom had

killed that pair, and only a few people in his inner circle knew about it to this day. Infuriated to think that one of his trusted soldiers had betrayed him and given this cheeky cunt ammunition to blackmail him, he had decided to pay the man a visit and find out exactly what he knew and who had told him before shutting him up for good.

So far, all the bloke had done was prattle on about Josie and Holly, and how he would tell Dom where they lived if Dom promised not to hurt him. For some reason Dom couldn't fathom, the man seemed to think that Dom had been in some kind of relationship with this Josie bird, and that she and her kid had spent the last thirteen years in hiding, terrified that he was going to kill them. He had no clue what that was about, but it was pissing him off that the dude still wouldn't give up the name of the traitor in Dom's crew, despite the kicking he'd already received. If Dom didn't know better, he'd think that the man genuinely didn't know. But there was no way he could have stumbled on this by chance. *Somebody* had pointed him in Dom's direction, and Dom wasn't leaving until he found out who it was.

'I'm getting tired,' he said, picking up the knife Austin had placed back on the table after escorting Suzie out to speak to the police. Moving round behind Rob, whose face was a bloody mess and whose breath sounded crackly as blood congealed in his throat, he ran the blunt side of the knife slowly across his neck. 'I'm giving you one last chance,' he said when the man stiffened. 'Give me the name.'

'I d-don't know,' Rob whimpered. 'I swear . . .'

Across the room, her face deathly white, the dark shadows surrounding her eyes, Suzie moaned, 'For God's sake! You can see he's telling the truth, so why are you doing this?'

'Oh, are we friends with him again?' Dom looked at her and raised an eyebrow. 'Only I got the distinct impression you weren't too happy with him when he told me about that bird and her kid.'

'They've got nothing to do with this,' Suzie murmured, so tired she could barely make sense of what was happening. 'You said you've never heard of them, so how could they be involved? Whoever this Harry person is who sent you here, he must have got it wrong.'

'Well, we know *someone's* talking shit,' Dom replied smoothly. 'But your man here still hasn't told me what I need to know, so . . .'

He turned the knife round and pressed the sharp edge of the blade onto Rob's neck.

'Don't!' Suzie cried, tears welling in her eyes when she saw blood trickle down Rob's chest. 'Please! He's telling the truth.'

'Last chance,' Dom said quietly to Rob as he increased the pressure. 'Tell me who told you, or I'm gonna slit your throat. And then I'll slit hers,' he added, looking over at Suzie. 'After I've had a bit of fun with her.'

'Harry . . .' Rob gurgled. 'It – it was Harry.'

'What was?'

'He – he told me about you,' Rob lied, feeling no conscience about dropping the old bastard in it if it saved his and Suzie's lives. Harry hadn't given a shit about him when he'd sent these men round to kill him.

'I told you that old cunt couldn't be trusted,' Austin muttered.

'Why would Harry tell *you* about me?' Dom asked Rob.

'It was when we – when we were in the Strange,' Rob spluttered, terrified to move his head in case the knife went in any deeper. 'He was bragging about knowing people who got away with murder. You've got to be tough to survive in there, and he – he used your name to scare them into leaving him alone. He made out like you were mates; said you'd come after anyone who touched him.'

'Why didn't you tell me this at the start?' Dom asked.

'I – I'm not a grass,' Rob croaked. 'And I thought he was my friend.'

'And you seriously expect me to believe that?' Dom sneered.

'It's true, I swear,' Rob insisted. 'It was three years ago and I'd forgotten about it till Harry rang me yesterday and asked to meet up. You can check my phone if you don't believe me. He withheld his number, but he sent me a text straight after with the address of the pub.'

'Why did he want to meet you?' Austin asked from the other side of the room.

'He – he wouldn't tell me over the phone,' Rob said. 'But when I got there, he said he was going to blackmail you.' He glanced up at Dom whose dark eyes were unreadable. 'He said he couldn't risk doing it himself 'cos too many people know him, so he – he needed someone from out of the area to do it. I said I didn't want to do it, so he brought me home and told me to keep my mouth shut.'

'So why did he give me your name and address?' Dom asked.

'I don't *know*,' Rob whimpered, tears trickling from his swollen eyes when it dawned on him that he'd probably just signed his own death warrant.

'Isn't it obvious?' Suzie piped up. 'He was covering his own back. He must have realized he'd made a mistake telling Rob his plan, and he sent you after him, hoping you'd kill him before he had the chance to tell you what was really going on.'

Rob almost stopped breathing when Dom narrowed his eyes thoughtfully. He could see that the man thought Suzie's explanation was feasible, and he silently prayed that it would be enough to save his life.

'Even if that's true, it still leaves us with a problem,' Dom said. 'You both know too much.'

'We won't say anything,' Suzie said sincerely. 'You have my word.'

Dom looked at her and gave a rueful smile. 'Sorry, darlin', but I can't take that risk.'

43

Gee, Davy and Ben had crept round the side of the car park and were now on the road at the side of the terraced row in which Suzie lived. Heading for the alleyway, Gee had decided to check if the BMW was still parked where he'd seen it earlier. Gesturing for the others to wait there in case the men inside were undercover cops, he pulled up his hood and headed over the road to the old church. If he found the men inside the car, he would tell them that he'd decided to check them out because he'd been concerned that they might be gang members waiting to start another war. It was a pretty flimsy excuse, but he would stick to it if confronted.

The car was empty when he reached it, and the doors were locked. Peering through the tinted glass of the passenger-side window, he saw a half-smoked spliff lying on the centre console and a partially full bottle of Jack Daniels in the foot-well, along with a mess of fast-food wrappers. Certain that the blokes he had seen couldn't be police, he gave a high, thin whistle.

''S up?' Davy, the eldest of Carol's sons asked when he and his brother Ben ran over.

'They're not cops,' Gees said, gesturing for them to look through the window.

'And they ain't from this estate, so they've got no business being here,' Davy said, pulling a lethal-looking flick knife out of his pocket and plunging the blade into the tyre.

'What you doing?' Gee hissed, watching in horror as Ben repeated the action on the other tyres.

'Like I said, they ain't from round here,' said Davy. 'And if they've got anything to do with what's going on at that house, this'll stop them getting away in a hurry.'

Hoping that he was right and the vehicle wasn't the property of an innocent developer, Gee looked nervously around to make sure no one had spotted them.

'Come on,' Davy said when he'd finished. 'Let's go see what's what.'

A mile away, sitting in their squad car outside McDonald's, finishing the burgers they'd bought from the drive-through, Dan Spencer crumpled his wrapper and, lowering his window, tossed it into the bin.

'You still thinking about that bird?' his colleague, PC Neil Hayes, asked, slotting the last piece of his own burger into his mouth.

'Yeah.' Spencer nodded.

'You and her got some kind of history?' Hayes asked, wiping mayonnaise off his chin.

'Not in *that* way,' Spencer said, guessing what the other man was thinking. 'Me and Jack have attended a few call-outs there.'

'Oh, yeah? What kind?' Hayes asked, chucking his own wrapper over the roof of the car and missing the bin. 'Make a habit of disturbing her neighbours, does she?'

'Not her, her boyfriend,' Spencer said. 'Or should I say *ex*, 'cos last time I saw her, she said she hadn't seen him in a while.'

'So what you thinking?' Hayes peered at him and hooked a piece of bread out of his teeth with a fingernail.

'I don't know,' Spencer said quietly. 'I've just got a feeling.'

'I bet you have.' Hayes grinned. 'I got quite a feeling myself when she answered the door dressed like that. Good-looking bird.'

Spencer frowned, irritated by the way the man was talking. But he couldn't blame him, he supposed. Suzie *was* pretty hot, and with only a pyjama top on tonight, her slim legs going on for ever, he'd had to force himself not to stare.

'Fancy a fag?' Hayes asked.

'No.' Spencer shook his head and started the engine. 'Something's bugging me. I think we should go back and make sure she's OK.'

'Mate, it's nearly an hour since we were there, so she'll be sleeping by now,' Hayes said. 'And we haven't had any more complaints from the woman next door, so surely you're not thinking of knocking her up again?'

'We'll just do a slow drive past,' Spencer said, reversing out of the spot.

'My man's got it bad,' Hayes teased, grinning as he clicked his seat belt into position.

Ignoring him, Spencer pulled out onto the deserted road.

'Any word from your brothers?' Carol asked, peering out through the glass in the door.

'Not yet,' her son Steve said, checking his phone. 'Want me to bell him?'

'No, they'll ring if they've got something to tell us,' she said. 'Anyone got fags?'

Steve tossed a cigarette to her and another to his brother before lighting his own.

Squinting as she sucked on it, Carol suddenly froze. 'It's her,' she said.

'Who?' Steve asked.

'The girl I was telling you about,' Carol said, quickly stubbing the cigarette out and stuffing it into her dressing gown pocket.

'Ma, what you doing?' both lads asked when she pushed the door open.

'Come with me,' she said, pulling the dressing gown tighter around herself before lurching outside.

Holly had been hiding for what felt like hours in the wardrobe. A man had come into the room and looked around a short time ago, and she'd almost pissed herself in fear when he had slid the wardrobe door open. Her heart had been pounding so hard in her chest she had thought she was going to pass out when he pushed his hand through the clothes on the hangers, but there were so many of them squeezed inside he hadn't spotted her cowering in the shadows behind.

She'd started breathing again when she heard him go back down the stairs, and when she had heard the kitchen door click shut she'd decided to risk climbing out and taking her phone over to the window to see if she could get a signal. The voices coming up from downstairs had been a lot quieter since the police called round, and she had begun to wonder if she had got it all wrong and they were actually friends of Suzie and Rob, that the screams she'd heard had come from a film they were all watching.

What about that laugh – the one from your nightmare? a voice had piped up inside her head. *You didn't imagine that, did you?*

Shuddering again at the memory, she peered out through the window and stared over at the flats. She'd thought her mum must have heard her voicemail when the police came round, but there were no lights on at the flat so she realized someone else must have called them.

A movement below the window caught her eye and a little cry of fear escaped her lips when she looked down and saw two men she'd never seen before staring up at her. Thinking that it must be the men from downstairs, that they had caught her, she was confused when she noticed her nosy neighbour, Carol, standing between them. Was this something to do with her? Had she sent someone round to beat Rob and Suzie up because of the argument she'd had with Suzie?

WITNESS

Carol was gesturing to her, and it took a few seconds before Holly understood that she was telling her to open the window. Terrified that it was a trick and the others were going to come up behind her and push her out, she bit down on her hand and twisted her head to look at the door before glancing back to Carol. The woman gestured again and, at last, Holly moved.

'Is someone in the house?' Carol whispered when the window was open. 'Are you in danger?'

Holly nodded and her eyes darted behind her again.

'How many?' Carol asked.

Holly mouthed *I don't know.*

'OK, climb out and drop down,' Carol hissed. 'My lads will catch you, I promise.'

Holly shook her head, terror flaring in her eyes at the thought of falling to her death.

'You can do it,' Carol cajoled. 'Come on, love, your mam's waiting for you and I promised I'd fetch you home to her.'

Holly's heart lurched in her chest. If her mum was home, why hadn't she answered her phone? And why were there no lights on?

Down below, one of the lads was showing his phone to Carol, and the woman's eyes widened when she saw whatever was on the screen. Looking up at Holly again, there was an urgency in her voice when she hissed, 'You need to jump right now! I'm not messing about love, just *do* it!'

44

'What was that?' Austin hissed, snapping his head round when he heard a noise outside the back door. 'Someone's out there.'

'Go check,' Dom ordered, still holding the knife to Rob's throat, his hand on the gun he'd stuffed into his waistband.

Gripping the baseball bat firmly between both hands, Austin edged towards the door. He'd almost reached it when he heard a muted thud, and he cried out in pain when the lock exploded inwards and blood seeped through his jeans.

'I've been shot!' he yelped, dropping the bat and clutching at his leg. 'I've been fuckin' shot!'

Three men rushed in, one of them brandishing a Samurai sword, another pointing a gun with a crude silencer attached to its nozzle at Dom.

'Drop it or I'll blow your fuckin' head off!' Davy said when he saw Dom's piece.

Dom gave a slow smile and dropped the gun before raising his hands.

'And the knife,' Davy barked.

'We cool,' Dom drawled, doing as he'd been told. 'No need to panic.'

'We ain't panicking, mate,' Davy replied coolly, gesturing for him to move away from the chair on which Rob was slumped.

'It's just business,' Dom said, moving slowly back. 'Nutt'n for anyone to get upset about.'

'They were going to kill us,' Suzie cried.

'It's over,' Gee said, eyeing Dom and Austin and praying that they didn't have any more weapons concealed anywhere as he loosened the rope that was binding her hands together behind her back and her ankles to the chair legs.

Out front, Holly was dangling out of the bedroom window as Carol's sons held out their arms to catch her.

'Let go!' Carol yelled at her, no longer bothering to be quiet in her urgency to get her away from the house since she'd seen the text Steve had sent to one of his brothers telling them that they were going in.

Holly squeezed her eyes shut and let go, squealing with fear as she plummeted towards the ground.

At the exact moment she landed in the arms of one of Carol's sons, a car turned the corner, its headlights illuminating their faces.

'Let me do the talking,' Carol hissed when she saw that it was a police car. 'Take her to mine. And warn your brothers!' she added, shoving her keys into Steve's hand and pushing them out onto the pavement.

'Stay where you are!' one of the two coppers who had jumped out of the car yelled as Carol's sons ran across the road with Holly.

'It's not them, they're my sons!' Carol hissed, rushing towards them. 'The ones you want are in there, and they're armed!' She pointed back at the house.

In the kitchen, Davy had received a call from his brother Pete. Still aiming the gun at Dom, he said, 'The pigs are outside and they're calling for armed backup. We need to get moving.'

Reacting instinctively when Dom lurched forward as if to make for the open door, Davy smashed the gun into the side of his head, sending him sprawling, blood pouring from a cut at his temple.

'I didn't mean you, dickhead,' he spat, grabbing a piece of the rope Gee had taken from around Suzie's ankles and quickly tying Dom's hands together behind his back while Ben did the same to Austin, who was crying out in pain.

'Go!' Gee urged at the sound of approaching sirens. 'I'll tell them it was just me here.'

'Don't you wanna come with us?' Davy asked.

'No.' Gee shook his head. 'I wanna make sure these two don't escape.'

Nodding, Davy pushed his brother out through the back door and they were quickly swallowed up by the darkness.

'Let me go, man,' Austin begged Gee as the sirens grew louder. 'My missus is due any day. It's our first kid and I need to be with her.'

'Should've thought about that before you broke in and terrorized this man and *his* missus,' Gee said.

'Don't do this, brother,' Dom said quietly, looking up at Gee from the floor. 'I can pay you *nuff* money, blood. You'll never need to work a day in your life.'

'I ain't your brother,' Gee said, staring down at him. 'And I don't want your dirty money.'

Dom hawked up phlegm in his throat and spat at Gee's feet. 'You is a dead man!' he snarled. 'Yuh hear me? You is *dead*!'

Outside, several vehicles screeched to a halt, their sirens deafening in the confines of the tiny kitchen.

'*ARMED POLICE!*' someone yelled at the front of the house, followed by a boom and the sound of wood splintering.

At the same time, the back gate flew open and the shout of '*ARMED POLICE!*' went up again as several dark figures rushed across the grass.

'It wasn't him!' Suzie cried when one of the armed men ran in and aimed a gun at Gee who was standing beside her.

'On the floor!' the man ordered. 'Both of you! Get down!'

The front door crashed into the wall as Gee and Suzie lay down on the floor with their hands raised.

'In here!' one of the officers yelled, his gun trained on Dom. 'Two restrained, one wounded, we need an ambulance ASAP!'

45

Carol's sons had taken Holly up to their mother's flat, and Steve had quickly stashed their weapons under her bed before doing a quick sweep of the living room to remove any traces of her weed and rolling paraphernalia.

Sitting on the sofa on either side of Holly, who was shivering despite the jacket one of them had placed around her shoulders, both lads nodded respectfully at the four coppers, two of whom were female, who walked in with their mum a short time later.

'Has she been seen by the paramedics?' Spencer asked, noting how pale and disoriented Holly looked. 'She's probably in shock.'

'You're the first ones who've come up since we got here,' Steve told him, standing up.

As one of the female officers spoke into her radio, requesting medics to come up to the flat, the other sat in Steve's vacated place, and said, 'Holly, my name's Annabel, and I'd like to talk to you about what's just happened, if that's all right?'

Holly's body jerked as if she'd been electrocuted and her eyes widened alarmingly.

'It's OK, love,' Carol said, waving for her other son to move so she could sit next to the girl. 'I'm here; you're not on your own.' Holding Holly's hand when she started to hyperventilate, she said, 'Just take a nice deep breath, sweetheart. In . . .' She inhaled deeply through her own nose to demonstrate. 'Then out . . .' she exhaled through her mouth. 'In . . . out . . .'

'Where are her parents?' one of the female officers asked.

'Her mum's sleeping,' Carol said, still demonstrating the breathing technique to Holly. 'She got attacked a few days back, and she's in a pretty bad way, so I thought I'd best leave her till we knew what was going on.'

'She's home?' Spencer asked.

'Yeah, came back last night,' Carol told him.

'My mum's dead!' Holly gasped, a stricken expression on her deathly white face. 'That – that man killed her!'

'No, she's not, love, she's safe in her bed,' Carol reassured her.

'Not that mum,' Holly wailed. 'My *real* mum. Anna.'

Questioning looks passed between the adults in the room.

'You're confused, love,' Carol said softly, stroking Holly's face. 'I promise you your mum's fine. I was with her not long ago. She's still poorly, but she's in bed.'

'*Noooo* . . .' Holly shook her head, tears brimming in her eyes and spilling down her cheeks. 'He killed her. He – he shot her.'

'I think someone had best go and get her mum to calm her down,' Spencer said when Holly started gasping for breath again.

'It's OK, we've got her,' Suzie said, walking into the room with Gee and a dazed-looking Josie.

'She must have woke up after youse came up here,' Gee explained quietly as they led Josie to an armchair. 'She was swaying at the top of the stairs when we came in after talking to the pigs. Sorry, *police officers*,' he corrected himself, remembering that there were four uniforms in the room.

'Don't worry, it's better than some of the shit we get called,' Hayes quipped.

'Ms Evans, are you all right?' Spencer asked, peering at her and wondering if she, too, had gone into shock after hearing of her daughter's ordeal.

'I think she's had strong meds,' Carol whispered. 'Looked proper out of it when me and Gee went to hers earlier.'

Nodding, Spencer squatted down in front of Holly, and said, 'Your mum's here now, Holly. Take deep breaths like the lady showed you . . .'

'She – she's not my mum!' Holly squawked, her eyes bulging. 'She's not my . . . *mum!*'

'OK, love, calm down,' Carol urged.

'She's right,' Josie said quietly.

'What?' All heads turned in her direction.

'She's right,' Josie repeated, the dazed look in her tearful eyes replaced by a look of sheer resignation. 'I'm not her mum. And her name's not Holly, it's Charlotte . . .'

Epilogue

Holly sat stiffly on the couch in the family liaison officer's office at the station. Suzie was sitting beside her, and they were waiting for Holly's case worker to arrive.

'Are you feeling OK, hon?' Suzie asked, touching her hand.

Holly nodded and forced a tiny smile, but it was a lie. She wasn't all right, and doubted she ever would be again. Her entire life had been turned upside down in the two months since Dominic Cooper had broken in to Suzie's house. The nightmares had already formed a crack in the wall she had built to protect herself from the traumatic memories, but the sound of Cooper's deep voice and sinister laugh had split it wide open – although she hadn't known why at the time. That was a blessing, because she would have been paralysed with fear and incapable of climbing out of the window if she had known she was listening to the voice of the cold-blooded killer who had murdered her mother. It wasn't until later, when she'd been taken to Carol's flat and the policewoman had said that her name was Annabel, that the wall had completely crumbled and she'd remembered everything.

The office door opened and Suzie squeezed Holly's hand when Vicky, the plump, kindly liaison officer who had been assigned to Holly's case, walked in.

'Sorry I took so long,' she apologized. 'Jenny will be with us in a sec; she's just getting coffees.'

No sooner had the words left Vicky's mouth than the door opened again, and Jenny, Holly's temporary social worker, came in carrying four lidded disposable cups between her slim hands.

'OK, let's get started,' Vicky said, sitting on one of the two chairs facing the couch while Jenny perched on the other. 'We've already talked you through the process, Charlotte, but we need to make sure you're ready to do this. We can postpone if you're not. It's totally up to you.'

'Please don't call me that,' Holly murmured, unable to get used to the name, even though she knew it was the one her real mother had chosen for her. She also couldn't get her head around the fact that she was actually seventeen and not fifteen, as she'd believed.

'Do you need more time?' Jenny asked, reaching for one of the cups. 'Or do you have any questions you need us to answer before you make a decision? Any concerns?'

Holly shook her head, but her eyes were downcast and it was obvious to the three women in the room that she was uncertain about something.

Clearing her throat, Suzie said, 'Can I ask . . . I know Holly's been staying with me since her mum – *Josie* – was arrested, but will this mean she has to leave right away? Only I'm happy to let her stay as long as she wants to.'

'That's her decision.' Vicky smiled.

'Is that what you want?' Jenny asked Holly.

Holly chewed her lip and gave a tiny shrug. She didn't know *what* she wanted yet, and a tiny part of her still longed to go back to how it had been before.

'Well, we can sort all that out later,' Vicky said. 'They're waiting in the next room, so when you're ready, let us know.'

Holly took a deep breath, then nodded.

'Are you sure?' Suzie asked quietly. 'This is huge, so you don't need to rush.'

'I'm ready,' Holly said.

Vicky got up and left the room, and Jenny sat forward and peered at Holly across the table.

'Try not to worry if you don't feel an instant connection,' she said. 'These things take time.'

'I know,' Holly said, chewing nervously on her thumbnail.

The door opened and Vicky appeared.

'Holly, this is Colin,' she said, holding her hand out to indicate the man who was hovering beside her.

'Hello, love,' the man said, taking a hesitant step into the room. 'It's so good to see you again. I – I looked for you.'

Holly slowly lifted her eyes and stared at Colin Haywood: the man who DNA tests had proved was Charlotte Hughes's biological father. He looked nothing like she'd imagined. In her fantasies he had been tall and movie-star handsome, with a thick head of hair and sparkling eyes, but this man looked quite ordinary, with a paunchy belly and receding blond hair. She could tell he was nervous by the way his eyes were swivelling and the tip of his tongue kept darting out from between his thin lips. She wondered if he was looking at her with the same disappointment as she was looking at him. Maybe he'd thought she would be gorgeous and he could proudly show her off to his mates. *Look at my stunning daughter* . . .

'Alison, my, um, wife is looking forward to meeting you,' Colin said. 'And the kids are, too,' he added. 'I know they're not your biological siblings, but—'

'How long have you been with her?' Holly interrupted.

Colin smiled and took another step forward, seeming relieved that she was responding to him after being warned by the liaison officer that it might take a while.

'Fourteen years this September,' he said, perching on the chair that Vicky had pulled out from under the desk for him and clasping his hands together between his knees. 'The kids, Jack and Livvy, are twins.'

'How old?' Holly asked.

'Fifteen.' Colin grinned. 'They're a right pair; always up to some trick or other. You'll fit in great, and we've already arranged to put a bed in Livvy's room for you.'

Holly continued to stare at him for several more seconds in silence, and Colin carried on grinning as if he thought he'd done a good job of winning her over. Then, snapping her gaze off him, Holly looked at Suzie, and said, 'Can we go home now?'

'Of course,' Suzie said, flicking a concerned look at Vicky.

'Colin, could I ask you to step out for a moment?' Vicky said, standing up and waving him towards the door.

'Oh, yeah, sure,' he said, his grin slipping as he got up. Hesitating, he said, 'Have I said something wrong, Charlotte?'

'Don't call me that,' she spat. 'My name's Holly.'

'Well, I know, but it's not really, though, is it?' Colin blustered. 'I mean, it's not the name we—'

'I said . . . my name . . . is *Holly*,' she repeated slowly, a fierce edge to her voice. 'And if you're so happy to see me now,' she went on coldly, 'if you've been "looking for me",' she made quote-marks in the air with her fingers, 'where were you all those times Anna and Devon got raided and I was sent to live with strangers? And why was there no mention of you trying to find me when I disappeared after they were murdered?'

'Of course I tried to find you,' Colin protested, his cheeks flaming. 'Everyone was looking.'

'You know I checked you out on Facebook the other week, don't you?' Holly replied smoothly. 'Before they tracked you down.'

'I don't understand.' Colin looked confused. 'What does that mean?'

'You've got an open page,' Holly elaborated. 'Which means I could see all your posts going back years. *Thirteen* years, to be specific. And there was no mention of me whatsoever.'

'Well, obviously that's not the sort of thing you'd post on

there,' Colin said. 'It was an upsetting time, and I'm a very private person when it comes to that sort of stuff.'

'Really?' Holly raised an eyebrow. 'If it was so upsetting for you, how come you were on there the whole time I was missing, posting pictures of *your* twins and gushing about them?'

'They were babies,' Colin protested. 'Of course I was going to talk about them.'

'But not about your *real* baby,' Holly shot back. 'The one you abandoned and never bothered with again, not even when social services contacted you to tell you I'd been placed in temporary care over and over again?'

'That's not true,' Colin spluttered. 'You've got to believe me, Charlotte, I—'

'Stop *calling* me that!' Holly yelled. 'And stop lying, 'cos I've seen the social worker's reports. They were concerned about my welfare for a long time before my mum – *Anna* – got shot, but you didn't give a toss. They asked you to take me, but you told them you had to put your *wife* and *her* kids first; that you already had your hands full and didn't need the extra responsibility.'

'Char— *Holly* – listen,' Colin held up his hands. 'It was a long time ago, and your mother was involved with some very dodgy people.'

'You know what, I don't even care,' Holly said dismissively. 'You're nothing to me, and you never will be. So, go on . . . get back to your wife and kids and forget you ever met me, 'cos I'm sure as hell going to forget *you*.'

* * *

Half an hour later, when they had finished talking to Vicky and Jenny, Holly and Suzie headed outside. Pausing to light a cigarette, Suzie blew her smoke into the air and peered at her friend.

'How you feeling, hon?'

'Better,' said Holly. 'I've been dreading this for weeks, wondering if he'd even bother to show up. I could tell he only did it because it's hit the news and he thought he'd better do the right thing. But it was way too little too late.'

'Well, I think you handled it really well,' Suzie said, hugging her. 'Remember when we first met and I said I was surprised you were only fifteen because you're mature? Now we know why, eh?'

'I guess so.' Holly smiled. 'Still feels weird knowing I'm seventeen and I can do whatever I want.'

'And what *do* you want to do?' Suzie asked. 'Because I meant it when I said you can stay with me.'

'I know, and thanks,' Holly said gratefully. 'I don't know what I would have done without you these past few weeks.'

'We're friends, and I'll always be there for you,' said Suzie. 'Speaking of which, have you got back to Bex yet?'

'I spoke to her last night; told her to call round after school today – if that's OK?'

'Course it is,' Suzie said, linking arms with her as they set off for the bus stop. 'Subject of school, are you still going to go in and sit your exams next week?'

'Yeah, definitely.' Holly nodded. 'I know I don't have to, but I might as well try to get some qualifications. That was the thing my mum was always worried about: me leaving with nothing and having to take shit jobs like her.'

'At least she got that right,' Suzie said softly.

'She got a *lot* right,' Holly countered. 'When she snatched me that night she was off her head with grief and guilt after losing her baby, and she convinced herself that I was Holly. She could have handed me back when she came to her senses, but she genuinely thought Dominic Cooper had seen me and would kill me if he found out where I was. That's why she did what she did: to protect me from him. And that's why,' she added, '*I'm* going to look after *her* when she comes out of prison.'

Suzie smiled and squeezed her arm. 'She's a lucky woman having a daughter like you.'

'And I'm lucky to have a mum like her,' Holly said.

Arriving back on the estate a short time later, Holly smiled when she saw Gee, Carol and Carol's four sons – Davy, Ben, Steve and Pete – waiting outside Suzie's house.

'Hey, how did it go?' Carol asked, rushing to her and giving her a hug.

'Horrible, but I said what I needed to say, so it's all good.' Holly smiled.

'She was brilliant,' Suzie said, unlocking her front door. 'Anyone fancy a brew?'

'I'd prefer a glass of this,' Gee said, grinning as he produced a bottle of Prosecco from behind his back.

'Me too,' Holly beamed. '*What* . . . ?' She held out her hands when Carol raised an eyebrow. 'I'm old enough.'

'Suzie . . .'

Turning her head when she heard the call, Suzie groaned, and said, 'What now?' when she saw Rob running towards them, his face still bearing faint bruises from the savage beating he'd received from Dominic and Austin.

'Can we talk?' Rob asked when he reached them, flicking a hooded glance at Holly and the others, as he added, 'In private.'

'I've got nothing to say to you,' Suzie said coolly. 'I gave you a chance and you betrayed me.'

'I didn't,' he argued. 'It was Holly he was after, not you, so I knew you'd be safe.'

'You're so full of shit,' Suzie sneered. 'He wasn't after Holly at all. He didn't even know who she was until *you* stuck your nose in, trying to get rid of her and make some money. You make me sick.'

'Please, babe,' he implored, reaching for her hand. 'Don't do this.'

'I haven't done anything,' she spat, yanking her hand away. 'It was all you.'

'I think that's your cue to leave,' Gee said, stepping between them and giving Rob a cold look.

'So do we,' Steve added, as he and his brothers flanked Gee.

Aware that he stood no chance, Rob backed off. 'This isn't over,' he said to Suzie. 'I love you, and I know you still love me.'

'If your definition of love is the violence I've been listening to through my wall for the last few months, you've got serious problems, young man,' May Foster said, coming out through her gate to join the others on the pavement.

'Spot on, May,' Suzie said, smiling at the woman who, in the last month, had proved to be an exceptionally nice lady.

'Why don't you do us all a favour and fuck off back to psycho Angie,' Holly piped up. 'No one wants you here.'

'Might've known *you'd* have something to say,' Rob hissed, glaring at her. 'Couldn't wait to get rid of me so you could jump into Suzie's knickers, could you?'

'That's news to me,' Dan Spencer said, walking up behind the group wearing civvies. 'Something you want to tell me, Suzie?'

'Ignore him, he's an idiot,' she said, smiling as she reached up to peck him on the lips. He had called round to check on her a couple of days after the siege, and she had invited him in for a drink. They had talked for hours, and she had realized that he wasn't only good-looking, he was also a genuinely nice man, so she had been happy to accept when he had asked if he could take her out for dinner sometime. They had been on several dates since then, but it was still early days, so she knew that the kiss was probably a bit forward. But he didn't seem to mind, and the look on Rob's face was priceless.

'Let's go in and get that bottle opened,' Holly said, heading for the door. 'Celebrate me getting my life back.'

'There's something else to celebrate, as well,' Dan said, closing the door on Rob's indignant face after they had all made their way inside. 'Dominic Cooper's going down for murdering your mum and—'

'*Anna*,' Holly corrected him, not yet comfortable about calling the woman who she now knew had pretty much neglected her in favour of Devon Prince her mother. 'But how did you manage to link him to it? I thought you said he might walk?'

'He probably would have if his sidekick, Austin, hadn't told us everything in an attempt to secure a lesser sentence for himself,' Dan said. 'He gave us the address of a flat we hadn't known about that Cooper used as a stash-pad, and we found enough there to pin him down. Anyway, we've got him for that murder and three others that had gone cold on us, so, all in all, Rob getting jealous of your friendship with Suzie did us a massive favour.'

Pausing, he turned to Suzie and gave her a mock-frown, saying, 'It *is* only a friendship, isn't it? Only I don't want to be treading on anyone's toes.'

'Pig's got game,' Davy chuckled, snapping his fingers in glee.

'Shut up, you idiot,' Holly laughed, slapping Dan's arm play-fully. 'She's fancied you from the first time she laid eyes on you.'

'*Holly!*' Suzie hissed.

'What?' Holly said innocently, following as Suzie, who was blushing brightly, headed into the kitchen and took glasses out of the cupboard. 'It's true.'

Gee opened the bottle and a poured a measure into each glass, and Carol handed them round before raising hers.

'To good neighbours.'

'The *best*,' said Holly.

'The best!' the others chorused, clinking glasses.

OUT NOW

RUN

Mandasue Heller

When there's nothing left, and no escape . . .

After being cheated on by her ex, Leanne Riley is trying her hardest to get her life back on track, which isn't easy without a job and living in a bedsit surrounded by a junkie and a mad woman.

On a night out with her best friend she meets Jake, a face from her past who has changed beyond all recognition. Jake is charming, handsome and loaded, a far cry from the gawky teen-ager he used to be. Weary of men, Leanne isn't easy to please, but Jake tries his best to break through the wall she's built around herself.

But good looks and money can hide a multitude of sins. Is that good-looking face just a mask? And what's more, what will it take to make it slip, and who will die in the process . . . ?

PRAISE FOR MANDASUE HELLER

'Mandasue has played a real blinder with this fantastic novel'
Martina Cole on *Forget Me Not*

'Captivating from first page to last'
Jeffery Deaver on *Lost Angel*

OUT NOW

SAVE ME

Mandasue Heller

When Ellie Fisher misses her train home one night, she has no idea that being in the right place at the wrong time will change her life forever.

That night she comes across Gareth, a young man about to take his own life because as far as he's concerned there is nothing left to live for. Putting her own life in danger, Ellie convinces Gareth that there is always something left. Her own life is no bed of roses, she explains, but she always pushes on.

However, good deeds aren't always repaid the way we want. Has Ellie unwittingly put her life in danger, or is the real danger a lot closer to home?

BRUTAL

Mandasue Heller

When Frank Peters' wife Maureen dies, he feels that his once-idyllic life on the Yorkshire Moors is over. And with a daughter emigrating to Australia and a son who has his own marital problems, Frank feels resigned to a life of loneliness. Then one night he finds a frightened young woman hiding at the back of his farmhouse. She explains that her name is Irena and was brought to this country by a man who promised her the world and then forced her into prostitution.

Frank offers her a bed for the night but it's the middle of winter, and when heavy snowfall prevents her from leaving the next day, he's forced to extend the invitation. But the longer Irena stays, the easier it gets for the men she's trying to escape from to find her.

People-trafficking could just be the tip of the iceberg, and Frank has no idea what these people are really capable of.